Promises to Keep

Promises to Keep

The Joy Business by Aisha Ford

A Change of Script by Lillian Meredith

Someone for Toni by Cecilia Dowdy

CROSSAMERICA BOOKS

CROSSINGS BOOK CLUB, GARDEN CITY, NEW YORK

The Joy Business

AISHA FORD

One

Audra Clayton tugged on a light cardigan and grabbed her briefcase, then headed toward the front door. Outside, she paused on the cobblestone path that surrounded her property and inhaled deeply a lungful of the cool spring air, then she sighed wistfully. It was good to be home from vacation, and heading back to work, but she knew that a few hours into her first day back, she would miss the serene and calm she had enjoyed during her two weeks at the beach.

"All play and no work will never build any character," Audra murmured, repeating one of her mother's favorite phrases.

As Audra rounded the path to her small guest house, she noted with curiosity that the vacant house next door was bustling with action. A huge moving van was parked out front, and several movers were scurrying back and forth, carrying boxes and furniture.

"It looks like I have new neighbors," she said to herself happily as she pulled open the guest house's front door. Inside, she was greeted with silence and chilly darkness. Audra rubbed her arms vigorously and flipped on a small lamp, then headed to adjust the temperature. As she made her way across the large room, she turned on the switch that controlled the lights on the several Christmas trees in the room.

After adjusting the thermostat to warm up the room, she took a seat at her desk. While sorting through the calls that had accumulated on the answering machine, she occasionally glanced through the wide bay windows in the room to see how things were progressing next door.

Minutes later, she saw a car pull into the driveway and park in the small lot out front. Audra returned to her work and was pleasantly interrupted minutes later when two of her employees, Laura Jenkins and Michelle Thorton, entered the front door.

Audra smiled brightly when they came in. "I didn't recognize the car, and I thought you two were customers."

Laura shook her head. "No, my car's in the shop, and I'm driving a rental."

Michelle added, "My car wouldn't start this morning, and we're late because I had to ask Laura to give me a ride."

"At least you showed up. I was starting to feel a little lonely in here all by myself. And I started coffee for us because we've got a ton of messages here. I think it's going to be a very busy spring."

Laura sat at her desk and looked at the stacks of mail. "It looks like we took our vacations just in time."

"No kidding," said Audra. "Did you guys have a good time?"

"Sure did . . ." Michelle launched into a vivid description of her vacation, and soon, the three of them were chatting and sharing vacation stories.

"So how's everything here at the office?" Laura asked when they were done. "The place is still standing. I guess that's a good sign." She laughed.

"Everything looks good . . . except I left the house in such a hurry to catch my flight, that I forgot to set the timers for all of the decorative lights," Audra told them. "I returned last night to a totally dark house. And the lights here in the office were off, too, which is pretty disappointing."

Michelle shrugged. "Don't feel too bad about it, Boss. My husband almost left the coffeemaker on before we left. It just so happened we noticed it when we had to turn around and head back because Ally had left her blankie, and we knew we would be miserable if we didn't go back and get it."

"You're right," Audra agreed. "No major harm was done. And I probably saved more than a few dollars on my electric bill, which is not an entirely bad thing."

"I see you have new neighbors," Laura said. "Have you met them yet?"

Audra shook her head. "I just found out when I stepped outside this morning. Whoever they are, they must have moved pretty fast, because I saw my old neighbor two weeks ago, right before I left. She had come over to check on the gardens and was pretty disappointed because her real estate agent said the house hadn't been shown in a several weeks. She'd been making payments on that house and her new house since last November, and it was getting to be pretty taxing financially. I asked her if she wanted me to pray for the house to sell, and we ended up praying right in the middle of her yard."

"Looks like the prayer paid off," Michelle remarked, glancing outdoors.

"I guess so, and I know Clare is relieved," Audra agreed. "Now I guess I need to find a housewarming gift and take it over soon."

Just then, the phone rang.

"I'll get it," said Laura, as she reached for the extension. "Joy Year Round," she spoke into the receiver. "Laura speaking, how may I help you?"

The second phone line rang, and Audra reached to answer it. "Happy to be back to work," she said, just before picking up the line. "Vacation's officially over."

"I'll pour some coffee," said Michelle, rising from her seat.

Nicholas Bryant paused from directing the moving crew long enough to glance out of the kitchen window of his new home. The small Connecticut neighborhood was highly picturesque, and although he had made the final decision about purchasing the home, he had asked the opinion of his mother, Sophie, and he could tell by the look of happiness on her face that she loved this home as much as he did.

His new home was a spacious white Cape Cod with green shutters and trim. It wasn't a mansion, but it was comfortable and more than roomy enough for just Nick and Sophie. The backyard consisted of a large perennial garden and a small swimming pool. The house sat on over an acre of land, and at the borders, the property was divided from the neighboring properties by a small, white fence. He smiled, satisfied to have met one of the more important goals in his life. His reverie was interrupted when his mother entered the room.

"Nick, guess what?" she asked.

Nick suppressed a smile. His mom loved asking him to guess things, even though he never got the right answer. "Mom, I need to run upstairs and make sure all of the furniture is ending up in the right place. I don't have time to guess anything."

Sophie frowned. "I was going to tell you that our next-door neighbor has Christmas lights on in her guest house."

"What?" Nick was confused. "It's the middle of April. No one has holiday decorations up this time of year."

"They do next door," his mother persisted. "And it looks so pretty." She smiled, her eyes alive with interest. "I was looking out of the family-room window and I saw some twinkling lights. I took a closer look, and it almost looks like there are several Christmas trees in the living room."

Nick's stomach churned a little. His mother had to be making this up, but he couldn't figure out why she would pretend about something like this, when she knew it would upset him.

But then again, she had never really taken his dislike of Christmas seriously. He sighed. If she was telling the truth, hopefully it was some kind of fluke that would be gone before the day was over. "Are you sure that's what you saw?" he asked his mother.

She nodded.

"All right, then, show me where you saw it." He followed his mother down the hallway toward the family room, but they were interrupted on the way by one of the movers.

The man cleared his throat and said, "Mr. Bryant, we have a slight problem with the desk you wanted us to put in the master bedroom."

"Yes, what's that?" Nick asked impatiently.

"Well . . . it won't fit through the doorway," the man told him.

"What?" Nick turned and headed toward the kitchen stairway, the man following behind him. "Please tell me you're kidding," Nick said, sighing loudly with frustration.

"I wish I was kidding, but we've turned it a million ways to Sunday and it won't go through that doorway," the man replied.

"And you're going to keep trying, because I want that desk in that room," Nick said firmly. When they reached the hallway, the men were still working with the desk, and Nick began barking orders and giving suggestions about how to get the desk through the doorway.

"Good night, girls, it's been fun." Audra smiled as Laura and Michelle got into Laura's car.

"And don't forget those lights on your house tonight," Michelle reminded her before they drove away.

"I won't," Audra assured her. As she slowly trudged back to her house, Audra noted that the moving van was gone from next door. It also appeared the new neighbors were gone, too. The house was totally dark, and if she hadn't seen the moving van there all day, it would have been easy to assume that the house was still empty. Audra was slightly disappointed, because she had wanted to walk over and introduce herself, but it seemed she would have to wait until tomorrow.

"Oh well," she told herself. "That just gives me a little more time to find a housewarming gift. I'll make that my project for the evening, since I wanted to give them something home-made."

The sky had already grown dark, so as soon as she was inside of the house, she flipped on the switch to the lights outside. Instantly, the exterior of her home was alive with color, and Audra stepped out onto the porch to admire the thousands of tiny Christmas lights that decorated the house.

"*I know I say this every night,*" she prayed softly, "*but I don't think You mind it too much. Thank you.*"

While most people who saw her home thought the display was "neat" or "interesting" and, in some cases, "gaudy," Audra looked at it as a big thank-you card to God, which she sent every night, her own way of proclaiming to the world that there was something more to life than what met the eye. God had given the world the opportunity to accept the greatest gift ever given, and most people never even thought much about it until the holidays rolled around.

But Audra had found a way to remind lots and lots of people about the precious gift, and urged people to accept and appreciate this gift.

A few minutes later, Audra went inside and started making her weekly batch of homemade bread. She planned to give her neighbor a freshly baked loaf tomorrow morning.

It was nearly eleven that night when Nick and his mother returned home. There was no food in the house, so he and Sophie had gone out to dinner, then stopped by the grocer's to stock the pantry. By the time they finished, they were both exhausted, and Sophie nodded off during the ride back home.

As Nick rounded the corner to his street, he became aware of glowing bright lights at the opposite end of the block, near his home. Concerned that something was terribly wrong, Nick sped up in order to see what was going on. As he drew closer, his stomach began churning for the second time that day. He couldn't believe his eyes.

His memory came alive as he remembered his mother's comments about his neighbor's home. But . . . hadn't she said the lights were in the neighbor's guest house? Nick pulled his car to a stop in front of the house. He sat there in astonishment and blinked several times as though that would make the terrible image disappear.

Several hours earlier, when he left to go to dinner, his neighbor's sprawling colonial had appeared normal, matching the beauty and tone of the other homes in the neighborhood. Now, it was ablaze with what was probably thousands of colorful lights, reminding him of a kiddie playland.

There has to be some logical explanation for this, Nick decided. Maybe it's someone's birthday . . . or maybe even a prank. He fervently hoped that one of these ideas was correct, or that there was some reasonable explanation for this garish display.

Nick took a deep breath and exhaled slowly. He would explore what was going on first thing tomorrow morning. Tonight, he would just pretend it wasn't there and would try to get a good night's sleep.

*T*wo

*T*uesday morning, Audra awoke earlier than usual in order to assemble a gift basket of homemade bread, jam, tea, coffee, and grapes for her new neighbors. As an afterthought, she impulsively added one of her homemade Christmas wreaths to the basket, along with one of her business cards. "It never hurts to do a little advertising," she joked to herself.

Just as she stepped outside, Audra saw a woman sitting in a rocking chair on the front porch next door. Audra hurried her steps, wanting to reach the woman before she decided to go back inside.

"Hi there," Audra greeted the woman as she made her way up the porch steps. "I'm Audra Clayton, and I live next door," she said, gesturing to her own home.

"I'm Sophie Bryant," the woman said, smiling warmly. "My son, Nicholas, just bought this house, and I live with him. Come have a seat," she told Audra.

Audra hesitated, knowing she had to get to work soon, but she decided a few minutes wouldn't hurt. She took a seat in the wicker rocker next to Sophie. "I've always loved this porch," she told Sophie as the two of them rocked back and forth. "Every summer, my old neighbor, Clare, would spend one entire day out here, just enjoying the view and the fresh air. When the sun got too hot, she'd just take her pitcher of lemonade and move to another side."

"Sounds like a mini vacation," Sophie said.

"It was," Audra admitted. "Last summer, I took a day off from work and joined her. We sat on the east porch and watched the sunrise, and ended the day on the west porch, watching the sunset. Of course, that night, I felt terribly guilty for having spent an entire day doing nothing but sitting in a rocking chair and talking." Audra laughed.

Sophie shook her head. "Sometimes a body needs a day off. Especially the way you young people run around nowadays, like you have to conquer the world. Sitting on the porch for an entire day seems like a good idea. I wouldn't mind doing that, myself. Just sit still and think, and sort things out. It could be therapeutic."

Audra nodded. "Clare used to call it her vacation for the soul. She said that one day helped clear the cobwebs out of her mind."

"How about you? Did you like it?" Sophie wanted to know.

Audra chuckled. "Too much, I think. I've been considering adding a porch to my own house, even if it only spans the front."

"Then you'll have to come over and teach me how to do it," Sophie said firmly. "We'll break in the whole porch."

"Oh, I wouldn't want to intrude on your time with your family," Audra said.

Sophie laughed quietly. "My family time is almost nonexistent. My youngest son, Alan, is away at college in Florida, and Nick spends all of his time working. He's the one who really ought to take a whole day and spend it doing nothing, but I'd never be able to talk him into it. The more conveniences he has, the more work he does." Sophie shrugged, shaking her head in disapproval.

"He got a cellular phone so he could spend more time away from the office, but whenever he's not at work, that little phone is ringing off the hook. It got so bad he had to get two cell phones and a pager. Then he got a laptop so he could do his reports at home. But now he takes those things everywhere, even to our family reunion picnic last year."

Sophie sounded so disdainful that Audra felt a pang of guilt for taking her own cell phone and pager to family functions, like her niece's dance recital and her nephew's Little League games.

"If he were still a little boy," Sophie continued, "I'd take all his little gadgets away and make him go outside and play. But he's too big for that now," she said sadly. "Even when he's at home, I rarely see him or talk to him."

Audra could almost feel this woman's loneliness, and she felt a brief surge of frustration toward Sophie's son. She had never really liked being around a workaholic, but she had no respect for a man who would neglect his own mother. And she was starting to like Sophie. She appeared to be in her late fifties or early sixties, but she was aging gracefully. Her nut brown skin looked bright and fresh, and although she wore more than a few wrinkles under her makeup, she didn't seem to be trying to hide them. Her ear-length black hair was liberally sprinkled with gray, but her posture was straight and confident. Sophie spoke quietly, but behind the soft-spoken tone of voice was a liberal measure of firm assurance.

"You remind me a lot of my mother," Audra said without planning to. She cringed inwardly, hoping Sophie didn't take offense at her impulsive statement.

Sophie lifted her eyebrows. "I just hope that's a compliment."

Audra smiled, relieved. "It is. Don't worry; I wasn't being sarcastic. I love my mom. And I miss her, too. Right now, she and my dad are on vacation." Audra remembered the gift basket, then picked it up and handed it over to Sophie. "I don't want to take up too much of your time, but I wanted to give you this."

Sophie happily examined the contents of the basket and thanked Audra for the gift. When Sophie came to the wreath, Audra saw a flicker of uneasiness pass over Sophie's face.

Audra figured Sophie was offended because she'd put the wreath and her business card in the basket, so she hurried to explain.

"I hope you don't mind that I added my business card. I own my own event-planning business. We do all kinds of occasions, but our specialty is Christmas functions. It's my favorite time of the year," Audra admitted. "The wreath and business card are kind of our logo, and I guess it was in bad taste to add it to the basket, huh?"

"Oh, no, I like it, but . . . well, we're not really into parties and things." Sophie seemed to be fumbling for words. She glanced over her shoulder, back inside the house, and said, "My son . . . Nick . . . he really doesn't like to celebrate holidays, and he gets in such a bad mood around Christmas, especially."

"Oh, I see," Audra said. She really *didn't* see, but she didn't want to pry, either.

"Did I see Christmas lights in your guest house yesterday?" Sophie asked curiously.

Audra nodded. "That's where my office is set up, and we have several Christmas trees in there. I hope your son didn't get upset."

Sophie shrugged. "I don't know if he even saw them."

Audra breathed a sigh of relief, then remembered something else. "I wonder what he thought about the lights on my house?"

Sophie seemed confused. "What lights?"

"I keep my house decorated for Christmas year-round. I don't know how anyone could miss it. It's pretty bright."

Sophie chuckled. "I was asleep when we came home last night, and I went right upstairs and fell into bed. And if he saw anything, he didn't mention it then, and I haven't seen him yet this morning. If he saw it, he might fuss for a while, but don't let him scare you. He's all bark and no bite."

"Oh," Audra said, feeling a little uneasy. *What an ogre*, she thought. She dreaded dealing with people who hated holidays. They never seemed to have any respect for her and her line of business.

Just then, the front door burst open and a man rushed out. Audra looked up and their eyes met briefly. He regarded Audra with a flicker of interest until he spotted Sophie. Zeroing in on Sophie, he said, "There you are, Mom. What are you doing out here so early?"

Audra assumed he was Nick, Sophie's ogre of a son. He had to be several inches over six feet tall, and although he seemed slightly perturbed, an attractive air of confidence surrounded him. She had to admit, he was a very handsome ogre. He was muscular but trim, and he looked every bit the successful businessman in his tailored navy blue suit. His hair was cut very close, and he had expressive dark-brown eyes.

Sophie looked up at her son. "I wanted to get a little fresh air." Gesturing to Audra, she added, "This is Audra, our neighbor. She stopped by to bring us a gift basket." She turned to Audra and said, "This is my son, Nick."

"Hi, nice to meet you," Audra said brightly, extending her arm to shake hands with him.

Nick reached out to shake her hand, and then suddenly withdrew. His eyes narrowed as he asked, "You live next door?" He jerked his head in the direction of her home.

"Yes," Audra said slowly. Judging from his reaction, it was safe to assume he *had* seen her lights and wasn't too pleased with them. "Right over there," she said, trying to keep the mood light.

He took two steps back and stared at her as if she had thrown flaming torches at him. His voice was no longer amiable as he asked, "What's the big idea with all the lights?"

Audra kept a compact little speech prepared for moments like this when people got upset about her display, but today, it was definitely misplaced somewhere in the back of her mental file cabinet. She tried and failed to retrieve the "Christmas lights" speech, so she decided to wing it. "Well," she began, "I just . . . just . . ." she trailed off, feeling totally confused. He had disarmed her with his good looks and then intimidated her with his steely glare.

Thankfully, Sophie started an explanation for her. "Audra owns her own party-planning business and her specialty is Christmas events. The lights are sort of her business card."

Nick lifted an eyebrow. "The last time I checked, this neighborhood was zoned residential. Since when did it become acceptable to advertise your home business by putting blinding lights all over your house? It seems pretty gaudy to me."

Audra inhaled sharply and tried not to lose her temper.

"Now, Nick, I don't think you're being very polite," Sophie tried to intervene.

Nick's eyes flashed, but when he addressed his mother, his voice was controlled and even. "Mother, I am not a little boy, so you don't have to worry about my manners. But I have a right to voice my opinion of that . . . *spectacle* next door."

Suddenly, bits and pieces of Audra's speech came into focus. She stood up and pointed at Nick. "For your information, that *spectacle* is more than just decorations and lights. It's a visual reminder of the gift of salvation. Jesus died so that people can spend eternity in heaven. I put up my lights to show how thankful I am, because I know I didn't deserve it, but God gave the gift anyway."

Audra felt like telling Nick what he deserved, but she held her tongue, knowing she had already put some serious dents into her witness. Sometimes it was so hard to be Christ-like, especially when infuriating people stuck their noses into her life and started spouting opinions.

Nick wrinkled his face with disdain. "I don't need to hear about church," he said, putting his hands out as if to stop her.

"Don't worry. I don't want to *tell* you about church." *It'll be a better place without you,* she thought. Audra hurried toward the porch steps but remembered poor Sophie, who was watching the awful scene with a worried expression. "I'm sorry that I can't stay longer, Sophie, but it was nice meeting you."

Sophie smiled weakly. "Thank you for coming over. We'll have to do this again sometime."

Audra shook her head. "I have the feeling that I'm not welcome here, but if your son doesn't have any rules preventing you from visiting *gaudy* neighbors, my door is always open." She gave Nick what she hoped was a withering look and headed back to her home.

When she was halfway there, she heard Nick call after her, "I'm calling the city hall about this. You'd better start looking for somewhere else to hang all that junk!"

Audra decided that she wouldn't even give him the satisfaction of turning around. She pretended that she hadn't heard him and promptly went to her office, since she was late for work. As soon as she was inside, she turned on all of the trees in the room, and took pleasure in hoping that Nick could see them.

Nick watched uncomfortably as Audra retreated to her guest house. She had seemed unfazed by his final threat, and hadn't even turned around to acknowledge that she had heard him.

Moments after she entered her guest house, he noted that she had turned on the lights of several Christmas trees. Nick felt his jaw twitch. He exhaled and turned around to complain to his mother about Audra's behavior. To his surprise, Sophie was gone. Nick figured she was probably a little upset with him, but he decided not to think about that fact right now. She would probably say something like, "Nick, I'm very disappointed in you," or something to that effect.

He checked his watch and realized he would have to eat breakfast quickly and head out soon if he was going to make it to work on time.

He found his mother in the kitchen, slicing a loaf of bread. "Do you want some toast and jam?" she asked him.

"Sure." While he waited, he scanned the newspaper to get a feel for what was going on in the world. He was going to have to get a TV installed in the kitchen so he wouldn't have to miss the news while eating.

Minutes later, his mother placed toast, jam, and grapes in front of him, along with a mug of coffee. Nick inhaled the aroma of the coffee and smiled with satisfaction. It was a very high-quality blend, but he didn't remember having bought it at the market the night before. He took a long sip and closed his eyes in delight. It was just what he needed to calm his nerves. His heart was still beating rapidly from the encounter on the front porch.

When he'd walked outside, he'd been instantly impressed with the beautiful woman who was talking to his mother. She was tall, with shoulder-length hair that was curled under at the ends. Her simple clothing was elegant and flattering, but not overdone. And she had a warm and genuine smile, and big brown eyes. When she had smiled at him so innocently, she had definitely thrown him off guard. And he had almost let himself become interested in her before he realized she was the owner of *the* house next door.

His mother cleared her throat softly, and Nick realized she was going to scold him.

"Nick, I was very disappointed with the way you treated our guest," she began.

Nick looked up from his paper and tried to look pleasant. "I know my manners were a little . . . skewed, but I will remedy that by not having any further contact with that woman."

His mother frowned. "Nick, she was only trying to be nice."

Nick shook his head and stood to leave. "I know I probably should have handled that a little better, but I don't regret a word I said. She claims to be a Christian, but look how she yelled at me."

His mother opened her mouth to interrupt him, but Nick held up his hand to indicate that he wasn't finished talking. "Mom, you can be disappointed all you want, but as long as I'm the one paying the mortgage, I will not sit here and let my property value go down because the free spirit next door wants to turn her house into some kind of year-round holiday wonderland."

His mother pursed her lips and stared at him. She would be upset with him for the next few days, so he might as well tell her all that was on his mind. "And I will take whatever legal action necessary to get those lights turned off."

His mother's face clouded with worry. "What are you going to do?"

Nick sighed. "For starters, I'm going to put a call in to that real estate agent who sold me the house and find out why she refrained from telling me about the circus next door. Then I'm going to call my lawyer, the mayor, city hall, the homes association, and whoever else can do something about this. I am not letting her get away with it."

"I see," his mother said, and then left the room. A moment later, she poked her head back in the room and added, "Don't worry any more about your manners. I've already thanked Audra for the gift basket she brought over this morning. Your breakfast was courtesy of your evil neighbor."

Nick felt sick. His mother was really rubbing it in. He vaguely remembered seeing a gift basket on the front porch near his mother's chair. How could his own mother have let him eat that food when she knew he wouldn't have touched it had he known who had given it to them?

Adding insult to injury, she hadn't even bothered to listen to his strategy for retaliation. Nick wanted to feel some satisfaction with his plans, but the two people he'd told so far had seemed uninterested. He should have been the one to walk away first, but both his mother and Audra had beat him to the punch.

Nick straightened his tie and lifted his chin. If he hadn't lost his touch, this conflict would be cleared up before the week ended. The only bitter part of the ordeal would be the fact that a very beautiful woman who lived next door would probably never speak to him again. Nick shrugged. It was a small price to pay in order to get the neighborhood back to normal.

Audra's face flashed into his mind and he shook his head to remove the image. Why did she have to be so pretty? Nick closed his eyes and struggled to focus. As he visualized the image of Audra's house, colorful and illuminated like a carnival ride, he cringed.

It was not a hard decision to make. And he would not let himself regret winning this battle before it even got started.

*T*hree

*A*udra was drained by the end of the day. Minutes after the confrontation, she was able to collect her thoughts and emotions, and only then did she realize how much she'd overreacted. She also realized that Nick would not easily forget all that she'd said, and would use it as fuel against her when he started making complaints in earnest.

After replaying the scene over and over in her mind, and giving it many alternate endings, she came to one conclusion: She wished she had been more civil. Audra fidgeted endlessly until Laura and Michelle joked that she was going to wear a trench in the new office carpeting. When she complained that they couldn't see the gravity of the situation, they took pity on her and tried to be reassuring.

"There is no way he can get your lights turned off," Laura said with confidence. "This is a free country, remember?"

"We have the right of personal expression," Michelle added.

"And pretty much everyone around here likes your lights. They'd be upset if you took them down."

"But what about the people who don't?" Audra argued. "They would join in with Nick's complaints if they heard about them, and then I'll probably have to take my lights down for good."

Laura had shrugged. "I seriously doubt that anyone who has the authority to take your lights down will actually do it just to please some arrogant newcomer who tries to change things his first day here." Laura punctuated her statement by flipping on the stereo system that played an assortment of Christmas CDs.

Audra had left work early to see about some last-minute details for the Neweler Foundation's annual company picnic, which was being held in a couple of days.

By the time she got home, she was too tired even to feel hungry. Discouraged, she changed into her soft cotton pajamas and stretched out on the family-room couch, watching an old black-and-white movie.

At eight-thirty, the phone rang, and Audra answered it to find Ryan Meyer, a friend from church, on the other line. Ryan got straight to the point. "Audra, you didn't make it to Tuesday Bible study tonight. Is everything okay?"

Audra had totally forgotten about Bible study, and she felt like a heathen because Ryan had called to remind her that she had missed it. She sighed and tried to think of how to answer him.

Things were far from being okay, but she wondered if it would be a good idea to share her concerns with Ryan. He was a solid Christian, perfectly mannerable, good-looking, and sincere: an all-around nice guy. A few years earlier, when they first met, he had been a good friend; eventually he had made it known that he was ready to move beyond friendship and into a more serious relationship.

Although Audra had made it clear that she didn't have any of those same feelings for him, he now seemed content just to wait for her to change her mind. Since then, Audra was always wary of sharing any personal information with him, fearing that he might mistake a sharing of confidence as the spark of romantic interest.

Just as she opened her mouth to give him a weak excuse, Ryan spoke up again, sounding concerned.

"Audra, are you sick? It just isn't like you to miss study and not call anyone to say you won't be coming. Did you have to work tonight?"

Audra shook her head, and then realized he couldn't see her. "No, it's not that. But I did have a long day at work, today, and then I went running errands. By the time I finished, I was so wiped out that I just came home and spaced out for a while."

Ryan, apparently, was not convinced. "Are you sure?" He cleared his throat nervously, and said, "I had several meetings today."

Audra leaned back into the oversized cushions and tried to prepare herself for a long, rambling story. Ryan was a successful executive at a local software company, run by a friend of her family. Though Ryan held a master's degree, Audra was convinced that most of his success was due to his thoroughness. Ryan never told the condensed version of anything, and when he began telling an anecdote, he had to tell the entire story— every little detail, from beginning to end, and that usually made for a very long account.

While Ryan recounted the details of his day, Audra let her thoughts wander back to Nick's threats. Even if Laura and Michelle thought his attitude was comical, Audra thought she had no choice but to take him seriously. She struggled about how she should show him that she wasn't afraid, not wanting him to get too cocky and unreasonable. Audra realized she hadn't even turned on the lights outside, and she wondered if Nick would view that as a sign of victory.

"So that's when I finally got to meet our new accountant," Ryan was saying.

"Oh. Is he a good accountant?" Audra asked, feeling guilty for not paying much attention.

"A great accountant. But he's not winning any awards for being a nice person. He's rude and inconsiderate. And way too conceited." Audra sat up and listened carefully. Ryan sounded angry, and it was highly unusual for Ryan to lose his temper. "And then, I couldn't believe how he started talking about you in a roomful of strangers."

Audra was totally confused. "What? Your new accountant started talking about me? Why?" Ryan's tone of voice didn't imply that the new accountant had been singing her praises.

"He said he just moved in next door to you. He started spouting off about how silly your lights were and how he was going to get them taken down. He said you yelled at him and treated him like a criminal when he made a harmless comment to you. When you didn't show up tonight, I put two and two together and figured you must be feeling pretty low."

Audra stood up and paced, carrying the phone with her. "What? Nick said all of this in a meeting?"

"Sure did. I defended you, of course. I told him what a wonderful Christian woman you are, and I told him that he needed to watch his mouth if he wanted to keep his job."

Audra took a deep breath and returned to the couch. As she sat down, she felt a wave of exhaustion wash over her. She felt emotions welling up in her chest and willed herself not to cry while she was on the phone with Ryan. "You did?" she asked weakly. This seemed totally out of character for Ryan. As a rule, he was pretty nonconfrontational, and he generally shied away from conflicts.

"Well . . ." Ryan began. Audra could picture him shrugging and looking a tad embarrassed. "I just didn't think he was being very respectful, and neither did anyone else."

"Oh?" Audra said, relieved. She was also glad to hear that Ryan wasn't her lone defender. For the first time in a long while, she felt comfortable speaking with him. It almost felt like the old days when they were just companionable friends. She briefly considered pouring out her thoughts and fears about the whole issue but decided against it. She wasn't going to whine to her friends about this, especially Ryan, who had already done so much for her. She also knew she needed to be truthful about her role in what had happened.

"Actually, he wasn't being completely dishonest. I did lose my temper a little with him this morning," she confessed. "I had gone over to take a welcome basket, and he came outside making threats about my lights and how annoying they were. I got defensive and said some things I shouldn't have. Of course," she added, "I feel terrible about it now, even if he did provoke me."

"He's not the easiest guy to get along with," Ryan agreed. "But if he causes any more trouble, feel free to call me. I would hate to see your lights go down, and I'll do my best to help you keep them up."

"Thank you," Audra said warmly. "But right now, I guess I ought to go over and apologize before this feuding-neighbors thing goes way too far. Hopefully, we can make some sense of things very quickly."

"Okay. And I guess I'll see you Sunday?" Ryan asked.

"Lord willing, I *will* be there Sunday morning, just like always."

Ryan didn't say anything for several moments, and Audra got the uncomfortable feeling that he might be gearing up to ask her out again. However, when he spoke, he just said, "Okay then, Audra. I'll look for you at church."

Audra let out a sigh of relief as she placed the phone back in its cradle. It had been embarrassing to admit to Ryan that she had lost her temper with Nick, but she couldn't let Ryan or anyone she knew think that Nick had been the only one who had been a little testy.

Feeling confident that her apology would put things in proper perspective with Nick, she quickly changed and confidently marched next door, only to find that no one seemed to be at home. The lights in the house were all dark, except for the small light on the front porch. *They must have gone out for dinner again,* Audra decided as she made her way back home. The apology would have to wait until morning. But just to play things safe, and not throw fat into the fire, she would leave her lights off just for this evening.

Nick awoke with a sigh of triumph. Last night, he and his mother had gone out to dinner again, and when they returned, Audra's lights were not on. He smiled as he got ready for work, feeling satisfied. Since she had changed her tune so quickly, he wouldn't have to pursue any of the routes he had previously considered. Victory always felt nice, but when it came this easily, it was even sweeter.

As he pulled out of the garage, he was surprised to see Audra crossing the lawn to his yard. He frowned, fighting off a growing uneasiness. The determined way she was walking suggested that she wasn't coming to admit he had won. He didn't really want to talk to her right now, at least not while he was still enjoying his win. And when he noticed the smile she had on her face, Nick's wariness grew. He couldn't think of why she would be smiling when she had so obviously given in to his complaint. Or had she really?

As she neared the car, Nick rolled the window down a few inches and waited for her to approach.

"Hello, Nick," she said, sounding happy and cheerful.

"Hi, Audra," he said slowly. *What does she have up her sleeve now?* he wondered. He remained silent and waited for her to speak.

"I came over to apologize for the way I acted yesterday," she began. "I lost my temper, and I said some things that were not appropriate."

"I accept," Nick told her. "But you really didn't have to come over and say all of that." He shrugged. "It's really not that important."

"You might not think so, but I thought it was pretty important," she replied, still smiling.

"Okay . . . so you got it off your conscience," he said. "Anything else?"

She looked taken aback for a moment, but she didn't yell at him again. She seemed to hesitate, but finally added, "Well, there is another thing." She smiled, apparently waiting for some type of response from him.

"If you don't mind, I'd like to get this over with. I'm going to be late for work," he said.

"Okay, I'll make it quick." She took a deep breath and continued. "I know we got off to a horrible start, and I imagine you probably can't imagine this now, but I am a good neighbor.

And I prefer to make friends instead of enemies. So I was wondering if you and your mother would be interested in coming to my church this Sunday. Afterward, you're invited to dinner at my house. Maybe then we'll be able to discuss some options about my lights," she said.

Nick's throat went dry. What did she mean by "discuss some options"? Wasn't the whole light thing settled and forgotten? He cleared his throat and voiced his questions. "What do you mean? I thought you had agreed to turn the lights off."

Audra blinked, then chuckled softly. "Not really. I didn't turn them on last night because I felt confused about what to do. We both needed to cool off, so I thought that might help. I was hoping we could talk this out and, somehow, come to an agreement."

Nick shook his head in disbelief. Did she actually think he was going to come to some tea party while she tried to convince him that she should be able to keep her lights up? "I don't think that's really an option. I don't want to work out an *agreement*. I want the lights *off*, plain and simple."

Audra frowned. "I'm sorry, but your demands are not acceptable."

Why did this woman have to be so frustrating? Nick shook his head. "We'll see about that. In the meantime, I'm late for work." Nick gently pressed on the accelerator to signal to Audra that he was ready to leave. She stepped away from his car, and he sped out of the driveway.

"All right, Mr. Yates . . . Yes, I see . . . No, no, I don't mind your asking at all. You have a right to be picky. A fiftieth wedding anniversary *is* a big deal. But I promise my event staff and I will take care of all of the details." Audra listened carefully to the older gentleman, who had been one of her first clients.

"And, Audra, don't forget, you promised to join the festivities," he reminded her.

"Yes, Mr. Yates, I will be there with bells on." She smiled. Normally, she did the preliminary consultations and arranged details, then let her staff run the actual events. However, since most of her clients were also her friends, they often expected her attendance as a guest, and such was the case with the Yateses' anniversary party.

After she ended her conversation with Mr. Yates, the phone rang again. Audra picked up the receiver and greeted the caller.

"Audra, this is Vickie Phelps," the voice on the other end replied.

"Hi, Vickie," Audra said tentatively. Although Vickie and her family attended Audra's church, she didn't know Vickie personally all that well. Mr. Phelps, Vickie's husband, was a lawyer, and Vickie herself was the town mayor.

Vickie was also a lawyer, but after she had had children, she had decided to be a stay-at-home mom. Vickie had been the mayor for the past three years, deciding to run for office after her youngest child entered high school. The city's residents numbered a little under one thousand, and most of the folks had known Vickie for several years. "Is there something I can help you with?"

"Not really." Vickie sighed deeply. "I just wanted to let you know that your new neighbor was in first thing this morning with a complaint about your lights."

"I see. Am I required to take them down?" Audra felt defeated.

"I'm not sure yet. You know I personally have no problem

with the lights, and as someone who knows you and understands the meaning behind the lights, I stand behind you completely. But I'm also the mayor, which requires me to be a little
more neutral."

"So what are you saying?" Audra asked. She hadn't even realized that Vickie even paid much attention to the display.

"I gave you a little time. I told him he'd have to take things
up with your subdivision's homes association. Hopefully, it will
be handled effectively without ever coming through my office
again. I hate the thought of you taking the display down, but I
can't take sides just because I know you. And as much as I
would like to, I can't just tell the man off. He's a citizen, too,
and I can't ignore his rights."

Audra remained silent, realizing just how much Nick was
willing to do to get his way.

"I know this call wasn't very encouraging, but I thought I
should let you know what he's up to, so you don't feel like anything's been going on behind your back," Vickie said. "And
isn't your brother the president of the homes association for
your subdivision?"

Audra nodded her head, even though she knew Vickie
couldn't see her. "Thanks. I really appreciate it. And my
brother *is* the president of the homes association, but I don't
think he'll be thrilled about the ordeal; it'll put him in an awkward position. As for Nick, he'll just get more and more worked
up if I manage to keep my display. What do you suggest I do?"
Audra questioned.

Vickie was silent for a long time. Finally, she said, "I would
recommend you pray. And I'll do the same. I'll see you at
church Sunday, and, hopefully, things will have calmed down
by then."

Audra replaced the receiver and sat, silently contemplating the depth of the situation. "Bad news?" Michelle asked sympathetically.

Audra shrugged. "I'm not really sure. But my neighbor has made it clear that he means business about my lights. He went to the mayor's office and complained."

"Wow." Michelle blinked. "You'd think he would have forgotten about it by now."

"Are you in any real trouble?" Laura questioned.

Audra shook her head in confusion. "I'm not sure about that either. And I don't know how to make things right with him, because it looks like the conversation we had this morning just made things worse."

"Let's pray about it," Michelle suggested.

"Good idea." Laura was up from her desk and at Audra's side immediately.

As they bowed their heads, Michelle led off in prayer and Audra was once again reminded how happy she was to have employees who shared her belief and convictions. Whenever one of them experienced trouble, they banded together in prayer to support one another through difficult and trying times.

"Go ahead, I'll be fine," Sophie told Nick.

"Are you sure?" Nick looked at his mother carefully. He hated to leave her alone, but she had flatly refused to accompany him, and he hated the thought of not showing up; it wasn't every day that one's boss invited a new employee to his fiftieth anniversary party.

And, whereas Sophie didn't particularly relish sudden invitations and spur-of-the-moment plans, Nick thrived on them.

He enjoyed activity and went to great lengths to assure that his calendar was always full. Stillness and solitude made him edgy, so events like this were icing on the cake. But he still felt unsure about leaving his mother home alone in an unfamiliar house.

Sophie interrupted his thoughts. "Stop sitting there looking like somebody spoiled your fun. You know I need time to get ready for things like this, but I don't mind if you go without me."

Nick looked at her, trying to decide if she was telling the truth. "I won't stay for more than a couple of hours."

Sophie waved her hand. "I told you, I'll be fine. Alan told me he would call tonight, and I don't want him to think his mother is too busy to listen to him." She glanced at the clock on the kitchen wall. "I'll just put your plate into the fridge, and you can have it for dinner tomorrow. But you'd better get going if you're going to make it there by eight."

Nick nodded and headed off to his bedroom to get dressed. As he looked for a appropriate suit to wear, he wondered again if moving here had been a huge mistake. Their old house was smaller and less showy, but it had been home to their small family for many years. And although he had previously worked long hours at his former job, the old neighborhood was home to plenty of Sophie's friends, who had regularly taken it upon themselves to look in on her and keep her company. Now, the hours he spent away left Sophie with long, empty days to try to fill since they hadn't gotten around to meeting any of the neighbors.

Except for Audra, Nick thought, feeling irritated. Although she was much younger than his mother, the two of them had seemed to hit it off well, as Sophie had phrased it. He shook his head and decided not to think about it right now. Tomorrow he would find some time to see about getting his mother involved in some activities or organizations where she could meet people. Right now, he had a party to attend.

Olivia Harper cornered Audra shortly after Audra arrived at the Yateses' anniversary party. As Olivia strode toward her, Audra noted that the woman had that "I need a favor" glint in her eye. She smiled in anticipation of whatever Olivia had decided that Audra needed to do for her.

The last time Olivia had approached her with that look was shortly before Christmas. When everything was all said and done, Audra had ended up spending five days baking and decorating one hundred dozen cookies for a party Olivia was coordinating at a women and children's shelter.

Olivia was involved with many local charitable and civic causes, both great and small, and she felt passionately about each of them. She was one of those people who was simply born to help others and had devoted most of her life to doing so. She had never married or even seriously dated anyone, as far as Audra knew. However, it wasn't because she had experienced a lack of suitors. Olivia just felt that she was called to help other families instead of starting her own.

A tall, elegant woman, Olivia wore her silvery white hair cropped and curly, framing her face and accentuating her dark gray eyes. She loved to get dressed up, and tonight was no exception. She was dressed in a long, jade pantsuit, along with a matching jade-and-gold duster that highlighted the gold undertones in her brown skin.

Her vivacious attitude and nonstop energy was her trademark, and though she had just turned sixty-five, she had no intentions of slowing down and spending her days in leisurely fashion, as many of her friends and acquaintances now did. In fact, some people said it appeared as if she had just gotten her second wind. She had recently pared her real estate career down to a few clients here and there, enabling her to devote more time to some of her favorite projects.

"Audra, I have a big favor to ask of you," said Olivia.

Audra put her hands on her hips and tried to look stern. "Aren't you going to even say hello?" she teased.

Olivia waved her hand, dismissing the suggestion. "Didn't you see me wave at you when you first came in? You know I don't like being repetitive."

Audra nodded, holding back a smile. "Of course, Olivia. So what is it you need?"

Olivia took a deep breath. "I need volunteers. I'm asking everyone here tonight, and, hopefully, I'll walk away with five or ten."

Audra raised an eyebrow. "What kind of volunteers?"

"Actually, I need tutors. As you know, I'm on the board of the Community Pastors Outreach. They've been wanting to get the ball rolling on a literacy program, and I'm in charge of co-ordinating all of the workers."

Audra frowned. "Oh, Olivia, I'd love to do something like that, but I have no idea where I would find the time. My schedule is always so hectic. Maybe I can donate money or supplies or something. Would that work?"

Olivia's smile fell, and Audra knew she was disappointed. "Oh sure, that would be fine, too. Every penny helps. But if you change your mind, I would only need you one or two nights a week. It's an ongoing program, so maybe down the road you could help out if your schedule allows. At least you have the ability *to* read your schedule book, whereas the people you'd be helping don't yet enjoy that luxury." Olivia looked at Audra pointedly. Olivia was not what one would call manipulative, but she rarely minced words.

Audra closed her eyes for a moment. She knew Olivia had a point, and she really would like to be involved. "Tell you what. I'll try it for a month. If it's just not working, I'll have to back out, but I'll do my best to try to stick with it. How's that?" Audra waited for her friend to answer.

Olivia grinned broadly, exposing a mouthful of beautiful white teeth. Audra figured that if Olivia drew upon all of her persistence and negotiating tactics, there wouldn't be a person at the whole party who could refuse that winning smile.

Audra made her way over to Mr. and Mrs. Yates and offered her congratulations. They had invited their entire church and many of their other friends and acquaintances to this event, and they seemed to be having the time of their lives. They were a dear couple and had been friends of Audra's family for many years. They had also been very gracious in providing Audra with an opportunity to plan events for their business when she had first started Joy Year Round.

Audra noticed her brother, Kyle, and his wife, Caron, at a table across the room, and she made her way to visit with them.

"You did such a good job with this party," Caron said. "I love these decorations."

"Thanks," Audra replied.

"I just wish Mom and Dad could be here," Kyle added.

Audra and Caron nodded in agreement. Their parents had been planning a month-long trip to the Caribbean, and by the time they realized their trip would overlap with the Yateses' party, it had been too late to cancel any of their plans without taking a loss. The Yateses had assured them that they wouldn't be offended and had urged Audra's parents to continue with their plans for their trip.

The three of them chatted for several minutes and were then joined by Ryan Meyer, along with Kate and Timothy Beem, a married couple who were friends of Kyle and Caron. After several minutes of small talk, Kyle announced that he was hungry and was ready to get something to eat. The rest of the group agreed and started moving in the direction of the buffet table.

As they traveled the length of the table, Kate kept them entertained with a comical story about the antics of her two-year-old son, and before long, she and Caron were sharing story after story about their children.

Kate and Timothy had a two-year-old son, a four-year-old daughter, and seven-year-old son. Caron and Kyle's two children were good friends with the Beem children, and the two families spent a great deal of time together. Kyle was Audra's only sibling, and Caron was an only child, so Audra held the distinction of being five-year-old Karee's and seven-year-old James's only aunt. Due to her busy schedule, Audra didn't get to see them as often as she would have liked, so it was fun to hear their parents tell entertaining stories about the kids' activities.

Not long after the group returned to their table, Audra glanced around the room, making sure the party was running smoothly. When she attended an event that she had coordinated, she sometimes felt intense pressure to see to it that everyone was having a good time. As she looked out among the crowd, she concluded that this was indeed a success. Everyone seemed to be enjoying themselves, Nick Bryant included.

Audra did a double take, hoping she was mistaken. Unfortunately, she wasn't. He was standing in the middle of a group of people and appeared to be their center of attention. Audra's stomach turned. What was Nick Bryant doing here?

Apparently, Nick must have sensed her disgruntled gaze.

Turning to look around, his eyes came to rest on Audra. Their gazes held for several moments. There was no discernible emotion on his face, and Audra wondered if he was ready to call a truce.

For a fraction of a second, Audra had the stomach flutters, a level of nervousness she hadn't experienced in years. The stomach flutters had barely registered with her brain when Nick's eyes grew cold. He frowned, then turned away as though he hadn't seen her.

Audra didn't know whether to be offended or relieved, but after a few seconds of deliberation, she decided on the latter.

At least he could have been a tad more polite and faked a smile or something. But he had to add insult to injury and pretend I'm not even here, she fumed.

While Audra tried to adjust to the fact that her scroogelike, but handsome, neighbor was completely ignoring her, he surprised her by extracting himself from the group he was speaking to and heading straight toward her.

Audra groaned silently. It didn't look as if Nick was going to give up any time soon. But it didn't matter, because she wasn't going to give up either.

Four

W*here are you going?* Nick ignored the internal question, partly because he didn't have an answer. He would figure out a somewhat reasonable explanation by the time he reached her table.

As soon as he began walking toward her, Audra abruptly turned away from him, giving him the impression that she didn't want to talk to him. Nick paused in his journey across the massive reception hall, wondering if he shouldn't go on.

What exactly was he going to say? He shrugged mentally. This was his boss's anniversary party, and Nick didn't want to make a bad impression on anyone here by continuing his argument with Audra. But he didn't want to rush over to her and beg forgiveness for asking her to remove her lights. He hadn't given up yet. For reasons he couldn't put his finger on, he just wanted to talk to her. As annoying as she and her lights were, there was something magnetic about Audra, and he was drawn to her.

He had been thinking about her off and on, for the better part of the day, and he couldn't even convince himself that all of his thoughts had been negative. From the little he knew about her, she was the type of woman he'd like to get to know a little better, except for the one glaring drawback concerning her case of Christmasitis.

Other than that, she was beautiful, smart, got along well with his mother, and he couldn't stop thinking about her.

Ironically, he'd hoped coming to this party would distract him from the battle that lay ahead. Instead, he'd walked in and found himself virtually face-to-face with his opponent—the same opponent who, at this very moment, was happily chatting away with Ryan Meyer, another person whom he didn't particularly care for. Nick had soon realized he wouldn't win many friends in this town trying to beat Audra behind her back after Ryan had jumped to her defense. Even the mayor herself had seemed a little hesitant to get involved, and Nick had a sneaking suspicion that she, too, was a friend of Audra's.

Nick stopped and considered yet another obstacle. He was ninety-nine percent sure that Ryan had shared with Audra the details of Nick's outburst concerning her lights, so even if he tried acting civilly toward her now, the people at her table might very well label him a total hypocrite. And who knew what the rest of the people there might think? He wasn't sure how many of them already knew about his attempts to cut off those lights. Would they also rush to her defense?

He rubbed his chin, wondering exactly how well Audra knew his boss, Mr. Yates. If they, too, were friends, the last thing Nick wanted to do was publicly offend a friend of his new employer.

Nick suddenly changed his course, veering away from Audra and toward the buffet table instead. While he drank a glass of punch, he grew wary of the people surrounding him. He had definitely taken a wrong turn somewhere with Audra, a turn that he wished he could reverse.

He now felt terribly out of place. Maybe things would be better if he just left. He found Mr. and Mrs. Yates and wished them a happy anniversary. Before he could tell them he had to leave, Olivia Harper joined them and grabbed his arm. "Mr. Bryant, how are you enjoying your new home?"

Nick stared at the woman who had failed to mention his neighbor's peculiar decorating habits when she had happily sold him his house. He opened his mouth to voice a complaint, then thought better of it. He had a feeling that both the Yateses and Olivia would be offended if he spoke rudely about Audra. He tried to remain calm as he said, "I'm not sure yet, but when I decide, I'll let you know."

She didn't seem to mind his cryptic comment. She grinned and said, "Since you're a permanent resident, I'd like to know how you feel about volunteer work."

Nick shifted his weight from one foot to the other, feeling uncomfortable. Mr. and Mrs. Yates were obviously waiting to hear his response. What could he say? "Well, I, ah, I'm not sure. Do you need a donation for something?" he finally managed to say.

Mr. Yates cleared his throat. "I think Olivia is referring to a donation of your personal time." He winked at Nick and added, "You would do well to go ahead and say yes, or she'll hound you until you give in."

Mrs. Yates playfully swatted her husband's arm. "Charles, you're scaring him."

Olivia jumped in before Mr. Yates could answer. "He's right, Nick," she informed him. "I need volunteers to tutor students enrolled in a local literacy program. It's just starting up, and we can't begin until we have enough workers."

Nick inhaled sharply. He really didn't have the time or patience for something like that. He'd much rather hand over a check for an acceptable amount rather than actually getting personally involved in an endeavor like this. He looked back and forth between the Yateses and Olivia, all of whom were waiting expectantly for his answer. What was he supposed to do? "I'd love to help," he said hesitantly. "But I don't know how productive I'd be. I've never taught anyone anything." He hoped that was a convincing excuse.

Olivia shook her head. "As long as you're willing to try, the students are willing to listen."

His heart sank. He wasn't going to get out of this easily. Trying another approach, he said, "An accountant's job is pretty demanding, Ms. Harper, and I want to give my job one hundred percent." He looked to Mr. Yates for support and asked, "Isn't that right, sir?"

Mr. Yates was thoughtful for a moment, then said, "Yes, that's true." Addressing the rest of the group as well, he continued. "Nick's résumé suggests that he's one of the best accountants I've ever hired, so by hiring him, I'm hoping for a return on that investment. I can't lie and say that I don't want my employees to give their all to the company, but I'd like to think that my employees care about more than numbers and figures. I want them to care about the community and the people around us, and to be willing to help when help is needed. I've been involved in quite a few volunteer organizations, and I've always hoped that I was setting a positive example for the people who work for me." He shrugged. "Maybe I haven't done as well as I'd hoped."

His wife patted his shoulder. "Don't say that. You've done a great job. Hasn't he, Olivia?"

Olivia nodded vigorously. "He has. And I'm not trying to pressure you, Nick. But if you can . . ." she trailed off, leaving the ball in his hands.

Nick felt trapped. He'd come to this party to make a good impression on his boss, and now he had the feeling that if he didn't help Olivia, Mr. Yates's opinion of him wouldn't be so high. Swallowing hard, he asked, "What do I need to do?"

Olivia lifted an eyebrow. "Are you sure this is what you want to do and you're not just trying to impress your boss?"

Though she was offering him a way out, Nick didn't think he should take it. "I can't promise you that, but I'm willing to give it a try."

Olivia nodded her head. "Sounds like a good start. I'll give you a call sometime this week and fill you in on all of the details."

Nick nodded, wishing he had stayed home from this party. First Audra, and now this. Almost as if he'd read Nick's mind, Mr. Yates said, "So, where are you living, son?"

"He bought Clare Phillips's old place," Olivia piped up.

"Oh, next door to Audra," Mrs. Yates smiled approvingly. "Audra coordinated this party for us," she told Nick. "Didn't she do a wonderful job?"

While Mr. Yates and Olivia murmured in agreement about Audra's wonderful planning skills, Nick nodded and forced what he hoped looked like a smile. He just could not get away from her.

"She has such an eye for color and decorating," Olivia said. "I've been trying to talk her into decorating display homes for some contractors I know who build new homes. I think she'd be a natural at it."

"Oh yes, I think she'd do an excellent job. Look at the way she arranged for all of the flowers here tonight," Mrs. Yates said, gesturing around the room. She and Olivia moved closer together and launched off into a discussion of Audra's many talents.

Nick stood silently, trying to determine how he could politely take his leave. The party had been merely uncomfortable earlier, but now it had become a downright nightmare, like something out of the *Twilight Zone*. Was he the only person in this town who did not think Audra was anything less than perfect?

"Ahem," Mr. Yates cleared his throat. Clapping a hand on Nick's shoulder, he said, "Don't think you have to help Olivia for my sake. I may want my employees to be involved in the community, but I won't force the issue by dangling their jobs as an incentive."

"Yes, sir, I understand," Nick said. He wished he could somehow back out gracefully, but he knew it wouldn't look right. Besides, he still had time to find a way out. He might even be able to get his mother to take his place. He let his gaze drift over to where Audra was seated, still laughing and talking with Ryan. Even though it didn't make sense, he wondered what it would be like to have a civil conversation with her. Ryan certainly seemed to be having a good time.

Mr. Yates turned his attention to where Nick was staring. "It looks like your new neighbor is much more interesting than I am," he said, chuckling.

Embarrassed to be caught staring, Nick turned away. "I think you're mistaken. To be honest, she and I have gotten off on the wrong foot."

Mr. Yates lifted his eyebrows in surprise. "Really? Audra gets along with everyone."

Nick hated to give out all of the details, but he decided to stick as close to the truth as he could. "Not with people who dislike her light display."

Mr. Yates grew serious. "Audra's light display is very important to her. It holds deep personal meaning, and she has a right to a personal expression on her own property."

Nick nodded. Now, this was a topic he was far more comfortable discussing. "She may have a right to a personal expression, but I have a right to object to it if her personal expression affects the view from my property."

"I'll leave that to you all to work out." Mr. Yates paused, then added, "But you'll be hard pressed to find anyone who doesn't love Audra or her light display."

"Is that a warning?" Nick asked, feeling a new wave of frustration rising up in his chest.

Mr. Yates smiled in a grandfatherly sort of way and shook his head. "Of course not. It's not a threat or a warning. I was just wondering if you might have a change of heart once you get to know her."

"Sorry to sound pessimistic, sir, but from what I've seen of her, I'm convinced it would be a long shot." Nick looked his boss in the eye and smiled a polite, but firm smile.

Mr. Yates just shrugged, and said, "Never say never, son."

"Sure." Nick could barely contain his sarcasm. "However, I need to be getting home. My mother couldn't make it tonight, and I don't like to leave her alone when I can help it," Nick said, looking at his watch for emphasis.

"Of course," Mr. Yates said. "Glad you could make it. See you in the office tomorrow."

Watching Nick stride purposefully out of the reception hall, Audra felt an odd mixture of confusion and disappointment. What had stopped him from coming over to the table?

To her left, Ryan casually draped his arm over the back of

her chair, and Audra felt uneasy. It wasn't that she *wanted* Nick to be interested in her, but she didn't exactly want him, or anyone else, thinking that she and Ryan were in any type of relationship that went deeper than friendship. Ryan was a great guy, but definitely not ideal husband material.

However, it bothered her that Nick might not know this. *Tell the truth: you're attracted to him.* Audra tried to ignore the warning signal her emotions were broadcasting. Still, she felt almost wistful when she stole a glance at the door through which he had just exited. *Get a grip, girl,* she scolded herself. Ryan's presence next to her was becoming more and more disagreeable. She needed to get away, if only for a few moments.

Audra stood and quickly excused herself to the ladies' room. The rest-room suite actually consisted of three separate areas, including a long, mirrored space and a huge, elegantly lit, carpeted room furnished with plush furniture, beautiful lamps, and exquisite artwork. Audra's own living room wasn't even decorated so beautifully. There were several women milling around, touching up makeup, smoothing hair, and preening in front of the figure-flattering mirrors.

Audra sat down wearily and tried to relax. Seconds later, she stifled a small yawn. It had been a long day, prolonged even more by this party. She loved Mr. and Mrs. Yates like her own family members, but she didn't think they would be offended if she left early. Before she could rise from her chair, a group of four women entered. They looked to be younger than her own age of thirty by at least two or three years.

As they paraded the length of the mirrors, one of them asked, "Isn't that new accountant good-looking?"

"Oh, yeah. Nick something," answered another.

"Nick Bryant," said the third.

Audra decided against leaving right away. Instead, she relaxed back into her chair and tried to act as though she wasn't paying attention to their conversation.

"Is he attached?" the first woman asked.

Woman number three shook her head. "Single. Thirty-three, lives with his mother."

The fourth woman finally spoke. "His mother?" she asked, lifting her eyebrows. "I knew there had to be a catch."

The second woman shrugged. "Big deal. I'm sure anyone smart enough to hook *him* could find a way to convince Nicky that he needs his own place."

"Ummm-hmmm," said the first woman. "And since his office is on the same floor as mine, maybe I'll have to pay Mr. Nick Bryant a visit tomorrow."

Woman number three tilted her head and placed her hands on her hips. "Maybe I will, too."

The second woman looked irritated, but managed a small laugh. "Why don't we all pay Nicky a visit? That way, *he* can decide."

The four conspirators laughed in competitive agreement.

Audra drew in a deep breath and bit her tongue. How dare they talk about Sophie like that? Nick might be arrogant and overbearing, but he seemed to care about his mother. Sophie and he shared a mother-son bond that wasn't likely to be broken up easily, even if the hopeful contestant was tall; built like a supermodel; wore designer evening dresses and three-inch heels; applied cosmetics expertly, and referred to him as Nicky. At least, Audra hoped not. Unwilling to listen to the rest, she hurriedly exited the room, sickened by the idea that she had let herself become a tiny bit jealous of those women.

Audra shook her head and sighed. Nick might have captured her emotions for a short period of time, but now it was imperative that she stick to her guns . . . starting with the light display.

From now on the display would be lit brightly every night . . . because as long as Nick was annoyed with her, she didn't have to worry about losing her emotions to a man who had a committee of women waiting in line for an opportunity to snag him.

Nick waited until he was sure most everyone else was gone home. At a quarter till seven, he stuffed a stack of papers into his briefcase and cautiously opened the office door. After making sure the coast was clear, he stepped into the hallway and locked the door to his office. If he could make it to his car without being stopped, he'd be home free — at least for today.

He'd taken maybe five steps when a voice behind him called out, "Nick?"

Nick whirled around, relieved that it was only Mr. Yates. "Yes, sir?"

Mr. Yates waved his hand. "Enough of that 'sir' business. You've been here nearly a month, and I think it's time you started calling me Charles."

Nick nodded. "If that's what you want."

Mr. Yates nodded emphatically. "I do." He began walking down the hallway toward the elevator. "So, tell me, how are the numbers looking?"

"The numbers look great, sir."

"You sure about that?"

"Positive." Nick had put in extra hours since day one on this job, checking and double-checking his figures against those of the other accountants to make sure he was absolutely correct. Mr. Yates's company was doing well financially. "Was there something you were concerned about?" Nick asked.

Mr. Yates shrugged. "I just got a little concerned since you seem to be putting in so many extra hours. You come early, hardly ever venture out of your office, and leave long after the rest of the staff does. I guess I just let my imagination get the better of me." Mr. Yates chuckled.

Nick nodded, realization dawning on him. His recent work habits had become a necessity for an entirely different reason. "Actually, I just needed some time to myself," he explained. "After your anniversary party, I must have developed a . . ." Nick inhaled sharply and searched for an explanation that wouldn't sound arrogant. "Ah, well, I guess some of the single women in the office have tried to strike up friendships with me . . ."

Mr. Yates had an amused look on his face. "Hmmm, well, yes, I had heard there was some interest."

"It's not that I'm antisocial," Nick explained hurriedly. "I just don't enjoy being . . . chased. So I try to come before they get here and leave after they go home." He sighed, relieved to get this off his chest. "They've brought me cookies, slid notes under my door, and asked me out on dates. I know I haven't done anything to encourage all that." He shook his head slowly. "I figured the only way to put an end to it was to just . . ." he trailed off, looking for the right wording.

"Be a hermit?" Mr. Yates smiled.

"I guess that's one way of putting it," Nick said. He was really starting to like working for Charles Yates. The man kept a sharp eye on every aspect of his company, and things rarely escaped his attention. It made an employee's life much easier.

"Tell you what, I'll discreetly address the subject in the weekly memo, and that ought to buy you a little freedom. You should be able to open your office door every once in a while, at least."

"Thank you," Nick said gratefully. The door to the elevator opened, and Nick stepped inside. He held the door, but Mr. Yates shook his head.

"I still have a few things to finish up," he told Nick. "I'll see you tomorrow."

"Thanks again for all your help," Nick said again.

Mr. Yates smiled wryly. "I didn't say it would solve all your problems, but I'll do my best. Of course, if you were seriously dating a young woman, or maybe even engaged, that would help."

Nick shook his head. "Oh, no, I'm not ready for all that yet."

Mr. Yates turned and headed back to his office. "Too bad. That would probably do the trick." He turned around just as the elevator door was closing. "Ever thought about Audra? I don't think she's dating anyone right now . . ."

Nick didn't hear the rest because the elevator doors closed firmly and the car began its descent to the parking lot. On the way down, he considered Mr. Yates's closing words.

He wasn't all that interested in Audra, but it did strike him as interesting that a man in the know like Mr. Yates had failed to realize that Audra was already dating one of his employees. At least, it had appeared that Audra and Ryan were together at the anniversary party. And although Ryan hadn't said anything to the contrary, he hadn't needed to. His arm draped over the back of Audra's chair and the constant attention he paid her had done all of the talking, effectively keeping any other potentially interested parties at bay.

Nick couldn't determine Mr. Yates's motivation for suggesting that he ask out Audra, but he decided not to dwell on it. *Forget about it*, Nick told himself. *The man had made an honest mistake . . . right?*

Audra hurriedly maneuvered her shopping cart through the grocery store, making good time in the midst of grocery-store rush hour. On most days, she disliked grocery shopping, but she absolutely loathed shopping when the store was crowded. As she rounded the corner to the frozen-foods aisle, she looked down at her list, trying to distinguish between the items she'd already gotten and the things she still needed to find. Seconds later, she and her shopping cart had an accidental collision with another cart and its guardian.

Audra rubbed her temples, embarrassed to be in this situation for the third time in less than six months. It seemed that when she was in a hurry, she became a total klutz with a shopping cart. "I'm so sorry," she said, not even daring to look up from the floor. The last two times, she'd been yelled at by the victims, first an elderly man, and then by a middle-aged woman.

"If they had grocery-store cops, you'd be on the receiving end of a traffic ticket," said her victim.

Audra snapped her head up, recognizing the familiar voice of Nick Bryant. This had to be the worst incident yet. "Hello, Nick," she said, managing a tiny smile.

He lifted an eyebrow. "I guess you're pretty mad at me—" He grinned "—but you'll have to get more creative." Nick leaned toward her and loudly whispered, "It's pretty difficult to run down a grown man with a little shopping cart."

Audra assumed he was kidding, but she wasn't quite sure. She'd seen him only once since the Yateses' anniversary party, when she'd walked outside early one morning to retrieve her paper. He hadn't acknowledged her wave, but had sped off in his car as though he hadn't seen her.

He'd also taken to leaving for work very early and getting home rather late, so there had been little chance for them to talk again. Of course, in this situation, no communication was good communication, since the disagreement about the lights tended to rear its head when the two of them spoke.

Audra carefully chose her words, not sure how long his good humor would last. "I honestly had no intention of trying to hurt you. It's just been one of those days, and I got a little careless. Forgive me?" she asked, mustering up all the charm she could after such a long day.

He paused, as though he were considering her request. Audra felt silly waiting for his reply. It was nothing more than a formality for her to say "I'm sorry" and for him to reply with a simple "I forgive you," but, as usual, he was being difficult.

She cleared her throat to get his attention, and he said, "Remember the meeting you wanted to have about your lights?"

Audra nodded cautiously, feeling dread rise up in her chest. "Yeah . . . I remember you wanted to try a different approach."

He looked sheepish, and Audra felt a twinge of guilt for making the comment, knowing that he hadn't gotten far in his complaint process. "But," she added for the sake of being diplomatic, "if that's what you want, I'm still willing to go that route."

He didn't seem to be offended. "I think that would be a good way to solve the problem, especially since we *are* neighbors. We don't want to come across to the rest of the community as being like the Hatfields and the McCoys, do we?" He looked hopeful, and Audra tried to suppress a smile, knowing that he was only taking this route because his previous attempts had made him look like the grinch.

But, for the sake of being Christ-like, she held back any impulse to be the tiniest bit arrogant and agreed with him. "That sounds very workable. After all, neighbors should get along, shouldn't they? My mother always said that neighbors can be just as close as family, and sometimes even closer, if they try hard enough. We shouldn't let a small disagreement stand in the way of friendship, should we?"

Nick raised an eyebrow at her burst of eloquence, and Audra felt her ears grow warm. She had spoken too hastily, and now it looked as though she were too eager. She had a feeling he would have some type of smarty-pants remark to answer her speech.

Surprisingly, he didn't say a word, just nodded. Assuming he was trying to think of a snappy answer, Audra figured she wouldn't look a gift horse in the mouth, and rushed on before he had the chance to say anything. "So how about Sunday?"

"Two-thirty okay?"

Audra nodded. "Of course, the offer to visit my church still stands. Service starts at ten-thirty."

Nick frowned, deep lines etched into his forehead. His eyes seemed to look right through her for a moment, as though his mind were somewhere totally different. He shook his head and gave a sharp laugh. "No thanks. Church never did anything for me or my family, and I don't think going now would help us any. We've done just fine," he practically growled.

Audra took a step backward, knowing she had gone too far, pulling Nick some distance away from his comfort zone. She held up her hands in defense, and said, "Okay, that's fine if you can't make it . . . this week." She probably shouldn't have added that last part, but it went against her character to stop inviting someone to worship after only one or two attempts. Nick's eyes narrowed, and Audra wondered if he would really yell at her in the middle of the grocery store. People were already slowing down their carts and staring at the two of them curiously, having no doubt already heard about their first disagreement. Nick also seemed to sense that it would not look good for him to voice his displeasure right here. Instead, he, too, took a step away and drew a deep breath. "I'll see you Sunday at three." His reply was curt and chilly.

Audra blinked, wondering if she should mention that they had previously agreed upon two-thirty, but she decided that an extra half hour on Sunday would be well worth a peaceful few minutes for the remainder of her grocery excursion. Nick was already walking away when she remembered to call after him, "Feel free to bring your mother—I'll cook dinner for three." He didn't turn around or do anything to acknowledge that he had heard her, and Audra hoped he would have the decency to inform her if he didn't want to do the dinner. However, the meal might make everything go much smoother. If the way to a man's heart was through his stomach, then hopefully, the route to easing troubled emotions and curbing rude behavior was pretty similar. Most people were considerably more reasonable after a good meal. Hopefully.

Five

Nick stared in disbelief as he watched his mother cross the lawn to Audra's. After reaching the front door, she rang the doorbell, and the door was soon opened by a surprised-looking Audra. After several moments, she invited Sophie inside, although she did look outside warily, as though she were expecting Nick to jump out and snatch Sophie away from her house. Eventually, she closed the door, apparently satisfied that Sophie wasn't involved in some type of elaborate scheme orchestrated by Nick. Several minutes later, Audra's garage door opened, and her car emerged with her and his mother inside. Nick peered from the blinds, watching until the car was no longer visible.

Nick plopped down on the overstuffed leather sofa in the den and fumed. He should never have mentioned Audra's church invitation to his mother. He had informed her that they would need to be at Audra's at three o'clock, and then had carelessly added that she had even wanted them to come to church, but he had flat out refused. He wanted to get along with Audra, but "enough was enough," he had explained to his mother. She had merely nodded, and told him she'd be ready on Sunday.

Much to his surprise, when he'd come down to start the coffeemaker this morning, his mother was in the kitchen, finishing her breakfast. She had matter-of-factly stated that she was going to attend church with Audra, and she would see him that afternoon at dinner. At first, he'd thought she was joking, but the more he protested, the more clear it became that she was serious.

"Mom, I know I've taken good care of you since dad left," he'd complained. "You yourself said that God didn't listen to your prayers. Can you explain to me why, after all these years, you feel the need to go back to church? When I was little, you said you would never step foot into another church, even if it was your own funeral." Nick could tell she wasn't going to change her mind, but he demanded some type of explanation.

Sophie's eyes had softened, and she'd wrapped her arms around him and hugged him. She hadn't hugged him like that in years, and Nick wondered if she had bad news. He uneasily pulled away from the embrace and looked her in the eye, frantic that something might be wrong. "What's wrong? Did something happen to Alan?" Nick tried to remember the last time he'd spoken to his little brother. Sophie shook her head and tried to reassure him.

"Everything's fine, honey. I just need to get myself back in church, that's all."

He frowned. "Why? You've been fine for all these years." He gently took hold of her shoulders and asked, "Are you sick?" Nick felt nauseated. He couldn't imagine losing his mother.

Sophie had chuckled and shook her head. "I'm perfectly

healthy, at least physically. But I've made all three of us spiritually sick, and I'm going to do something about it by setting an example for you and your brother."

Nick sat down at the table, his heart still beating overtime from getting so worked up. "You don't need to set any examples for me. You already did when you left that place, and it turned out for the best."

"I know," Sophie grew serious. "It was bad enough that I turned my own back on the Lord, but I had no right to try to poison your opinion of Him." She sighed and sat next to him. "You used to love church, but you felt compelled to do what your mother did." She placed her hand on his arm and patted it gently. "I watched you grow angry and bitter at the Lord, and didn't discourage it because I felt the same way, and somehow, it made me feel better." She broke off suddenly, and Nick watched as she brushed away several tears.

Nick felt helpless. He hadn't seen his mother cry in many years, and he didn't know how to make her feel better. Silently, he waited for her to finish crying. Then she spoke again. "Having Audra next door has been a real wake-up call for me." She shook her head slowly. "I can't go on like this. I can't let the past ruin my future, and I pray that you won't either." With that, she stood up and opened the kitchen door. "See you later," she had said before she left him to spend the morning at Audra's church.

Now, Nick sat with his lips pursed, wondering what she could have meant by, "I can't go on like this."

Like what? He shook his head, confused. She had everything she could ever wish for. A new house, plenty of clothes . . . Nick had graduated from college with honors, and his brother would soon do the same. She had raised two sons she could be proud of, and they both doted upon her.

They were doing a better job than his father had, Nick thought, feeling those always present feelings of bitterness well up again. Nick stood up, too disgusted even to think about it any longer. He would take a long shower and then think about it. As he made his way to his room, he cast a rueful glance toward Audra's home, and he hoped deep down that wherever she was, she could feel his disdain. *What had Audra done to his mother?*

"Does anyone want pie? It's apple," Audra suggested hopefully. Sophie gave a strained smile and said, "Apple pie is one of Nick's favorites. Isn't that right, Nick?"

Nick grunted in reply and reaffixed his gaze toward the window out of which he had been staring during the entire meal.

Audra didn't wait to hear whether anyone wanted to eat dessert but rushed off to the kitchen to retrieve the pie—and balance her thoughts. The day had been quite full of surprises, starting with Sophie's knocking on her front door and asking to attend church with her. Audra had been certain Nick had put her up to it for some odd reason, but as she and Sophie had gotten an opportunity to talk on the way to the service, she realized the woman's desire to come was genuine. She didn't know exactly what Nick's family had been through, but she had the impression they were nursing some pretty extensive injuries.

Audra stole a glance into the dining room while she gathered the pie and serving plates. The atmosphere was uncomfortably quiet, with Sophie giving Nick pleading stares and Nick maintaining the stony demeanor he'd had since he'd come over for dinner. Audra had given up on trying to make conversation after Nick had accused her of "trying to brainwash" his mother in response to her asking if he wanted any peas. The three of them had picked over their meal, and she seriously doubted anyone would eat pie, but she decided that serving dessert would stall the more unpleasant task of talking about the lights.

His attitude was almost enough to make her give in to his demands. But if he had a right to complain, she had a right to decorate her house the way she pleased. Audra retrieved a carton of ice cream from the freezer and slammed the door shut in frustration.

Calm down, she admonished herself. *He is not worth all of this trouble.* Of course he wasn't worth it, but she couldn't help but wonder if he would have been more pleasant had his mother not decided to come to church this morning. *He didn't have to mention it to her*, Audra decided. Or maybe I shouldn't have mentioned church to Nick that day at the grocery store.

But, apparently, the Lord wanted Sophie to come to church with me this morning, Audra realized. *And if I had kept my mouth shut, she might not have come.* "So even though Nick's in a sour mood because of it, I can't let him make me feel ashamed for asking them to church," Audra murmured as she made her way back to the dining room, where she was met with complete silence.

Standing in the doorway, she said, "Why don't we have dessert in the great room, so we can sit and talk?" The great room was one of her favorite rooms in the house, with its glossy, honey brown hardwood floors; oversized, but cozy furniture; and the fireplace that was nearly four feet tall. She had decorated the room greens and golds, sprinkled with deep, jewel-toned reds as an accent. The room featured a full wall of windows, ushering in the delightful feeling of sunlit warmth for most of the day. Spending a few minutes in that room couldn't help but cheer someone up when they were feeling grumpy, Audra decided.

Audra led the way, and Nick and Sophie followed. Audra cut slices of pie more as a formality, figuring no one had any desire to eat it. Then she brought up the subject of the lights.

"I guess the real reason for this meeting is to determine how to find a balance between what I want and what Nick thinks I should do with my lights." She looked back and forth between Sophie and Nick. "Any suggestions?"

Sophie looked away, and Audra got the impression that she didn't want to get involved. Audra took a deep breath. It was between her and Nick from this point on.

Nick cleared his throat. "Obviously, you want the lights up, and I want them down." He shook his head. "Unless one of us changes our mind, no one will be satisfied."

Audra shook her head slowly. "Well . . . You're right, to a degree. But I'm not totally against a compromise. I just don't want to be the only one making a compromise. If this is going to work, we're going to have to do a little give and take."

Nick gave her an odd look, and Audra felt self-conscious. Apparently, she had said something he didn't like, but she couldn't see anything wrong with her point of view.

"Give and take?" Nick snorted. He stood up and jammed his hands into his pockets. "We're not married. We're just neighbors. This is about property value, not give and take."

Audra was indignant. "What do you mean, property value?"

"I'm talking about the amount of money I paid for my house. And the amount of money I should gain if I ever sell it. As long as this . . . spectacle is next door, I'll be lucky to get what I put into it. I might as well kiss equity good-bye."

Audra stood to face him and narrowed her eyes. "If this was

so important to you, maybe you shouldn't have paid so much for the house. No one forced you to buy it."

"No one mentioned that there was a three-ring circus next door, either."

"What are you talking about?" Audra was genuinely confused.

"I'm telling you that had I known about all of this before I made the offer, I wouldn't have bought it."

"You mean you never saw the lights?"

Nick shook his head. "Not until after I moved in. Why did you wait until after I moved in to turn them on?"

"I didn't. I always have my lights on . . ." Audra trailed off, thinking back to when Nick had first moved in. "Oh." She sat down, feeling slightly reticent. "I was on vacation when you bought the house. When I got back, I realized my timer hadn't been set properly. My lights never came on while I was gone."

Nick stared at her, suspicion veiling his eyes. "Oh really?"

"Really."

"How convenient." Nick sat down, too, apparently out of steam.

"I'm sorry," Audra said, feeling some compassion for him. It was one thing to buy the house *knowing* about her display, but it was something entirely different for him not to have seen the lights until *after* he had moved in.

"Right. I just bet you are."

"I am. But I hardly think that my expression of my personal beliefs would contribute to a loss in property value. You can check with the homes association. Houses here are selling well, and at good prices."

Nick didn't answer, but Audra sensed that she had made some progress. She leaned closer to Nick and said, "I think the problem here is that I love Christmas and I celebrate it year-round. You dislike Christmas. What if you hated yellow and I painted my house yellow? Would you still feel the same way?"

"We're not talking about paint," Nick countered. "It's different."

"How?" Audra stood her ground.

Nick opened and closed his mouth, but didn't speak immediately. He turned slightly and sat as quiet as a stone.

Audra had the feeling that Nick's dislike of her lights stemmed from something about Christmas itself that he didn't like. As far as she knew, she wasn't affecting any of the neighborhood's property values so it was possible that he was reacting to something other than that issue.

"Nick?" Audra ventured gently, trying not to sound antagonistic.

"Yeah," was his gruff reply.

"Well, I was just wondering . . ." Audra hesitated, remembering that Sophie had been the one to tell her that Nick disliked Christmas. Sophie had already hinted that Nick hadn't been too pleased about her attending church with Audra, and she didn't want to cause any further problems between Nick and his mother.

Audra glanced at Nick and found him staring at her, his emotions unreadable. "You were saying?" he prompted.

"Yes." Audra took a deep breath and forged ahead. "I just wonder if you have a personal preference to dislike Christmas. That doesn't give you a right to make me hide my love for Christmas. I'm a Christian. Christmas is a celebration of my savior's birthday. It's part of my religious freedom."

"And what if *I* don't believe in Christmas? Wouldn't that mean you were violating *my* religious freedom?" Nick argued.

Audra was shocked at what she was hearing. Although Nick claimed not to believe in Christmas, she didn't believe for one second that he was being honest. Just that morning, Sophie had mentioned that she had attended church on a regular basis when her sons were younger.

"Nick, I don't believe that you don't think Jesus is real," Audra said, careful to keep eye contact with him.

Nick lifted his eyebrows. "I didn't say that."

Audra shrugged. "You might as well have. You said you don't believe in Christmas."

Nick looked toward Sophie. "Mom, it's time to leave." Turning back to face Audra, he said, "Where are our coats?"

"In the hall closet," she said, gesturing in the general direction. "I'll get them for you." She hurried to the closet, Nick at her heels, Sophie a few steps behind them. As she went, she inwardly lectured herself. *You just had to go and push Nick's buttons, didn't you? Now look at what's happened. I'm offended, Nick's just plain mad, Sophie's hurt, and I just destroyed any chance of getting this dispute resolved in a nonconfrontational manner.* The so-called "peace" meeting had turned out to be degrees short of disastrous.

When she handed the coats to Nick, he looked as if he could have snatched them from her, but made a great show of saying "Thank you," then gently helped Sophie into hers.

As her guests prepared to leave, Audra implored, "I'm really sorry this turned out to be so awful. I want this to be resolved as much as you do, Nick." He seemed to be ignoring her, and Audra felt her skin grow prickly and warm. Having people ignore her was one of her main pet peeves. She spent so much of her life trying to make people feel as if they mattered, and she generally took great pains to listen to each and every person when she was engaged in a conversation. Now that Nick seemed to be blatantly dismissing her, she felt indignant.

Feeling the need to say something, anything, to get his at-

tention, Audra said, "I'll tell you what. I *will* compromise."
Both Nick and Sophie stared at her. Pleased that she had his
full attention, Audra hesitated. She didn't really have a compromise in mind, but she had the feeling if she didn't come up
with one quickly, Nick would suggest something she couldn't
or wouldn't be able to agree to.

"And? What is it?" Nick probed.

What can I do? Audra mentally raced down corridors of her
brain, trying to piece together something reasonably acceptable. "Well, I'll admit my behavior today was, well, a little . . ."
Audra looked for a word that wouldn't make her feel *too* con-
victed.

"Antagonistic?" Nick offered.

And you weren't? Audra wondered. Biting the inside of her
lip, she fumed for a few seconds. Finally, she answered, "Okay,
I guess we could use that word. Anyway, here's my offer. I will
turn my lights off for one week, giving you a chance to cool
down. At the end of one week, I will resume my normal light
procedure. At that point, if you have sufficiently cooled off, we
may be able to talk about this in a more civil manner."

"Which lights?" Nick had an infuriating look of victory
etched into his face.

"All of the exterior lights on my house. I will not turn off my
interior Christmas decorations, and I will not turn off the lights
at my office. Any problems with that?"

Nick seemed to consider for a moment, then said, "Fair
enough."

"All right then," Audra confirmed. She opened the door to
allow Nick and Sophie to leave. As they exited, Sophie reached
out and squeezed Audra's hand. With that small gesture, Audra
knew that Sophie wasn't angry with her, and she drew comfort
from it. As she watched Nick and his mother cross the lawn,

she wondered what was really bothering Nick. He carefully held Sophie's arm as they walked, an obvious display of care and affection. How could a man who loved and respected his mother so much be so disrespectful and rude to other people?

I can't say that I'm completely perfect, either, Audra decided. This situation with Nick was going to take lots of prayer and more than a careful choice of words when she encountered him.

Six

Nick shuffled a stack of papers for the third time and looked at his watch. The day was passing far too slowly. Actually, the past four days had passed way too slowly.

Since his Sunday meeting with Audra, Nick hadn't been able to shake the nagging feeling of guilt that had shadowed him without end. The feeling of triumph that he'd expected to feel had faded away Sunday evening when he'd checked to make sure Audra was true to her word. Of course, the exterior lights were off, and the only light to be seen outside of her home was the lone porch light at the front door. Even though he had demanded it be done, something about the sight of that dark house made him feel as though something was missing. Each night that he looked out the window and saw that dark house, he felt more and more at fault. He shouldn't have let Audra take the blame for the meeting having gone awry. He'd acted sullenly during the meal and had egged her on during the meeting. Then, feeling spiteful, he'd let her assume all of the responsibility for its outcome and had accepted her week-long compromise without even saying thank you. Since that day, he hadn't seen his neighbor, even though he had hoped to be able to say thank you and to try to let her know he was sorry.

The ringing of a phone somewhere down the hall inter-rupted his thoughts. Nick took a look at the papers on his desk and decided today would be a good day to take his lunch away from the office. He had to attend a meeting tonight with the lit-eracy program he'd volunteered to work with, and he needed to get some air before he could effectively finish his work.

He gathered his jacket and notified his secretary that he would be out of the office for lunch. As he left the building, Nick decided to head for one of the cafés downtown, about a ten-minute walk away.

As he walked, he saw a man leaving a small florist's shop with an armful of roses. His mother loved flowers, and Nick hadn't given her any in some time. Thinking he would have an arrangement delivered to his mother, he went in. As he browsed, looking for African violets, one of his mom's favorites, he overheard another customer saying she wanted to purchase some daisies and send them to her sister, with whom she'd re-cently had a disagreement.

He had never sent flowers to anyone for an apology, but he wondered if he should send a small bouquet to Audra and a note to say he didn't mean to be so gruff the other day.

He went to the counter where a short thin woman took his order. For his mother, he selected a large table vase full of the violets, and he debated what he should send to Audra. She seemed to be the type of person who would like roses, but he didn't want to send the wrong impression. He knew that differ-ent roses had different meanings, and he was too embarrassed to stand there and ask the lady at the counter to give him a rundown on which rose meant what, so he finally decided on an arrangement of brightly colored spring flowers. The clerk then handed him two cards to include with the flowers. Nick filled out one for his mother, but couldn't think of what he should say to Audra. He handed the card back to the clerk and double-checked to make sure that the flowers were on their way to the correct addresses.

As he continued to a café, he felt slightly relieved that he had started to make amends. As for any formal apology, he would wait for a few days until he could be absolutely sure that he could keep his emotions under control. He had overreacted twice in conversations with Audra and he didn't intend to do it again.

A little after two o'clock, Audra was finishing up the last loose ends in order to end up for the day. After work, she planned to go shopping with her sister-in-law, Caron, who had told her she needed to get her mind off of the situation with Nick. Her family and friends understood why she had made the decision to snuff out the lights, but they had also agreed that her decision might have been too hasty, giving Nick the impression that she had given in too quickly, which might make it more difficult when she wanted to turn the lights back on. She glanced at her watch and decided that she would call it a day soon. She had to attend Olivia's meeting for the literacy program volunteers tonight after visiting with Caron.

"Looks like we have a delivery," Michelle remarked, glancing outside. "Are we expecting something?"

Audra looked outside and saw a delivery van from one of the

local florists. Shaking her head, she said, "I don't think so. I definitely don't remember ordering any flowers."

Laura grinned. "Then it looks like one of us is going to be the recipient of something from the florist." She walked to the door and opened it just as the deliveryman made it to the door. In one hand he held a clipboard, and in the other, he held a large crystal vase filled with a variety of colorful flowers.

"Looks like somebody's husband was in a generous mood today," Audra teased Michelle and Laura.

He checked his clipboard and said, "I've got a delivery here for Audra Clayton."

Audra looked up, surprised. "I'm Audra," she said, walking toward the door. When she reached the deliveryman, she asked, "Can you tell me who sent this?"

He flipped through a few pages on his clipboard and shook his head. "Sorry, but there's no name listed."

"Really?" Audra signed on the line he had indicated, and reached for the flowers. "They're beautiful." She smiled.

The man shrugged. "Don't thank me, I didn't send them," he said good naturedly. "But this street is pretty popular today." He gestured toward Sophie and Nick's house. "I just delivered a big arrangement to the lady next door."

"Oh?" Audra asked, feeling a little more curious. "Do you know who sent Sophie her flowers?"

He paused, apparently trying to remember. "I'm not sure, but I think she said they were from her son." He gave a little military-style salute and said, "I've gotta get back to work. Enjoy your flowers."

"I will," Audra murmured as she looked through the arrangement, hoping to find a card of some sort.

By this time, both Laura and Michelle were thoroughly curious. They looked on intently, and Audra was disappointed to inform them that no card had been included.

She placed the vase on her desk and took her seat once again. Looking at Laura and Michelle, she said, "I really have no idea who these could be from, but I love them."

"They're gorgeous, and I'm a tiny bit jealous. My husband hasn't sent me flowers in forever." Michelle laughed.

"Don't get too jealous. I'm almost positive that Caron and Kyle sent these." She shrugged. "Maybe even my parents. They called the other night, right after I'd told Nick I would turn the lights off for a week. I was pretty down about it, and they sounded concerned."

"Maybe," Laura said, "but didn't the delivery guy say that Nick sent flowers to his mother? Maybe he sent you some, too."

"Yeah, right." Audra laughed. Then she grew serious. "Actually, I thought about that at first, but I decided it was way too far fetched."

Michelle and Laura didn't say anything, but they looked unconvinced.

"Really," Audra explained. "You would believe me if you had seen how upset he was."

Michelle shrugged. "You never know . . . Underneath that rough exterior, he could be a big teddy bear, or . . ." she paused, thinking.

"A real puppy dog," Laura filled in.

"Enough with the animal comparisons, unless you're going to use the term 'vicious wolf' or 'slithering snake.' Audra laughed. Shaking her head, she added, "I can't imagine Nick as a sentimental softy."

"You never know," Laura said.

"You're right," Audra agreed. "Underneath, Nick might be a

nice guy. But I just don't think I'll ever see that side of him. I'm already dreading the next meeting."

Michelle and Laura instantly seemed to sober. "Is there anything we can do?" Michelle questioned.

"I don't think there is," Audra shook her head, starting to feel hopeless once again. Several moments later, she changed her mind. "Actually, you can do a lot. Keep me lifted up in prayer, and especially pray that I can keep my temper under control the next time I see him. As things have gone so far, I'm doing a terrible job of being a good witness. He has an extreme dislike of anything concerning Christianity, and I'm starting to realize that if any Christians he's come in contact with are anything like me, I can understand his point of view."

Laura and Michelle agreed to keep her in their prayers, and Audra decided that before she met Caron to go shopping, she would spend a little extra time searching the Scriptures for a blueprint for how she should conduct herself when she saw Nick again.

It would help her immensely to have a Scripture under her belt to quote to herself if things got rough.

Nick got turned around reading the directions Olivia had given him and ended up arriving ten minutes late. When he found the place, he grew uneasy, not having realized previously that the meeting would be held in a church. The small church parking lot was crowded, and as Nick drove around, searching for a space, he briefly considered skipping the meeting. He seriously doubted he would even be missed, but he decided to go as planned, realizing that Mr. Yates would probably end up asking him how he was liking the volunteer work. He didn't relish the thought of telling his boss that he had decided to quit before he'd even started.

When he finally located a space nearly a block away, the light sprinkling of rain that had been falling most of the afternoon became a downpour. Nick fumbled around underneath the passenger's seat to find his umbrella.

Drawing in a deep sigh, he got out of his car, ready to start the wet walk to the church. Before he could even take five good steps, another car pulled up and parked right behind his own car. Nick instantly recognized that car as Audra's, and he wondered if she, too, was involved in this program. He wondered if she knew that he would be here tonight. He also wondered if she would have found some way to bow out tonight if she had known he was coming. While she parked, Nick stood and waited. There was no reason the two of them couldn't walk to the meeting together.

Audra opened her door and got out of the car. She was wearing jeans and a deep blue blazer, but she didn't have a raincoat or umbrella.

She reached back into her car and retrieved her purse. Regarding Nick warily, she said, "As soon as I curled my hair, the rain clouds decided to let loose." She smiled softly, placing her hand over her head as she began walking.

Nick hurried to catch up with her, then moved close enough so that his umbrella would shield them both. "You know what they say about April showers," he said, trying to sound relaxed and cheerful.

Audra looked up at him, and he could tell she was probably trying to decide if he was genuinely trying to be kind.

He gazed down at her. "You can relax. I'm not going to strike out with a surprise attack."

Smiling, she said, "Good. I'd hate for us to get off on the wrong foot for the third time."

Nick didn't say anything but nodded. They walked a good amount of the distance in silence. Nick wondered if she had received the flowers and if she had liked them. He was very curious, but he held back from asking, not wanting to make her more suspicious of him. He had to admit that if he were Audra, he'd have a hard time believing someone who'd been highly upset with him could turn around and send him flowers four days later.

He'd tell her about the flowers some other day. Maybe. Right now, it was time to start being civil and start acting like a gentleman. He looked at Audra and said, "You know—" He was interrupted by Audra, who started speaking at the same moment.

"Nick, I—"

Their eyes met and they both laughed, albeit somewhat stiffly. Nick had the feeling that he and Audra felt they were walking on eggshells whenever they encountered each other. Nick gestured to Audra and said, "Ladies first."

She shook her head. "Why don't you go ahead? I think you started talking maybe a millisecond before I did." Her eyes twinkled with a spark of mirth for the first time, and Nick felt he was on more solid ground.

"Well, I was just going to say that . . . I'm sorry about what happened Sunday. I was out of order, and I shouldn't have been so unreasonable."

He looked at Audra to see if she was accepting of his apology. Getting the impression she needed more convincing, Nick rushed on to add, "I know this whole apology seems really ironic and probably pretty meaningless since I apologized to you last week in the grocery store, and then turned around and got all upset again."

Audra nodded slightly, confirming his suspicions.

Nick paused and cleared his throat, knowing he was looking

like a big phony. But he'd already started the apology, and he had to finish it and try with all of his energy to abide by it. "I let some personal issues get in the way of resolution, and, frankly, I don't know what came over me. I would never pull a stunt like that at work, so it was inexcusable for me to act like that with you. You were trying your best to smooth things out, and I goofed." After he'd spoken, Nick realized that Audra had been a little difficult herself, but he decided, for the sake of the apology, he wouldn't mention her part.

Audra held up a hand before he could get any further. "I appreciate your trying to be diplomatic, but I was hardly blameless. I contributed to the situation, too, and I feel terrible about it. I'm sorry, too, and I have been praying about my temper."

Something inside of Nick's chest tensed when Audra mentioned prayer, and he could feel her watching his face for a reaction. Determined not to fail another test, he pushed the feeling of discomfort aside and smiled. "So it looks like we're back on the right foot."

"Right." Audra flashed him a smile that sent surges of warmth racing through his heart. Feeling magnanimous, and confident that Audra had gained new respect for him, Nick opened his mouth and was unable to stop himself from adding even more to what he'd previously said. "And since you were so generous with your compromise, I want to return the favor."

"Oh?" Audra looked up questioningly.

Nick felt his pulse start to race. What had he been thinking, just idly talking on and on? Now she expected a compromise on his part, one he hadn't planned to offer.

They were steps away from the door to the church entrance, and Nick briefly wondered how hard it would be to rush into the church, head to the men's room, wait a few minutes, then join the meeting. By that time, Audra would have found a seat somewhere, and by the time the meeting was over, maybe she would have forgotten about his compromise. It wasn't that he didn't want to offer one; he had just let it slip out, without even considering what the compromise might be.

No, he couldn't do that. He had to say something, and say it fast, before she figured out what he was up to.

Audra put up a hand, "Nick, I don't want you to feel I've rushed you to a decision. If you don't want to talk about this now, I understand."

Nick's good sense told him to take the loophole she'd just extended him; However, his desire to be chivalrous surged ahead and knocked his logic aside. "No, I do want to be fair. You can turn your lights back on, and I won't say a word in complaint. In a week or so, I'll take you out to dinner and we'll talk about a way for both of us to agree on a permanent solution." Nick felt pleased. He'd come up with a reasonable-sounding plan in a matter of seconds. He doubted Audra would have any objection.

"Dinner?" Audra questioned, her eyebrows lifted slightly. "That's not really necessary. We can meet at my house or your house, you know."

Nick shook his head. "Let's not attempt to go that route again. Hopefully, if we're out in public, we'll both remember to be on our best behavior."

Audra seemed to consider for a moment, then nodded in agreement. "You've got a point there." She laughed.

Nick held the door for Audra, and they entered the church. Several people were milling around just inside the doorway, including Olivia, who rushed over when she caught sight of them. "Well, isn't this neighborly? I knew it was just a matter of time until you two finally noticed each other."

Audra laughed. "Olivia, this isn't a date. Nick and I happened to get here at the same time, and Nick was kind enough to share his umbrella, since I'd forgotten mine."

Olivia looked back and forth between the two slowly, then wagged her finger and said, "You're only trying to convince yourselves. I can tell there's definitely something brewing here."

Audra looked flustered, but Nick laughed. Brewing was an accurate term, but not the way Olivia had meant. If she'd been a fly on the wall at Audra's last Sunday, she'd have an entirely different view about just what was "brewing here."

"Believe what you want, Olivia," he said as he took hold of Audra's elbow and led her down the hallway to the room where people were congregating for the meeting.

"Why did you tell her that?" Audra asked. "Now she'll *never* let the subject rest."

Nick didn't answer, just kept heading in the direction of a seat for them.

"Did you even hear what I just said?" Audra asked.

Nick paused next to a row where there were two empty chairs. "Yeah, I heard."

"So? Why didn't you set her straight?"

He shrugged. "Why try? She's going to believe what she wants, no matter what we tell her. Just because she thinks it's true doesn't change the fact that we barely know each other, and have only had one civil conversation."

Audra nodded and silently took her seat. She kept quiet the rest of the meeting. Afterward, while he was talking to some of the other volunteers, she slipped away without his noticing.

On the drive home, he pondered his last words to Audra. If things between them hadn't started out on such a rocky path, he might have believed that his comment about their not being a couple had bothered her.

Still, the fact that she had as much trouble being nice to him as he had being polite to her caused him to dismiss that line of reasoning. It wouldn't bother him one bit if she was interested in him, but it was highly unlikely. If anything, he had probably unwittingly said something to offend her.

When he arrived home, Nick was troubled to see that Audra hadn't turned her lights back on. While he didn't enjoy the sight of them, it would have made him feel less guilty if she had turned them on, even if only to make him feel miserable.

Seven

*F*riday morning, Audra awoke at six o'clock with a scratchy throat. Thankfully, she didn't need to be at work until noon, so she decided to snuggle down under the comforter for a few more winks, but she was unable to rest, her throat crying out for relief.

Although she wanted a mug of hot tea, she put off making some for a little while. The house was generally chilly in the mornings, and she dreaded the idea of exposing her feet to the cold floor while she made her way to the kitchen. Audra leaned over and grabbed the television remote from the bedside table and flipped through the morning news shows.

After ten minutes of channel surfing and not finding anything she felt like watching, Audra decided to give up and brave the cold to venture down to the kitchen. She pulled on a thick pair of wool socks, and, wrapping herself in a bathrobe made from sweatshirt material, she slowly walked to the kitchen, re-

alizing along the way that her walk to the car after the meeting
had rewarded her not only with a sore throat, but with a cough,
as well.

Yuck, a cold. Audra shivered and rubbed her arms. Usually,
she made tea the old-fashioned way, in a teapot that actually
whistled to signal the water was ready, but she felt so awful that
she pulled a mug from the cupboard and decided to zap some
water in the microwave and have a quick cup to get her started.
While she waited for the water to heat, she perused her extensive tea collection and picked a decidedly indulgent blend that
was supposed to taste like butter toffee. Caron and Kyle had
given her a gift set of several unusually flavored teas a couple of
months earlier, and she hadn't gotten around to trying any of
them yet, but this morning seemed like a good time.

As soon as she added the tea bag to the hot water, Audra
could tell she would like this tea. The aroma that wafted up
into the air truly did smell like butter toffee, and she hoped it
would taste just as delicious.

After adding her requisite teaspoon of honey, she took the
mug and padded down the hallway to the great room. There,
she curled up on the sofa and sipped the tea, watching the light
patterns and shadows on the wall change as the sun rose. The
tea did live up to its name, and Audra thoroughly enjoyed it.
She was halfway through the cup and contemplating making
another mug when the front doorbell rang. Wondering who
could be at her door so early, Audra hurried to answer it.

She swung the door open and found Nick standing on the
front porch. Audra fought the urge to close the door, run to a
mirror, and give herself a once over, then come back to see
what Nick wanted. She put a hand to her hair and determined
that it wasn't sticking out in odd directions. At least she had remembered to wrap her hair in a scarf the night before.

She looked down at her comfy but decidedly nonglamorous robe, her pink-and-lavender-striped flannel pajama pants, and her green wool socks, and reasoned that, although she wasn't exactly a fashion plate, she was grateful she wasn't wearing the neon orange and green nightgown her great aunt Myra had given her for Christmas last year. Just thinking about it made Audra shudder, and she made a mental note to leave that poor nightgown in the box for eternity.

"Looks like I woke you up," Nick said. He, of course, looked well put together, dressed in a dark-blue suit and a tan overcoat.

Audra shook her head and held up her mug. "Actually, I was just having breakfast." She cleared her throat and took another sip of tea, amazed at how scratchy her voice sounded.

Nick's forehead wrinkled in concern. "Are you sick?"

Audra nodded. "I guess I caught a cold."

"You shouldn't be out here without a coat," Nick said, waving her farther inside the house. As she retreated into the foyer, Nick followed, and she smelled the woodsy scent of his cologne. "You should have waited for me to walk you to the car. I looked around and you were gone."

Audra shrugged. "I didn't want to interrupt you."

"It wouldn't have bothered me." He frowned. "Did you take some medicine?"

Audra was torn between feeling flattered by his attention, and feeling defiant that he was treating her as if she were a six-year-old who had caught a cold after playing out in the rain when she wasn't supposed to be outdoors.

After a moment, she decided not to get upset, since Nick was in such a good mood. "Actually, no, I haven't. I was thinking about running to the store to get an arsenal of cough syrup, lozenges, and orange juice."

"I could run out and get you some," he offered.

She shook her head. "I know I don't look so great, but I'm really not that sick."

"Well, take care and get lots of rest," Nick admonished. Turning to leave, he added, "I'll have my mom check in on you later."

Audra blinked. Nick was sending his mother to check on her? He must really feel sorry for her. She didn't want to hurt his feelings, so she didn't argue, and said, "Thanks. I'll probably go into the office around one or so, but I'll be looking out for her."

"Are you sure? Shouldn't you stay home and rest?"

"I think I can manage," she told him. Teasing, she added, "Shouldn't you be at work?"

He laughed. "Okay, I can see I'm wearing out my welcome." He turned to leave but stopped short. "Wait, the reason I came over in the first place was to ask you why you didn't have your lights on last night. Did I say something wrong?"

Audra paused, trying to think back. "Actually, I think I just forgot. I guess I was already starting to feel a little under the weather when I got home."

"Oh." Nick looked somewhat relieved. "I'll see you later then."

Audra held the door for Nick and watched as he walked out to his car. She was forced to close the door because she was overtaken with a bout of shivers. Feeling suddenly tired, she decided to take Nick's advice and rest for at least a few more hours.

Later, Audra awoke to the sound of the phone ringing. Her body felt like one huge ache, and she groaned as she reached over to grab the phone and croaked out a hello.

"Audra, it's Laura. Michelle and I are at the office and we

were concerned since you weren't here. You sound like you don't feel too good."

"I feel awful," Audra admitted. "But I feel even worse for not even showing up at work. Listen, give me a little while and I'll come down."

"Audra, don't you dare come out of that house. I know you have a need to do things yourself, but we are very capable of doing the job you hired us to do."

"Well . . ." Audra sank back into the pillows, trying to convince herself to stay put. "I will today, but call me if you need anything, and I'll get over there."

"Don't worry about us, we'll do fine. Now you relax and we'll see you when you feel better."

Audra gratefully accepted the instructions and hung up the phone. She snuggled back into her covers and immediately fell asleep. Later, she awoke again, this time to the sound of her doorbell ringing.

She stumbled out of bed, threw on her robe, and hurried downstairs. She opened the front door and found a worried-looking Sophie holding a huge stainless steel pot in her hands and pacing the front porch. When she saw Audra, her face creased into a frown. "Oh dear, are you feeling any better?"

"A little," Audra said. "Why don't you come in?" she asked, gesturing to Sophie.

"I got a little anxious when you didn't answer right away. I was debating whether or not to call someone and ask for help. I didn't know if you were too sick to come to the door."

Audra was really touched by Sophie's concern. And she was even more surprised that Nick actually had asked Sophie to check in on her.

"I made you some soup," Sophie said, lifting the pot she held.

"I love soup." Audra smiled. "Why don't you bring it into the kitchen?"

As soon as they made it to the kitchen, Sophie busied herself preparing a bowl of soup for Audra, while Audra sat at the kitchen table, feeling like a limp noodle.

Sophie told Audra she didn't believe in microwaving food, so she put the pot on the stove to heat. While she waited, she rummaged around in the refrigerator and found some orange juice.

As she handed Audra a glassful, she frowned. Placing her hand on Audra's forehead, she announced, "Child, you're burning up with a fever. Take this juice and get to bed. I'll bring this soup up to you when it's hot."

Part of Audra felt embarrassed that her neighbor had come over to nurse her, but the other part of her was too tired and worn out to protest the attention. In fact, she felt relieved that someone knew she was sick. The last thing she wanted to do was call her parents on their vacation and whine about having a cold, and her brother and his wife had their own family to care for.

So it was comforting to know that Sophie had thoughtfully looked in on her and was treating her as if Audra were her own child. "Thank you," Audra murmured. Wearily, she shuffled up the stairs and buried herself under the tangle of covers that had been her home base throughout the day. By the time Sophie came with a huge bowl of steaming soup, Audra realized how hungry she was.

She sat up and dug in with gusto. "Sophie, this is wonderful." She smiled. "I can feel my strength coming back already. What's in this?"

Sophie gave Audra one of her trademark gentle smiles. "Basically, it's just turkey noodle soup. Leftover turkey, carrots, onion, celery, and my homemade noodles. Then, of course, there are a few other secret ingredients I can't tell you about. But I've been making it for over thirty years, and it always perked up Walter and my boys when they were sick," she answered as she settled into an oversized armchair next to the bed.

"Walter?" Audra stopped eating and inclined her head. She didn't remember ever hearing Nick or Sophie mention anyone named Walter. Did Sophie have another son?

Sophie looked down at her hands, silent. Audra sensed she had stumbled onto foreign territory and tried to remedy her blunder. "I'm sorry. Sometimes I have trouble reminding myself to stop being so nosy," she offered.

Sophie shook her head. "No, no, I'm not offended. I haven't mentioned Walt's name out loud in so long, and it just slipped out." She laughed softly. "I guess I feel pretty comfortable with you to have just blurted it out like that."

For several awkward moments, Sophie stared across the room, gazing out the huge windows, while Audra busied herself eating soup, trying to think of some way to change the subject. If Sophie didn't want to talk about this Walter, she wasn't going to pursue the subject.

Audra was busy making a great show of loudly stirring her soup and spooning out mouthfuls when Sophie suddenly announced, "Walter was my husband." Sophie didn't lift her eyes, but wrung her hands and said, "Actually, he still is, but he left us when Nick was ten years old." Glancing at Audra, she added, "We don't talk about him much at all anymore."

Audra stopped midchew and stared. She almost always felt discomfited when people she didn't know very well suddenly announced surprising revelations; this happened to her quite a bit when she interacted with her customers.

Her family had always said she had a very honest and safe

personality, and she supposed they were right. Many times, after two or three meetings with a client, they began to feel very
trusting of her; in the course of a normal conversation, family
secrets and skeletons inevitably came tumbling out of their
closets, and their owners often seemed relieved to share them
with *someone*, namely Audra.

Of course, the fact that Sophie had once been married
didn't surprise Audra, and it was probably nothing to be secre-
tive about, but something about the way Sophie brought it up
had unnerved her. She had wondered about Nick's father, and
not having the nerve to ask of his whereabouts, she had supposed he had passed away.

Audra put the half-finished soup on the table next to the bed
and leaned back into her pillows, her appetite gone. She didn't
know what to think. Was she supposed to follow up this news
with a question or a reply? Either way, what could she say?
Somehow, she didn't think Nick would be elated to find out
she knew this about his family. He had never mentioned any of
this himself, and she guessed he had done so purposefully.

The pounding headache she'd been trying to ignore grew
more persistent, and she rubbed her temples, trying to relieve
the tension. She was disappointed to think that just as she and
Nick had been able to be civil, things might take a turn in the
opposite direction again. "I'm sorry, Sophie," she said, trying to
decide whether or not to ask any questions.

"Oh, my. I've gone and burdened you with my problems,
and I made you feel even worse," Sophie said.

"No, that's not it." Audra sighed deeply. "I just . . . I didn't
know what to say. I didn't want you to think I didn't care if I
didn't ask any questions, but I didn't want you to think I was being nosy by asking *too* many questions. I guess what I'm saying

here is, if you do want to talk about your husband, I understand, but if you don't, then I understand that, too, and if you don't want me to, I won't even mention it again."

Sophie laughed. "Audra, it's not your fault that I mentioned him." Shrugging, she said, "I guess it's time for me to think about this and talk about the situation." She smiled. "But I think you need a nap right now, so we'll finish this conversation later."

Relieved that she and Sophie had come to an understanding, Audra closed her eyes and concentrated on getting some rest. As she tried to get more comfortable, Sophie said, "I'm going to run next door for something, but I'll be right back. If you need me, I'll be in the great room downstairs. Just yell for me, okay?"

Audra nodded, already drifting off to sleep. She slept like a rock, a deep, rejuvenating sleep. The next time she awoke, the sunset was already in progress, the room growing darker by the minute. Taking a general survey of her symptoms, she realized she felt much better. The sore throat was nearly gone, and the cough was well suppressed by the cough syrup Sophie had insisted she take earlier in the day. As far as she could tell, her fever was gone, and most of her strength had returned. Audra took a moment to thank the Lord for blessing her with good health. She was rarely forced to take to her bed to recover from anything, because when she was ill, she usually didn't feel horrible for longer than a day or two.

Tomorrow she would be up and around again, back to business as usual. And even though being sick was no picnic, her body was probably just warning her to slow down and take life at a slower pace for a while. She had, after all, come through the winter's flu season with not even a single case of sniffles, and she had bragged about the fact to her family and coworkers. How ironic that now, in mid-May, she would succumb to some leftover bug. She smiled wryly, wondering if her pride had been the cause of her forced day off.

She glanced at the clock and saw that it was nearly seven o'clock. She should find Sophie, thank her for coming, and try to assure her that she could go home now. Nick would probably be home soon and start to wonder where his mother was.

Figuring Sophie might be reluctant to leave, Audra decided to take a quick shower, knowing from experience with her own mother that if she looked as good as she said she felt, the assertion that she was better would be more believable. After her shower, she hurriedly dressed in a comfortable, soft cotton T-shirt and a pair of khakis. Not wanting to fuss with her hair, she pulled it back into a ponytail and decided to forgo any makeup. She didn't have to leave the house, so getting all dressed up wouldn't be too practical.

As she descended the stairs, she heard a very familiar male voice coming from her kitchen. Pausing at the landing, she listened carefully. Nick and Sophie were in her kitchen, conversing, and Audra was pleased to note that he sounded as if he was in a good mood.

When she entered the kitchen, Sophie was busy stirring a pot on the stove, while Nick was chopping vegetables on a cutting board. Nick saw Audra and grinned. Nudging Sophie, he said, "Mom, look who's up and around."

Sophie turned and smiled. "Looks like you're feeling much better."

Audra grinned. "Thanks to a certain angel who came bearing turkey noodle soup, I think I'm out of the danger zone."

"Praise the Lord," Sophie said.

"Amen," Audra agreed. The word slipped out of her mouth before she could even think about what Nick's reaction would be. She glanced at him from the corner of her eye and found that even though his smile had faded slightly, he didn't appear to be angry. Turning to Sophie, she said, "I would hug you, but I don't know how many germs are lingering, so I won't. I'll have to find some other way to thank you."

"You don't have to do anything special," Sophie said, waving Audra's suggestion off.

"No, really, I mean it. I might still be up in that bed if you hadn't come over and looked after me," Audra said, taking a seat at one of the barstools that she kept at the large island.

"If you want to thank somebody," Sophie told her, "thank him." She pointed at Nick, who was suddenly very diligent about his chopping duty. "He was the one who told me I needed to come over and make sure you were okay. He was the one who said I *needed* to make the soup." Sophie grinned and patted Nick's shoulder.

Audra smiled, surprised. Nick cared about her that much? "Well, thank *you*, then," she said, turning toward him. "I still appreciate it."

Nick looked up with a teasing glint in his eye. "So what do I get? You had promised to get something special for my mom. Since it was my idea, all the rewards should transfer over to me."

"Really?" Audra teased back. When Nick was like this, he was such fun to be around.

Nick stopped chopping and firmly put both hands down on the counter, his shoulders squared. "Really."

Audra put a finger to her chin and pretended to think. Finally, she asked, "Okay, what do you suggest? I don't see you as the type of guy who would get all excited about a gift basket or some potpourri."

He quirked an eyebrow. "You're right about that." He put a

finger to his chin, as though he was in deep thought. Then he said, "But I'll take the hug you offered my mom. Or maybe even . . . a kiss," he said, grinning.

Sophie burst out laughing, and Audra rolled her eyes. "Sorry, mister," she told him. "I don't think so."

"Why not?" he challenged, shrugging.

Audra cleared her throat and tried to look serious. "Two reasons. One, I still have germs. And two, I make it a practice not to go around kissing strange men."

"We're neighbors. I didn't think we were strangers," Nick said innocently.

Audra laughed again, feeling a tiny bit embarrassed at Nick's insistent teasing. Refusing to reply to his last comment, she turned her attention back to Sophie. "Whatever it is you're cooking smells delicious. Can I help?"

Sophie shook her head. "I'm making my special meat loaf and green beans, and Nick's doing a salad. You just sit tight and relax." She playfully shook her spoon at Audra and said, "You cooked for us on Sunday, and now it's our turn. Go sit in the great room and read a book or something. We'll call you when dinner's ready."

On her way out, Audra glanced at Nick, who was still chopping the veggies. In the great room, Audra glanced over her bookshelves, and selected a new mystery novel she had purchased at the Christian bookstore, and sat down on the couch to read it. Reading was not really one of her hobbies, but every now and again, she found a novel that caught her interest and bought it, intending to read it when she had some free time. Currently, she had nearly fifteen books that she had never gotten around even to opening. It had seemed that she never had time to sit down and spend time just reading, although she did make time for her morning Bible study.

After making herself comfy on the couch, Audra tried to read, but her mind kept wandering back to Nick's behavior in the kitchen. He was being so friendly, and his latest attentions toward her were almost flirtatious.

While his attention was flattering, Audra knew that a relationship between the two of them would be impossible, given Nick's current attitude toward the Lord. He had many qualities she would consider as ideal in a husband, but she could never marry a man who didn't love and serve God. She wondered if Nick had ever seriously dated anyone. Had he ever been in love? He was thirty-three, three years older than she was. She had dated off and on throughout college but had been more career-focused during the past several years. She'd had friendships with other Christian men, but she hadn't met anyone who really seemed to be someone she'd want to spend the rest of her life with. Of course, she wanted to get married and have children someday, and she was at an age where marriage should be seriously considered.

Audra wondered if her interest in Nick was just a resurgence of her own longing to be a wife and mother. At any rate, she couldn't let herself grow too attached to him, knowing where he stood on matters of faith. If the Lord moved in Nick's life and drew him back to Himself, then things would be different. But if it didn't happen, she would be nothing more than a friend and witness to Nick. With that issue firmly settled in her mind, she turned to her book again. Perhaps she could get a chapter read before dinner.

Eight

Nick entered the house, tossed his briefcase on the kitchen counter, and poured a glass of water. The house was empty, and his mother had left a note, saying she had gone for a walk with Mrs. Melendon, a neighbor she had met at Audra's church.

Over a month had passed since Sophie had first attended church with Audra, and his mother continued to go each week. In addition, Audra's lights shone brightly every night, but Nick had decided that his heart wasn't really up for the battle. He'd been incredibly busy at work, and he and Audra had never gotten around to their proposed dinner to decide the fate of her decorations. Currently, the light issue had been neatly tucked away, out of mind.

Still, he didn't really want to argue about it. Over the past month, since their talk at the volunteers' meeting, the two of them had gotten better acquainted. Although Nick now considered her to be his friend, he hoped that one day, something more might develop from their relationship.

During the early stage of their developing friendship, Nick had hinted to Audra that he was attracted to her, but apparently the idea didn't sit well with her. She had almost immediately withdrawn from him. The relationship had stalled until he had adjusted his attention to be more friendly and less romantic. From that point on, he and his mother had spent a great deal of their time next door, and vice versa. They went on walks together, helped each other with yard work, and cooked together on Sundays after Audra and Sophie returned from church. Audra had often suggested he join them, but he flatly refused and gave no explanation for his refusal. He was sometimes tempted to say yes because he knew it hurt her feelings when he wouldn't go. She was deeply religious and always talking about the Lord, even though he tried to ignore those comments.

He figured Audra was one of those women who wouldn't date a man unless he shared her beliefs in religion, and he had wondered if his attending church would change her opinion of him.

However, his own conscience, left over from his churchgoing days, wouldn't give him clearance to begin such a charade. In a way, he was happy about this roadblock, because he had a feeling it would only cause heartache and confusion for them if their relationship grew more romantic under false pretenses. Still, Nick couldn't help but think that he and Audra would be an ideal couple. Nick took a sip of water and shook his head, realizing that this would be a near impossibility. Just as he was draining the last of the water from the glass, Sophie burst in the kitchen door, vibrant and full of energy.

"Hi, Nick," she greeted him.

"Hi, Mom," he said, giving her a hug. "How was the walk?"

"Excellent," she announced. "It always feels good to get these bones moving."

Nick laughed, happy to know that his mom was adjusting well to their new neighborhood. He had worried that she would feel misplaced, but he had to admit, since she'd been attending church, she'd made friends and was gone so much that he sometimes was a little jealous. Currently, his main social activity was the volunteer work he did twice a week at the literacy center.

Nick suddenly remembered that he had to teach tonight. Glancing at his wristwatch, he noted that he would have to leave in almost twenty minutes in order to get there on time.

On his way to change into more casual clothes, he wondered if Audra would want to ride with him this evening. The June air was warm enough for him to open the sunroof in his car, and maybe they could even stop for a sandwich after they were done teaching.

After getting dressed, he reached for the phone to call her, then changed his mind, deciding he would just walk over and ask. Outside, he stopped at the mailbox and retrieved the mail, which his mother had probably forgotten about. Their previous house had had a mail slot in the front door, so they never had to go outside to get the mail. Now that they had a curbside mailbox, both he and Sophie were having a hard time remembering to bring the mail in each day.

Nick flipped through the stack, finding a couple of bills, some catalogs and flyers, two cards for his mother, and one business-sized envelope addressed to him. There was no return address, and it had been forwarded from his previous address. Wondering who had sent him an actual letter in the age of e-mail and fax machines, Nick paused, then tore open the envelope.

As he read the opening line, Nick's heart skipped a beat, then resumed, with a deep, pounding rhythm.

Nick exhaled, feeling overwhelmed, then returned his attention to the letter again.

> *Dear Son,*
>
> *I am sorry that our first communication after all these years had to come in the form of a letter. Please forgive me, but I couldn't work up the courage to face you boys or your mother in person. I don't know the best way to apologize to you, but I want to make a start. Would it be possible for us to meet and talk? I know you have many reasons to be angry with me, but I'm begging you to put your anger aside and consider at least seeing me just once. I will be waiting for your answer.*
>
>   *Sincerely,*
>   *Nicholas Walter Bryant, Sr.*

His hands shaking, Nick returned the letter to the envelope and stuffed it into his pocket so he could dispose of it while he was away from the house. There was no way he wanted his mother to know his dad had written after all this time.

His mouth had gone dry, and he licked his lips repeatedly while he composed himself. He was angry, but he didn't want anyone to know his emotional turmoil, or the cause of it, at least not right now.

While he was standing next to the mailbox, trying to decide if burning the letter or tossing it out of the window on the highway would feel more gratifying, Audra emerged from her office and called out to him.

Arranging a calm look on his face, Nick waved and asked if she wanted to ride to the tutoring session with him.

"Sure," she told him. "Just let me lock up the office and grab my purse."

"I'll get the car," he said. Nick took the rest of the mail in to Sophie, then drove over to Audra's driveway and waited for her to come outside.

A couple of minutes later, they were on their way, enjoying the warm weather and extended daylight late spring had bestowed on them.

Audra chatted on about her day and related some funny stories about her clients, but Nick was only half listening. The majority of his thoughts revolved around the letter and the proper response. He supposed the polite thing to do would be to write back, informing his dad that he'd prefer not to have any contact with him. Actually, it might not be the polite thing to do, but it was *honest*, and he didn't think his dad expected polite from him after all of this time.

Of course, he could just pretend the letter had never come. After all, the letter had been sent to his old address, and, in all actuality, lots of mail had probably never been forwarded to his new home. He could just pretend that this piece had never come, either. Still, *he* would know it had come, and as much as he didn't want to acknowledge it, the fact of the matter was that his dad had written him and was now waiting for a response.

After twenty-three years of no contact, his dad had shoved the ball into his court as if nothing had happened at all, and it made Nick angry. He stared ahead, growing more agitated. How would his dad feel if Nick waited twenty-three years to answer this letter?

In an instant, Nick's attention was abruptly pulled back to the present with the sound of a loud car horn. "Nick, watch out!" Audra yelled.

Ahead of them, a sudden traffic jam was forming, forcing all cars on the road to come to a complete stop. Nick pushed down on his brakes, trying to stop before hitting the car ahead of him.

His car was slowing, but not as fast as he would have liked. If he didn't pull into the next lane, he would hit the car ahead of him. Nick started to swerve to the right lane, but was forced to pull back over because another car was in that lane. There were cars all around him, and he was trapped; either way, he was going to hit something. "Lord, help us," he said. Bracing himself for impact, he reached out his right arm to keep Audra from hitting the dashboard.

Just before impact, his car managed to reach an abrupt stop. Nick glanced at Audra, who was shaking. Not knowing what to say, and feeling shaken up himself, he put his hand over hers in an attempt to reassure her. Then he checked to be sure no cars were about to hit them. The car behind him cruised to a smooth stop, leaving plenty of distance between the two vehicles. Nick couldn't believe it.

He opened the door and got out of the car, just to be sure no damage had been done to the car ahead of him. Upon further examination, he realized that only about two inches marked the distance between the two bumpers. He returned to the car to see how Audra was doing.

He waited a few seconds before he said anything.

"Is everything okay?" she asked, her voice much quieter than usual.

He nodded. "I'm really sorry about that," he told her. "I should have been paying attention."

The traffic jam was clearing up, and the cars began inching forward. Nick cautiously put his car into gear and advanced.

Once the congestion cleared up, he returned to a safe speed and gave his complete attention to driving.

When they pulled off the exit ramp, Audra looked over at him. For a long while, she didn't say anything, just stared at him intently. Nick figured she was probably calming down enough to get angry with him for endangering the two of them. He looked straight ahead, waiting for what she had to say.

Finally, she spoke. "Nick?"

"Yeah?"

"I thought you didn't believe in prayer."

"What?" he asked, confused.

"I distinctly remember you telling me once that God didn't answer prayers."

He shrugged. "Yeah. That's what I believe. I never changed my mind."

"Then . . . why did you pray?"

Nick looked at her, not understanding what she was referring to.

"Just then, when we were about to hit that car, you prayed. You said, 'Lord, help us.' "

Nick pulled into the church parking lot, eager to find a parking spot and get inside. He vaguely remembered saying those words, but he wasn't sure those words really counted as a prayer. And if they did, he didn't know how to explain it to himself, let alone to Audra. Shrugging, he said, "Everyone prays when they're in trouble. Even bad people in movies."

Audra nodded, but didn't let the topic rest. "But I'm not talking about bad people in movies. I'm talking about you, just now. We were about to hit that car, and you prayed and asked the Lord to help us. Why?"

"I don't know." He pulled into an empty space and turned the car off.

"But, Nick. If you knew God wouldn't answer you, why did you even bother praying?"

Nick felt trapped. Audra had never pressed religion on him, but all of a sudden, because of an unwitting flap of his lips, she was arguing her case like a trial lawyer.

He sighed. "Look, I told you I don't know. God doesn't answer my prayers."

"He did just then," Audra said quietly. "We didn't have a wreck."

"But remember, I said 'Lord help *us*.' You're the one who prays all the time. Maybe He didn't want *you* to get hurt."

"So you're saying that God did stop the wreck from happening?"

"No. God has not cared what happens to me for a long time. I got where I am today because of my own hard work and persistence, not by praying, because it doesn't work. For me to start praying now would be hypocritical. Even if God did answer prayers—which He doesn't—I doubt He would listen to me now." Nick opened the door and got out, but Audra didn't move. Several seconds passed, and he ducked his head back inside to see what was taking her so long. "Are you coming?"

"Do you think God answers anyone's prayers?" Audra asked.

Nick sat back down in the car, frowning. It seemed as though today he was a magnet for problems. First a letter from his dad, now Audra's barrage of questions. "I guess he might answer some people's prayers, like yours or people at your church."

"What about your mom's?"

Nick inhaled sharply. Audra was treading on shaky ground, asking about his mom's prayers. In his opinion, it seemed God had all but forgotten his mom existed, and she had agreed until she started going to church recently. He didn't know if his mom prayed anymore, and he didn't know if her prayers had been answered, but he knew one thing for sure. If God had really wanted to make an impression on him, He had missed his chance when He failed to bring his dad home twenty-three years earlier. To answer Audra's question, he said, "I said I don't know." Nick got out of the car once again and shut the door. He was walking to the church door when Audra caught up with him.

"Nick?" she said, placing her hand on his arm.

He looked down at her and saw urgency in her eyes. "Yes, Audra."

"Why didn't the wreck happen?"

Nick let out an exaggerated exhale. "I guess God wanted to protect you. I bet you prayed, didn't you?"

"Yes."

He threw his hands up in the air. "That's why. It wasn't my prayer. It was yours. *You* prayed, and since God listens to *you*, He stopped the wreck from happening." He moved forward, but she stopped him. He looked down at her, annoyed.

"Is that what you really believe?"

He hesitated. Did he believe that? He had long ago given up praying, but the one time he picked to pray, it appeared that it had been answered. Was it a coincidence, or had he just been lucky that Audra was in the car to pray?

"What do you really believe, Nick?" Audra persisted.

He turned to face her. "This is what I believe about religion. I believe God exists. I believe He answers prayer. I believe He has favorites, and I'm not one of them, so I don't pray. This is what I believe, and I don't want to talk about it anymore." He held the door for Audra, and they walked inside. Just before they entered the meeting, Audra gave him an impromptu little hug so quickly that he almost missed it. Then she squeezed his hand and whispered, "Jesus loves you, Nick. And I think you love Him, too."

Too tired to argue about it, Nick said nothing, relieved that they were about to start tutoring, and Audra wouldn't be able to bug him anymore. He couldn't take any more of this soul searching today. It hurt too much.

Audra climbed into bed, thoroughly exhausted, but happy. She closed her eyes and spoke to the Lord as she did every night, telling Him about her day, and thanking Him for all He had done for her and the rest of the world. To close her prayer, she added a special thank-you. "Lord, I just want to continue to pray for Nick. I know he was a little annoyed with me, and I admit I got a little carried away, but I just got so excited that he admitted to praying. Even though he says he doesn't think You will listen to him, I know he has to be wondering about what happened after he prayed today. I just want to ask You to keep speaking to him. I have a feeling he wants to believe, but he can't or won't right now. But I'm going to keep praying for him." Audra fell asleep wondering how Nick felt about the whole situation, and hoping his perspective might be changing.

Nine

*S*unday, on the way home from church, Audra and Sophie stopped at a cafeteria for lunch. Nick was out of town on business, and the two ladies had decided they weren't up to cooking a big meal.

As they ate, Audra couldn't help but wonder if Nick had mentioned anything about the near wreck to Sophie. She was too polite to ask, but she got her answer soon enough.

"I'm afraid something's happening with Nick, and I don't know if it's good or bad," Sophie announced as they were enjoying a dessert of coconut cream pie.

Audra lifted her eyebrows in response. She nearly had to bite her lip to keep from blurting out what had happened the other day. If Nick hadn't told Sophie yet, she wouldn't feel right about telling her.

"Thursday afternoon, he was in such a good mood. But by the time he got home from teaching, he was in such a dark mood." Sophie shrugged her shoulders in confusion. "I don't know what got into him. He started throwing all these questions at me about praying, and whether or not prayer even worked." Sophie hung her head. "It's all my fault, and God is punishing me through Nick." She looked across the table at Audra, tears welling up in her eyes.

Audra's heart ached for Sophie. How could this sweet woman blame herself for Nick's troubles? Audra gently patted Sophie's hand. "I'm sure whatever Nick's going through isn't your fault."

Sophie pulled a handkerchief from her purse and sobbed into it. Sophie couldn't be comfortable sitting here in a restaurant full of people, feeling anguished over her son's behavior, so Audra decided it was time to leave. As she led the older woman from the restaurant, Audra felt a little miffed at the way Nick's attitude had affected his mother. How could he have gone on a business trip when Sophie was feeling so vulnerable and guilty?

In the car, Sophie's restrained weeping developed into a flood of tears and hiccupping sobs.

Audra petted Sophie's arm as she drove back to their neighborhood. She debated with herself over taking Sophie to her own house or having her spend the afternoon with Audra at Audra's place. Finally she decided Sophie was coming with her. She needed some cheering up, and Audra didn't think having any reminder of Nick's presence would help the woman feel any better.

Once they arrived, she sat Sophie on the wicker loveseat in the kitchen and proceeded to make tea. When it was ready, she joined the other woman, and the two of them sipped their tea in silence.

Soon, Sophie was calm enough to speak. "Walt and I got

married when we were in our mid-twenties. Neither of us had ever attended church on a regular basis. We were poor, but we were happy, at least at first. A few months before Nick was born, Walt lost his job, and we almost lost our apartment. Our landlady was a Christian, and she gave us a little time to get back on our feet. She helped me find a job doing day work, and a few weeks later, Walt got another job.

She invited me to go to church with her, and to make a long story short, I got saved, but Walt didn't have any interest in my new life. I was determined to make him get saved, but I guess I only made things worse. Nick was born on Christmas Day, and I just knew he was a special gift from God. I took him to church with me and taught him about Jesus, and he loved it. He was so sweet and gentle. Nine years later, our second son, Alan, was born, but by that time, Walt wanted a divorce. He was spending more and more time away from home, and he said that I was making him miserable, trying to get him saved. Sometimes he would stay gone for days, but he would always tell Nick that he had to be gone so much for work. Walt and I fought terribly, and Nick would get so upset." Sophie burst into tears again, and Audra hugged her while she cried.

"Sophie, I'm so sorry," Audra said, feeling weepy herself. Nick and Sophie had already been through so much.

Sophie composed herself again and resumed her story. "Walt would yell about how I was no fun anymore, and I would yell back about what a sinner he was. Nick would cry and cry, and I told him to pray to Jesus about it, that He would be able to fix things." Sophie shook her head. "That's where I went wrong. The day before Nick's tenth birthday, on Christmas Eve, Walt left for good. He just packed and left. We didn't hear from him again."

"Oh, Sophie, that's not your fault," Audra said, trying to be comforting.

"No, there's more." Sophie blew her nose, then continued. "I was scared and alone, with two little boys to care for. At first I prayed for God to send Walter back. Nick was depressed, and couldn't eat or sleep; he missed his dad so much. I tried to pretend I was okay, letting people at my church pray for me and help with the boys and our expenses, but after a few months, I just got angry. I knew Walter wasn't coming back, and I felt like God had let me down. I got a job and decided I was going to be the best mother I could be to my boys, and I thought I was doing a good job. Alan was too little to know what was going on, but Nick still wanted his dad back. He whined and cried, and it just hurt me so bad to see *him* hurting. He would ask me when his dad was coming home, and I didn't have an answer. When my faith ran out, I stopped going to church. I stopped reading Bible stories to the boys. Nick was so faithful, though. He prayed every night, and read his little Bible the church had given him.

"One day, I came home from work, tired and grumpy, and Nick was going on and on about how God was going to bring his daddy back. I felt angry, because I felt like Nick didn't think I was a good enough parent, and I snapped at him and told him that God didn't answer our prayers. I yelled and told him how I had prayed for Walter to come home, but God hadn't listened. He argued that our pastor said that God always listens, and I told him God must have been ignoring us."

Audra inhaled sharply, recalling what Nick had said to her about prayer. Had Sophie's comment affected him that deeply for all of this time?

Wringing her hands, Sophie said, "When I told him that, he just looked at me. I was his mother, and I had always been honest with him, so he believed me. He didn't cry or anything, he just went to his room. The next morning, he seemed like his old self, just quiet. I didn't even realize anything was wrong, until I was cleaning his room and I found his little Bible in the trash can. He quit saying his prayers at night, and I knew I should have repented and gone back to church, but by then I was too bitter. I was resentful, and I poisoned my own son, because it felt good to have someone on my side.

"From then on, we never talked about God or church anymore, and I watched Nick grow more and more hardened. He was never really disobedient, and I never had many discipline problems, but he was always so self-reliant, and not in a good way. He had to do everything for himself, and wouldn't let other people help him. I guess he figured if God wouldn't help him, who would?"

Sophie wept quietly while Audra digested all of this information. This conversation had suddenly given her brand-new insight into why Nick was the way he was. She couldn't imagine how he must have felt when his mother told him that God didn't care about him. She could understand why he hated Christmas and anything having to do with Christmas, since the holiday was connected to so many bad memories. And, more important, she could understand his confusion about Sophie returning to church now. He probably felt as if his mother was now betraying him, telling him that what he believed was wrong.

"Oh, Sophie . . . I can understand how both you and Nick feel, and I know that God has forgiven you. You don't have to feel guilty about this."

Sophie nodded, and said, "But what do we do about Nick?"

Audra's shoulders sagged. What could they do about Nick? If he felt as if they were teaming up against him, he would not be appreciative. Audra realized there wasn't really anything she and Sophie *could* do.

She put her arm around the woman's shoulders and said, "I don't think there is anything we can do to make him different. But we can pray about it. I know God will listen. And we're going to have to trust God to work this out."

Sophie nodded, and Audra could sense uneasiness on her part. Her faith was undoubtedly being tested again, with the opportunity to lay her deepest troubles at the Lord's feet and trusting Him to solve them.

She turned to Sophie to look her in the eye. "Listen, I know you might feel a little worried about this. But we have to trust him. He will listen to our prayers, and we'll trust Him to change Nick."

Sophie nodded in agreement. "I know. I'm just worried about Nick. He's been like this for so long, and I've never really explained to him why I turned my back on the Lord. If I tell him that I'm putting all my trust in the Lord now, he'll just argue about his dad not coming back. He'll say that God doesn't answer prayer, and I'm not sure I have an answer for that."

"Sophie," Audra said, "If our hearts are in the right place, God always listens to our prayers. And He answers, too. But we have to understand that God doesn't work according to our schedule. He may hear a prayer, and answer it, but we might not see the results for some time. But we have to be willing to accept His answer, even if we don't agree with it. And if we're going to be successful, we have to be willing to live our lives like that."

A smile spread across Sophie's face. "That's right. When he gets home, I'm going to tell him that." She hugged Audra, and stood up. "Thanks for listening to me. I know I wasn't very cheery company, but I feel so much stronger now. Since I've gone back to church, and gotten right with the Lord, I knew that soon I would tell Nick that I had been wrong, and I've been dreading it. But I'll tell you something else. I've been praying every day for Nick and Alan to come to the Lord—and Walter, too, wherever he may be, and I'm excited to see what's happening to Nick. I think the Lord is speaking to him, and that's an answer to my prayers already." Her eyes, still damp from tears, shone with excitement. "We'll just keep praying and see what happens."

"That's exactly what we'll do," Audra agreed.

Monday evening, Nick didn't go home between work and his tutoring session. He didn't want to see his mother or Audra, didn't want to have to listen to their ramblings about prayer and the Bible.

Instead, he sat at his desk, eating takeout from the Chinese restaurant down the street, dreading having to face both his mother and Audra. It seemed they had become united against him while he was out of town and, according to his mother, had started some type of prayer campaign to get him back on the right track.

Late Sunday night, he had come home exhausted and almost immediately his mother had started telling him how she had been wrong to stop going to church when she did.

Nick shook his head in disbelief. What was he supposed to do, jump up and run to church now that his mother had changed her mind? She had told him that prayer didn't work, and because his dad hadn't come back, he had believed her. Now, she was saying that prayer did work, and God's answer must have been no.

That explanation hadn't set well with him. He had politely

listened, then informed her that he was an educated adult, and as far as he was concerned, his current philosophy was working well for him. He was living a successful life without having to depend upon the imagined, or placebo, effects of prayer.

He had spent a long and restless night, though, wondering if he really was wrong. Was it just a coincidence that, after his mother returned to church, he received a letter from his dad? He had always heard people say that God answers prayer in His own time, and his mother had repeated the phrase last night. Was this contact from his dad really an answer to their prayers from back when they had first been abandoned?

Nick couldn't convince himself that this was true. For one thing, they didn't need his dad now. They had already faced and survived the most difficult times alone. If God had really wanted to help them, why hadn't he sent his dad back when they were struggling to pay the rent and buy groceries? Or maybe when Nick was working two jobs while he attended college? Wouldn't that have been a real answer to prayer?

The fact that his dad was just now willing to make an appearance made Nick only more upset. What was the use? They were doing just fine as they were. They had money in the bank. They had a new house. Nick had been able to help support his brother for two years after he graduated from high school while Alan decided what he wanted to study in college. Now, at the age of twenty-four, Alan was a junior in college, earning a degree in music performance, as a classical pianist.

Although he felt uneasy about hiding the letter from his mother, he had made a decision to do what was best for the family. He didn't want to falsely raise his mother's hopes when she was so vulnerable, naively thinking that her prayers might finally be answered.

No, this was not an answer to prayer. In fact, if he believed in prayer, he would pray that his dad never try to contact them again.

Nick stood and cleared his desk in preparation to leave for the tutoring session. Of course, he would see Audra there, and he hoped that she would be considerate enough to keep her religious rhetoric to herself.

"Now we're going to talk about what it sounds like when you see the 'y' after the 'g,'" Audra said to her newest student, Violet Huber. Mrs. Huber was a seventy-three-year-old grandmother who had not attended school past the fourth grade. She had been one of the first people to sign up for Olivia's tutoring program, and had been one of the most constant attendees. Her granddaughter faithfully drove her to the church twice a week, and Audra greatly admired the meticulous approach Violet took in studying her lessons. She was progressing rapidly and had even expressed an interest in becoming a tutor herself once she was able. Olivia had been thrilled to hear this and had lavishly praised Audra's teaching ability, but Audra shifted all of the applause to Violet herself, who displayed a tenacious desire to learn.

Violet was a joy to work with, and each time she showed up to work, Audra felt more and more pleased that she hadn't found some way to wiggle her way out of this job.

Many of her students were elderly, and although they had trouble reading, they possessed a wealth of wisdom in matters of life, and she never failed to leave without having gained some new insight.

They had also discovered that she had more than a passing

interest in Nick, and in a kind way, they teased her mercilessly about it.

Audra smiled as she stole a glance over to the table where Nick was working with his students. Olivia had insisted on making all of the student-teacher assignments, and Nick had ended up with a table full of ten- to twelve-year-olds, all of whom had been referred to the program by their teachers at school.

At first, Nick was intimidated by his group of students, but as time passed, Audra could tell that Olivia had made a good choice. They looked up to him and tried hard to get their work done. Nick had really grown to enjoy working with them, and had admitted that he actually looked forward to Monday and Thursday evenings.

Nick seemed totally at ease this evening. Both he and his students were laughing and smiling, and Audra wondered just how much tutoring was occurring that night. From the looks of things, no one was getting much studying done. Still, she was happy to see Nick looking so relaxed, since Sophie had called her at work to tell Audra that Nick hadn't taken Sophie's admission and apology too well.

Earlier this evening, he had strode in and gone directly to his table without even a hello to Audra. She felt disappointed. She and Nick usually shared good-natured banter during their times together. It hurt that he simply hadn't acknowledged her presence.

Considering that she had promised herself to not get too close to Nick, she shouldn't be feeling so out of sorts. She would just have to spend a few days reminding herself that Nick wasn't very likely ever to see eye to eye with her about matters of faith, and then she would start to feel better.

With a deep sigh, Audra forced her attention back to her table, and patiently began explaining to Mr. Jacobs the difference between the combination of "ou" in words such as though, bough, and through.

Nick was well aware of the fact that seven pairs of eyes were intently watching him as he scribbled numbers on a sheet of blank notebook paper. Feeling self-conscious, he moved his arm over part of his paper to hide his work, his frustration rising when he came up with the wrong answer. Again.

He frowned and bit the end of his pencil, wondering what the kids would say when they realized that he, a grown man, a a professional accountant, couldn't solve a sixth-grade math problem.

Jake had been struggling with the problem for the better part of a half hour when he had finally asked Nick for help. Nick had smiled, realizing how much Jake reminded him of himself when he'd been younger. He had sometimes spent hours toiling over his homework, refusing Sophie's help in order to relish the satisfaction of figuring it out for himself.

Although Jake had trouble with his reading skills, he was an excellent math student, and Nick enjoyed helping the boy when Jake asked for assistance.

Now, fifteen minutes had passed since he'd begun working the problem, and Nick was wondering what he would say when he admitted that he couldn't reach the answer in the back of the textbook. Of course, it was possible for him to save face by making up a way to reach that desired number, and give some complicated answer about how he had come to that resolution, but that wouldn't be any help to Jake.

Nick looked up from his paper and met seven pairs of somewhat worried eyes. His credibility as a reliable tutor was now officially on the line.

"So?" Jake looked wary. "You figure it out or what?"

Nick's mouth went dry. He cleared his throat and pushed his chair away from the table. "Almost. But I need to get a drink of water," he told them, trying to sound more hoarse than he really was. "I'll be right back, but for now, why don't we all get back to our homework?" he suggested with a wave of his hand.

Nick hurriedly stood up and headed to the water fountain. As an afterthought, he went back and retrieved the sheet of paper he'd been writing on. Knowing those kids as well as he did, they'd be all over that paper, and by the time he came back, he'd have a lot of explaining to do concerning his inability to solve the problem.

He folded the paper and stuffed it into his pocket as he walked out to the hallway. There was a very tiny chance they'd forget all about it.

At the water fountain, he encountered Audra, who was filling a large cup full of water.

"Playing hooky?" he teased.

Audra grinned. "No, just feeling a little—" she shook her head "—restless, I guess. How about you? Tough crowd tonight?"

Nick blew through his lips loudly. "No kidding." He lowered his voice and leaned toward Audra. "They're watching my every move like a hawk because I'm having trouble solving one of Jake's math problems."

"Sixth grade?" Audra asked, surprised. Teasing, she added, "And you call yourself an accountant?"

Nick ran his hands over his head. "Tell me about it. I feel pretty silly right about now."

Audra laughed. "I can't believe you're getting so worked up over this. It's probably a typo or something."

Nick saw light at the end of the tunnel. "You think so?" he asked, hoping she was right.

Audra shrugged. "Maybe."

"Good idea. I think I'll try that one." Nick leaned over the fountain and took a drink of water.

"You better have a pretty good reason to back it up," Audra warned. "You know how kids are. They can tell when you're just trying to be right for the sake of being right."

"Yeah." Nick was silent for a moment. He really would have to do some convincing. He glanced at Audra and caught her staring at him. She looked away, realizing she'd been caught.

He wondered, for the first time in several weeks, if Audra might be attracted to him. He wondered if the issue of religion was still a barrier to prevent a romance between them. "Yeah, you're right, but sometimes people believe what they want to believe. What about you?" he asked.

Audra blinked. "Me? What about me?"

"Can you tell when somebody's trying to be right for the sake of being right?"

She looked puzzled. "I would hope that I wouldn't be misled by someone who was trying to trick me, if that's what you mean."

"But what if you really wanted to believe them? Would you just hope they were right and pray that you had picked the right person to believe?"

Frowning, Audra said, "I don't think I fully understand you."

He shrugged, and moved closer to her. "Like me, for instance. I know that you wouldn't consider dating me unless I was a Christian, like you are."

Audra nodded but didn't say anything.

"And we both know my stance on religion. But—" he held

up a finger "—I'm attracted to you, and I think you might feel the same way about me."

Audra took a step away from him and looked back toward the fellowship hall.

Nick continued. "So what if I just showed up at your church on Sunday? Would that change things any? Would that convince you or would you need some deeper evidence?" He took another step closer. "Would you be overjoyed and relieved to know that I've gotten my life right? Would you be willing to be more than my friend?"

"It would depend," Audra said flatly.

Nick crossed his arms and leaned back against the wall. "On what?"

"On whether or not you really meant it."

"How would you know? You can't read my heart. I could spend the next twenty years sitting in the pews and singing hymns, but you wouldn't know if I believed your religion or not."

"I can't read your heart, but if you were really changed, I would be able to tell by your actions," she pointed out.

"How? Anybody can fake being a Christian. How do you spot a phony?"

Audra shook her head. "I can't say for sure. The Bible says to look at people's actions, but it also says that God is the only judge. For my own benefit, I would have to trust God and pray that I would not be tricked into a relationship under false pretenses."

Nick leaned his head to the side. "And you expect God to protect you from a lie?"

Audra nodded. "God always answers prayer, and He protects His children."

"Always?" Nick challenged.

Heading back to the fellowship hall, Audra said, "Always." She stopped and turned to face him. "Except sometimes we don't know what He's protecting us from, so it may seem like He's forcing us to endure the very thing we wanted protection from. But that's the beauty of His wisdom. He's God, and He knows everything, while we can only see part of the big picture. But if we really trust Him, he'll take care of us—in accordance with His will, of course." She patted Nick's arm, then left him alone in the hallway, thinking.

Ten

*F*riday afternoon, Nick took a longer than usual lunch break in order to attend an appointment he'd scheduled with Jake's math teacher. The kids had not wanted to believe Nick's assertion that the problem was printed wrong, and he wanted to redeem himself.

Nick had asked Jake for the teacher's name, then looked it up in the phone book. He'd called her early Thursday morning and asked for ten minutes of her time to review a question concerning Jake's homework assignment. She knew who he was because Jake mentioned him often, so she agreed to meet him at the school during the lunch period.

At the school, he found the principal's office and explained about his appointment with Ms. Grey. The principal, Mrs. Atwater, led him to the cafeteria and pointed out Ms. Grey's table.

As he crossed the room, he wondered if the principal had

sent him to the wrong table. The woman at the table was beautiful. She was tall and thin, with short, curly black hair. Her skin was the color of caramel, and her eyes were a glittering deep brown, so dark they could have been black. Ms. Grey was wearing a very flattering yellow pantsuit that reminded Nick of a warm summer day.

One thing was for sure: when he had been in elementary school, summer-school math teachers hadn't ever looked like her.

As Nick moved closer, he cleared his throat, and Ms. Grey turned to face him. "Hi, I'm Nick Bryant, and I spoke with you on the phone," he said, extending his hand.

She smiled warmly and shook his hand. "Please, call me Kameelah."

She turned her attention to the kids at the table, all of whom had lost all interest in their lunch once Nick made an appearance. "Finish eating," she told the kids. "Lunch is over in ten minutes." Then she turned to Nick. "Mr. Bryant, why don't we have a seat?" She headed to a vacant table a few feet away and gestured for him to sit down. After they were seated, she smiled and asked, "Now what seems to be the problem?"

"Call me Nick," he said.

"Okay, Nick then," her glossy eyes twinkling. "What's the problem?"

Nick tried to remember the argument he had prepared for this occasion. Unfortunately, Ms. Kameelah Grey's striking appearance thwarted his plan. He had been expecting an older, matronly teacher, the type he had been used to dealing with during his own days as a student. This woman was his age, and she was distractingly good-looking. He didn't want to offend her by pointing out flaws in the math homework she'd given out the night before.

He tried to think of something else to talk about, but his mind went blank. Ms. Grey glanced at her watch. "Nick, in five minutes I have to get my students back to class. Did you have anything of importance you wanted to discuss, or did you schedule this meeting so you could sit here smiling for no apparent reason?" She smiled, playfully reprimanding him.

"Well, I wanted to talk to you about number seven on the math homework you gave out yesterday." He fumbled around in his pocket, trying to find the sheet where he'd tried to work the problem.

A slow smile spread across her face. "Were you referring to one of the long-division problems?"

"Yes. That's right. And I hate to tell you this, but something must be wrong."

"Oh?" Kameelah lifted her eyebrows.

"Yeah." Nick held out the sheet and showed it to her. "I'm an accountant, and I solved that problem fifty different ways and still couldn't get the answer in back of the booklet. Neither could Jake." He steeled himself for a teacher speech, figuring she would deny having made any mistake.

"I know. It's impossible," she told him.

Ignoring her reply, Nick forged ahead with his point. "Well, I don't know what you're trying to do here, but there just has to be a mistake. Jake got what I'm sure is the right answer when he tried to work it, but—" Nick stopped, realizing what she'd said. "What did you say?"

"I said it was impossible to get the answer in the answer key. Good for you and Jake. You're both very honest."

"What are you talking about?"

Kameelah leaned toward him and lowered her voice. "Nick, this is the first week of summer school. I get a lot of kids in my class. Some of them want to learn, and some just want to get by. I like to sort them out as early as possible so I can figure out which ones need special attention."

"I see." Nick leaned back, feeling a little less noble than he had anticipated. "It's a test?"

Kameelah nodded. "I want to make sure all the kids get the most out of this course, but I get off to a better start when I can quickly determine which kids will work with me and which ones won't."

"Isn't that a little unfair, not to mention dishonest?"

She laughed. "Don't worry, I told all of the kids this morning. And most of them told me the same thing you came to tell me. They had really worked hard on that problem and most of them were convinced it was a typo."

"And what about the ones who just copied the answer?"

"They got a gentle reprimand, and I think the suspicion that there might be more 'typos' in the lessons has given them a reason to pay more attention to the future assignments."

"Oh." Nick still had his doubts about this method, but figured she knew what she was doing. "Then I guess I should get back to work." He looked back to the table of Ms. Grey's students. "Where is Jake now?"

"He's in library detention for the lunch period."

Nick lifted his eyebrows. Jake was not exactly an unruly kid. "What did he do?"

"He was being disruptive this morning, and even though he's usually a good kid, I couldn't let him get away with it, so the principal sent him to the library."

"Could I see him?" Nick asked.

"I guess so. He's actually supposed to join the class again after lunch, so his time is about up anyway."

"Could you point me in the right direction?"

She nodded and gestured out to the main corridor. "Down that hall and to the left."

"It was nice meeting you," Nick said, extending his hand to Kameelah once again.

She shook his hand. "I agree. Maybe we can meet again sometime. For fun," she said, lifting her eyebrows.

Ms. Grey was asking him out. Nick smiled. "Maybe we can do that."

"You have my number," she told him, before returning to her students.

Today is shaping up to be quite satisfactory, Nick thought. His math skills were no longer in question, and he all but had a date with a very attractive math teacher. Now if he could just find out what was troubling Jake that had caused him to misbehave.

In the library, Nick told the librarian that he was Jake's tutor and that Ms. Grey had given him permission to speak with the boy for a few minutes. She nodded, and pointed to the table where Jake sat.

The boy was sullen, staring uninterestedly at his untouched lunch in front of him.

Nick took a seat across the table from him. "I guess you already know about that math problem, huh?"

Jake looked at him, but didn't flash his usual smile. "Yeah. Why are you here?"

"I came to find out why we couldn't figure out that problem, and then Ms. Grey told me you had gotten into trouble this morning."

Embarrassed, Jake looked down at the table. Nick felt a measure of relief, knowing that if Jake felt some remorse, he wasn't too far gone.

"Can you tell me what happened?" Nick gently probed.

Jake shrugged. "I didn't feel like coming to school today. It's summertime. I want to play outside."

"But summer school only lasts for five weeks. It'll be over before you know it."

Jake scowled.

Nick figured something else besides summer school was bothering the boy, but he didn't want to push him. Instead he said, "Your teacher said you're supposed to go back to class after lunch. Please tell me you won't get into trouble again."

Jake blinked several times, and Nick saw tears welling up in his eyes. His mouth went dry. Of course he should pursue finding out what was wrong, but he was treading on unfamiliar territory. Maybe this should be left up to Ms. Grey or some other school personnel. Nick looked around for the librarian but didn't see her. He stood up partially and turned, trying to see if she was behind one of the shelves.

"My dad left us last night," Jake said, beginning to sob.

Nick spun around to face the boy. Jake was crying in earnest now, face buried in his arms, his small back heaving. What could he do to console him? Nick sat quietly, waiting for Jake to continue.

Teary-eyed, Jake looked up. "They sometimes fight a lot, my mom and dad. When I got home last night, he was packing his suitcase. He gave my sister and me a hug, and then he just left. He didn't tell us where he was going or anything, and Mom said she didn't care." This admission sent a new wave of emotion over the boy, and he buried his head in his arms again.

The librarian heard the commotion now and came rushing over. Nick quickly whispered an explanation to her and told her he would try to calm Jake down.

Moving around the table, Nick took the seat next to Jake, trying to sort out his own emotions. This situation reminded him of his own dad's departure, and Nick knew he didn't really have any comforting advice. He put his arm around the boy's shoulders and patted him for several minutes.

Finally, the sobs grew less frequent, and Jake sat up and wiped his eyes. "Nick, does God answer prayers?" he asked, looking at Nick earnestly.

Nick's heart leapt into his throat and stopped. He felt as if he was frozen, unable to talk or move or even breathe. For a frantic moment, he wondered if he were having some kind of attack. Suddenly, his heart began beating again, racing wildly. Jake was still waiting for an answer, and Nick didn't have one.

"What?" Nick was finally able to say.

"In my church, my pastor tells us to pray about everything and God will answer. But I prayed for my parents to stop fighting, and they didn't. I prayed for my dad to come back last night, and he didn't. Do you think God is mad at me?"

Nick couldn't answer. His hands were shaking, and he clenched and unclenched his fists several times to get control over his errant muscles. He wanted to shout at the top of his lungs that praying was useless. He wanted to tell Jake exactly what he felt about God and prayer, and rant about what his own father had done. He wanted to tell Jake that he needed to toughen up and lean on no one, because that was the only true way to reach the path of success. But he couldn't.

Looking at the sad and innocent little brown face with the big chocolate eyes next to him made Nick think carefully before speaking. Jake was a good kid. How could his father just walk off and leave this child and his sister and his mother?

Although he didn't know Jake's father, Nick was angry with the man. Jake deserved better than this, but Nick didn't know how to tell him that life was like this sometimes.

He opened his mouth and blurted the first thing that came to mind. "Of course God isn't mad at you. He listens to everyone's prayers."

Mentally, Nick tried to ignore a number of troubling questions. *What in the world am I talking about? Have I lost all sense of logic? And why did I just lie to this kid?*

Jake managed a small smile. "Do you really think so?"

Nick swallowed, nodding. Of course he didn't believe any of what he'd just said, but what could it hurt to tell Jake? Right now, the kid needed anything other than depressing reality. "Sure," Nick said, firmly gripping Jake's shoulder.

"But why didn't God make my dad stay home?" Jake pleaded.

"Well, you know . . ." Nick tried to remember what Sophie and Audra would say. "God doesn't always answer prayer right away. He knows the whole picture, while we can only see a small part of everything."

"So I should keep praying?" Jake asked hopefully.

"Sure. I have a friend who says that God always answers prayer. He may say yes or He may say no, but He still answers."

Jake grinned, appearing to be much more settled. He stood up. "Thanks, Nick. I really needed that."

"Glad I could help." Nick was happy that he didn't have to continue this farce with Jake. *Good thing kids are so resilient,* he decided.

"Guess I better go back to class, huh?"

"You bet. I'll walk you there." Nick stood and informed the librarian that Jake was going back to class. On the way there, Jake chatted about his plans for the summer and his neighborhood baseball team, while Nick walked silently beside him.

At the classroom, Nick opened the door for Jake and poked

his head inside to say good-bye to Kameelah. She gave a small wave and mouthed, Call me.

Nick nodded and shut the door to the classroom. On his way to the car, he thought about the turn his day had taken. His math skills were still competent, and Ms. Grey was definitely interested in him.

But, was he still true to himself? He had blatantly lied to an eleven-year-old about matters of faith, and the kid had believed him. However, the most troubling part of the whole thing was the nagging sensation that he himself took comfort in what he had told Jake.

Nick sat in his car and rubbed his forehead, feeling the beginnings of a tension headache. Was he starting to fall for Audra's talk about God because it sounded good? Or was it because it was true?

Nick jerked his car into gear. He had let things with Audra go too far, because of his attraction to her, and she, along with his mother, had been gently brainwashing him. Now was the time to draw the line in the sand, and he would do it today. If he waited, it would be too late, and he had no intention of falling for feel-good religious rhetoric for the second time in his life.

"Hi, Audra," Caron said as she and Kyle slid into the pew next to Audra. "Where's Sophie this morning?"

Audra chuckled. "She called right before I left for Sunday school and told me she'd overslept, and she was going to drive her car and try to make it to the worship service. Apparently, she and Olivia Harper were up late last night playing Scrabble."

Clare smiled. "I'm just relieved to hear she isn't sick or something."

Audra shook her head. "Sophie is one of the healthiest people I know. She told me herself that she hasn't had a cold in ten years."

"Hey Audra," Kyle leaned over and patted her knee. "Did you know her son filed a complaint with the homes association yesterday?"

"No. What's the complaint about?"

"Your lights." Kyle looked grim.

"My lights?" Audra repeated, placing a hand on her chest. "Why?"

Kyle shrugged. "Dropped the papers off at the office last night. Said he was tired of having his rights trampled."

Audra pursed her lips, fuming. How could he! She had spent the past three days praying for him after their hallway conversation Thursday night. "I don't understand," she murmured. "We've been getting along so well, and he hasn't said a word about the lights. I thought we were good friends."

Kyle shrugged. "He didn't talk like he was your friend."

"So am I supposed to take them down?" Audra asked defensively.

"You're not required to. I told him we'd put it on the agenda for the next homes association meeting, and the residents would vote and make the final decision."

"But the next meeting isn't until the end of October! That's more than four months from now. I won't be able to stand it if he harasses me from now until then."

"Just try to stay away from him," Caron said, wanting to be helpful.

Audra gazed at Caron. "I live next door to him," she replied. "How am I supposed to stay away from him?"

"Hello, ladies." Audra and Caron looked up and saw Sophie standing at the opposite end of the pew. She walked over and sat down next to Audra. "Sorry I missed Sunday school. Do you think I could take a look at your notes sometime this week?"

"Sure," Audra said, trying to sound normal. She felt odd talking to Sophie; it almost felt as if she were somehow hurting her own cause.

"How is Nick doing?" she asked, feeling more than a little suspicious. Had Nick and Sophie decided to befriend her in order to make her feel at ease, knowing that she would feel more vulnerable when they made their attack?

"Actually, he's not doing too well," Sophie confessed. "He's been acting strangely all weekend. Not angry or anything, just really quiet. And then he just announced he was going on a date last night."

"A date?" Audra echoed. Now she really was hurt. Thursday, Nick had all but announced that he was seriously interested in her. For the past few days, she'd been thinking that he was close to making a decision about his faith, and hoping that there would be a real chance for a deeper relationship between the two of them.

But no. He had been plotting surprise complaints about her lights and filling his social calendar.

"Yes," Sophie answered. "I didn't even get to meet her, but he said she's a teacher at the elementary school where one of the kids he tutors attends."

"Oh." Audra felt as if she were hollow inside. "I'm glad for him. He always complains that he doesn't have a social life." *I guess the handsome new bachelor in town couldn't stay unattached forever,* Audra reasoned. *He deserves happiness, too, even if he is dishonest, sneaky, and annoying. But he can also be kind and sweet, and honest . . . or at least I thought he could be. Maybe it was my own imagination.*

Sophie sighed softly. "Honestly, Audra, I had sort of hoped

that you and Nick would fall in love and get married. Provided, of course, that he returned to the Lord." She shrugged. "Guess it was my own wishful thinking, hmmm?"

Audra didn't have an answer for that, so she merely murmured, "Hmmm." Changing the subject, she asked, "Did Nick tell you that he filed a complaint about my lights with the homes association?"

Sophie's eyes widened. "No, he didn't. Are you sure?"

Kyle leaned over and answered. "I'm sure. He filled out the paperwork yesterday."

"Oh, my. I had no idea." Sophie bit her lip. A moment later, she put her hand on Audra's shoulder. "Audra, I don't know why he did this now, but I'm sorry. I'll see if I can talk him out of it, okay?"

Audra nodded, staring straight ahead. Pastor Walls was up on the podium, talking to the choir director, and Audra prayed fervently that the service would start as soon as possible. She didn't know how much longer her emotions could take all of this talk about Nick.

Lord, please help me to put my emotions back in their proper place, she prayed as the choir sang a lively chorus.

After the service, Kyle and Caron invited Audra and Sophie to have lunch with them. Sophie offered her regrets because she had a roast in the oven, and Audra declined because she felt a headache coming on and she wanted to take a nap.

Normally, after church, Audra and Sophie rode home together, and if Sophie had driven her own car, they stopped and chatted for several minutes, but today, they both felt some type of barrier between them, so they went their separate ways immediately after church.

On her way out the door, Audra met no one other than her trusty friend, Ryan Meyer.

"Are you feeling all right? You don't look so well," he said, sounding concerned.

"I'm just fighting a little headache," she assured him. *Not to mention heartache*, she thought.

He held the door for her, and they both stepped out into the hot, sunny air. "You know, I wanted to talk to you about something," Ryan said.

Audra was tired and not really in the mood for one of Ryan's digressive dialogues, but she reminded herself to be patient. After all, he was one of her most steadfast friends.

"Sure, go ahead," she invited. They had reached her car, and she unlocked and opened the driver's-side door. "But let's sit in the car. It's way too hot out here. I'll turn the air on."

Ryan went around to the passenger's side while Audra got the air conditioner going. The cool rush of air had an immediate refreshing effect on her headache. She looked over at Ryan, waiting for whatever it was he had to say.

"I'll be totally up front with you, Audra. I like you. You're a solid, levelheaded, attractive woman who loves the Lord like I do. I'm attracted to you, and I know you don't feel the same way about me, but maybe you haven't given me a fair chance. I think we should spend more one-on-one time together and make an effort to learn more about each other."

Audra didn't know what to say. She had been down this road with Ryan more than a few times, and she had never varied her thinking, but today, his suggestion didn't seem so far-fetched.

He continued. "I mean, I want to get married someday, and I know you do, but neither of us has seriously dated anyone for quite a while now. Don't you think we should at least consider each other? I may not be the man of your dreams, but I would treat you with love and respect. And I think that, in time, you could love me. What do you think?"

"Well . . . this is really kind of a surprise. I hadn't expected it."

"I know," Ryan said, placing his hand over hers. "And I don't expect you to give me an answer right now. But promise me you'll at least consider it. Please?"

Audra didn't like the way Ryan had proposed more of a contract than a relationship, but it wouldn't hurt to think about it. She did want to have her own family, and Ryan did, too. They shared the same beliefs, and they would probably make a good husband-and-wife team. In addition, Ryan was a very handsome guy. He was tall, almost reed thin, and very distinguished looking, with a close haircut and dark skin nearly the same color as hers. There were plenty of women who would love to have a husband like Ryan, and he was still interested in Audra. She owed it to him to think about it, and to herself not to let the opportunity slip away. He was responsible and never said anything harsh or rude to her. He wasn't the most exciting person in the world, but, as her mother often said, "There is no verse in the Bible that says you pick a husband by how exciting he is."

"Okay," Audra decided. "I'll think about," she added, before she lost her nerve.

"Thanks." He grinned and gave her hand a warm squeeze. "I'll call you in a few days, okay?"

"Okay." Ryan got out of the car, and as he walked away, Audra thought she saw a new lift in his step. Could she have been overlooking her ideal mate all along?

Refusing to think about Ryan or Nick, she drove home. As she pulled onto her street, she noticed Nick's car sitting in front of his house. Just then the front door of his house swung open, and Nick emerged with a very pretty and graceful young woman.

They were dressed casually, and the woman was carrying a

kite while Nick held a picnic basket. Sophie stood in the door-way behind them, smiling, and Audra felt betrayed. Sophie has said herself that she would have liked to see Nick and Audra end up together. How could she change her mind so quickly?

Audra felt herself getting teary-eyed, and she willed herself not to let a single tear drop until she was inside of her house, where no one could see her.

Get a grip, she told herself. *You have no logical reason to take Nick's going on a date so seriously. You made your position clear to him, and you had to stick to it. He obviously didn't agree with you, and he's made his decision. Now you have to respect his freedom to choose and at the same time be glad that you didn't compromise.*

Audra blinked back tears and waved to Nick, Sophie, and the woman, smiling as though today was the happiest day of her life. She had made the right choice, and even if it didn't feel so great right now, she knew she would have been miser-able and guilt-ridden had she decided to date Nick given his current lack of faith.

Eleven

*N*ick looked down at the sheet of paper where he had scribbled the number. Instead of picking up the phone, he had rewritten the number over and over again, as if somehow that might make the conversation easier.

Over a month had passed since the day he'd gotten the letter from his dad, and for the entire time he had carried the letter around in his briefcase. Every night, he would read it, then try to make himself throw it away. And every night, he would end up returning the letter to his briefcase, putting off the decision until the next evening.

Then this afternoon, he'd checked the mailbox and found a second letter, also sent to his previous address. His dad was still asking for forgiveness and wanted a chance to talk to him. This time, his dad had not only given him an address where he could be reached, but a phone number and even an e-mail address. In this letter, his dad extensively mentioned the Lord and the Bible and prayer, and by the time he was finished reading, Nick was furious. How could his dad even suggest that God was on his side?

Nick thought back to his childhood. He remembered lying on the floor in the living room of the family's small apartment, playing with Alan, who was a small baby at the time.

His mother and father had been in the kitchen yelling for some time.

Nick was used to their arguing and had ventured out into the hall outside of the kitchen to hear what they were yelling about. His mother had wanted his father to attend Christmas Eve service with the family. Of course, his dad had refused to go, and Sophie had gotten upset.

"You and this church!" Walter had yelled. "Don't you realize that none of it is true? I'm not stepping foot into that place. God doesn't care about us!"

"But Walter, I'm just asking you to come tonight at least," Sophie pleaded. "Nick is in the Christmas program, and he'll be disappointed if you don't come. The other fathers will be there. Can't you set a good example just this once?"

"Yeah, I'll set an example all right. You go to church and he can stay home with me. Church is for women and weaklings. Real men don't need church. We don't pray, and we don't let some old book tell us what to do."

Nick had quietly crept back to the living room and prayed that his daddy would come to church with him.

Back then, he had had supreme faith that one day, as a result of all his prayers, his dad would wake up and announce that he was going to attend church with his family and stop yelling at Sophie forever.

Nick's stomach knotted, and he pushed away the painful recollection. Of course, his dad hadn't attended church with them that night. And after church they came home to an empty house. His dad's clothes were gone, along with a good deal of Sophie's household expense money.

For a few days, Sophie had figured that Walt had gone to the racetrack, but eventually she learned from one of Walt's cousins that he had left for good.

Nick had been scared at first, but then resolved that he should simply pray harder. When Sophie had fussed that he was wasting his time, he had believed her. Why would his mother lie to him? He had thrown away his Bible and hadn't even touched one since then.

He remembered Jake and his anguish. At least Jake's dad had the decency to hug his son for the last time instead of sneaking away like a thief. Jake's dad had been gone for almost a month, and Jake was coping moderately well. He reported that his dad called lots and came on weekends to visit him and his sister.

Of course, there seemed to be a permanent sadness that had etched itself into the boy's demeanor, but he seemed confident that his prayers were going to prevail. Every time Jake talked about that part, Nick's stomach wrenched.

Watching this scenario replayed before him brought back all the little-boy anger and hurt that Nick thought he had gotten rid of. Sometimes Nick thought it was more difficult to watch someone else go through this.

Still, it troubled Nick to realize that Jake's father was not totally missing from his life. More troubling was his wondering if Jake's prayers really were the reason his father hadn't abandoned them completely. All of this reasoning never failed to bring Nick back to his original question. Why hadn't his own childhood prayers worked?

Nick stared at the phone number again. There were too

many questions neither he nor his mother could answer. Only one person had the answers, and Nick didn't think he would rest until he heard them from that person. Nick picked up the phone and dialed the number before he could change his mind. Now was the time for some answers.

Laura sorted through the mail and handed Audra a big lavender envelope. "I don't even have to guess who this is from."

Audra smiled and read the return address, confirming that this was another card from Ryan. Emotionally, she winced every time he did something like this. In the two months since she and Ryan had been dating, he had been nothing less than gallant in his actions toward her. He sent flowers, wrote her e-mails, and sent flowery cards that walked the line between friendship and love.

He gave freely and from his heart, and, in return, Audra gave . . . nothing. She respected him, of course, but she had always respected him. What she couldn't give him was love. She had tried and failed.

There was simply no romantic interest for him on her part. She knew it hurt him. He had been incredibly patient with her, but she couldn't expect him to be patient forever. Two nights ago, they had gone to dinner with her parents, and when he walked her to the door, he had asked very politely if he could kiss her.

Audra's heart had caught in her throat, feeling strangely sad at the way he had wistfully asked for a kiss. He deserved to be with someone who *wanted* to kiss him, someone who wouldn't mumble some excuse about being tired and having a busy day tomorrow and turning to flee inside the house.

She rubbed her temples, feeling the ache of tension. She

liked Ryan. They got along well. They laughed together, went to church together, spent time together, and she had fun. But her heart shrank back from his every attempt to be more than friends.

Yet, in spite of her uncertainty and aloofness, he had sent her a card today. Audra placed it in her desk and didn't open it, not wanting to think about the situation. It was mid-August, and Ryan was already hinting about Christmas presents, which made her uncomfortable. When they went shopping, he'd casually steer her toward jewelry-store windows, and linger long enough to let her know he was thinking of a serious purchase: "commitment jewelry," as Laura would say.

Audra rested her chin on her hand and absently stared out the window. Nick's car was in the driveway, along with Kameelah's little silver coupe. Nick and his new girlfriend had been dating for roughly the same amount of time as Audra and Ryan had, but she envied their relationship. She saw glimpses of them every now and then; they seemed to spend most of their free time together.

Sophie had told Audra Kameelah's name, but not much more. She had the impression that Sophie liked Kameelah well enough, but she also knew that they weren't close friends.

Sophie used to drop over for tea, and they would visit together during the evenings. However, those visits had tapered off during the month of July, when Alan had come home for a few weeks before returning to school.

Sophie now drove herself to church, so the Sunday dinners had come to a halt as well; she now spent Sunday afternoons with Nick and Kameelah.

Audra sighed wistfully. Sometimes she couldn't help but feel a little jealous of Kameelah. In the moments when she was completely honest with herself, she could admit that she cared for Nick more than she had dared let on. She had never said as much to Sophie, but she supposed Sophie had realized it.

Michelle cleared her throat. "Audra, it's hard to see you like this."

Audra tore her glance away from the window. "Like what?"

"Pining away for the man next door. It's like a sad movie."

Audra lifted her chin. "I am not pining away for Nick."

"Yes, you are," Michelle persisted. "And it's not at all fair to Ryan."

"You mope constantly," Laura added. "It's so not like you to get down like this. In a couple of weeks it'll be September."

Audra blinked. "And?"

"It'll be time for you to start planning your annual Christmas party."

Audra shrugged and began sorting through some order forms she had on the desk. "The Christmas party is not that hard to do. I've done it for so long, I think it plans itself."

Laura wore a look of disapproval, and Audra realized she sounded like a cranky little kid.

"Audra, I hate to say this, but I have to." Michelle looked her in the eye and announced, "You have lost your Christmas spirit."

"What?"

"You don't have it anymore."

"I do too. Look at this place," Audra gestured around the room. "It's fully decorated all year long. I just added a new tree last week."

Michelle and Laura did not appear to be convinced, so Audra kept talking. "I got new wreaths for the windows in the front of the house, and I'm having my brother put some new lights up around the front porch railing."

"Nope. You're not fooling us," Laura said gravely.

"You guys. I'm a party planner. I am always in the holiday spirit. I own a company called Joy Year Round." She sighed exasperatedly. "I'm in the Christmas spirit business."

"Audra?" Michelle asked. "Do you remember when I first came to work for you?"

Audra nodded.

"It was in March. I really needed this job. Dave had been laid off, and we were down to our last hundred dollars in savings. Two days after I came to work, Alyssa fell out of a tree and broke her arm. Of course we had no health insurance, and the last thing we needed was another bill. Remember?" Michelle prodded.

"Yes, I remember. You were depressed."

"Yes, very much so. You gave me a check to cover the cost of the emergency-room visit, and when I asked you how you were going to deduct the extra money from my paycheck, you said you weren't. You told me it was a Christmas present."

Audra nodded, still not understanding Michelle's point.

"I told you it was way too early for a Christmas present and insisted on a way to pay you back. But you told me that Christmas was a day on the calendar, but Christmas spirit was year-round." Michelle's eyes were brimming with tears. "You taught me that Christmas spirit isn't about decorations or caroling or shopping or parties or eggnog." Crossing her hands over her chest, she said, "You taught me that Christmas spirit is being thankful for the birth of Jesus and how much He did for us. You said that it meant being willing to forgive people even when you didn't want to." She paused and brushed tears away with her sleeve, and Audra wiped away tears from her own eyes.

"You said sharing this gift with other people every chance you get is the real Christmas spirit. You said that made you happier than any Christmas present could. You told me that was the reason behind your joy. Every day, all year long, and not just in December."

"Yeah," Laura added. "You told me that sharing the Gospel with people was our duty as Christians. You said it was the—"

"Real joy business," Audra said, in unison with Laura. They were right. Somewhere in between wanting to prove to Nick that she was a good Christian witness and then falling in love with him without even realizing it, she had lost sight of the joy that had been an integral part of who she was. And now, she felt miserable and had nothing to lean back on. Nick had moved forward, and her lights were just . . . lights.

"You two are right. Somehow, during the fight for my right to keep the lights up, I allowed myself to think that those lights and decorations were the reason behind my happiness. And while I fought to keep my exterior lights shining bright, I let the light in my heart fade." She sighed a deep heaving sigh. "But I did learn something." She stood up, crossed the room, and flipped the power switch that controlled the Christmas trees in the room. "You can't artificially manufacture real joy. Not even if you buy a new Christmas tree every day of the year."

"That's the spirit," Michelle agreed.

"So now what?" Laura asked. "Do we have the old Audra back?"

"I think so," Audra said. "I may stumble now and then, but that's why you guys are here. We keep each other on track. The next time I get all mopey, ask me where my joy is."

"Where's your joy?" Michelle asked, smiling.

"I'm messing up already?"

Michelle shrugged. "Just testing. So what's the answer?"

Audra considered. "My real joy is in knowing that I have the best Christmas present anyone can receive. It's called salvation, and it was made possible when God sent His son to Earth to die for my sins. Of course, I didn't deserve this gift, and that's what makes it all the more special." Grinning, Audra asked, "How's that?"

"Laura," Michelle said, "I think we've got our old Audra back."

"Good." Audra sat down at her desk and fished around for a blank sheet of paper. "About my annual Christmas party." She paused dramatically. "I think I want do things a little differently this year. Get out some paper, because I want you to take notes."

"Oh, Nick, look at this one." Kameelah pointed to another ring. It was a round-cut solitaire and at least two carats. It would look great on Audra's hand.

He cleared his throat. "I thought you wanted to buy a bracelet for your sister's birthday."

Kameelah frowned, something she did often, and it was starting to wear on Nick's nerves. "I do, Nick. But it's fun to window shop, too, you know. There are exactly three months till Christmas."

"Really?" Nick asked dryly.

Kameelah nodded. "I guess you forgot Christmas even existed after your neighbor turned off those silly lights, but it's September twenty-fifth."

Nick frowned when he heard Kameelah refer to Audra's lights as "silly." He looked around for an escape from this overpriced jewelry store and found it in the form of the Christian bookstore across the hallway. He patted Kameelah's shoulder. "Take all the time you need to pick your sister's bracelet. And while you're at it, you'd better get a head start on buying your Christmas gifts since it's sneaking up on you so fast. I'll be across the hall at the Christian bookstore."

Kameelah frowned, but Nick was expecting it. "Don't tell me you're letting your deadbeat dad's religion rub off on you?" Placing a hand on her hip, she continued. "Or is it your mom's constant little sermons that have you acting so holy all of a sudden?"

Nick decided it would be best not to answer that question, and wordlessly headed to the bookstore. He had been putting this off for some time, but after this trip to the mall ended, so would his relationship with Kameelah.

Entering the bookstore, he breathed a sigh of relief. It was unlikely that Kameelah would set one of her high-heeled feet in here, even if he browsed for the next two hours. He grinned, and then sobered, realizing that he had visited this store for the first time only a couple of months ago. He guessed that miracles did happen, but he wasn't in any hurry to invite Kameelah in and have his moment of peace disturbed right now.

He headed to his favorite section of the store and perused the shelves for something new.

A store clerk passed by and paused. "Hey, Nick. You back already?"

Nick grinned sheepishly. "I guess so. Got anything new?"

The man shrugged. "I figured that study on Romans and James would keep you occupied for a while." He scratched his head. "Have you done the book of John yet?"

"Last month."

"I'll check the computer and see what has come in. If you keep at this rate, I don't know how we'll be able to meet your demand for study guides." He headed toward the counter, while Nick continued to scan the shelves.

Seconds later, he saw Audra enter the store. Nick watched her as she stopped and picked up a little figurine on a display table.

He missed her. He missed the shared rides to tutoring, the Sunday dinners, and her smile. Still, he hadn't been able to bring himself to go knock on her door and apologize. Sophie had been furious at him for filing a complaint with the homes association, and he had been too proud to drop it at the time.

In truth, he rarely saw Audra. She and Sophie didn't get together much anymore, and Nick himself stayed at work longer than normal to talk to his dad on the phone. Kameelah almost always monopolized the free time he did have with her restless need to be out and about.

He winced inwardly, recalling the sight of Audra's once-again dark house. He felt like the big bad wolf each night when he looked out his window and saw no lights shining next door. For the past month, the lights had been out, and he hadn't yet come up with a way to get them turned back on without making Audra feel as though he were lording some type of authority over her. He knew that if he suddenly dropped the complaint, she wouldn't trust him. In order to get her lights back on, he would have to lose the vote at the homes association meeting. And, although he was very much a changed man, he didn't relish the thought of having his complaint publicly tossed out—even if he did want to lose. Worse yet, he had nightmares that he would actually win the vote, and then what could he do? Audra would be forced to take her lights down for good, and it would be entirely his fault. Nick shuddered, hoping things wouldn't get that out of hand.

He wished for what seemed like the millionth time that he had been able to agree with Audra about faith issues before he had met Kameelah. As things were now, he was about to break things off with Kameelah. Meanwhile he knew from Sophie and assorted sources at work, including Ryan Meyer himself, that Audra and Ryan were a couple.

Now *he* was feeling the way he suspected Audra must have felt in her friendship with him. It was hard to have a romantic relationship with someone who didn't share your faith. And, as his dad had pointed out a couple of weeks earlier, the Bible said it was wrong to do so.

Audra passed by the study-guide section and went to the next aisle over, where the fiction titles were. The shelves were not much taller than five and a half feet, and as things were, he and Audra were facing each other with a bookshelf between the two of them, but she hadn't noticed him yet. He watched her as her eyes traveled from side to side, and she finally reached out and selected a title. Nick cleared his throat, and she finally noticed him.

Her eyes widened. "Nick? What are you doing here?"

He looked around in mock surprise. "Do I need a pass to get in or something?"

She looked embarrassed and shook her head. "Of course not." She eyed him intently, and Nick wondered how he should tell her about all that had happened to him over the past few months.

Some of it was intensely personal and private, so much so that he hadn't even told Sophie. He sometimes thought his mother suspected but was waiting to hear the words directly from his mouth.

Nick was the first to break the silence. Peering over the shelves, he asked, "So what'd you get?"

Audra shrugged and held up a book with a flowery cover. "I was in the mood for something new, so I thought I'd try this one."

Nick walked around to her aisle and perused the cover, reading the little blurb at the bottom. The story didn't particularly interest him, but he wanted to be polite. "A romance, huh?"

Audra looked away, then back at him. "It's a Christian romance, mister. It's not vulgar or anything, if that's what you're wondering."

He smiled at her, amused about her shyness over the book but impressed with her standards. "I didn't say it was. And, lately, I'm a big fan of clean fiction." He cleared his throat, hoping she hadn't gotten the wrong impression. He didn't read romance novels at all—Christian or mainstream. "Not that I have ever read a romance novel." Inclining his head toward the general fiction section, he said, "Actually, I'm a fan of action adventure and mysteries."

Audra nodded but smiled, indicating she hadn't misunderstood him.

He guessed he had beat around the bush too long. It was time to get to the nitty gritty. "I hear you and Ryan are pretty serious. Congratulations, I guess," he said.

Audra shook her head. "No, we're not. We broke up about a month ago."

Nick was surprised. Ryan had indicated that he wasn't likely to let Audra go anytime soon, and most people knew he was serious. One of the other accountants had told him that Ryan had been waiting for Audra to marry him for years, and Nick had accepted the fact that an engagement would probably be announced soon. In recent weeks, he had steered clear of Ryan at the office because he didn't want to think about Ryan and Audra as a couple.

Unfortunately, his curiosity was not satisfied, because Audra changed the subject without supplying any additional information. "How is your mother?"

Nick nodded as he answered. "She's doing really well."

"And Kameelah?"

Nick stopped nodding. So she did know about Kameelah. He guessed it would be hard to ignore her, since Kameelah insisted on coming over to his place so much. "She's ah, well, she's doing good. We're not actually dating . . . really . . . anymore." And he was about ninety-five percent truthful. Their relationship had been going downhill for some time, and this afternoon he planned to end things officially.

"Oh." Audra tilted her head to the side. "I didn't know that." She glanced at the books, then back at him. "I'm sorry."

Nick chuckled. "Don't be. Really."

Audra nodded.

His curiosity was getting the better of him. Why had Audra and Ryan broken up? "Should I be sorry about you and Ryan?" he asked, hoping she would give more details.

Audra blinked, and didn't say anything for a few seconds. Sighing, she said, "No, not really."

Nick couldn't tell if this was a good or bad thing. He wondered if Ryan had done something to terribly hurt Audra's feelings but found that idea highly unlikely. Ryan treated Audra like a queen, and it was more probable that Audra had been the one to end the relationship. But why? Had she met someone else?

"So how have you been?" she asked.

Nick could hardly contain his joy. He couldn't decide where to start; he had so much good news. "I've been excellent," he confessed.

Audra smiled. "You sure sound like it."

"I've been praying. A lot."

Audra nodded, but she didn't look as surprised as he had hoped she would. "Aren't you even a little surprised?"

"I've been praying, too. For you," she said.

"Looks like God answered your prayers."

Audra chuckled. "It's pretty funny hearing that line from you."

Nick agreed with her. Over the past few months, he'd done a complete three-sixty turnaround, and he couldn't remember ever being happier. He leaned closer to Audra and said, "Guess what else?"

Audra glanced up at him expectantly, her eyes level with his chin.

"I prayed the salvation prayer." He was grinning from ear to ear, and he knew he probably looked goofy, but he didn't care. Lately, he had realized that salvation wasn't called the "good news" for no reason!

"I know Sophie's pretty excited."

"You look pretty excited yourself. I mean, you sound excited, and you've always been pretty, in my opinion."

Audra's smile faded, and he realized he'd overstepped his boundaries.

He needed to change the subject. Fast. "Actually, I haven't told my mom yet. I want to surprise her."

As relief visibly washed over her face, Audra laughingly groaned. "Nick, she'll be surprised no matter when you tell her. You don't have to wait for some special occasion to break the news. You could tell her today and she would be surprised and happy."

"I know . . ." Nick said, realizing that Audra was probably right. "But I have a reason for wanting to tell her on a special day." He paused, wondering if he could say what he really wanted to say.

"And what's the reason?" Audra asked.

"Actually, that's where I need your help."

Audra took a step away. "My help?"

"Yeah. Your help." Nick looked around for a place for them to sit down. "C'mon," he said, leading her to the children's section, where there was a platform for children to sit and watch cartoons. Thankfully, there were no children around at the moment.

Once they were sitting down and facing each other, Nick took a deep breath, then spoke. "I've been in contact with my dad."

Twelve

Audra gasped. "Oh, Nick, I'm so happy for you." Her eyes were shining, and he could tell her expression of happiness was genuine. "How long have you been speaking to him?"

"A few months, three or four, I think. He wrote me a letter, and I called him. He lives in Boston."

"Does Sophie know?"

He shook his head. "Not yet, but she will soon. He's planning to come for Thanksgiving when Alan will be home, and I want to surprise her."

"So where do I come in?"

"His plane comes in Tuesday night, and I need you to hide him until Thursday at dinnertime."

Audra thought for a while. "I guess I could let him have the guest house. I don't have much work to do that week, and Laura and Michelle have the week off. He could have some privacy and relax that way."

Nick could barely restrain himself from hugging her. "Thank you so much. I'll be in touch with you about the details."

Audra grinned. "It's no problem. I always love to be in on a good surprise."

They fell silent again, until Nick spoke. "You know, I think I will tell my mom about my getting saved. I just won't give her all the details yet. Her surprise will still be a surprise. The part about my dad, I mean."

Audra nodded her head, smiling warmly. "I think she'll love both surprises. And I take it your dad is excited about seeing your mom?" She looked somewhat troubled.

"Oh yeah. He still loves her, and I think she still loves him. Of course, they have to get reacquainted, but this time they'll have Jesus in common." He looked across at Audra. "That ought to make a relationship a lot easier, don't you think?"

She nodded but didn't get a chance to reply; she was interrupted by a plaintive voice echoing from the front of the store. "Nick?"

He cringed, recognizing Kameelah's voice.

Audra threw him a questioning glance, and he felt slightly panicked. He vaguely recalled telling her only a few minutes earlier that he and Kameelah had broken up. It didn't exactly look that way now.

"That's Kameelah," he said.

"I know," said Audra. She looked calm, but questions filled her eyes.

"Nick? Are you in there?"

In his mind's eye, Nick could envision Kameelah standing at the perimeter of the store, in the mall corridor, as though coming inside might contaminate her with Christian germs. As much as he didn't want Audra to misinterpret things, somehow, it made matters worse to have Kameelah standing fifty feet away, yelling for him. Now everyone was going to be staring at him, and he felt like running and hiding in the storeroom.

He sighed. "I'll explain this later," he told Audra. He stood up, turned around, and was alarmed to find himself face-to-face with Kameelah.

She glared at him, then turned her gaze to scrutinize Audra. "If it isn't Ms. Joy Year Round herself."

Audra stood and extended her hand. "Audra Clayton, but yes, I do own Joy Year Round. You must be Kameelah."

Kameelah stared at Audra's hand and took her time before she extended her own arm. Nick was mortified. "Yes, Nick's girlfriend." Her lips were in a tight line.

"I see." Nick willed Audra to look him in the eye, so he could make her know the truth, but she didn't even glance in his direction.

She bent to pick up her book from the ground, then moved toward the front of the store. "I'd better get going. Nice seeing you two," she said as she hurried away.

Nick turned to Kameelah, who was staring after Audra with a stony glare. "Let's go," he suggested.

"What was that all about?" she demanded.

"This is not the time or place for this discussion," he warned. "Let's get going."

Kameelah didn't move an inch. "Why were you hiding from me? Did you plan to meet *her* in here?"

Nick shook his head, inhaled, then exhaled. "No, we just ran into each other."

"In the back of the store?" Kameelah challenged. "It looked like a planned meeting to me. Why didn't you answer when I first called you?"

Nick laughed. Poor Kameelah. He would have to remember

to pray for her. "I'm telling you the truth, take it or leave it. But just think about it for a second." He gestured around the area where they stood. "We're in the children's section of a Christian bookstore, sitting on this little kiddie bench. Who would arrange some kind of rendezvous right here, in the middle of the day?"

Kameelah pursed her lips and shot him yet another glare, then turned and walked away.

As much as he felt like pretending she didn't exist, Nick realized the air outside was chilly and, since she didn't have the keys to his car, he didn't want to be mean and leave her standing out in the elements long.

Overwhelmed with a sense of obligation, Nick left the store and headed for the mall exit.

Audra tried to sort out her emotions as she drove home. No, she wasn't angry, but she *was* indignant. She wasn't *embarrassed*, but she did feel as though her intelligence had been out and out *insulted*. She didn't want to believe that Nick had been feeding her a string of lies back in the store, but she had almost no choice but to accept it.

He'd gone on about how he'd gotten saved and had reconciled with his dad. Even had the nerve to hint that now that they had the same spiritual footing there might be a chance for a relationship between them. Audra had fallen for the lot of it, like a fish after a pretty lure.

She had wanted to be swallowed into the floor when Nick's model-gorgeous girlfriend came in the store and gave her the once-over. Never before had she remembered feeling like such a frump.

She was shorter than the willowy Kameelah. She wasn't overweight, but she definitely carried a few more pounds on her frame than Kameelah did. Her nails were cut short, while Kameelah's were long and manicured, painted a pretty shade of mauve. Kameelah's hair was cutting-edge fashionable, while Audra's was everyday-plain-old-boring just-below-the-shoulders straight-with-the-ends-curled-under. And as far as makeup was concerned, Audra didn't even want to go there right now. She usually managed to get some powder, mascara, and lipstick on for work and church, but she couldn't remember the last time she'd worn a full face of makeup to run to the mall.

Audra pulled her car into the driveway and jumped out, realizing the temperature had dropped significantly on her way home. The sky looked as if it might just dump a load of late September snow on the city, and Audra was glad she had bought the novel. Tomorrow, for the first time in several months, she had a full Saturday completely to herself, with no work to do, no chores to complete, and no assorted errands.

If she was going to be snowed in, it was going to be nice to have the book and all of its characters for company.

She pushed thoughts of Nick aside and decided to visit the woodpile to bring some logs inside so the fireplace would be well stocked.

Nick cupped his hands together and blew them as he ventured out to the parking lot. Again. Still no trace of Kameelah.

Discouraged, he trudged back inside, wondering what his next step should be. Snow flurries were starting to fall, and Nick wondered why so many people had decided to come out and shop when a storm was threatening.

At any rate, it was time he stopped lying to himself, thinking he could sift through all of the people inside the building and somehow find Kameelah.

He glanced at his watch, noting that just around forty-five minutes earlier, she had left him in the bookstore. He hadn't lingered behind for more than a minute, but by the time he got out to the car, she wasn't there. Figuring something in one of the store windows had caught her eye on the way out, Nick had sat in the car, waiting.

Ten minutes passed, and no Kameelah. A little miffed, Nick had gone back inside, checking some of her favorite stores. When he realized he had wasted almost half an hour, he'd come back outside just now to see if she were out there waiting for him.

Just inside the mall entrance, Nick paused, looking around. No, he wouldn't find her by himself. He was heading toward the mall security booth when his cell phone rang.

Sophie was probably calling to ask him to pick up something at the store. He pulled the phone from his pocket and flipped it open. "Hello?"

"Nick, where are you?" It was Kameelah. "You should have been home ages ago. I called your mom and she said you hadn't gotten home yet. I was worried about you."

He blinked. And he had been worried about her. He silently counted to five and asked, "Where are you?"

"I'm at home," she replied impatiently. "Where are *you*? I hear a lot of voices."

"*I'm* at the mall, looking for the person who I came with since she didn't have the decency to tell me she had a different ride home."

Kameelah yawned. "Sorry. I took a cab. I didn't want to pull you away from your precious Bibles. Why don't I come over to your place tonight? You could pick me up on your way there."

Nick shook his head, even though she couldn't see him. "Don't think so. I'm tired."

"Well, you don't have to get all worked up about the things I said about your little friend," she snapped.

"I'm not worked up. But I realize that our relationship is over. We're not a good match anymore since I got saved."

"What?"

"I said it's over."

"You find that excuse in the Bible somewhere?" was her snide retort.

Nick forced himself to sound pleasant, despite the fact that she had played a stupid, childish trick on him. "Actually, I did. Good-bye, Kameelah." Before she could protest, Nick ended the call. He then called Sophie and told her not to worry because he was on his way home.

Feeling as if a load had been lifted from his shoulders, Nick barely felt the biting wind as he again walked out to his car. All he could think was that he was truly free.

The next morning, a fine layer of white dust carpeted the ground. Audra peered out of her windows, somewhat disappointed. She loved a good old-fashioned snowstorm every now and then, and she had been in the mood for a little snowy adventure this weekend.

She would still find time to read her book, but first, she would get out and take a nice walk, something she hadn't done in a long time. Heading to the gym was a part of her normal schedule, and she was usually faithful about keeping to the plan, but taking a walk for fun was something she rarely had time for.

She enjoyed a breakfast of warm granola with blueberries, then got dressed.

She stepped outside and shivered. It hadn't snowed much, but the temperature was colder than she had expected. She popped back inside to change to a warmer jacket, then found a scarf and pair of gloves in the hall closet.

She went outside again, feeling much more insulated. At the end of her driveway, she hesitated, deciding whether to pass Nick's house and head toward a nearby park, or go the opposite direction toward the community walking trail.

She finally decided she would head to the park so she could sit and look at the lake. Although it wasn't frozen yet, the surface was likely to be frosted over.

Just as she passed Nick's home, the front door opened and Nick emerged, wearing jeans and a sweater, rubbing his hands to keep them warm. "Where are you headed in this cold?" he called.

Audra froze. She suspected Kameelah was somewhere nearby, and she didn't want to have any additional run-ins with that woman. "To the park," she answered, hoping Nick wouldn't probe any further.

"Do you know how cold it is?" he asked.

"I'm dressed for this better than you are," she informed him.

He held up his hand, and said, "Hold on a second, I'll come with you. Let me grab a coat." He disappeared inside before she could protest and returned moments later wearing a knee-length wool coat and a pair of gloves.

Audra began at a fast pace, leaving Nick trailing behind her at first. He jogged to catch up with her, then took hold of her arm, gasping for breath. "Hey, can we slow down a little? I haven't been to the gym in ages, and I'm really feeling it."

Audra relented and slowed her pace. "The trick to taking a walk in cold weather," she teased him, "is walking fast, instead of at a snail's pace. That way, you stay warm."

"It's not *that* cold out here, and if it were, I don't think you'd be taking a walk to the park. But that's not why I'm here. About yesterday," he began.

She shook her head. "No, you don't have to explain."

"I don't have to, but I want to, so please hear me out."

Audra nodded and waited for what he had to say.

"If you thought I wasn't being honest with you, you were right. Kameelah and I hadn't broken up yet."

Audra wasn't surprised at the truth of the statement, she could tell he and Kameelah were still together during the confrontation yesterday. However, she was surprised that he was admitting to this.

"I had been planning to break up with her sometime this week, and I didn't tell you the entire truth. But we did end our relationship last night. I hope you're not going to hold this against me. I want us to be friends again."

Audra didn't answer him right away. She wanted them to be friends again, too, but she wanted them to be honest with each other.

"Let's start over, Audra, from the beginning." His voice was quiet but urgent. "I know things can be different."

"How?" Audra asked, wanting reassurance. "We've started over once before, and we're not any better off today because of it."

"But we are," Nick interrupted. "I mean, I think we can be. I'm a Christian now, and I think that counts as better."

"Of course that's a good thing, but I'm still a little unsure about the two of us trying to turn back time again." She shook her head. "I know I shouldn't feel like this, but I don't think I trust you. And it's not that I don't want to." They were nearing the park, and Audra could see sunlight reflecting off the lake like millions of little stars.

Neither of them said anything more until they were seated on a small bench facing the lake.

"This is so pretty; it's worth the cold," Audra said.

"I guess it is," Nick said. "But you have a scarf."

Audra giggled and unwrapped the scarf from her neck. "Here, take mine," she said, handing it to him.

Nick stared at her offer, then shook his head. "Never mind."

"You said you were cold. Take the scarf."

"It's purple. I can't wear a purple scarf."

"Lavender," she corrected.

"I really can't wear a lavender scarf. It's a girl color."

She shrugged. "There is no such thing as a girl color."

Nick said, laughing, "Oh yes, there is."

"Then name some."

"Yellow, pink, *purple*, and anything pastel."

"And what are boy colors, if you don't mind my asking?"

He cleared his throat. "Brown, blue, gray, those are *man* colors."

"Okay, so now I know which colors are which. Do tell me how you came to this determination."

"Women gravitate to girl colors. Men gravitate to boy colors. Like right now, you're wearing a pinkish-colored jacket, with a purple scarf and gloves. I'm wearing a navy blue jacket and matching gloves. There's your proof right there."

Audra shrugged and looked at the scarf, which lay on the bench between them. "You sure you don't want the scarf?"

"Positive. Not only is it purple, but it smells."

Somewhat offended, Audra inhaled sharply.

"Like perfume," Nick amended, realizing he had made a mistake.

Audra knew he wasn't trying to be mean, but she frowned and said, "I think I'm really offended."

"I didn't say it smells bad," he hastened to explain. "In fact, it smells really good, like flowers . . . and fruit or something. C'mon, Audra, don't let that make you mad. You smell great. I just don't want to smell like perfume."

Audra laughed. "You should have seen the look on your face. I'm not mad at you. I wouldn't want to smell like your cologne, either."

"So you think my cologne stinks?" he wanted to know.

Audra held up her hands in defense. "No, I did not say that."

Nick sniffed the sleeve of his coat and held it close to her nose. "Take a whiff and tell me what you think."

"I can't believe we're having this conversation," Audra told him, but she sniffed the jacket anyway. Of course, it smelled good, like pine needles and fresh air, but she just nodded and shrugged her shoulders, as though she were still trying to make a decision.

"So what's your opinion? I just got it a few days ago."

"Did Kameelah buy it for you?" Audra asked, her curiosity overtaking her politeness.

"No, she didn't. Actually, my mom bought it for me."

"Then I love it."

"Hmmm. That perfume you're wearing . . . I know I said I liked it, but . . ." he trailed off, grinning broadly.

"Ryan didn't buy this perfume. I've worn this scent forever."

"I know," Nick admitted. "I was just teasing."

Audra shivered. "Scarf or no scarf, I'm getting cold. I think I'm ready to head back." She stood up, ready to go.

"You're right. It's getting colder. I think I'll have to go find out where my scarf is when I get back home."

"Don't say I never offered you my scarf. If your neck freezes, it's not my fault."

Nick shrugged. "It wouldn't be any fun to have just the scarf. I really don't mind the perfume, but really, I'd rather just be standing next to you." He draped his arm over her shoulder and kept it there the rest of the walk home.

At her house, he walked her to the front door, but declined the offer to come inside for tea, saying he had work to catch up on. "You keep warm, okay?" he instructed, gently cupping her cheek in his gloved hand. Audra nodded, and he smiled warmly. Removing his hand, he said, "I guess I'll see you at church in the morning."

"Okay. Have you told Sophie yet?"

"I will today."

"All right, then." She hurried inside as he made his way next door. She changed into comfy clothes and puttered around the kitchen, preparing tea to sip while she read. Her time with Nick that morning had been a surprise, a pleasant one. She could tell by the sense of peace that surrounded him and by the way he seemed more relaxed that he was a different man.

She just hoped the change was genuine, so that the trust could be reinstated between them.

Sunday morning, when Nick and Sophie walked into Sunday school, Audra was happy to see how pleased Sophie was. She was practically beaming she was so proud of Nick.

At the end of the service, Nick went forward to formally join the church. When the pastor asked him if he had accepted Jesus into his heart, Sophie cried tears of joy when Nick answered yes.

After church, the three of them went out to dinner at a small restaurant that Sophie had wanted to try. That evening, while Audra got ready for work the next day, Sophie called to thank Audra for praying for Nick and for not giving up on him.

She listened as Sophie poured out her heart about how she was still praying for Alan to accept Christ, and Walter, too, wherever he might be.

Audra could hardly hold back her smile when she remembered that Nick's dad had already accepted Christ, and she wondered what Sophie would say when he showed up for Thanksgiving.

Audra was not the best secret keeper, and she wondered if she would be able not to let on anything about Nick's dad. She prayed that she wouldn't. Before Sophie could hang up the phone, Nick asked to speak to Audra.

"Hey," he greeted her.

"Hey to you, too."

"I don't want to keep you long, but I just thought I'd see if you wanted a ride to tutoring tomorrow; I have an empty seat in my car for you."

"I'd like that," Audra told him.

"Then I'll see you tomorrow," he said. "Good night."

"Good night."

As Audra got ready to go to sleep that night, she thanked the Lord for the evidence of His hand in Nick's life and prayed that Nick would continue to grow in the Lord. And just before she fell asleep, she added, "And Lord, you know better than I do that I'm attracted to Nick. I'd be interested in a deeper relationship with him, but only if it's Your will. Please help guide my emotions where Nick is concerned and even take them away if Nick is not the person You want me to spend the rest of my life with. In Jesus' name, amen."

Audra went to sleep, feeling at peace about her relationship with Nick. From now on, things were in the Lord's hands, and she trusted His judgment completely.

Thirteen

*T*he month of October passed in a blur, but Audra enjoyed every minute of it. She, Laura, and Michelle were gearing up for the busy season, the time of year when people threw a seemingly endless string of parties for the holidays.

The amount of planning the company took on this year reached a record high, and Audra hired even more event employees to ensure that all parties would be well staffed.

Since issues with Nick were no longer a problem, Audra and Sophie spent much more time together. Many times, Sophie even accompanied Audra to activities with Audra's mother, Deborah, and Caron.

Audra's entire family enjoyed spending time with Sophie and Nick, and they all hinted and guessed about whether or not Audra and Nick were ever going to "officially" go on a date.

Audra and Nick had agreed to spend time together, but not force themselves into a relationship just "because." Since they had both ended relationships, they wanted to be sure before beginning a new one. They were, of course, attracted to each other, but Audra's trust in Nick had been severely damaged, and while she had forgiven him, she didn't feel comfortable trusting him with her emotions. Nick, in addition, wanted time to grow in his faith and knowledge of the Lord without the distraction of a romance with Audra, so he, too, felt comfortable with the slower pace of their relationship.

The one point of stress stemmed from the question of what they should do about Nick's complaint concerning Audra's lights, now that the homes association meeting was fast approaching.

Nick wanted to drop the complaint, because he said he now had no problem with her lights. Audra felt no qualms about waiting for the other residents to vote on whether or not the lights were a nuisance. She wouldn't mind turning them back on, but she wanted to be sure that no one else would be offended by them.

One day, at work, Laura and Michelle had urged her to take Nick's advice and let him tell Kyle he wanted to drop the complaint, but Audra had resisted their efforts.

"I thought you used your lights to witness to people," Laura had said. "Don't you still want to do that?"

"The last thing I want to do is stop sharing the gospel with people," Audra admitted. "But the lights are not the only way I can share." She shrugged, adding, "Most people around here know who I am, and they know about my lights."

"And because they've seen the lights, they know what they stand for," Michelle added.

"Maybe, maybe not. But I don't know if I've given people the wrong impression."

"What do you mean?" asked Michelle.

Audra grinned. "Take, for instance, what happened with Nick. I was shoving my lights in his face in the name of salvation, but look how I treated him. I had a hard time controlling my emotions, and it made him think even worse of Christians."

"But he still got saved," Laura pointed out.

"Yes, he did, but I wonder if I slowed the process down some. I started to think about why I needed my lights so much the day you guys told me I had lost my Christmas spirit." She rested her hand in her chin, searching for the right words. "I think that, in my desire to have this big display of how thankful I was for salvation, I forgot what the display was about. And when Nick came and seriously questioned my motives, I got way too defensive. Instead of drawing him closer to the Lord, I was pushing him away."

Laura shook her head. "I still don't get your point. You were praying for him, Sophie was praying for him, and Michelle and I prayed for him. Eventually, he changed. Where do you think you messed up?"

Audra grabbed her Bible from her desk drawer and pulled it out. "The Sunday after the three of us had that conversation, Pastor Walls preached First Corinthians eight. You know, the chapter that talks about how we should be careful not to exercise our freedoms to the extent that it causes confusion or a stumbling block for someone else who has questions about what we are doing?"

Laura nodded. "Yeah, but that's for people who are already Christians. Nick wasn't."

Audra shook her head. "Some people interpret it that way, but I think it applies to everyone, including people who we might be witnessing to. Of course, it doesn't mean that we should give up things that God has commanded us to do, like praying and obeying the Bible in general. Those things are mandatory. But I don't have to have my lights on in order to be a Christian, so if it's causing me to have an ungodly argument with someone, then the lights should go."

"Wow." Michelle nodded. "I'd never thought of it like that."

"Yeah . . ." Laura agreed. "Wouldn't it be awful to get to heaven and find out that your self-inflicted rules had made someone decide not to get saved?"

"That's my point," Audra said. "It was my own pride standing in the way of my witness, even though I was complaining about Nick needing Jesus." She giggled. "I used to always shake my head when we read about Jesus and the problems He met when he was on Earth. Remember how some people got upset when Jesus healed a lame man on the Sabbath and pointed out that it would be unlawful for the man to take up his bed and walk since the law forbade work on a Sabbath?"

"Or when the Pharisees questioned Jesus about letting his disciples pick grain on the Sabbath because they were hungry."

"And Jesus asked them if they knew the meaning of the part in the book of Hosea that said, "I desire mercy, not sacrifice.""

Audra nodded. "I went home and looked for that verse, and here's what it says." She flipped to Hosea chapter six and searched for the verse. "Here it is," she announced. "Verse six says, 'For I desire mercy, not sacrifice, and acknowledgement of God rather than burnt offerings.' That's where I was missing the point. My lights had gotten to be more about a personal show instead of my relationship with God, and that's where I made my mistake." She took a deep breath. "So that's why I'm waiting to hear from everyone at the meeting about my lights. If it's hurting someone, I don't need them."

Michelle and Laura nodded gravely.

"*But*," Audra said, pausing dramatically, "if no one cares, I will be more than happy to turn them back on. I do miss seeing all those twinkling colors every night."

"I guess you'll find out for sure tomorrow night," Laura said. "But I miss the lights, too, so I'll be praying no one else objects."

"Me, too," Michelle chimed in.

"Thanks," Audra said, grinning. She wiggled her eyebrows comically, and added, " 'Cause I'm praying the same thing."

Nick parked the car in front of Kyle and Caron's home but didn't get out right away. He looked over at Audra in the passenger's seat and asked, "Are you sure about this? I checked with Kyle, and I can still withdraw the complaint, you know."

Audra smiled warmly, and his heart turned over. He loved the way she was handling this. Her beloved light display was on the line tonight, and she was smiling at him as if she didn't have a care in the world.

He knew one thing for sure; he was falling in love with her. Maybe he already had; he wasn't sure when it had first become apparent to him. But every day, his heart grew more full of love for this woman. He just prayed that the day he told her, she would be able to say that she loved him back.

Audra reached across the seat and squeezed his hand. "You look more nervous than I feel. But I'm sure about this. I want everyone to vote so I can be sure that I'm not hurting anyone." She let go of his hand and opened her door. "Now let's go in and get this over with."

Nick got out of the car and followed Audra inside, dreading every second he had to wait until the subject could be settled. He didn't know if anyone else disliked the lights, but he felt badly that he had been so selfish about the whole situation. Audra still hadn't turned the lights back on, and even though people around town knew that he was now a Christian, they didn't know what to make of the fact that Audra's house was no longer lit. They blamed him personally for the lack of lights, and he didn't know what type of reception he would get tonight.

Inside Kyle and Caron's home, dozens of people were milling around, enjoying refreshments until the meeting began. The house was large, but the space was tight, and Nick wondered why the association didn't rent a hall or something for this meeting.

"Hey buddy," Kyle came up to him and clapped a hand on his shoulder.

"Looks like you've got a full house tonight," Nick said.

Kyle agreed. "We should have rented a space. But, you know, we usually don't have this many people. These meetings are pretty boring, and only the real sticklers ever bother to come." Kyle lowered his voice and added, "I think the real draw is the vote about Audra's lights."

Nick felt queasy. Of course, the largest crowd ever *would* show up to vote about his silly complaint. "I feel really badly about this," he told Kyle. "I wish I hadn't been so obnoxious about it."

"She still won't let you drop it?"

"No. And when I threatened to do it anyway, she said she would complain herself, to make sure people voted about it."

Kyle shook his head. "That's my stubborn little sister. I guess we'll just have to hope that most people here want to see those lights back on."

"Yeah," Nick said grimly. "But from what Audra's saying, she won't turn the lights back on if even one person has a problem with them, so you'd better pray instead of just hope."

Kyle managed a nervous laugh. "I will, buddy. I will."

Nick couldn't imagine eating anything, even though Caron had prepared a huge buffet of finger foods, so he went downstairs to the family room where the meeting would be held and took a seat in one of the chairs.

Shortly after he sat down, people started filing downstairs, taking their seats. There was an air of excitement that seemed to reverberate throughout the room. Nick was the recipient of many stares and looks, some curious, some angry, and several friendly. He was relieved when Audra came and sat beside him, hoping everyone noticed that he and Audra were getting along.

His hopes were dashed when he heard a woman a few rows behind him loudly whisper to someone, "Look over there. That Audra Clayton is such a bleeding heart. She would give the shirt off her back to someone, no matter how awfully they treated her. I'm glad I came tonight. I'll be proud to vote for those lights to stay up."

Nick grimaced, and glanced at Audra. She had heard, too, but she didn't look upset. She turned around, gave the woman a cheery smile, and waved. Then she reached over and grabbed Nick's hand. "No matter what, we'll still be friends when this is over," she told him softly.

Nick felt a small measure of relief, but he knew he wouldn't rest until the matter was behind them. Shortly afterward, Kyle went to the front of the room and urged everyone to take a seat so the meeting could begin.

In the beginning, everyone gave Kyle their full attention, but as the meeting wore on, Nick sensed people were getting restless.

Matters such as snow removal, trash and leaf collection, and the annual garage sale were discussed in great detail—almost excruciatingly so, in Nick's opinion. They discussed the beautification of the neighborhood park until Nick felt like standing up and yelling that he would pay for all of the flowers, both impatiens and petunias, if they could just move on.

Nearly two hours after the start of the meeting, after the Easter egg hunt committee had been appointed, the moment of truth came.

"That concludes all of our regular business," said Kyle. "Tonight, however, we have another issue on our agenda that will need to be resolved through a vote. I'm sure you all know the subject of this vote from your newsletters," he said, looking out across the crowd. The audience immediately grew quiet and the passive atmosphere grew tense once again. "Does anyone need me to go into detail?" asked Kyle.

One older gentleman, near the back of the room, raised his hand. "Yes, Mr. Martin?" said Kyle.

The man stood up. "In my opinion, this is a silly issue and a waste of our time. If we're going to all vote on something, we should vote about whether or not Mr. Lewis should be able to get away with painting his house orange and purple. Audra's lights are pretty, but Mr. Lewis's house is the real eyesore."

Chuckles spread across the room, and Nick was glad for the relief. Audra warned him beforehand about the legendary feud between Mr. Martin and Mr. Lewis. It was true, she had admitted, that Mr. Lewis, who painted his house every year, *did* pick some odd color combinations, and Mr. Martin, who lived across the street from Mr. Lewis, complained every year. However, the association never really did anything about it, because Mr. Lewis was always careful to stay within the rule book's code requirements, picking colors that were acceptable, but using strange combinations.

The orange and purple Mr. Martin referred to was *actually*

burnt sienna and deep maroon. And, although it *was* indeed a ghastly combination, both colors were acceptable according to the rules. The matter had been brought before the residents several times, but the vote had always gone in favor of Mr. Lewis, since Mr. Martin complained about almost everything and most people agreed that he was too grouchy.

"Mr. Martin, I understand your frustration," said Kyle, but you need to file another complaint for the next meeting."

"Oh, sure," the man grumbled, taking a seat. "By that time, his house'll be neon yellow and hot pink."

"That's not a bad idea," Mr. Lewis said loudly, from the other side of the room.

Incensed, Mr. Martin leapt to his feet. "It's a house, not a Post-it note!" he yelled, pointing at Mr. Lewis.

Mr. Lewis shrugged nonchalantly. "They paint them like that in the Caribbean, you know."

The crowd was roaring with laughter. Mr. Martin rushed toward Mr. Lewis's side, yelling, "This is Connecticut, not some island, you jerk!" He made a sudden lunge toward Mr. Lewis, but a couple of other men nearby stopped him.

Mr. Martin was ready to fight. "Let him go!" he yelled to the men who restrained Mr. Lewis. Nick couldn't believe two elderly men were ready to go to blows over this, but, remembering how heated things had gotten with he and Audra, he wasn't entirely surprised. In the seat next to him, Audra was giggling so hard, tears were forming in her eyes.

"Okay, let's get some order here!" Kyle yelled over the roar of the crowd and the two men. "Mr. Martin, Mr. Lewis, if you want to be a part of this meeting, go back to your seats and calm down. Otherwise, you will *have* to leave."

The two reluctantly returned to their seats, and Kyle continued. "Back to the issue at hand. As you may know, Nick Bryant turned in the complaint, but he has since changed his mind. He no longer has any problem with the lights."

A woman in the front said, "Then what are we waiting for? Let's go home."

Kyle shook his head. "My sister wants the vote to continue as planned. She wants to make sure no one has any problem with her light display."

A murmur rippled through the crowd, and Kyle had to ask everyone to quiet down. "So, if no one has any objections, we'll go ahead with the vote. Everyone needs to take a sheet of paper and write down whether or not you are in favor of having the lights turned off."

Mr. Martin stood up. "Why go to all that trouble? Nobody wants the lights down. Let's do a show of hands."

Kyle shook his head. "No, we need to make sure no one feels forced to take a particular side."

The people started grumbling again, and the general tone was that everyone preferred the show of hands. Kyle finally relented.

Mr. Martin stood up again, looking around the room. "Why don't we have a show of hands about whether we should do a show of hands?" Before Kyle could protest, he asked, "Who wants to vote by show of hands?"

Every person in the room raised a hand, with the exception of Audra and Kyle, and Nick knew they just wanted to be impartial.

"Okay, okay, we'll do a show of hands," Kyle said. "All in favor of the lights being turned off, raise your hand." No one moved. "All in favor of keeping the lights on, raise your hand." Everyone raised a hand, and Nick was able to breathe a sigh of relief.

"Then it looks like the lights stay on," said Kyle. "Does any-one have any additional comments?"

Someone started clapping, and the whole room joined in the applause. Nick realized he was still holding hands with Au-dra, and he leaned over and gave her an impromptu hug. The crowd cheered even more, and Audra smiled at him with tears in her eyes. She looked just as relieved as he felt, and Nick was happy the whole thing was over.

"Don't cry," he whispered.

"I'm not crying," she answered.

"Yes, you are." He gently wiped the trail of tears with his fin-gers and looked her in the eye. "Now will you please turn those lights back on?"

She nodded, still crying.

Nick was touched by her patience and her desire to make sure the issue was decided fairly. She had such a heart to do right, and that added to her beauty. Impulsively, Nick leaned forward and gently kissed her. "I love you," he whispered.

Audra's eyes widened, and Nick felt a twinge of guilt. He should have waited longer before doing that, but he couldn't help himself.

The crowd was still clapping and cheering as if the happy ending of a movie had played out in front of them. Nick moved away from Audra and self-consciously looked around him. Au-dra also looked a little flustered, and Nick wished the meeting would end for good so they wouldn't be under so much scrutiny.

"All right, everybody," said Kyle. "This meeting is ad-journed. Thanks for coming, and I hope to see you all next year. There are still refreshments upstairs, so feel free to stay and visit for a while."

People got up and started milling around once again. Several of them stopped to congratulate Audra on her victory, and they gave Nick friendly glances as well.

One lady patted Audra's shoulder and said, "Honey, you be sure and get those lights back up again. My kids really miss them."

Audra nodded and said, "I'll do that." After the crowd thinned out some, she turned to Nick and asked if he was ready to leave. "I'm worn out," she told him.

"Me, too." He took hold of her hand and led her to the car.

"I'll bet Sophie is wondering what took so long," she said once he started the car.

"Yeah. Who would have thought it would take so long to pick a date for the community garage sale."

Audra laughed. "Or what about Mr. Martin and Mr. Lewis?"

Nick laughed, too. "I'd forgotten about that one." Kyle's home was only a few blocks away from his and Audra's street, and they laughed about some of the meeting's funnier moments during the ride home. Neither one of them mentioned the kiss. As he pulled into Audra's driveway, Nick said, "I'm sorry if I embarrassed you in there with the kiss and everything."

Audra shook her head. "You didn't embarrass me. I just didn't expect it, that's all." She hesitated, and added, "I guess no one else minded either. I didn't think they were going to start clapping like that."

"Yeah. I guess it turned out to be quite a show, as far as they were concerned."

Audra groaned. "Of course, word will get around, and people will start speculating."

Nick shrugged. "There's not that much to speculate about. Everyone thinks we're a couple anyway. They just couldn't understand why I didn't withdraw my complaint. With that issue out of the way, we look every bit the happy couple."

"But we're not, really. At least not now," Audra pointed out.

"But we could be," Nick said.

Audra looked at him questioningly, and he continued. "I meant what I said. I do love you. I'm willing to commit to a serious relationship if you are."

Audra didn't say anything for several moments, and Nick's hopes diminished as the seconds ticked past. Apparently, Audra didn't love him back.

She sighed. "Nick, I'm still not sure. I'd really like more time to pray about this, if you don't mind."

Nick was discouraged, but he didn't argue. "Sure. Take as much time as you need," he said. He watched while she unlocked the door to her house, then pulled out of the driveway after she was safely inside.

He hadn't been thrilled with her answer, but he had to trust the route she was taking. He firmly believed in the power of prayer, and as long as she was going to pray about their relationship, it wouldn't hurt for him to continue praying as well.

Two weeks later, Audra sat in her great room, on the floor in front of the fireplace, enjoying her quiet time and sipping a cup of tea.

Emotionally, she was confused. She knew she had hurt Nick's feelings when she hadn't responded that she loved him back after the kiss, but she had been too shocked to say anything.

Before the day of the meeting, Audra was aware that her feelings for Nick were growing into something more than friendship, but she was afraid to admit it, fearing that he wasn't ready for love. She had convinced herself that she wasn't really *in love* with him, yet, and when he'd admitted he loved her, she had sat there, numb, wondering if she had imagined it, because he'd whispered so quietly. Even after they left, during the ride home, she had wondered if she had been hearing things.

She hadn't known for sure until he had said so again, and then she'd been overcome with a case of nerves and didn't know what to say. So, she'd promised Nick she would pray about it, and she knew he would pray as well.

Now, she sat in front of the fireplace, having poured her heart out to the Lord about the matter. Deep in her heart, she knew she loved Nick, but she was reluctant to admit it to herself, let alone to anyone else. The problem lay in all of the false starts she and Nick had faced in their relationship. What would prevent them from facing any further roadblocks and obstacles?

She had shared these concerns with her mom, who had offered only one piece of advice. "No relationship is ever perfect, but a relationship with Jesus prominently at the center will have an excellent chance of survival, provided He remains the center."

Audra felt confident that she and Nick would be willing to make the Lord the center of their relationship, and ultimately their marriage, but she didn't want to rush the issue. She had spent many hours in prayer over the matter, and she had a feeling Nick had done the same. God knew both of their hearts, and He would make it clear to them when it was time for them to take the next step forward in their relationship. As she and Nick both had learned, God's timing was always impeccable.

The day before Thanksgiving, Audra stood in the bitter cold as Nick stood perched on his roof, trying to hang Christmas lights. Ten inches of snow had fallen the day before, and the city was blanketed in a thick carpet of the white stuff, making travel difficult. Nick had taken a few extra days of holiday vacation time to spend with his family.

Alan, home for Thanksgiving break, stood on the ground with Audra and Sophie, teasing Nick's amateur efforts. Alan was a younger version of Nick, looks and all. He also loved to tease and crack jokes. "Hey, Nick, you sure you should be up there? Maybe you should call in a professional, like Audra. Now she knows how to hang some lights," said Alan.

Nick stapled another length of lights to the edge of the roof. "Why don't you come up and help me if you're such an expert?"

"No, thanks," Alan said. "In fact, I think I'm going to go inside and warm up. I'm more suited to a warmer climate. These fingers can't play the piano if they're frozen, you know." Alan turned and headed inside, rubbing his hands together to warm them.

Nick was determined to put lights on his house for the holidays, and he had insisted that Audra go with him to buy the decorations. Audra had been delighted to go with him, pleased to see more evidence of the Lord's work in Nick's life. Only eight months earlier, Nick had shied away from anything having to do with Christmas, and now, he was excited to be putting up Christmas lights on his house.

Audra watched Nick struggle with a tangle of lights and grinned. Knotted lights were not part of the fun at all, as she well knew. Nick looked down at her and winked. "What are you staring at?" he teased.

"The handsome guy up there on the roof," she teased back. "You think you can introduce me to him?"

"Only if his name is Nick," he laughed, continuing his task.

The wind howled rather treacherously just then, and Audra

shivered. Sophie looked at Audra and grinned. "I don't mind a good snowfall now and then. It's the cold that's hard to handle."

"Yeah, the snow's fine," Audra agreed. "It adds to the holiday feeling. It would be great if we could have snow and eighty-degree days at the same time."

"Yeah, in a perfect world. But as long as I've got both my boys here, I don't care what the weather's like," Sophie said happily.

Audra smiled and bit her tongue, knowing that in a few hours, Sophie's entire family would be together for the holiday. Although Nick's dad had originally planned to come a few days earlier, he'd had to change his flight arrangements, and he was now due to arrive at the airport later in the evening. Audra couldn't wait to see the look on Sophie's face when he showed up.

Nick and Audra had both agreed that Sophie might get suspicious if one of them suddenly left in the middle of the special dinner Sophie had cooked, so they had drafted Kyle to pick Walter up from the airport and smuggle him into Audra's guest house where he would remain hidden until the next morning. Then Audra would take him next door, where he and Nick would explain to Sophie and Alan the events leading up to the surprise.

"Okay, that's the last of the lights," Nick announced. "It won't be as fancy as the house next door, but it's a good start for someone who has never done this before. We'll have the big lighting ceremony tomorrow night." He picked up the staple gun and walked back to his ladder.

"Be careful, it's slippery up there," Sophie warned.

"Yeah, Mom, I am," Nick said, already halfway down the ladder. Suddenly, his foot slipped, and in an instant, he had fallen off the ladder and into a cluster of evergreen shrubs growing beneath.

Sophie and Audra ran to where he had fallen. Nick groaned, half hidden in a mass of shrubbery.

"Nick, can you hear me?" Sophie yelled, patting his cheek.

Nick groaned again but didn't speak. Audra ran inside and called for Alan to help get Nick inside.

Alan rushed ahead of Audra to where Nick lay, still in the bushes. Sophie continued patting his cheek, but he appeared to be unconscious. When Audra got closer, she realized Nick also had a large cut on the side of his forehead.

Her heart beat double time, and she didn't know what they should do. Alan took over and suggested they get Nick in the house.

Nick was a total dead weight, and the bushes made the logistics of getting him up difficult, but somehow, the three of them managed to lift him and half drag, half carry him inside.

Because Nick remained unconscious through all of that, Audra decided they should take him to the emergency room. So the three of them worked and got Nick situated in the backseat of his car.

Sophie rode in the back with Nick, and Audra directed Alan, who wanted to drive.

During the ride to the hospital, Nick awakened several times, then drifted back into unconsciousness. Sophie prayed aloud during the entire ride there, and by the time they reached the emergency room, Nick was awake and a little disoriented.

The emergency-room staff immediately admitted Nick and began running tests on him, and some time passed before Sophie, Alan, and Audra heard anything. Finally, the doctor came out and told them that Nick had a concussion. They wanted to keep him at least overnight to make sure he would be okay. The cut had been stitched, but it hadn't been deep enough to cause a major blood loss.

He had lost consciousness again while they were running tests, so the doctor suggested that the three of them go in and talk to him to help keep him awake for the next few hours.

They found Nick looking tired but alert, sitting up in his hospital bed. The four of them were pretty well shaken up, but they all thanked God for protecting Nick from serious harm.

They talked, watched TV, quizzed Nick's memory, and talked some more until Nick became slightly cranky. "I'm not a baby," he said. "Don't be so overprotective," he told them.

Sophie ignored him and began a whole new round of quizzing.

Audra, standing behind Sophie, met Nick's eyes, as he did his best to answer every question Sophie posed.

It was well into the evening when Audra remembered about Nick's dad. She checked her watch, realizing Walter had arrived nearly two hours earlier. She slipped out of the room to find a phone to call her brother.

"Audra, where are you!" Kyle exclaimed.

"Where's Walter?" she asked.

"He's with me, at our house. I picked him up, but when I went by your house, no one was there. Your car was there, and Nick's front door was wide open."

Audra vaguely recalled that after they got Nick into the car, no one had gone back to shut the door.

"I went in and checked for intruders, but everything's okay," Kyle reported. "So where are you? I tried calling your cell, but I kept getting the voice mail."

"We're at the hospital, and they made me turn it off. Nick was putting the lights on his roof, and he fell off the ladder coming down. He has a concussion and a few stitches, and the doctor thinks he'll be okay."

"Whoa. Hold on a sec, I'll tell Walter. He's been pretty worried."

Audra waited while Kyle relayed the information to Walter. When he finished, he said, "Walter wants to come. What room is Nick in?"

"Well," Audra hesitated. "I'm not sure Nick wants to see his dad for the first time in all these years while he's in a hospital bed. Why don't you take him to my house. Hopefully, Nick will be out tomorrow and everything can go as planned."

"Okay, I'll try to convince him. Is the key to the guest house still under the doormat?"

"No, it's under the fake rock in the flower bed. Make sure you turn the heat on in there, okay? And tell him I said hello, and for him not to worry."

"I will. You take care now," said Kyle.

Audra returned to the room, where Sophie was asking Nick to name the fifty states.

"Where'd you run off to?" asked Nick.

"I called Kyle and told him where I was so he could get in touch with me if he needed to." Nick's eyes lit with under-standing, and Audra felt herself begin to relax, seeing that he really seemed to be doing well.

A children's holiday cartoon came on the television, and since Sophie had run out of quiz topics, the four of them set-tled down to watch TV.

Audra sat on the wide windowsill of the room and let Sophie and Alan sit in the two chairs.

The day had been long and taxing, and Audra nodded off to sleep several times. She wanted to go home, but since she hadn't driven her car, she would have to wait until So-phie and Alan were ready to go, unless she called Kyle or someone to come and get her. She didn't really want to do that because of all of the snow, which made for difficult driving conditions.

Audra was halfway asleep when she heard Sophie gasp loudly, then cry out. Worried that something was wrong with Nick, Audra jerked awake, nearly falling off of the windowsill.

"Hey, be careful there," Nick warned. "We don't need two of us in here."

Audra regained her balance and saw what had caused Sophie's cry. In the doorway stood a man who bore such a striking resemblance to Nick that there was no mistaking his identity.

Fourteen

Sophie stood frozen in place, her hand covering her mouth. Walter was overcome with emotion, and he wept openly. Finally, Sophie looked toward Nick, tears also streaming down her face.

Nick struggled to sit up straighter. Looking to Audra, he said, "I was hoping you had asked Kyle to take Dad to your house, like we planned. I didn't want to meet him sitting in this bed."

Audra shrugged. "I tried, but I guess he made his own decision."

"You both knew about this?" Sophie asked.

Nick and Audra nodded. "It was our Thanksgiving present to you," Nick said.

Walter stepped inside the room and crossed to Alan, who was looking back and forth between Walter and Sophie.

"Dad?" Alan asked.

That was all Walter needed. He wrapped Alan in his arms,

both of them weeping. "I know you don't remember me, but I am your dad," Walter told him.

When Walter pulled away from Alan, he moved to Sophie. "Hello, Sophie."

Sophie was shaking, but she managed to say, "Hello, Walter." He reached out hesitantly, and she flew into his arms. The two of them cried and held each other for several moments, and Audra worried that she was intruding on a private family moment. Nick seemed to sense her concern and gestured for her to come and stand next to him. When she reached the bedside, he grabbed her hand and held it tightly. By this time, everyone was crying, including Audra.

When Walter came and stood on the other side of Nick's bed, Audra bit her lip to keep from wailing louder than anyone else. Walter didn't hesitate this time; he leaned over and hugged Nick so tightly that she wondered if he was hurting him. Nick winced slightly but didn't complain, and Audra knew that being hugged by his dad was far more important to him than any discomfort he felt.

The four members of the Bryant family began talking all at once, and Audra gave Nick a quick kiss on the cheek, then went out to the hallway, where she figured Kyle would be waiting for her. Sure enough, he was right outside of the doorway, his eyes suspiciously wet.

Audra playfully jabbed him in the arm. "Go ahead and cry like the rest of us," she told him. "You don't have to be all macho."

Kyle tried to laugh, but a few tears leaked from his eyes instead. He and Audra hugged for a few moments while they wept. Finally, Kyle drew away, and Audra knew her big brother had been deeply touched, for she had rarely seen him cry. "It looks like the Lord is putting Nick's family back together, doesn't it?" asked Kyle as they were on their way to the parking lot.

"It sure does," Audra agreed. "But a lot of prayers went into this reunion, starting with the prayers of a little boy, nearly twenty-three years ago."

"You know, I'd like to know how this all came about," Kyle said. "How did Nick get back in touch with his dad?"

"It's a long story, but I'll try to remember all the details," Audra said, wearily climbing into Kyle's SUV.

On the way home, she explained what Nick had told her. After leaving his family, Walter had traveled around the country for the next ten years, making a living by gambling, whether in a casino or a racetrack or a poker game.

When his luck ran out, he joined a support group for gamblers and started working as an auto mechanic in Washington. He thought about his wife and sons on a regular basis but didn't want to go back and have to deal with Sophie's religious beliefs, so he didn't try to make contact with them. Still, he hoped they were okay, and he never got involved in any other relationships.

Finally, three years ago, on a whim, he used some of his savings, got a small business loan, and bought a small mechanic shop in Boston, sight unseen. He packed up and moved across country to start his own business. The shop was located next door to a church, and the pastor of the church reached out to him again and again, until Walter finally decided to let Jesus into his heart two years ago. From that point on, he went back and forth, trying to decide if he should contact his family. He wasn't sure if Sophie had remarried, or if she wanted to have anything to do with him, so he decided against writing her. He realized Alan wouldn't even remember him, so he decided to contact Nick, and that was what got the ball rolling. Audra was so tired, she fell asleep at that point. Kyle, understanding she had had an emotionally exhausting day, let her sleep.

Audra was so exhausted when Kyle dropped her off at home that she went inside, got in bed, promptly fell asleep, and didn't move until the phone rang the next morning.

"Hello?" Audra said, her voice all groggy.

"Oh, dear, I woke you up," said Sophie.

Audra sat up, fully alert. "Is Nick okay?"

"He's fine, and they're releasing him in an hour. We were wondering if you wanted to come with us to pick him up. We'll be leaving in about a half hour."

"I'll be there," Audra said, flying out of bed. She rushed into the bathroom, washed her face and brushed her teeth, then took a shower in record time. She wanted to look nice for Nick, so she curled the ends of her hair, and even put on a little makeup. She dressed in a deep maroon crushed velvet blazer and a pair of nice jeans, hoping she looked festive and dressy, but not too formal.

She rushed next door and found Sophie, Alan, and Walter in the kitchen enjoying cinnamon rolls and coffee.

"I know you don't drink coffee, so I made you a cup of tea," Sophie said when Audra came in.

Walter stood up and greeted her with a hug. "The famous Audra. Sorry I didn't get to meet you yesterday, with all of the commotion."

"Oh, it's no problem," Audra told him. "Nothing went according to the plan, did it?"

"No, it didn't. And Nick was not happy about us leaving him there all night my first night here."

"Walter was telling us about what's been happening with

him all this time," Sophie said. "I guess he can tell us the rest on the way, if everyone's ready."

Everyone agreed that they were ready to go, so they piled into Nick's car, with Alan driving. From the backseat, Walter told them more of his story.

"By the time I convinced Nick to get in touch with me, I was pretty caught off guard," Walter began. "The Nick I remembered read his Bible every day and never hesitated to tell me how he was praying for me. I had expected him to be happy to hear that I was saved, but the first time he called, I hardly got a chance to say anything, he was fussing so much. I went to my pastor and told him I had made a big mistake in contacting him. He told me to pray for my wife and kids, and to let the Lord do his work. I agreed to do that, but I wasn't going to try to talk to Nick again.

"A few weeks later, he surprised me by calling me back and wanting to talk. I tried to talk about the Lord, but he made it clear that he didn't want to hear any of that. So, we would just talk, sometimes about nothing but the weather, but we were still talking.

"He was really getting concerned about whether or not prayer worked, and he would ask me questions sometimes. If I got too carried away in my answer, he would change the subject."

"Audra and I were praying for him," Sophie said.

"He knew," said Walter. "It bothered him a little, too. One time he told me he could almost feel the prayers working." Walter paused to take a breath. "He talked about you lots, too," he said to Audra. "He was really impressed with you, but he was scared to get too friendly with you because he was so busy running from the Lord. But eventually, one day, we were talking, and out of the blue, he just said, 'Dad, I want what you and

Mom and Audra have. Can you tell me how to get that peace?' "

"Were you surprised?" Sophie wanted to know.

Walter's eyes got big. "I was shocked, but I didn't waste any time. I led him in the prayer of salvation as quick as I could. And I guess the rest is history. We started making plans for me to come, and everything was on schedule until yesterday."

They were at the hospital, and they made their way to Nick's room, eager to take him home. Dressed in his clothes from the day before, he was sitting on his bed waiting for them. A pair of crutches rested next to him. "Get me out of here," he said, grinning broadly.

"What are the crutches for?" Audra asked, concerned.

Nick shrugged. "In all the excitement yesterday, no one realized I had twisted my ankle, since I wasn't doing any walking. We learned about the ankle when I tried to get up late last night. When I put weight on my leg, I fell down. Thankfully, a nurse was out in the hallway when it happened."

"Are you okay? From the fall?" Sophie asked.

"I guess so. I have a big bruise to show for it, but it won't be permanent. I've already done all the paperwork, so we can go." He carefully placed the crutches under his arms and slowly began hobbling out of the room. They filed down the hall behind him and waited while a nurse found a wheelchair for him.

Nick balked at the idea of leaving in a wheelchair, but the nurse sternly informed him that it was the hospital policy, and he had to obey. Grudgingly, Nick sat in the chair and let Alan push him out to the car.

"I'll drive," Nick announced when he saw they had brought his car.

"Not with a sprained right ankle," Audra told him. "Alan's driving, but you *can* sit in the front seat with him."

"You let Alan drive my car?" Nick asked, grimacing.

"How do you think you got here yesterday?" Audra challenged. "Now get in that car, mister."

Nick silently obeyed, frowning all the while. When they got home, Sophie, Alan, and Walter started preparing the Thanksgiving dinner, while Audra kept Nick company, his foot propped up on the couch.

They talked for a long time about his dad and how his mom and Alan were taking the surprise.

"Alan doesn't know what to think. He was just a baby when Dad left," Nick informed her.

"What about Sophie? What do you think they'll do now that they're both Christians and they're reunited? Will they live together?"

Nick thought for a while, then nodded. "I think they will. I'm just not sure if they'll live here, or in Boston."

"I'm glad they're going to be together, but I'll miss Sophie if she goes to Boston," Audra admitted.

"Me, too," Nick said quietly. "We'll both be lonely, and I won't have anyone to keep house for me." He laughed at his joke.

Audra laughed, too, but sobered thinking of what a great friend Sophie had become.

"There is a way to remedy the problem," Nick said.

"What's that?" Audra was curious.

"You could marry me." Nick was smiling, and Audra thought he was joking.

"Oh, yeah, that's a great idea. Or, you could just hire a maid. It might even be cheaper than having a wife."

"No, I'm serious," Nick sounded more earnest. "You know I love you. I said it before, and I meant it. Do you believe me?"

Audra nodded. "I do. And I love you, too."

"So will you marry me? Nick put his foot down from the coffee table and tried to get down on one knee, but he accidentally banged his shin against the solid wooden leg of the table and yelped in pain. Walter and Sophie came running from the kitchen, followed by Alan.

"What's wrong?" Sophie said, sounding panicked.

Nick shook his head as he sat down and propped his leg up on the table again. "Nothing's wrong. I just made a clown of myself trying to propose to Audra."

"Oh." Sophie grinned, her eyes dancing with interest. "What did she say?"

Nick sighed in exasperation. "I haven't finished asking her yet. But since you're all here, why don't you stick around to see what she says." He turned to Audra and began again. "I know we didn't exactly get off to a great start, but we both know the power of prayer, and I know that if we keep the Lord at the center of our marriage, we have a good shot at making this work. So, what do you say?"

Audra was thrilled to hear Nick reaffirm her feelings about marriage, and she knew what her answer would be. But first, she decided to tease him a little. "What do you say?" Audra repeated. "What kind of proposal is that?"

Nick groaned playfully. "It's a proposal from a sick man. If you accept now, I'll think up something more eloquent and propose in front of everyone at your Christmas party."

"All right, I guess so." Audra laughed.

"What do you mean by 'All right, I guess so?' " Nick asked. "What kind of acceptance is that? Shouldn't you say something a little more legally binding?"

"I promise to come up with something more eloquent for the second proposal," she informed him.

"Of course, I don't have a ring yet," he told her.

"That's okay."

"I'll have it at the party, though." Leaning closer to her he added, "This will have to do for now." He cupped her face in his hands and gently covered her lips with his. "For now," he repeated.

Audra nodded her head in agreement. "So it looks like we're engaged."

"Officially sort of engaged," Nick corrected. "This is a kind of dress rehearsal for the real thing."

Walter cleared his throat. "Since we're on the subject, Sophie and I have decided to have a small ceremony as soon as possible. We know we're still married, but we want to start over with the Lord's blessing. It'll probably be sometime this week, but you're all invited."

Audra, Nick, and Alan clapped and cheered while Walter took Sophie in his arms and kissed her.

When they finished, Sophie added, "And Walter's going to sell his business and move here."

Audra and Nick cheered even more. "You know you're welcome to stay with me, Dad, for as long as you need."

"Actually," said Sophie, "We were hoping you two would get engaged, so we could buy one of the two houses from you. I have some money saved, and so does Walter."

Audra and Nick looked at each other. "So whose house do we sell?" he asked.

Audra lifted her shoulders toward her ears. "I don't know. Let me think about it."

Nodding, Nick turned to his parents and said, "We'll let you know at the official proposal, okay?"

Epilogue

December 23
Joy Year Round's Annual Christmas Party

Nick caught Audra's eye, signaling that he was ready. He took her hand and led her to the front of the large reception hall. He motioned to the quartet to stop the music for a moment, and the crowd focused their attention on Nick and Audra.

Audra spoke first. "On behalf of myself, and all of my employees at Joy Year Round, I want to thank you all for your support. We appreciate each and every one of you. Many of you expressed your support for me when I had my Christmas lights off earlier this year, and some of you, even a few of my employees, expressed concern about my Christmas spirit being dampened. Well, it was. But during this year, I have learned that Christmas lights don't make Christmas spirit. Christmas spirit is in your heart. It's all about the gift of salvation and how you use it. You can hold on to it so tight that no one else can see it, which ultimately makes it difficult for you to enjoy. Or you can share it with others, and share freely, without conditions or self-imposed rules, and that is the way that you'll find the most joy."

Everyone clapped, and Audra leaned her head on Nick's shoulder. She had learned so much from him, and though things had been rough in the beginning, it was all worth it in the end.

Nick cleared his throat to get everyone's attention again. When the room was quiet, he began. "Many of you might know that when I moved here in April, I was not a very happy person. So I guess it was a good thing I moved next door to a lady who was in the joy business."

The crowd chuckled, and Nick continued. "A lot of you know that we've been engaged for about a month, but I was unable to propose the way I wanted to, and I promised Audra that I would do a better job at this party. So here goes."

Nick got down on one knee. "Audra, I love you, and I want to spend the rest of my life with you. Would you do me the honor of being my wife for forever and ever?"

Audra nodded. "Yes, I will." Nick pulled a ring from his pocket and slipped it on her finger.

He stood up and kissed her while the people clapped enthusiastically.

Audra held her hand in front of her and looked at the ring. "Do you like it?" he asked.

"I love it."

He held her hand gently and pointed to the triangle-cut diamond in the ring. "That's to make sure we remember," he whispered.

She looked at him quizzically, and he added, "About keeping the Lord at the center of our marriage. See, He's the point at the top and we're the two points at the bottom. Every time we look at the ring, we'll be reminded of our promise."

"So we remember not to lose our tempers," said Audra.

"And hold on to our joy." Nick smiled.

About the Author

AISHA FORD was home-schooled during her entire academic career. She lives in Missouri with her parents and sister. In her writing, she hopes to show that our best guide for living is to follow the biblical example of Jesus Christ. No matter how hard it seems or how much it may hurt to do things His way, God's way of living life will always be the best way—the route by which we will reap the most lasting rewards. And though none of us is perfect, and we all make mistakes, God is the inventor of grace, and He is patient above and beyond what we can ask or imagine.

Aisha's home page on the web can be found at:
http://www.aishaford.com

A Change of Script

LILLIAN MEREDITH

One

The car made a groaning noise. Again. "Please, please, please, just make it to Aunt Marla's." Natalie Jacobs groaned in frustration. "After that, I promise you can sit still for a few days."

A road sign came into view on her right—STERLING: 20 MILES. "Hey, car, did you see that?" she asked. "Twenty miles isn't that bad, is it?"

The car responded with two more foreboding groans that sounded like grinding metal. It did not sound healthy. But healthy had never been a part of this car's vocabulary. For the next few moments, Natalie considered pulling over to let the car rest, or cool off, or whatever it needed to do, but decided against it. Considering the car's track record, it was currently on a roll. She'd been driving nearly two hours without any major problems. But if she stopped the car now, it might not start again.

Collecting all of her resolve, Natalie did her best to ignore the increasingly frequent grating sounds and kept going.

"Ten miles," Natalie said as she passed another sign. "You can do it," she said in an imitation of a very energetic aerobics instructor.

Natalie breathed a sigh of relief as she reached the exit for Sterling. Exiting from the highway, for nearly a mile she followed the road that led to the town, her car growing more and more creaky by the minute. As she drew closer to the main entrance to Sterling, the car began rattling and jerking back and forth as she tried to drive forward. "No, not now," was Natalie's plaintive whisper.

The car ignored her appeal and finally choked to a complete and utterly silent standstill, barely five hundred feet past the town entrance.

Natalie sat very still, feeling highly embarrassed. Six years ago, she had left Sterling right after graduation, and she vowed never to come back until she had reached the height of fame as a Broadway actress. Now, she was limping back in a car that had decided to upstage her by giving its own dramatic performance right on Main Street.

Natalie looked around, hoping that, somehow, no one had noticed. True, she *was* sitting on Main Street, but it was after dusk, and according to her memory, most of the residents of Sterling, Missouri, would be at home for the evening, sitting at their dining-room tables.

She took a deep breath and slowly opened the door. She was going to have to walk to Aunt Marla's and come back later for the car. The sun was setting rapidly, and she didn't like the thought of walking in the dark, but Marla's house wasn't too far. She also didn't relish the thought of leaving most of her luggage and possessions in the car. She had haphazardly piled what she could fit into her car earlier that afternoon, and even though it didn't look that neat and orderly, she had assumed she would be able to park the car in Marla's garage once she got here. Now, her things were out in plain view for any and all to examine.

In a matter of hours, someone was bound to report that a broken-down vehicle was sitting on Main. And by dawn tomorrow morning, she'd probably find a newly formed committee of some sort standing around her car, peering into the windows and trying to determine to whom it belonged.

Natalie shook her head. Two days from now, the newspaper's headlines would read, LOCAL ACTRESS COMES HOME IN WORSE SHAPE THAN WHEN SHE LEFT, or something to that effect. She simply had to get back here before morning and get her things home.

Natalie swung open one of the back doors and tried to decide what to carry with her to Marla's. What she wanted to take was her suitcase, but she didn't even want to imagine what people would assume if they saw her walking through the town lugging that big old thing behind her.

The fact was, she didn't want to be seen carrying any of this stuff. So she shut the door, made sure the car was locked up tight, and started home with only her purse and what she hoped was a confident expression on her face.

She had not taken three steps when a dark-colored, older-model jeep rounded the corner and headed in her direction.

"So much for going unnoticed," she grumbled, turning her back to the advancing vehicle.

The car pulled to a stop behind her, and she heard a door open and then slam shut. Natalie heard footsteps moving toward her and struggled to keep feelings of apprehension at bay.

From what she remembered, Sterling was not exactly Crime

Central, USA, but her years of living as a single young woman in Kansas City had taught her to be on the lookout for people who might be searching for someone to take advantage of. And, though she might not have given this car and its driver a second thought a few hours earlier, the fact that the sky was growing darker by the minute put a whole new perspective on the situation. She sped up her pace and glanced over her shoulder, her heart jumping in her throat when she saw a man walking toward her.

Frantically searching her memory for some of the moves she and her roommate, Kelly, had learned in self-defense class, Natalie whirled around and took what she hoped was an assertive stance.

The man stopped in his tracks. "Whoa!" he said, putting his hands out in front of him. "I'm not trying to hurt you."

Natalie thought he seemed familiar, but she couldn't quite put a name with his face. Unwilling to trust him just yet, she placed her hand on her purse and told him to stay where he was. "I've got pepper spray," she warned.

To her surprise, the man laughed. "Natalie, it's me."

Still trying to remember how she knew this guy, Natalie took another step away. From his statement, she ascertained that she did know him at least, which was slightly comforting.

He took a cautious step forward.

"You *are* Natalie, aren't you?"

Hesitant, Natalie nodded, wishing it wasn't so dark so she could at least see him clearly.

He moved toward her even faster now. "C'mon, don't you remember me? I'm Brad Owens," he said, placing his hands on his chest. "We dated a few times in high school," he said, trying to jog her memory.

Exhaling the breath she hadn't realized she'd been holding,

Natalie was relieved to remember she *did* know him. In high school, everyone knew Brad Owens. He had been the star of the school's barely functioning basketball team and had been very popular with the female population at school. Brad, however, had always been focused on his studies and sports activities, rarely dating much. In fact, Natalie had been shocked when Brad had asked her to the junior prom. Flattered, she'd accepted the invitation, and they had even gone out a few other times, but nothing had really come of the relationship. By the time senior year began, they were once again just acquaintances. Natalie again wished she could see him better. He looked somewhat similar, but he'd changed enough over the years that she hadn't recognized him at first. His shoulders had broadened more, and his formerly skinny frame was now more muscled. The past six years had resulted in a different Brad Owens than the one she remembered, but she supposed that she, too, had changed as well.

During her senior year at college, she had finally lost her baby fat, much to Natalie's relief, right on target with Aunt Marla's prediction that most of the women in their family did so when they were in their early twenties. During her adolescent and teenage years, Natalie hadn't considered herself overweight, but a little more rounded than she had appreciated.

She didn't remember exactly when the change took place, but one day, early in her senior year, she woke up and found herself to be a nearly different person. Her figure was slimmer, her cheekbones were more prominent, and her entire demeanor had taken on a more mature appearance. Natalie had tearfully noted that she bore a striking resemblance to old photos of her mother.

"You do remember me, right?" asked Brad, interrupting her reverie.

Natalie nodded, smiling. "It took me a few seconds, but yes, I remember you." He didn't say anything.

Natalie had never liked awkward silences, so she started a new topic. "So . . . how've you been?" she said, trying to get the ball rolling.

He nodded before he spoke. "Good. And how about you?" He paused, then grinned, adding, "Your aunt's been telling everybody you work as an actress in Kansas City."

Natalie laughed. Aunt Marla sometimes tended to exaggerate things just a little, especially when it came to people she cared about. "Well, I do some acting, here and there, but I haven't given up my day job."

Brad nodded. "That makes sense. I hear the theater is a pretty fickle business. All the actors are at the discretion of the director's mood."

Natalie pursed her lips, her pride was slightly wounded, but she refrained from any snappy retorts. Instead, she changed the subject. "So what about you? What keeps you busy these days?"

"Oh, this and that," he said, walking around to the front of her car. "You know I got my education degree at the U of Missouri in Columbia. Now I teach history for all grades at the high school, and this past year, they decided to make me the basketball coach," he said.

Natalie laughed, remembering her own high school days. "I'm actually a little surprised they still have enough people to make a whole team."

Brad chuckled. "Actually, the basketball team is the best it's ever been. Football team's a little weak in the depth chart, though." He pointed to the hood of her car. "Having some car trouble?"

Natalie smiled wryly. "It looks that way, doesn't it?"

"Want me to take a look at it?"

Natalie hesitated. She doubted the car was repairable, and she didn't want to stand there while Brad took twenty minutes to diagnose an unfixable problem.

She tried to look nonchalant. "Nah. I think I'll leave it there tonight and head on over to Aunt Marla's."

"At least let me drive you over," he insisted. Without waiting for her to answer, he walked to his jeep, beckoning for her to follow. "I'll just put some of your bags into my car," he said, reaching his hand out for her keys.

"No, that's really okay. I'll come back later tonight with Marla's car and get everything."

"Are you sure? It'll save you work later if we get some of it now."

She shook her head, determined not to let him change her mind. "That's okay. You've been helpful enough, really."

"I'll still take you home, though," said Brad, heading toward his jeep.

Natalie followed and slid into the passenger's seat. During the brief ride to Marla's, she listened while Brad made small talk, mostly about his job.

Not feeling much in the mood for chatting, Natalie simply nodded her head, "hmmm-ing" and "ah-ing" at appropriate moments. Less than five minutes after they started, they reached Marla's home, where her aunt was sitting out on the front porch swing. When she saw Natalie get out of the car, she jumped up from her seat and ran out to the street to greet them.

Natalie threw her arms around the woman who had been her complete family for almost as long as she could remember. Several moments later, Marla stepped back from the embrace and took a long look at Natalie.

"Child," she said, smiling broadly, "it's good to have you home. I was starting to wonder what was taking you so long. But never mind that now. I've got dinner warm in the kitchen for you. Nothing fancy, just some salad and sandwiches, but I figured you wouldn't want anything heavy after all your driving."

Natalie laughed. "Aunt Marla, I called you before I left, and that couldn't have been more than three hours ago. What did you expect me to do? Fly?" she teased.

Marla laughed heartily. "I guess it just seemed like a long time since I was so impatient to see you." Marla looked over and seemed to see Brad for the first time. He had been standing a few feet away while the women exchanged greetings.

"Hello, Miss Marla," Brad said respectfully.

Marla waved her hand. "Don't you 'Miss Marla' me, Bradley Owens. I'm not your teacher anymore. How many times do I have to tell you to call me Marla?"

Brad shook his head. "I've tried, but it doesn't seem right. I've been calling you Miss Marla since I was five, and it just feels comfortable now."

Marla smiled fondly but shook her head. "I guess it doesn't matter much. Most people around here call me Miss Marla, even the ones I never taught. As far as the people of Sterling are concerned, it looks like the word 'Miss' has been permanently affixed to my name." She looked over at Brad's jeep. "So how did you end up bringing my Natalie home?"

Natalie, who had been getting used to the feeling of being back home, suddenly remembered her car problems. "Oh, my car broke down right after I got into town. Brad saw me walking and offered to drop me by here." Then she added, "I was hoping you would let me borrow your car so I can run over and get my things out of mine."

Marla nodded. "Oh, sure, honey. We'll head out right after you eat something." She turned to Brad and gestured back toward the house. "Why don't you stay for a bite?"

Brad smiled, but shook his head. "Sorry, Miss Marla, but I promised my mother I'd be over for dinner tonight. Maybe some other time?" he asked. "You and I could spend some time catching up," he told Natalie.

Natalie felt her mind go blank as she tried to come up with an answer to what Brad had just said. Was he asking her out? Natalie tried to discard that idea, but it wouldn't go away. Surely he wasn't . . . But then again, he might be. But why? They'd dated a few times in high school, but her priorities had never meshed with his. After all these years, he was content still to be living in Sterling, while she was hoping to leave the minute she got back on her feet again.

She was almost certain that he was just being friendly, but to be on the safe side, she nodded and said, "Some other time then." Realizing she had probably sounded a little harsh, she added, "And thanks so much for bringing me home. I really appreciate your help." There. She'd been polite, but hadn't really been overly encouraging about the prospect of their spending any time together.

Unfortunately, Marla didn't see any harm in encouraging Brad to come back. "Actually," her aunt told him, "I was hoping to keep this a surprise, but I've been playing with the idea of having a little get-together for Natalie on Sunday after church. Maybe you can think of some other people to ask, Brad. Some of the folks you two went to school with."

Natalie jumped into action. "Oh, no, that's totally unnecessary, Aunt Marla. I don't need any party." The last thing she wanted was to sit around for hours on a Sunday afternoon and field questions about her currently failing career. "Please don't. I don't want to make any trouble for you," she appealed for the second time.

Marla looked surprised. "Nonsense. And it's not putting me

to any trouble. I want everybody to know you're back. It's been years since you've been home, child."

"I have too been home," Natalie corrected her aunt, and then felt remorse because she knew she sounded whiny.

Marla frowned. "I'm not talking about those two- and three-day visits. And, when you did come, you insisted on holing yourself up in your room to study your lines. Then you were gone so fast, I started wondering if I had just imagined you'd even come home at all. Now that you're here to stay, I want to make a big deal out of it, and I will."

"I didn't know that you were planning on staying," Brad said, clearly surprised.

"Well . . ." Natalie glanced over at Marla, and decided not to burst her aunt's bubble right away. She'd tried to tell Marla that she didn't plan to stay for long, but she realized Marla was sincerely hoping that Natalie would change her mind. She would let things ride for a while, then gently break the news as the time for her to leave drew closer.

"Now, let's see . . ." Marla was saying. "I know we'll want to have Janet Murphy. And remember Emily and Kyra? You used to be in drama club with them." She turned to Natalie. "Who else would you like to invite?"

Natalie sighed. "Let me think about it, okay?"

Marla eyed her doubtfully. "Just remember it's Monday. I want to let everyone know by Wednesday at the latest. That way, more people will be able to make it."

Natalie stifled a groan and said, "I don't think we should worry too much about that. In Sterling, you could whisper the word 'party' Sunday morning at the crack of dawn and everyone would be there with bells on."

Brad laughed heartily. "You've got a point there, Natalie.

But that's part of the beauty here in Sterling. Everybody's so close."

Natalie wanted to roll her eyes. *Close* was not the word for it. The town had more than its share of busybodies, and she couldn't wait to get away again.

Before she could answer, Brad spoke up. "I guess I'd better head to my mom's. She'll be upset if she has to keep dinner warm for too long. You sure you don't want me to come along while you get your stuff?"

She shook her head. "No thanks, we'll be fine."

He nodded. "I'll see you around. And I'll be waiting for your whisper Sunday morning," he said.

After he left, Natalie sat alone on the front porch for several minutes. He was different than he had been when they were younger, particularly more good-looking. He perfectly fit the description of what her roommate Kelly would call "beautiful." Beautiful men were far and few between, yet Natalie had driven into her old hometown in her cantankerous little car and had the experience of being rescued by one such member of the male species. *Kelly would be jealous*, Natalie thought, smiling.

She immediately began thinking of how she would describe him when she talked to Kelly. He was tall and ruggedly hand-some, with a sculpted nose and jaw, strong full eyebrows, and a stubbly beard and mustache. His skin was the color of golden pine, and he had the look of a person who loved being out-doors—taking walks, canoeing, hiking, and other adventurous activities. His voice was wonderfully resonant and low-pitched, but mellow and gentle. He didn't just walk, he strode, and his shoulders were squared with purpose. This man exceeded the description of beautiful. Natalie chuckled, thinking she was probably going a little over the top. If she didn't stop soon, Kelly would come down to Sterling and demand to meet him.

Natalie leaned back in her chair, wondering if and why she might not want Kelly to meet Brad. She laughed aloud again, remembering that her friend Kimbra always said she never introduced a guy to her friends unless she was sure she wasn't interested in him. Natalie had never really felt that way, but maybe it was because she had never met anyone she was deeply interested in.

However, this wasn't really an issue with Brad. She *had* dated him a couple of times, but that didn't mean anything now. In fact, he was probably engaged, or, at the very least, he had a girlfriend.

For a moment, she wondered what might have happened if she and Brad had continued their relationship. Would they have been married by now? Had a few kids? Natalie shook her head slowly. She just couldn't see herself as a small-town teacher's wife, not even if the teacher was as handsome as Brad. Not unless . . .

Natalie stood up suddenly, not willing to consider the idea further. She was pretty happy with the way her life was, and the fact that she was suddenly in what-if mode was most likely due to her being tired. Her imagination always tended to get more creative when she was tired.

"Natalie?" Marla called from inside. "I have a sandwich for you before we go and get your bags from the car. Why don't you come inside and eat?"

"Here I come," Natalie told her aunt. She wasn't hungry, but she managed to eat half of the sandwich to please Marla. After the quick meal, the two of them left to gather up Natalie's things from her car. She had a feeling she hadn't totally put the subject of Brad to rest, but she would think about it later on, when she had less to do.

During the drive to his mom's, Brad wondered why Natalie had even come home. When Marla had commented on Natalie coming home to stay, Natalie had evaded the issue, and he could tell by the look on her face that she hadn't been ready to agree with Marla. Brad figured she probably had no intention of coming home to live in Sterling for any longer than she had to.

He frowned, wondering what really might have brought her home today. She had a mountain of luggage in her car, and he got the impression she had made a sudden decision to come home. Ever since she'd left for college, Natalie had made very few trips back to Sterling, as Marla had mentioned. He'd seen her a few times on those short visits, and in their brief conversations, she'd made no attempt to hide the fact that she would be going back to Kansas City as soon as she could. She made it seem as though she were doing everyone a favor by stopping in for a one- or two-day visit.

Today, she had looked almost pained when he'd asked how long she'd be staying. He wondered if there was some reason why she couldn't go back to Kansas City. Maybe the acting business wasn't turning out to be as lucrative as she'd thought it would be.

Brad chuckled softly, remembering how she'd looked so afraid before he'd told her his identity. As soon as she'd realized who he was, her face had dissolved into relief.

He'd almost not recognized her, either. She'd always been pretty, but she had changed since high school, especially over the past couple of years, and in his opinion, she was now stunning. Her tightly spiraled hair had grown and now hung just below her shoulders in what seemed like thousands of longish curls. Her skin, the color of suntanned honey, was sunny bright, and she had a news-anchor smile that lit up the room — when she chose to smile. Her face had taken on an aura of maturity, her cheekbones more defined. She had always been tall, but now she seemed even taller, and she was undoubtedly pretty skinny, or what his mother would call willowy. She still had the same wide, childlike eyes that gazed out at him with nonthreatening genuineness, and seemed almost hesitant at times. When she spoke, her voice was soothing, tempered with grace and care, even though he had gotten the distinct impression that she didn't particularly *care* for the idea of catching up with him, and of possibly building a friendship. He pulled his car to a stop at a red light; while he waited for the light to change, he wondered if her nice demeanor was all an act. After all, she did claim to be an actress. Maybe she wasn't as nice as she seemed. Maybe she was up to something.

After mulling the idea over, Brad laughed to himself. He doubted Natalie had changed *that* much. Even as she tried to remain aloof, she couldn't remain totally distant. There was something about her . . . a trueness, an openness that Brad found highly attractive. If she were really up to no good, she wouldn't let on that she didn't want to be here.

Brad couldn't fault her for feeling that way. He also couldn't deny the fact that he'd had times in his life when he didn't particularly like the circumstances that he was facing. However, the Lord had always managed to bring him through those times. He knew Natalie had once had a close relationship with the Lord, and if she was, indeed, facing one of those times, the Lord would help her get through this time safe and strong.

Though there was a heavy sense of unhappiness around her that made him want to fix the problem, he faced similar feelings with other friends. He had learned in these cases that usually the Lord was more interested in what he, as a fellow Christian, could *be* for these friends, rather than what he could *do* for them. He would be a friend and pray for her, but that was all. If something needed to be done for Natalie, the Lord would take care of the doing.

That night, unable to sleep, Natalie gave up tossing and turning, realizing she was only growing more and more awake. She sat on her bed and quietly did some of the stretching exercises that usually helped her to relax, and thought about some issues that were troubling her.

She *should* have been nicer to Brad when he had tried to be friendly to her, at least for her aunt's sake. Although Marla hadn't directly admonished her, Natalie could tell her aunt wasn't pleased with Natalie's attitude during her exchange with him.

Natalie knew she had probably sounded ungrateful, but she couldn't dredge up much remorse for her belittling remarks about Sterling. She couldn't remember the last time she had actually enjoyed being at home, and it didn't seem likely she could make herself fall in love with the town after all of her time spent away in the real world.

However, she decided that no matter how bad the situation got, she shouldn't allow herself to hurt Marla's feelings anymore. She would have to find a way to make up for her sarcasm. Her problems were her own, and there was no need to take her frustrations out on her or anyone else.

Two

The next morning, Natalie awoke before the sun and lay in bed a few extra moments to enjoy the beautiful shade of blue violet the sky had turned. A cool summer-morning breeze was playing with the lacy white curtains in her windows, and she was tempted to close her eyes and drift back into a delicious predawn catnap, but her promise to make things up to Marla nipped at her conscience.

Drawing up her willpower, Natalie quietly dressed and made her way down to the kitchen. As she passed through the dining room, she caught a glimpse of her natural curls in the mirror and cringed. As usual, they were all over the place, and each spiral was firmly convinced that it alone was headed in the right direction. It wasn't glamorous, but it would have to do for now. Natalie was relieved that no one was expected for breakfast this morning, because it was going to take a good coaxing with lots of water and conditioner to get her hair tamed again. Grabbing handfuls of her hair, she pulled it away from her face and fastened it with a scrunchie.

Once she reached the kitchen, she fell into the comfortable rhythm of cooking breakfast. She knew that Marla enjoyed an old-fashioned breakfast, but she also knew that Marla never cooked a hot breakfast unless she was cooking for someone else. This small gesture was the least Natalie could do to show some of her appreciation for her aunt.

Natalie felt relaxed and calm as she worked. No matter how much she disliked being in Sterling, the boundaries of Marla's house represented home to her, and she appreciated her aunt's generosity in raising her.

Natalie's mother, Andrea, was Marla's niece, and when Marla's sister Carol and Carol's husband, Wayne, drowned during a boat outing, just before their daughter Andrea's wedding, Marla had stepped in and become like a mother to Andrea.

Two years later, Natalie was born, and her parents were happy to remain in Sterling and live with Marla. Marla had been a part of Natalie's life for as long as she could remember. When Natalie was six years old, her parents had gone on a two-month missions trip to Africa; because they didn't want to take Natalie with them, Marla volunteered to keep Natalie until they came home. Two months passed, then three, and Natalie's parents didn't return. They had now been gone for nearly twenty years, and still nothing had been heard from them.

Most people assumed they were dead, but Natalie still had a hard time accepting that. Marla never tried to discourage her from believing they were still alive, but after the first couple of years, she never spoke much about that possibility.

After their disappearance, Marla, who had never married, stepped into the role of mother, caring full-time for her great-niece. Although Natalie felt the void left by her parents, Marla had done her best to make sure Natalie was raised with love and tenderness; as Natalie grew older, she realized what a great task Marla had undertaken in raising a child who was not her own.

As Natalie removed a tray of biscuits from the oven, Marla walked into the kitchen. "Child, what is all of this?" she asked.

"Just sit down and relax. I'm cooking for you today, Aunt Marla." Natalie pointed toward a chair and motioned for Marla to sit down.

Marla slowly sat down and waited while Natalie fixed her breakfast. She strained her neck to see what Natalie was doing over by the stove.

Natalie took note of Marla's anxious looks and grinned. "What?" she challenged playfully.

"You sure you don't need any help over there?"

"Now what are you so worried about? Didn't I learn how to cook from the best chef in Sterling?"

Marla returned the grin as she relaxed back into her chair. "I know I taught you how to cook, but I haven't seen you this skinny since you were in elementary school. Either you forgot what I taught you or they don't have much food in Kansas City."

"Aunt Marla, your eggs are going to get cold," Natalie said, changing the subject. She put a plate in front of Marla and waited for her to taste her meal.

Marla looked up at Natalie. "Well, aren't you going to eat? You look like you could use a good meal more than me."

Natalie put her hands on her hips, biting back a retort. Leave it to Marla to criticize her thin frame when everyone else she knew said she looked good.

Seeing the concern in her aunt's eyes, Natalie softened. After losing many of her relatives, including a sister and a niece, Marla tended to worry about anyone she didn't see for long periods of time. And this concern wasn't completely unfounded. Natalie had seen lots of friends sacrifice their health to reach a certain look.

She couldn't honestly say the thought hadn't ever crossed her own mind. She skipped more meals than she'd really care to admit, and maybe broken down and overdone things a few times when she felt too weak to resist temptation, all the while telling herself she wasn't as extreme as some of her friends.

Natalie sighed, knowing if she didn't give in right now, Marla would have an absolute fit. "If I ever plan to get an acting job again, I definitely need to watch my weight now," she told her aunt, in a last effort to stand her ground.

Marla lifted her eyebrows and stared silently at her until Natalie relented.

"Oh, all right. I'll have a biscuit and little piece of sausage," she said. Inside, she was a little relieved to have Marla's eagle eye watching her for a change. It felt a little comforting to be accountable to someone other than herself, and Marla was way more honest than any of her friends would dare to be. Before she sat down, she remembered her abandoned car. "First, I need to call a garage and get someone to tow my car. Hopefully, it can be fixed for a relatively low price."

"Why don't you call George Milton's garage?" Marla suggested. "I'm sure George would give you a pretty good discount. He's one of my oldest friends, you know. And he's the only mechanic I've ever let work on my car."

"Okay. What's the number?" Natalie asked.

"It's on the refrigerator. And this breakfast is delicious, Natalie, honey," Marla said.

"Thank you," Natalie said, then leaned over and kissed her gently on her forehead. "I'll just give Mr. Milton a call and see about my car really quick."

Natalie picked up the extension in the kitchen and dialed the number of the garage.

He answered after the second ring. "Milton's Garage. This is George."

"Hi, Mr. Milton, this is Natalie Jacobs—Marla's niece."

"Hi, Natalie. What can I do for you?"

"Actually, I need to get my car towed. It's sitting at the corner of Main and Forest."

"Hmmm . . . What kind of car is it?"

She gave him the make and model.

He was quiet for a few seconds, then said, "I think we have your car here already. Can you hold for a bit while I check?"

"Sure." While she waited, she told Marla, "He thinks my car has already been towed in. But I'm not sure how that could be."

A few moments later, George returned to the phone. "Natalie, it looks like George Jr. towed your car in last night. We've got a pretty full schedule, but if you can get the key down here, we'll look at it as soon as we can and let you know what's going on with it."

"But how did my car happen to get towed in last night?" Natalie asked.

"Well, Brad Owens called and asked George Jr. if he would mind bringing it in. He figured you wouldn't want it sitting on the street all night."

Natalie was pleasantly surprised, but she wondered just what Brad's generosity suggested. She decided not to spend too much time worrying about it. To Mr. Milton, she said, "Then I need to find out how much I owe you for the tow."

"Oh, we won't worry about that now. We'll figure something out after we find out what's wrong with the car."

"Okay," Natalie said. "I guess I'll let you go, then, and I'll be down with the key this morning."

"Don't worry about her; she's in good hands," George said before he hung up.

Natalie returned to the breakfast table and told Marla how Brad had called George Jr. about the tow.

Marla smiled knowingly and said, "That Brad always was a nice boy. Didn't you like him much?"

Natalie shrugged. "I don't know. We never really spent that much time together. I know *about* him, mostly from what people have told me, but I didn't know him that well personally."

Marla finished the last of her eggs. "Maybe you should rethink things a little."

"Maybe. Maybe not. We're pretty much strangers to each other."

"I'm not trying to tell you what to do," Marla said as she stood up. Pushing her chair back underneath the table, she added, "You'll have to follow the Lord's leading there."

"What are your plans today?" Natalie asked her.

Marla smiled. "I thought you'd never ask. Remember that special project I told you about over the phone?"

Natalie nodded, swallowing a piece of her biscuit. "Yeah. Are you ever going to tell me what it is?"

"I'll show you. Why don't you come up to the attic and see what it's all about."

Natalie pushed her plate aside and stood. "Let's go," she said. Just as they left the kitchen, the front doorbell rang.

"That's probably Florence, coming to find out about the church dinner. I'll find out what she needs," said Marla, "and then we can get back to the project."

"Don't rush because of me," said Natalie. "I'll be in the kitchen. I saw some 'help wanted' ads earlier that I wanted to check out."

While Natalie sat at the table, she heard Marla laughing and talking with the visitor. Assuming that one of Marla's church friends had come for a visit, Natalie decided to say hello.

To her surprise, she rounded the corner and found Marla chatting with Brad. Natalie took a step backward and ran her hands over her hair. But it was too late. He'd already seen her. Brad gave her a broad smile and waved. "Hi, Natalie."

Natalie stood still and tried to arrange a smile on her face. Mentally, she vowed that she wouldn't let her vanity send her running from the room just because her hair wasn't perfect.

"Thanks for having my car towed in. I hated to leave it out in the street all night," she told him. "I was going to call you later on, but since you're here . . ." Natalie trailed off, unsure of how to finish.

"You're welcome," said Brad. "I didn't want to take up too much of your time. I just came over to ask Marla a few questions about her project."

Natalie frowned. For some reason, she had expected to be the first person Marla told about her project. Now she felt a tad left out. Apparently, Marla and Brad had been chatting away about whatever Marla was planning to do.

Marla stood up and said, "I still haven't gotten a chance to tell Natalie about it, but if you both come on upstairs, I can explain it a little better." Without waiting for an answer, Marla turned and started toward the attic; Natalie and Brad fell into step behind her.

They followed Marla up two flights of stairs up to the large third floor of the house. Although the floor was finished, Marla had never used the area for anything but storage of her assorted collections of papers, clothing, and items that held special meaning to her.

As a child, Natalie had often begged her aunt to let her "go exploring" up in the attic rooms. For Natalie, the biggest draw was Marla's collection of antique trunks that held old clothes and accessories. Natalie had loved putting on the old-fashioned dresses and hats, and she had spent hours making up little plays for her and her friends to perform for Marla. When Natalie stepped into the costumes, she felt as though she were stepping into the shoes of a person other than herself. She loved imagining who that person might be and what her life was like, and she tried to reflect these ideas into her skits.

As she grew older, her enthusiasm for the contents of the attic faded, but her love of performing had continued to develop, and Natalie decided to pursue an acting career.

After they walked up the final flight of stairs, Marla opened the door and led them into one of the larger rooms. Natalie looked around, her curiosity growing by the moment.

She hadn't been up in the attic for several years, but immediately she could tell that a great deal had changed. Years ago, boxes and boxes had been piled and stacked in no particular fashion, collecting dust. Now, it appeared that Marla had been doing some organizing. Neat stacks of paper lined several tables. Clothes had been removed from the trunks and were hanging on clothing racks.

"Wow," Natalie said. "I didn't even realize most of this stuff was up here. You always kept so much of it in boxes. Are you getting rid of it or something?"

Marla shook her head. She smiled broadly and told them, "No, I'm just finally getting around to using it all."

Natalie tilted her head and waited for Marla to continue. She didn't quite understand how Marla could really use any of this old junk.

Marla walked over to one of the windows and stared outside for a few moments. Concerned that something was wrong, Natalie joined Marla and placed a hand on her shoulder.

Unsure of what to say, Natalie looked at Brad and lifted her eyebrows, hoping he might know what to say to Marla.

Marla turned to face Natalie. "I've been collecting this stuff for years," she said, gesturing toward the items in the room. "At first, it was my hobby. It was interesting to hold bits and pieces of history. Some of it belonged to family members, and other things I just picked up here and there. By the time you graduated from high school, Natalie, I knew I wanted to share it with other people."

Natalie nodded, wanting to hear the rest of Marla's story. She felt relieved to know that nothing seemed to be seriously wrong.

"So . . ." Natalie said slowly. "Are you saying you're going to give all of this away?"

Marla nodded. "In a way. But I want to do more than just give away. I want to turn the house into a museum."

Natalie stared at her aunt, unable to say a word. Aunt Marla was going to move from the house that had been in her family for years and open it to the public as a museum?

"You're selling the house?" Natalie blurted out.

Marla chuckled softly and shook her head. "Not exactly. But this house is way too big for just me, and you're never around much anymore. I'm going to start out using the first floor for the museum, and I'll use the second floor for my living quarters. Eventually, I'll convert the third floor into an apartment and use the first and second floor for the museum."

Natalie tried to remain calm. "Are you sure this is what you want to do?"

Marla looked at her carefully. "I think so. I've never had the time before, and now it makes good sense to start. But I won't do it if it upsets you."

Natalie shrugged. She didn't particularly love the idea of Marla opening up the house to the whole town, but she didn't feel that she had much say in the matter. She hadn't been home very many times over the past few years, so she didn't feel she had any right to stop Marla from pursuing her dream. "Aunt Marla, if this is what you really want to do, you shouldn't let anyone talk you out of it," she said, trying to smile.

Natalie didn't think she had been dishonest in her reply, but she felt a little unsettled about what her place in Marla's life would be once the museum got up and running.

Although her own goal had been to live her adult life away from Sterling, she'd always been welcome to return if she needed to, just as she had yesterday. Now, even though she was happy for Marla, Natalie felt as though the open invitation to return home had just been withdrawn, and it made her uneasy.

Natalie swallowed back her troubled emotions and tried to focus on what Marla was saying to her.

"So that's why I want you to help me, Natalie. At least while you're here. I think you might really enjoy it," Marla said.

Natalie blinked in surprise. Marla wanted her help? "Well . . ." Natalie began. She tried to think of a polite way to refuse. Part of her was pleased that Marla wanted to include her, but another part of her felt that this museum project would be one more thing that tied her to Sterling.

Just as she decided to tell Marla she didn't think she would be able to help, she noticed the hopeful look on her aunt's face. Natalie instantly felt guilty about thinking of refusing to help. She also remembered about her plan to show Marla how much she appreciated all she'd done for her.

How can I be so ungrateful? Natalie chided herself. *Marla's spent over twenty years caring for me and encouraging me, and the only way I've shown any thanks was to go away and leave her here alone.* "I guess I could help for a little while," Natalie said uncertainly.

Marla beamed. "I knew it. I knew my girl would come through for me. I've been imagining all the fun we're going to have, and I'm so happy you said yes."

Natalie turned to Brad. "You knew about this already?"

He nodded. "Since I majored in history, she asked for my input. Plus, I'm teaching Black history this year, and I'd like to work this into the students' coursework."

Marla spoke up eagerly. "That's the part I'm really excited about. We need to get more young people interested in our history."

Natalie's mind began to wander as Brad and Marla began discussing ideas about the project. An overwhelming sense of dread enveloped her as her aunt and Brad planned out a work schedule.

Once again, she was back in Sterling, feeling boxed in. It seemed that the harder she tried to stay away, the harder some invisible force pulled her back home, like a giant magnet tugging on a paper clip. She hugged her arms around herself and shivered, in spite of the heat in the attic. *Will I ever be able to leave this town for good?* she wondered.

Three

Natalie looked at her watch and realized she was going to have to end this call quickly. Despite the barely two-hour distance between Sterling and Kansas City, long-distance prices were in effect. As happy as she was to be talking to her former roommate, Kelly, Natalie didn't have money to burn on an extended call.

"So I checked with the storage place," Kelly told her. "And you can get the first month for free. After that, it's thirty-five dollars a month. So what should I do with the hundred dollars you left?"

"Hold it until I can get back and put everything into storage, of course," Natalie answered.

"Well, I wasn't sure," Kelly sounded hesitant. "Remember, you were thinking you might not store your things. You said you might be able to get back down here and take the stuff to your aunt's. I didn't want to spend the money unnecessarily."

"Thanks for being so thoughtful," Natalie said. "But right now, I really don't want to start bringing more stuff up here. It feels like everything I bring here represents more time I'll end up staying here. So I'm definitely going to get back down there in a week or so to store everything."

"If that's the way you want to do it," Kelly said. "You could actually keep everything in the apartment. There's plenty of room here."

Natalie hesitated. "But what about you? I feel bad enough about having to leave so quickly. You still need to find a roommate to take up my part of the rent."

"It doesn't really matter right now. You left me two months' worth of rent money, and since I haven't found another roommate, you have the right to store your boxes and stuff here for at least two more months. That's only fair."

Natalie smiled. Kelly was one of those people who always tried to be fair, and people got along with her well because of that. That was the reason Natalie felt so badly about leaving without much notice. Both women made modest salaries with their daytime jobs. Natalie worked as a secretary, and Kelly worked as a librarian. Both held college degrees and could have gotten better jobs, but they decided against it, choosing to pool their money and share an apartment in order to have flexible schedules, enabling them to audition for theater jobs. So far, they had not been very successful. The extent of their theater work had been community theater, which involved many hours of rehearsal but no pay. They both held out hope that, one day, they would be able to break into the competitive field and earn a paying position.

Unfortunately, a recent string of car breakdowns and the subsequent mechanic bills, along with a rent increase and an emergency root canal, had depleted Natalie's meager savings account and forced her to use her emergency credit card. She and Kelly had gone over their budgets repeatedly, trying to come up with a plan that would help Natalie to stay afloat financially, but in the end, even after Kelly had offered to make Natalie a loan, Natalie had decided to cut her losses and go home for a while. She would take a full-time job, rebuild her savings, and then return to Kansas City and get back on track with her career plans.

Natalie had taken her last paycheck and given almost half of it to Kelly to cover the next two months' rent. With the other half she paid her share of the household expenses, and she used the remainder on gas to finance her trip back to Sterling.

She had packed up all of her clothes and piled them into her small car. The rest of her belongings she had packed into boxes and asked Kelly to hold until she could get them into storage.

"Kelly, you've been more than fair," Natalie told her friend. "I'll take you up on the offer to store my things in the apartment for a while. I got a job this morning working at a little café here, and I start tomorrow. Once I make enough money to get my car fixed, I'll come up and put everything in storage. But promise me that if you find a new roommate before two months you'll let me know. I'll find a way to get there and get all my stuff out of the way."

Kelly sighed. "All right, I will. But I'm hoping that I don't have to get a new roommate. I still want my best friend to come back."

"I'm working on it," Natalie assured her. "But I probably need to get off the phone. Aunt Marla needs my help up in the attic this evening with that project I was telling you about."

"Oh, yes," Kelly said, and Natalie could almost hear her friend smile. "The project and the very handsome ex-boyfriend who comes along with the deal. No wonder you're not in any hurry to get back here."

Natalie groaned playfully. "It's definitely not like that, Kelly."

"Why not? You said he's a Christian," Kelly pointed out.

"So? I can't marry every guy who's a Christian."

"Well, it's a definite requirement, right? For whatever guy you end up marrying," Kelly prodded.

"Yes, it's a requirement," Natalie admitted.

"And it doesn't hurt that he's so aesthetically pleasing, either," Kelly laughed.

"Okay, he's good-looking, but Christianity and good looks can't be the only thing. How about the way Brad and I actually feel about each other? As of right now, there is absolutely no chemistry between us."

Kelly made a *tsk-tsk* sound and said, "Nat, chemistry doesn't always just explode. Sometimes the components have to combine for a while before anything happens."

"I understand what you're saying, but trust me, it doesn't take a rocket scientist to figure out that water and oil don't mix. He loves it here, and I can't wait to leave. Romance does not spring from a foundation like that."

"I don't know . . ." Kelly sounded thoughtful. "Just because love *shouldn't* grow from that kind of foundation doesn't mean that it *won't*."

Natalie sighed loudly. "Now I know I need to get off the phone. Warning bells go off in my head when you start feeling compelled to give me a lesson about the similarities of science and love. Don't you think that's a little risky, given the straight C's you made in college science?"

Kelly cleared her throat, then stated in a dramatic manner, "The science of love is hardly difficult to master."

"Umm-hmmm. Then I'll remind the scientist that if her favorite roommate falls in love and gets married, the scientist will have *permanently* lost her roomie. That should give Dr. Science of Love pause."

"Of course, I want you to come back, but I have a feeling about this, Nat," Kelly said. "I love having you for a roommate, but I know I want to fall in love someday, and I want the same for you. It's only fair. And, if something is God's will, you'll have a hard time getting away, no matter how fast you run."

"Okay, okay, thanks for caring, but I really better get off the phone. I don't think the phone company will be nearly as sympathetic as you are if I can't pay my bill. Talk to you later, Kelly."

"All right, Nat. And I hope your job goes well. Make lots of tips so you can get back sooner."

Natalie smiled as she hung up the phone. She really did miss Kelly, but part of her wondered if she would make it back to Kansas City. Maybe Kansas City wasn't the right place to be for a person who seriously wanted to be a stage actress. Back in her college years, she thought the best way to break into the business would be to start small and work her way up, but she wondered if she would have been better off to move to a bigger city and then look for work. Natalie wrinkled her forehead in thought. After she paid off her bills, maybe she should move to a city that had more theater work and bigger, more publicized shows—like New York or Chicago.

As she made her way downstairs where she was supposed to meet with Marla and Brad, Natalie promised herself that she would seriously devote more time to that idea.

Brad looked up from the papers Marla had laid out on the dining room table just as Natalie entered the room. "Looks like you finally made it," he teased her. "I was starting to wonder how a person could be late to a meeting in her own house," he said, smiling.

Natalie checked her watch and apologized. "I was just tying up some loose ends back in Kansas City," she told them. She took the seat closest to the dining-room entrance and looked at them expectantly. "So what did I miss?"

Marla jumped in before Brad could say anything. "Don't worry, honey. We were actually discussing your party this Sunday. I went ahead with the plans because you haven't objected any more. I invited only a few people, so you won't feel overwhelmed."

Natalie opened her mouth, then closed it and sighed. Brad knew she wasn't thrilled with the plan, but he was happy she hadn't objected. He smiled to himself, knowing that Marla's "few" was probably way more than what Natalie had in mind. Natalie looked over at him at that exact moment.

"Did I miss a joke?" she asked, her eyebrows lifted.

Brad shrugged.

"Then let's get started," Marla said. "I'd like to start by creating a schedule to project the opening date. Of course, all three of us will work at repainting these main rooms and getting our furniture upstairs. Then I'm in charge of sorting and cataloguing all of what's in the attic. Brad's going to head up the student volunteering, and I'd like for Natalie to decide how we should display the items."

Natalie looked at Marla with surprise. "Me?"

Marla smiled proudly. "Of course, you. You're the more creative one. Maybe you could draw on some of your acting jobs to help us figure how we should place everything."

"You mean, like props?" Natalie asked.

"I guess so," Marla answered. "I thought we could turn the

parlor into a room that gives information about the founders of the city. Maybe the dining-room display would focus on national and local Black history, and in the living room, we'd display other items that don't fit anywhere else. I'll let you figure out what to put in the den and the library.

"Well," Natalie said slowly. "I guess I could do that. But I don't know about my hours at the café yet. That's going to determine how much time I can spend with you all on the museum."

Marla waved her hand at Natalie's response. "I know that. Brad has to start school in a couple of weeks anyway, so I'm going to be the only one who'll be able to work on this full-time. I don't want either of you to sacrifice your work for my project."

While Marla talked, Brad stared at Natalie, wondering what it was about her that had so fully captivated him in the few short days since she'd returned. He shouldn't let himself get so distracted by her being here, but he hadn't really done anything to make himself stop thinking about her. *Pay attention to the conversation*, he told himself.

"Okay. So what's your target date for opening?" Natalie asked.

Marla titled her head upward and stared at the ceiling for several seconds. Finally, she said, "I'm not sure. I'd like to see it open as soon as possible, but I don't want to rush things or interfere too much with your lives. It's the end of August right now, and I'd love to see us open in February to coincide with Black History Month, but I think that would be rushing things. I think we could aim for May, instead."

"May?" Natalie asked, looking panicked. "That late?"

"That's about nine months from now," Brad said. "We don't want to do a rush job. And besides, it'll give my class a project for the entire school year."

"That's fine, but I'm not sure I'll be here that long," Natalie said quietly.

Brad was surprised. From the way Marla had been carrying on, he'd let himself believe that Natalie was home for good. Now it looked as if that wasn't Natalie's plan after all. Or maybe it was. *C'mon*, he argued with himself. *You remember how she hates it here. Why'd you even let yourself imagine that she really wanted to come back?* Though Brad tried to ignore his thoughts, he couldn't help listening to them all the more. *She doesn't like you; she never did. And you're hurting yourself if you let your emotions take over while she's here. It would never work.* Brad's heart sank, but he knew his thoughts were probably accurate. Natalie was not a small-town kind of girl. It was best to keep things friendly with her, but definitely nothing more.

Clearing his throat, he spoke up. "Maybe we should just do what we can, when we can. If we get all of your things moved upstairs before school starts, that will help to get things going because we'll have space to start tinkering with displays. And after school starts, I'll probably bring my students over once or twice a week to do whatever you need them to do," he told Marla.

Looking at Natalie, who still seemed a little disturbed, he added, "And if you have to leave before the opening, I'm sure Marla and I will understand. You have a life in Kansas City that you need to get back to, and we won't try to keep you from going back." He had been a little more harsh than understanding, but he didn't feel any remorse. Yet.

The room was heavily silent, and Marla was frowning.

Uh-oh, he'd gone too far. That speech had been his own way of keeping his developing feelings about Natalie under wraps, disguised as reassuring words for Natalie. And he'd hurt her. He could tell by the way she was looking down at the table, not saying anything.

"Listen, Natalie," he began, "I didn't mean it like that. What I'm trying to say is, well . . . this is for the town, not for us, so I hope that we'd all take our commitment to getting it done seriously." He looked back and forth between Marla and Natalie, hoping they weren't offended.

"No, you're right." Natalie suddenly looked up at him. "It is for the town, not for us. But I don't appreciate your suggesting that I wouldn't do my part of the work."

Brad felt humbled. He'd wrongly judged her. But he felt a little irked that he'd been wrong. "I'm sorry," he said simply. "I was too presumptuous. I just wouldn't want you to take on a job you knew you might not finish and then have to bail out without any kind of warning before the job is complete. And I'm not trying to pick on just you. All of us should work under that principle. It would put unfair pressure on the rest of the group if any one of us suddenly up and left our jobs in everyone else's lap."

Natalie stood up. "I forgive you. But I need to get to bed early. I have to start work in the morning. Since you seem to have all of the planning done already, I'll take my leave now. In the future you can just *tell* me what I need to do." She smiled a hollow smile and briskly left the room.

Great job. Just run her out of a meeting in her own house, Brad mentally reprimanded himself. Brad turned to Marla, whose lips were pursed in a thin line. He stood up and gathered his papers together. "It looks like I ruined your planning meeting. Tell Natalie I'm sorry."

Marla shrugged. "You already told her. But I don't think she really heard you." She followed him to the door and held it open for him.

"If it's okay, I'll come over tomorrow morning and start moving your furniture up to the second floor. If it's okay," he added again.

"Fine with me," Marla said. "But if you don't mind a little advice from an old lady like me, be patient with Natalie. She may be saying one thing, but I know her, and I don't think she's sure what she wants from life. She needs patient friends, like you and me."

"I'll let Natalie decide what she wants to do. With the museum *and* her life," he told Marla. "Unless she really wants my opinion and asks for it, I'll keep my mouth shut."

Natalie tried to ignore the ache in her lower back as she lifted another stack of clean plates and returned them to the cabinet. Anyone who ever said being a waitress was easy had obviously never spent an entire day running back and forth between the kitchen and dining room, taking orders and dealing with varying stages of general human crankiness in order to make a living.

The fact that her mind had been constantly replaying the scene with Brad didn't make matters any better. It had eaten at her concentration several times, resulting in more than a few mistakes with customer orders. Still, she couldn't bring herself to forget it.

He had definitely hit a raw nerve last night. She just didn't fully understand what had made it so bad. She could deal with the fact that he didn't want her helping with her aunt's project. It looked as if, while Natalie was gone, Brad had learned about Marla's plans and decided that he wanted to be in charge of things.

But why? Natalie had asked herself that question repeatedly but still hadn't come up with a good answer. She didn't think the museum was going to turn out to be a real moneymaker. Then again, Brad loved history, so it could be something he had grand plans for. But Marla appreciated his help. And Natalie hadn't had any intentions of standing in his way. Until last night.

From the looks of things, she thought Brad wanted her out of the way. He'd tried to give her the boot—to make her leave early—and had sounded so condescending when he'd said it, even twisting his words to sound as if it was for her benefit, so she would feel free to return to Kansas City. And that's why she had decided to stay and see the whole thing through. It would give her great satisfaction to prove to Brad that he couldn't second-guess her.

But it wouldn't have been so irksome if he hadn't tried to make it look as if she thought she was too good for the project. Then he'd insinuated that she didn't care about the town. And that was the confusing thing. She didn't care about the town. At least she didn't think she did.

Do I care? Natalie wondered. She shrugged. *Not really,* she decided. *Then what did he say that was so offensive?* She dug around in the nooks and crannies of her mind to find the answer. Finally, it came to her in a sudden rush of insight. It wasn't about the museum. It was the feeling that he couldn't stand for her to be around him. What made her so repugnant to him? Her own feelings about him were the opposite. She liked him, or at least she *had* before the meeting last night.

Natalie drew in a sharp breath as she realized what she had just admitted. Brad did not figure into her life like that. At least, he shouldn't. She was acting like a schoolgirl with a crush! And she didn't have a crush. She knew she didn't. *I do not have a crush on Brad Owens,* she repeated in order to reassure herself.

She glanced up at the clock, noting that the café would be closing in ten minutes. She swished her hands around in the warm, soapy water, promising herself that she would indulge in a bubble bath when she got home. Whenever that was. Her new boss, Sharon Bates, had apologized for the long shift that Natalie had to work on her fist day. But two of the other waitresses were out sick with something, which left Natalie and Sharon running around trying to do their work as well as that of the two absent waitresses. In addition, a couple of the kitchen staff were on vacation this week, which meant that whenever things slowed down in the dining room, Natalie and Sharon rushed back to the kitchen to wash dishes, fill salt shakers and ketchup bottles, and resupply the napkin holders.

The kitchen had never fully recovered from this haphazard system; it was going to take a good amount of time after closing to get things in order again for the next day. But that would be a breeze, Natalie reflected, as long as the door was locked and there were no customers constantly demanding attention.

At six minutes until closing, Natalie peered out the front windows. Seeing no one in sight, she suggested that Sharon lock up for the night.

"If I did, I'd never hear the end of it," Sharon said, shaking her head. "The town would gossip about my false advertising, since my sign says we close at nine. In fact, I usually don't lock up until five after, just to make sure I don't miss anyone."

Natalie sighed and headed back to the kitchen.

"Hey, Natalie, I'll take a turn at those pots and pans if you'll start wiping down the tables," Sharon offered.

Natalie accepted gratefully. Her hands were beyond the prune stage, and bending over to wipe tables seemed better than plunging her arms up to her elbows in that murky water one more time.

While she worked, she kept one eye on the door, vowing that anyone who tried to come in before closing would remain her mortal enemy for life. When the bells above the door jingled at one after nine, Natalie thought she would scream. She instantly felt repentant for the many times she had breezed into a restaurant minutes before closing and kept some poor, tired waitress working. As she wiped the tables, she listened to the sound of footsteps trudging across the floor.

Too weary even to protest slightly, Natalie looked up and found herself gazing into Brad Owens's deep brown eyes.

Apparently, she was too tired to talk, because she couldn't say a word. Brad smiled, revealing the dimple in his chin that she had long ago forgotten existed. Natalie couldn't believe she hadn't noticed that dimple until now.

"I know I'm a little late, but I didn't cook dinner for myself," he told her. "I've been at your aunt's all day, and I didn't want to trouble her or my mom to cook for me so . . . I thought I'd stop in and get something to go."

Natalie's resolution to tar and feather anyone who came in right before closing dissolved. She especially didn't have the heart to be mean to Brad. After all, the poor man had been working hard all day, and he was hungry. "All right, what can I get for you?" As Brad gave his order, she listened, memorizing it.

"Aren't you going to write that down?" he asked her.

Natalie shook her head. "I'm an actress. Memorizing is my specialty." She grinned.

Brad didn't say anything, but his smile faded slightly. Natalie wondered if she had food in her hair or something. She reached up to smooth back a few rebel curls, hoping she didn't look like a complete and total mess. If Brad had been working all day, he certainly didn't look it. His jeans and polo shirt were a little dusty, but didn't look any the worse for wear. *Why do I even care how Brad looks?* she wondered. *Besides, it's probably the lighting in here. I'll bet everyone looks better than they normally do,* she decided.

"You look like you've had a rough day," Brad said.

Okay, everyone looks good in this lighting except me, Natalie thought, feeling humbled. "I look that bad, huh?" she asked him.

"I didn't mean it like that. Please don't get mad at me about that."

"Don't worry. I've forgotten about it already." She smiled. "And I know I look tired because I am tired."

"Can I give you a ride home?" Brad asked.

Natalie nodded, feeling grateful, even though "home" was only four bocks away. "Sure. I'll get the cook started on your order, and by the time he's done, I'll try to be ready to leave."

Brad sat down at one of the tables. "Take your time, I'm not in a big hurry." He smiled again, and Natalie's heart jumped again at the sight of that lone dimple.

As Natalie hurried back to get John started on Brad's order, she wondered if he'd had a change of heart since last night. Or maybe she had read too much into what he had said.

Since she'd come back to Sterling, she'd felt off balance, and her emotions had been on edge. Maybe she had been feeling a little too self-absorbed, as Marla had quietly suggested after Brad had gone home last night.

She was willing to give him the benefit of the doubt, as long as he wasn't antagonistic toward her. They could probably get to be good friends if they gave each other a second chance. She would just have to be careful to keep her emotions in check and not let her feelings run away with visions of love and romance. After all, the way things stood now, he probably wouldn't even be interested in a long-term relationship with her. As long as things continued along the path of friendship and no one got their emotions mixed up, they could avoid a situation that almost always resulted in hurt feelings.

Four

 S unday morning, Natalie dutifully awoke early to attend church with Marla. Although Brad had offered to pick them up, the two of them decided to drive over in Marla's car. They needed to get home quickly after the service in order to ensure everything was ready for the brunch Marla was hosting in Natalie's honor.

Shortly after they arrived, Marla left Natalie alone while she chatted with her own friends. As she stood on the large landing at the top of the stairs, Natalie briefly felt abandoned. She spent the next few minutes feeling uncomfortable and was tempted to take the car and go home. Knowing her aunt would be deeply hurt and even embarrassed if Natalie just up and left, she resigned herself to watching the people who were milling around. Some nodded to her politely, but no one struck up a conversation or even seemed to notice her until Brad came along. His face lit up with a smile when he caught sight of her from the parking lot. He waved and headed in her direction, and Natalie moved to meet him halfway. She had last seen him when he'd given her a ride home from work. The two of them had chatted about how they had spent their day, and when she climbed out of the car, he'd said, "See you later." As things turned out, with their schedules keeping them so busy that they were unable to work on the museum project at the same time, later had turned out to be today. And since she had resolved to view Brad as just an old friend, rather than an old *boyfriend*, she was honestly happy to see him. At least now she would have someone to chat with until the service started.

Before she could cover any distance to Brad, Natalie heard a woman yelling her name; she looked around to see Janet Murphy, with a big smile on her face, coming toward her from the other side of the street.

Natalie waved to the woman who had been her best friend, and she wondered what had kept her from staying in touch with Janet after high school.

Janet ran the rest of the distance to Natalie and enveloped her in a warm hug. Pulling away from her, Janet exclaimed, "I just can't believe you're really back here!"

Natalie was at a loss for words, knowing that she didn't have an equally cheerful reply to Janet's exclamation.

Janet linked her arm through Natalie's just as they had done back in high school. "Emily told me that you got here Monday, but I held back from calling until I knew you were settled in. I figured you'd call when you got some free time, but I'm so glad that I got to see you today."

Natalie felt a pang of guilt. Until now, she hadn't even thought about Janet, much less about calling her. She did remember that Marla had invited her to the brunch, so she asked if Janet was going to be able to attend.

"Of course I am. And I told Eric I wanted to be there on time, so his mother is going to take the little ones home from church with her so we can head right over."

"Eric?" Natalie asked. "Eric who?"

"Eric Summers." Janet had a puzzled look on her face. "And don't *even* try to pretend you didn't know. By the way, I know we sent you a card, but I wanted to thank you in person for the glassware you sent us. We absolutely loved it. I was so disappointed you couldn't make it, but Marla told us about your audition in New York."

Natalie had a fleeting memory of Marla telling her that Janet was engaged to Eric. But the only time she had been to New York was for a fall workshop nearly three years ago. And as far as the glassware Janet was referring to, she didn't have a clue. She'd have to get details from Marla when she had a chance. Natalie swallowed and tried to adjust to the fact that Janet was someone's *wife*. It didn't seem possible.

She and Natalie were the same age, and Natalie remembered them pledging they wouldn't marry until they had lived life to the fullest and led exciting and independent lives as single women. They would wait until they were more down to earth and serious before getting married. Natalie took another look at Janet, who didn't exactly look old and matronly. She'd cut her hair a few inches shorter to chin length, and she was wearing very minimal makeup, but her clothes were still stylish, and she looked extremely happy. This whole conversation seemed unreal. Things had drastically changed, and Natalie hadn't even been aware of it.

"Natalie, what's the matter?" Janet was shaking her arm. "You look like you're in pain or something. Are you okay?"

Natalie shook her head and looked around for Brad, as if she might gain comfort from just seeing him. At least *he* hadn't changed all that much. "I'm fine. I just zoned out for a few seconds, that's all."

Janet shook her head. "You don't look fine. Let's sit down." She pulled Natalie over to a small bench and practically pushed her down into the seat. Janet quickly placed her hand across Natalie's forehead. "It's probably this summer-fall weather; you never know what it's going to be like. One day it's ninety degrees, and the next day it's chilly, like today. It's a good way to get sick, that's what. You would never believe this was August if you didn't look at the calendar."

Natalie had the vague impression that Janet was treating her like a little kid, which was totally out of character for her friend. The Janet she remembered believed in letting people do things on their own, and made it a practice not to interfere, which was why she was such a good friend. Natalie felt somewhat irritated by Janet's take-charge attitude, but she didn't voice her complaint. Instead, she said, "You're right. Plus I'm so worn out from the hours I've been working at the café."

Janet nodded, taking on a wise look. "That doesn't help matters any. When you can, try to get a day off and just relax. Sometimes it can really be refreshing to just—"

"Honey." The towering figure of Eric Summers, who was holding a baby carrier in one hand and balancing a fidgeting toddler on the other arm, approached.

Natalie was relieved at the interruption. The little boy shyly glanced at her, then buried his head in Eric's chest. "Aren't you the shy one?" she asked cheerfully as she stood up. "What's your name?" The boy mumbled something that Natalie couldn't hear. She turned to Janet and was about to inquire who his parents were when she was hit with the realization that these two babies were the "little ones" that Janet had referred to earlier. Now Janet was a mother. A mother of two, at that.

Natalie sat back down, feeling as if the world had passed her by. At least she knew how Janet had come to acquire her sudden maternal streak.

Janet retrieved the boy from his father's arms and said, "This is Eric Jr., and little Olivia is somewhere under all of those blankets. I'll show her to you once we get inside and out of this wind. But right now, Eric needs his diaper changed." Janet headed toward the church, and Natalie followed.

"How old are they?" Natalie asked, feeling numb.

Janet was beaming with pride. "Eric will be two in November, and Olivia is nine weeks old."

"Wow," Natalie was once again at a loss for words. "They're . . . so . . . sweet," she finally finished. Janet looked at her strangely but didn't say anything. Once they were inside, Eric whipped the blankets off of Olivia and held her up for Natalie to view.

Natalie smiled as she caught sight of the infant attired in a puff of pink and lace. Even in sleep, the little girl was adorable, with milk chocolate brown skin and a mass of teeny-tiny curls that covered her head. Natalie spent a few moments cooing over the baby and even held her while Janet and Eric looked on. Eric began squirming in his mother's arms, but Janet appeared not to notice until his huge brown eyes filled with tears and he opened his mouth to let out a wail that was highly surprising, considering his small size. Janet immediately began trying to console him. "It's definitely time for a diaper change," she told Natalie. "Do you want to come with me while I step into the nursery?"

Natalie felt uneasy at the prospect and shook her head. Changing diapers was definitely a mother thing in Natalie's book. You had to have the hormones to stomach it. "You know, Marla's probably looking for me, so I'll just head on into the sanctuary. If I don't see you after church, I'll see you at the brunch." Janet nodded as she hurried away with the wailing Eric in her arms. Shortly after Janet departed, Olivia felt the need to harmonize with her big brother's song, and she began a loud, high-pitched tune of her own. Eric began jiggling her in his arms and pacing back and forth. Natalie crept away and headed into the sanctuary, where she took a seat in the pew where Marla had always sat.

While she waited for her aunt to join her, Natalie tried to focus her thoughts and emotions. Part of her was glad to see that Janet was so happy, but another part of her wondered if a person could truly remain happy living such a chaotic life. Currently, Janet and Eric's every move was dictated by their children's moods. *How*, Natalie wondered, *do they ever find time for themselves?* And even though the children were precious, she didn't think she'd ever want to do the mothering thing herself. At least not right now, she hastily added. But maybe one day . . . Natalie shook her head. What was she thinking about? Marriage was not in her plans for several more years, and here she was thinking about children. She'd always envisioned being happily married for several years before she and her husband decided to have children. And that was supposed to be years off, maybe even in her forties, certainly not in the near future. Natalie did not relish the thought of trying to balance a theater career with raising young children. Neither did she want to have children and leave them with others on a regular basis, as her parents had done with her. Of course, whenever they left, they were going off on a noble cause, but it still hurt to remember the many times their missionary work took them away from her, resulting in her barely having any memory of them at all.

Natalie became aware of a movement at her side and looked

over to see Brad sliding into the seat next to her. "You look like you're trying to come up with the formula for world peace and justice," he said.

Natalie looked up at him and chuckled. "I looked that serious, huh?"

He shrugged. "Maybe. Am I close?"

Natalie grew serious. "Actually, no. I just had a conversation with my old best friend, and I can't figure out if she's drastically changed or if I'm just being a nonmaternal stick in the mud."

"Oh . . . Eric and Janet," he said thoughtfully. "They love being parents, don't they?"

"Mmmm," was all Natalie said. She remembered that Eric and Brad had been good friends during school, and she wondered how he'd been affected by Eric's marriage and new family. Both Brad and Natalie were silent, as though neither of them wanted to say anything negative.

"I guess mothers have to be . . . motherly," Natalie finally said.

This time, it was Brad's turn to say, "Mmmm." He added, "I'll admit, I've had days when I've seen them coming and intentionally headed the opposite direction. They tend to get a little overly enthusiastic about showing those two little ones off. But it's not that I don't love kids. I work with them every day, and someday I want to have several of my own. But, for right now . . ."

"It's nice to *occasionally* hold someone else's baby," Natalie finished for him.

"Right," Brad nodded emphatically. "You can always hand them back. But I have a feeling that having kids is like being called in to service. When it's your time, it's your time. Only—" he tilted his head and looked thoughtful "—it's a little different. When it's your own child, you feel like you have the most precious gift God could ever give you."

He looked Natalie in the eye and said, "My mom always says that my brothers and I are the only people in the world she didn't have to grow to love. She says she loved us instantly, and I think that's probably true for most parents. And that," he said tenderly, "is what I'm waiting to experience."

Natalie's heart warmed, as she realized that Brad had shared a deep desire of his heart with her. He had always been the type of guy who could be understanding and caring, but he had never before spoken to her in such a candid and sentimental manner.

"I think you may be right," she told him. While her own mother hadn't been around long enough to impart such information to Natalie, and since Marla wasn't her biological mother, she had to take his word for the scientific explanation. But she had a feeling that Brad's mother was telling the truth.

She felt a tiny twinge in her heart and realized that maybe she wanted to get married and have children much earlier than she had led herself to believe.

Brad reached over and gently squeezed her hand. "So did I cheer you up any, or what?"

"I think so." She smiled.

"And don't worry. Eventually, you'll get used to seeing all your friends being married and having children. I know I did."

"There you are, Natalie," Marla slid into the pew from the other end. "I realized after a while that I had gone off and left you all by yourself. But it looks like you're not too lonely."

Natalie felt slightly alarmed. Her aunt had already put in more than a few well-meaning comments about Brad, especially after he'd given her a ride home from work. Although

Natalie had convinced herself that Brad wasn't such a bad guy, she didn't want Marla presuming there was something developing between the two of them, especially since Brad hadn't made any clear moves in that direction. *Never give in to a crush unless you're sure he feels the same way*, she reminded herself.

"Actually, I've been pretty well occupied. I met Janet *Summers*, and, if you don't mind, I'd like a little more information about the *glassware* I sent to her and Eric's wedding. That way, if she mentions it again, I won't have to stand there with my mouth hanging open." Natalie grinned.

"I did you a little favor since you couldn't make it to the wedding. I knew you were short on money from planning your trip to New York, so I bought it and put your name on it."

Natalie was embarrassed. "Thanks, Aunt Marla." She stood up with the rest of the congregation and tried to focus on the song the choir was singing. While the rest of the congregation made a joyful noise, Natalie stared blankly at the hymnal and tried to battle the wave of thoughts that assaulted her conscience.

She felt like a heel for not even paying attention to the fact that one of her friends had gotten married. Back then, as long as she didn't have to be in Sterling, everything about it had seemed far and distant to her. Her aunt could have told her that Martians had landed on Main Street, and Natalie would have just said, "Oh really?" and proceeded to let the announcement fly in one ear and out of the other.

In fact, Natalie couldn't even honestly admit that she hadn't totally zoned Marla out when her aunt mentioned people in Sterling. Natalie simply hadn't wanted to hear it. That system had worked well in the past four years since she'd last come home. It would have continued to work if she hadn't been forced to come home and face daily reminders of all she'd tried to pretend didn't exist anymore.

The only person in Sterling she had allowed herself to miss was Marla, and Natalie had always planned to take Marla with her when she moved to New York.

Yet, in the back of her mind, she knew that Marla and Sterling were inseparable, and if she wanted Marla, she'd have to take Sterling, too. And she couldn't stand the thought of that, so she'd simply chosen to put it all out of her mind. Natalie sighed. Why did moments of self-contemplation usually make her feel like such a cold and shallow individual?

The congregation sat down to listen to the sermon, and Natalie followed along. Brad looked at her. "You okay?" he whispered.

Natalie managed a nod. There was no way she could explain to anyone what she was feeling. "Fine." She picked up her Bible and flipped to the chapter she was supposed to be reading.

"Natalie, tell us more about your life on the stage," Kyra Mills said.

Natalie felt her face grow warm as all eyes in the room turned toward her. What was there to tell that would be interesting, without her having to come up with some extravagant story that was far from true. *I never made it to the big time, but they don't want to hear that. And I don't want to look like a failure at my own party.*

"Well . . . There's not much to tell," she began. "Theater is hard work. Late hours and lots of memorization. You put your heart and soul into becoming a character and hope the audience believes you." Natalie stopped, hoping that was enough to satisfy everyone's curiosity. At least she wasn't lying. Community theater was just as challenging as professional work. The auditions were rigorous, and the competition was fierce. The people she worked with were all good enough to be professionals, and it showed. The only problem was, professional work wasn't nearly as profuse as nonprofessional opportunities.

"What's it like? Sleeping late and going to the theater to pretend for a few hours every night . . . rubbing shoulders with famous people . . . sounds like a dream job to me." A hint of wistfulness could be heard in Leva Emory's voice.

"Yeah. Ever meet any Hollywood stars?" Jake Bryant's booming voice echoed loudly through the living room.

This was getting out of hand. As much as she hated it, she was going to have to admit she didn't have a dream career, nor did she make loads of money. In fact, she hadn't made one single cent on an acting job.

"Listen, everybody," Brad spoke up. "This is Natalie's welcome-home party. She's here in good old Sterling to get a break from the glitzy world of showbiz. My guess is, she'd rather use her vacation getting caught up on all of us here instead of having to talk about her job all of the time. Isn't that what any of us would want out of a vacation?"

Relieved, Natalie sent Brad her warmest smile. Either he was tired of hearing about her work, or he was genuinely intuitive that the subject was uncomfortable for her. At any rate, he had pushed that line of conversation aside for now and was now drawing everyone into a discussion of recent movies.

Since the attention had shifted away from her for the time being, Natalie escaped to the kitchen for a few moments of silence. She poured herself a glass of ice water and listened to the people sounds coming from the front of the house.

Marla had turned on the heat since the morning had been cool, but now the temperature had risen slightly, and the house was starting to feel overly warm. Natalie opened the kitchen door and stood outside to get a breath of fresh air.

Hearing footsteps behind her, she turned and found Janet entering the kitchen. "I needed some fresh air," Natalie said, hoping Janet didn't think she was trying to ditch the party.

"I had the same idea." Janet stood next to Natalie and fanned herself. "I also had a little too much of Marla's apple shortcake," she admitted, patting her stomach.

Natalie grinned. Marla's apple "shortcake" was very well known to the citizens of Sterling. The simple dish consisted of a round of corn bread, sliced in half, layered with apple compote and topped with whipped cream. Marla had contrived the dish many years before Natalie had even been born, and the recipe had been copied and passed around in the years since its conception, but folks still considered it a treat when Marla herself made the dish.

"I had a rather large helping myself," Natalie agreed.

The two women stood silently for several moments until Janet spoke again. "Remember sitting on these steps when we were little?"

"Every day after school." Natalie nodded in agreement. "Marla would bring us a snack, and we would have pretend tea parties."

"Remember the 'tea' she used to give us?" Janet laughed. "Hot apple juice, but we thought it was the real thing."

"Yeah, we thought we were so mature." Natalie sat down on the steps and rested her chin on her hands.

"Remember singing in the church choir?" Janet sat next to her. "I think that was my first major brush with jealousy."

Natalie looked over to Janet for an explanation.

"You had such a beautiful voice. And I could barely carry a tune, let alone harmonize."

Natalie chuckled. No one could ever accuse Janet of being destined for a singing career, but it was startling to hear Janet's sudden confession. "You sing perfectly well. Don't start putting yourself down to make me feel good."

Janet stared at the ground for a moment, then looked up again. "I think that's when I started to realize God had something special planned for your life. And you had the guts to step out in faith to seriously pursue something you were good at. I've admired that about you."

Natalie felt a lurch in her chest. The combination of God and her career hadn't seemed real to her in a long time, yet the words seemed to roll off of Janet's tongue so freely. "I don't know about that," she began.

Janet held up a hand to silence her. "Don't be modest, Nat. You sacrificed what was familiar to journey into the unknown. Like Abraham did when he followed the Lord's leading. And look how things turned out for him."

Natalie chewed the inside of her lip. Putting a religious spin on her career didn't appeal to her. There had been a time when she had been more devoted to her faith, but lately, matters of faith and devotion to the Lord had taken a backseat to the simple task of searching for the always-elusive big break and keeping pace with the bills.

It made her antsy that Janet seemed to be heading in the direction of a serious conversation. When they were younger, she and Janet had been able to talk about anything and everything, but right now she wasn't comfortable with the prospect of having a heart-to-heart with this former best friend whom she hardly recognized. In fact, it would probably be easier to have a serious conversation with Brad than with Janet. Natalie stood up. "I probably ought to get back inside in case Marla starts looking for me."

Janet looked up at her in surprise, and Natalie felt guilty for sounding rude. "It is your party, isn't it?" Janet said, a tight smile on her face. She gestured toward the house. "You don't want to keep your audience waiting."

"You coming in?" Natalie asked.

Janet nodded. "Yeah, but Eric and I need to pick up the kids and get them down for a nap before it's too late, so we'll be leaving soon."

"Maybe . . . we can get together or something," Natalie suggested, knowing Janet was probably feeling a little slighted.

"I lead a women's Bible study on Thursday nights at seven," Janet answered. "And if you don't mind being around the kids, feel free to drop by anytime during the day. I'm usually at home."

Neither of the two suggestions was highly appealing, but Natalie resolved to do at least one of them in order to smooth things out with her friend. "I'm not sure what my schedule will look like this week, but if the other waitresses come back from sick leave, then I should be able to stop by."

"Okay. I'll be looking forward to it."

Inside, Natalie sat down on the sofa and tried to appear interested in the festivities. The party was far from being a disaster, but her heart had never been in it. She put herself into acting mode and tried to look as if she was having the time of her life, when, in reality, she was waiting for the whole thing to end.

Mercifully, most of the guests had to get up early for work the next morning, so the party broke up a little after seven o'clock. Natalie spent the night turning back and forth in a restless sleep, apprehensive of what emotions and conflict the next day might bring.

Five

"*A*m I mistaken, or is there a rift between you and Janet?" Brad poured another measure of paint into the tray.

Natalie didn't answer right away. Brad had picked her up from work today and rushed her home so they could get started painting the dining room. Marla had a sewing circle dinner to attend, so for the past two hours she and Brad had been working on getting the main-floor rooms ready for exhibits. She held her arms out in front of her, surveying all of the tiny cream-colored dots of paint that had splattered on her brown arms. She would definitely be making an appointment with a hot bath tonight.

Dipping his paint roller in the tray, Brad asked, "Am I being too nosy?"

Natalie shrugged but didn't answer right away. She probably *had* ruffled Janet's feathers yesterday, and she would have to go and make amends soon. She planned to stop by Janet's house sometime this week and try to smooth out the rough edges she had created. "Why?" she finally asked Brad. "Did she say something to you about me?" She held her brush at her side and looked up at Brad, who was now perched at the top of the ladder, painting the top of the dining-room wall.

"No." Brad shook his head and kept painting.

"Then why are you asking?"

"I don't know . . ." Brad climbed down from the ladder and headed over to the tray of paint. "You two used to be a lot closer back when we were in school, and now it looks like you don't even know each other." He quickly climbed back up the ladder and resumed his work.

"Maybe we don't," Natalie said, sighing. The long day on her feet at the café was starting to catch up with her, and her body was begging for a break. Natalie sat her brush in the pan and sat cross-legged on the floor, thinking about Brad's comment while she watched him paint. He was very perceptive; that was for sure. She and Janet *didn't* know each other anymore. She didn't like the idea of letting a friendship just dissolve without any particular reason, but she didn't know if trying to bridge the gap would be worth the effort. By the time she and Janet were on strong footing again, Natalie would probably be ready to leave, and then their friendship would suffer the same fate all over again.

"So you're willing to let your friendship with her end, just like that?" Brad wanted to know. He climbed down from the ladder once more.

Before Natalie could answer, her stomach growled loudly. She stood up, grinning. "Why don't we break for the day and finish this conversation over some dinner?"

"Good idea. Where do you want to go?" he asked.

Natalie laughed. "The kitchen."

Brad looked surprised. "You don't want to go out?"

Natalie shook her head. "Look at me. I'm covered in little pin-sized dots of paint; my hair's being difficult; and I'm exhausted. If we went anywhere, I'd probably fall asleep in the car on the way there. I'll just peek in the refrigerator and see what I can find. Is that okay with you?"

Brad seemed satisfied with this answer. "Fine with me. I just didn't think you'd feel like cooking."

Natalie put her hands on her hips, playfully challenging him. "Yeah . . . or you just didn't think I knew how to cook."

"I won't answer that one," Brad said. "But I will clean up all of this mess while you get started cooking."

Natalie went to the kitchen and checked the pantry and the refrigerator and decided that she would serve turkey sandwiches along with some of Marla's potato salad.

She put plates and bread on the table, along with glasses of ice water. Afterward, she got to work slicing tomatoes, which she added to the other items on the table. By the time Brad walked into the kitchen, she was tearing apart a head of romaine. She handed him a butter knife and pointed to the mayonnaise and mustard on the table. "I didn't know what you liked, so I decided you could do your own thing with these sandwiches." Natalie picked up the platter of lettuce and carried it to the table.

The two of them sat and bowed their heads while Brad said grace. While they assembled their sandwiches, Brad returned to the subject they had been discussing in the dining room. "What are you going to do about Janet?"

Natalie shrugged. "I wish there was an easy answer. But I think maybe it's best to leave things the way they are. I think we both probably miss our old friendship, but we've gone in totally different directions."

"I take it her new life doesn't appeal to you?"

"It's her life, and if she's happy, then good for her. But I'm not married, and I don't have kids. All of my friends are single and career-focused. Janet is a stay-at-home mom. We don't click anymore."

"I see. You're giving up because you're too different now?" Brad looked her in the eye, and their gazes locked for several moments. The look on his face suggested he disapproved of her reasoning.

She didn't know why, but she didn't want to disappoint him. "I'm not saying that I don't care anymore. But why invest the effort when I'll be leaving at some point."

Brad nodded abruptly and pushed back from the table in a jerking motion. "So you *are* leaving. I thought so."

Natalie pushed away from the table as well. "I never said I was staying."

"But you never said you were leaving. In fact, Marla seems to think you're home for good. When were you planning to tell her?"

Natalie looked away. She hadn't gotten around to telling Marla that she was planning to leave. "Okay, you're right. I haven't told her yet. But I will."

Brad looked skeptical. "When? She's under the impression that you're here to settle, and, frankly, so was I."

Natalie blinked. Why did Brad care if she was here to stay? "I'll tell Marla soon," she repeated. He looked unconvinced, and Natalie's temper flared. Why did he feel as if he could tell her what to do all of a sudden? She took a bite of her sandwich to keep from saying something she would later regret.

Brad pulled his chair back to the table and resumed eating. Natalie glared across the table until he held up his hands in defense. "Okay. I'm sorry. I was a little harsh."

Though Natalie had doubts about his sincerity, she accepted his apology. "I forgive you."

He lifted his eyebrows, as though he was waiting for something more from her. "And," she added stiffly, "I'm sorry for losing my temper."

"And I forgive you, too." He took a bite of potato salad and swallowed. "I just feel badly for Marla. She'll be hurt, you know."

Natalie nodded, her anger fading quickly. Marla would be hurt, and Natalie didn't like to think about that happening. She'd been pushing the thought away for as long as she could. "I'll miss her, too. I'm not entirely heartless, and I would prefer for her to come with me, but you and I both know she loves this town. It's her home."

"But isn't this your home, too?"

"Not really. I don't belong here." Natalie closed her eyes and laughed sharply. "Although it seems like I can never get away for good."

"Maybe there's a reason for that," Brad suggested. "Have you prayed about it?"

"Oh, no. Don't even go there. Janet said the same thing to me."

Brad looked as if he was fighting back a grin. "What did she say?"

"She thinks that I should let the Lord make my career decisions for me."

"And what's wrong with that? He's the only one who won't mess things up." Seeing her frown, he quickly added, "Not that I think you are." After an uncomfortable silence, he clarified his sentence, adding, "Messing things up, I mean."

"Good," Natalie agreed. "So let's change the subject. Pick a topic, any topic—except this one."

He inclined his head, thinking. "Tell me about your life in Kansas City."

"Well . . . that's a pretty broad topic. Let's try something a little narrower."

"Okay. Where do you work? What are your friends like? What kind of acting jobs have you had? Are you dating anyone?" Leaning back, he folded his hands in front of him. "Is that better? Lots of topics to pick from."

Natalie took a deep breath, and answered, "I'm a secretary. I have lots of acquaintances and a few close friends; the closest one is my roommate, Kelly, and I'm not dating anyone." Exhaling, she said, "Now you answer all those questions."

"I'm a history teacher, my best friend is Jake West, who was always my best friend in high school, and no, I'm not dating anyone either." He paused, and then added, "I didn't mean for this to be a Q and A session. I thought maybe we could have a back-and-forth conversation. Plus, you didn't answer my question about your acting."

Natalie nodded and placed her hand over her mouth, covering a yawn. "It's not all that interesting. I've done lots and lots of community theater, but paying jobs have never seemed to come my way." She shrugged. "The market is pretty tight, especially in theater. I've done more commercials than paying theater roles."

"You've done commercials? That's pretty impressive," Brad said.

Natalie took a while to answer. "I guess so," she finally admitted.

"You don't sound that excited. What's so bad about commercials?" Brad questioned.

"There's nothing wrong with commercials. But for someone

who wants to be on stage in live theater, it would be like you having a teaching degree, but only being able to find a job as a part-time substitute."

Brad frowned. "I don't think it's as bad as you're making it out to be, but I won't argue with you. You got paid, didn't you?"

"Yes." Natalie sighed. She wished Brad would stop grilling her about her lack of success. There was no way he could understand. No one in this town could understand, which was why no one had ever taken her career plans seriously. No one, except for Marla, who had wished Natalie could be an actress and still live in Sterling. Natalie began clearing the table in an effort to get Brad to drop the subject. He was a nice guy, but he would be much easier to get along with if he wasn't so persistent.

She carried an armful of dishes to the sink, and Brad followed with the leftovers. He put items away in the refrigerator while Natalie washed dishes.

"Can I help?" Brad wanted to know.

Natalie shook her head. She was tired, and she really wished Brad would just go home. "I've got them."

He leaned sideways against the counter while she worked. "So under what circumstances would you stay here in Sterling?"

Natalie shot him an irritated glance. "I thought we put this subject to rest."

"I'm just curious. What if Marla begged you to stay? If she needed you here?"

Natalie looked down at the sink full of soapsuds and considered. Brad's phrasing of the question made her feel somewhat guilty. She had considered the issue several times in her heart over the past few years but had never come to a solid conclusion. If Marla were sick and needed someone to care for her, what could Natalie do? Marla would never leave her home, so getting her to move to Kansas City or Chicago or New York with Natalie would be out of the question. The right answer, of course, would be to move to Sterling and care for Marla. Marla had given a great many years of her life to being a mother to Natalie's mother, and then to Natalie. Natalie's heart sank. Did Brad know something she didn't? Had Marla confided something to him?

"What are you saying?" she demanded of Brad. "Did she tell you something? Did she say she *needs* me here?"

Brad smiled easily and shook his head. "No, she didn't. But I guess I have my answer for that question."

In a huff, Natalie began drying dishes. How could he upset her like that just to make her answer his question? She looked sideways at him. "I never answered your question," she said pointedly. "You can assume all you want, but your assumption might not be true."

"Then what is your answer?"

She gave him a smug smile. "The answer is that Marla would *never* ask me to stay here. She knows how important my goals are to me. And," she added in concession, "if I were needed, of course I would come back."

He nodded. "Anything else that would keep you here?" Exasperated, Natalie sighed. "I don't think so." She gave him a false cheery smile and took the dishes to their proper cabinet. When she was done, she put her hands on hips and asked, "Is there anything else?"

"Yeah." He cleared his throat. "Since it looks like you'll still be here Friday, I was wondering if you wanted to come to the annual teachers' dinner with me? I need a date," he added, as if to clarify his request.

"Sure," Natalie said. Brad looked surprised at her quick answer, and Natalie had to hold back a smile. "This isn't really a date date, is it?"

Brad seemed to be collecting his thoughts, then his words came out in a rush. "It could be if you wanted it to be. Do you?"

She shook her head. "No. I just thought it would be fun to do something besides going to the café and working on the museum for a change." She laughed. "You could have asked me if I wanted to go for a ride in the country or visit a petting zoo, and I would have accepted."

An unreadable look passed over Brad's face, but it was quickly replaced with a stiff smile. "I have to spend most of my time this week getting my lesson plans and classroom ready, so you might not see me around too much until Friday. But I'll call you and let you know what time I'll be around to get you. Is that okay?"

"Fine with me," Natalie said.

"I'd better get going. Thanks for dinner," he said. Brad turned and walked to the front door. Natalie followed and let him out. As he walked to the car, Natalie wondered if she had hurt his feelings. She shouldn't have made fun of his asking her out, even if it was just a friendly date.

And it is friendly, she told herself. *Brad said so himself.* Her conscience piped up with a clarification. *He didn't say it was friendly until you said you wanted it to be.*

Walking back to the kitchen, Natalie groaned aloud in frustration. Why did she seem to be offending so many people lately? First Marla, then Janet, and now Brad.

She paused in the middle of the hallway, and closed her eyes. "Lord, please help me to be nicer . . . more polite or something." Natalie opened her eyes and continued back to the kitchen. She poured herself a glass of milk and sat at the table, not ready to go to bed. Something was bugging her, tugging at her mind.

Two things, actually. For one thing, she hadn't prayed outside of Sunday-morning services in a long time, and the fact that she had just said an impromptu prayer bothered her a little. She couldn't place the feeling, but it was somewhere in between feeling hypocritical and feeling relief. Since coming back here and being around a large amount of people who attended church on a regular basis, she had been acutely aware of the fact that her relationship with the Lord wasn't all it used to be.

She closed her eyes and prayed again, apologizing for allowing herself to drift away, little by little.

Her second concern was about Brad. Having grown up in the same town with him, and knowing his family, she knew a great deal about him. He was upright, handsome, and kind without being a pushover. And he was single—something that could be dangerous to her own agenda.

Why had she agreed to the date so quickly? There was no harm in a friendly date, but she had been the one to define the date as friendly.

Natalie rinsed her milk glass and walked up to her room, still deliberating. She had made a point not to fall in love with anyone in this town before she'd graduated from high school. In Natalie's opinion, too many people missed chances in life while still in high school because they made up their minds about who they wanted to marry, how many kids they would have, where they would work, and where they would live. By the time graduation rolled around, they had already decided which holidays they would spend with which in-laws.

Natalie had determined when she was young not to fall into that trap. She rarely dated and, in truth, had gone out with

Brad because he was popular. And he was very handsome. He had expressed more than just a passing interest in her, but because she was scared of developing feelings for him, she'd broken the relationship off before things could even get started.

Marla had kept her up to date about whom Brad was dating and, most often, whom Brad wasn't dating, but Natalie had refused to think about it. She'd come home recently, fully expecting him to be married or engaged, or at the very least in a steady relationship.

But he wasn't. And she was going on a date with him. He was definitely the type of man who would be a good husband, and someday she wanted a husband and a family. Still, she wasn't ready to abandon her career plans for a family, and Brad wouldn't pursue a relationship with her once she made that clear to him.

Deciding not to trouble herself any further for the night, Natalie made her way to her room, careful to leave the lights on for Marla, who still hadn't come home.

Six

Natalie knocked on the door again, glancing at her watch. She'd been given a one-hour break this afternoon, since business was slow, and she'd hoped to be able to clear things up with Janet. Unfortunately, no one was answering the door at Janet's house.

Natalie turned to go back to her car. The poor little thing, which should have been in a junkyard somewhere, had just gotten out of the shop, and Natalie thought George Milton and his crew had worked a minor miracle on it. When she'd gone to the shop to retrieve it, he'd warned her that it was working moderately well, but she might have trouble with it again as the weather grew colder. She knew he was right, and she was saving for another car as well as replenishing savings, which would allow her to return to Kansas City.

Natalie sighed as she turned the ignition. She was on the

right track, but in all of her experience, she had never seen a financial crunch such as the one she faced now clear up quickly.

She was just about to drive off when a honking horn alerted her that a minivan was parked right behind her. Natalie turned and saw Janet jump out of the driver's side of the vehicle and run toward her.

Natalie rolled down the window to talk to Janet. "I thought I'd stop by for a quick visit, but I guess I should have called first," she explained.

Janet shook her head. "No, no, I just had to run out on a quick errand. Do you still have time to stay?"

Natalie checked her watch. "I have about forty-five minutes before I have to get back to work."

"Then come in." Janet sounded enthusiastic. "Let me run and get the kids out of the van, though." Janet ran back to her vehicle and began unlocking her kids from their car seats. Natalie followed and stood watching, feeling a little useless. Both of Janet's children had been asleep, and they were fussy at having been awakened. Little Eric cried loudly, which caused Olivia to wail all the more. Janet lifted him out of the seat and placed him on the ground, but he apparently was not in the mood for walking, so he promptly sat down on the grass, still crying.

Natalie looked down at the little boy who was now pulling on Janet's pant leg, an endless stream of tears sliding down his rounded cheeks.

"Can I help out?" Natalie asked Janet.

"Yes." With that, Janet handed Natalie a bundle containing Olivia. At least, Natalie assumed Olivia was somewhere under all of those blankets, since she could hear the baby crying.

Carefully making sure she had a firm grip on Olivia, she followed Janet into the house. Eric had calmed down almost immediately after Janet gathered him into her arms and carried him inside.

Janet led Natalie to the children's room and sat Eric on the changing table. "Give me a minute to put him down for a nap and then we can talk, okay?"

Natalie nodded and looked down at the still-crying bundle of Olivia. Janet nodded at the bundle and said, "You can take her into the family room and peel some of those layers off. She's probably hot by now."

Natalie nodded but didn't move immediately. "She's still crying. How should I stop her?" she asked.

Janet laughed. "You should see your face. Just take her out of the blankets, smile at her, and play with her."

Natalie turned and went back to the family room and began removing blankets from the baby, finally uncovering Olivia. The baby had stopped crying now, and she lay on Natalie's lap, her eyes still moist from tears. Olivia made a gurgling noise and kicked her legs.

Afraid she might drop her, Natalie lifted Olivia and placed her on a baby blanket. Olivia made happy-sounding noises, and Natalie played with the tiny hands and feet, tickling the bottoms of the miniature toes. The baby girl was easy to entertain, and Natalie wondered why she had been so apprehensive about helping Janet with the baby. She had always thought kids were cute but hadn't ever really baby-sat, and she didn't have any siblings to bond with.

She was singing a medley of all the nursery rhymes and lullabies she had ever heard when Janet came in.

"See, I told you you'd be okay." Janet laughed. "She's about to fall asleep." She sat down on the floor across from Natalie and patted the baby's stomach. "So what brings you here? Just wanting to chitchat?"

Natalie cleared her throat. "Actually, I wanted to come over and apologize. I acted a little . . ." Natalie wondered how to explain her behavior.

"Surprised? Uncomfortable? Distant?" Janet supplied.

Natalie watched Janet closely for any signs that she might be upset. Nodding in agreement, she said, "Yeah, I guess you could use all of those. Standoffish, too. I hope you're not upset with me."

Janet shook her head. "Nope. Let's be honest here, Natalie. After high school, we took different paths. In the beginning, I was a little hurt that you didn't make any effort to keep in contact with me, but I didn't let myself get bitter about it."

"But I didn't even realize you were married and had a family," Natalie pointed out. "Does that seem even just a little bit terrible to you? I've been so self-centered since I left. Maybe even before I left."

"Yes. Definitely before you left," Janet agreed, smiling.

"So why did you keep being my friend?"

Janet shrugged. "Because I like you. You're not perfect, and you had your annoying habits and stuff like that, but we've known each other since we were kids. I know that, sometimes, friendships aren't meant to be long term, but I had my hopes." She grinned, a gleam shining in her eyes. "Do you remember when you used to make me promise that we wouldn't just get married and be mothers, but first we would become famous at doing something, and I could never decide how I wanted to become famous?"

Natalie laughed, remembering that she'd told Janet that she could be her personal wardrobe designer if she couldn't come up with any other ideas. After all, Janet had been known to sew some magnificent outfits for the fashion dolls they played with. Natalie had solemnly vowed to wear Janet's designs to all of the parties she would attend, thereby making Janet the designer whose clothes were in demand.

"Well," Janet continued, "While you imagined us riding around in limousines and living in fancy hotels, I imagined us falling in love with handsome men, living next door to each other, raising our kids together, and getting old and gray sitting on our front porches." She looked at Natalie and winked. "I didn't tell you, though. I just nodded while you were talking and imagined my own dream. So don't feel too badly about the way things have gone. You're living your dream, and I'm living mine." Olivia was starting to fuss and Janet picked her up and bounced her up and down. "I love my life, Natalie. But I do wish we could have had the same dream."

Natalie remained quiet. Her best friend had just told her that in the twelve-plus years of their friendship, Natalie had never bothered to listen to what Janet really wanted. She felt stunned, but Janet was right.

Janet seemed to be examining her closely, a concerned look on her face. She reached over and touched Natalie's sleeve. "Natalie, don't get upset about it. It's all in the past now."

Natalie nodded, in admiration of the fact that Janet had forgiven her so easily. She wanted to be like Janet. She didn't necessarily want to have the same life as Janet, but she wanted to be able to forgive and live her life without carrying around heavy emotional burdens.

"Natalie," Janet said firmly. "I understand about your needing to be an actress and live in other cities, but while you're here, let's not think about it. Let's just be friends again, and when you have to leave again, we'll go back to our separate lives. But until then, we can get caught up on each other's lives, okay?"

Natalie grinned. "Janet, you are incredible. If you had done the same thing to me, I don't think I could have forgiven you so easily."

Janet placed Olivia, who was now asleep, back on the blanket. "Yes, you could have, Natalie. That's part of being a Christian. It's hard sometimes, but we can do it." Janet was interrupted by the sound of Eric calling her from his room. Janet flashed Natalie a wry smile. "Short nap, huh?"

Natalie laughed. As she and Janet stood up, Natalie remembered that she had to get back to work. "I'd better get going," she told Janet, "but I do want us to keep being friends. Maybe sometime later this week we can get together."

"How about Friday night?" Janet wanted to know. "We could sit around and watch old movies."

Natalie smiled at how Janet remembered how much she enjoyed old movies. Janet, who had never cared for the black-and-white films, preferred newer romantic comedies. Natalie shook her head. "We'll watch something that you really like, okay?"

Janet laughed. "We'll take turns. How's that?"

"Sounds fair to me, but I can't this Friday," Natalie said, remembering her date with Brad.

Janet quirked her eyebrows in a silent question.

"I'm going to the annual teachers' dinner with Brad," Natalie told her.

Janet looked surprised but didn't ask any more questions, and Natalie was grateful that she hadn't.

"Mommy?" Eric called again.

"I'm coming, sweetie," Janet called to him. "Let me walk you to the door," she told Natalie. Janet reached over to lift Olivia and led Natalie to the front door. Before Natalie stepped outside, Janet said, "Thanks for coming, Nat. It really means a lot that you still want to be friends." She looked down at Olivia and said, "I'd hug you, but I don't want to wake her. She's been fussy for a few days."

Natalie gently touched one of Olivia's little feet and nodded. "I'm glad I came, too. I feel like a weight has been lifted off my shoulders. I'll see you at church on Sunday if not before then." With that, she turned and walked to her car, feeling as if her shoes were made of clouds. Maybe the reason she had put off coming home wasn't because she hated Sterling. She was slowly realizing that she had many doubts about how she would be received if she didn't return home as a star. She had left everyone behind, not caring about their lives, in her quest to become famous, and when she fell short of getting past the bottom rung on the ladder, she'd been too embarrassed to come back as anything less than great. The humbling part of this was the fact that she still had people who genuinely cared about her in the town.

Visiting Janet had really cheered Natalie's spirit, giving her the boost she needed to begin repairing other friendships she'd conveniently forgotten about after leaving Sterling. For the rest of the day, Natalie couldn't hold back the silly grin that spread over her face. She couldn't explain it, but she felt better than she had in years.

Seven

 *B*rad straightened his tie one last time as he strode up the sidewalk to Marla's front door. Before he could even ring the doorbell, Marla swung the door open and invited him inside. "Natalie's still getting ready, so you'll have to wait a couple of minutes."

Brad followed Marla inside to the kitchen, the only room downstairs that wasn't empty in preparation for the museum. Yesterday he and Eric Summers had come over and moved all the rest of Marla's furniture up to the spare bedrooms on the second floor. He had teased Marla that she was the only person he knew whose living and dining rooms had been relocated to empty upstairs bedrooms. She had joked with him that she felt as if she were living in some fancy apartment building since all she needed was on one floor, with the exception of the kitchen.

As they got settled in the kitchen, Brad noticed that Marla had brought a number of the boxes down from the attic. "Look at what Natalie and I brought down from the attic this morning," she said, pointing to the table. Spread out on the big kitchen table were what appeared to be hundreds of old magazines and newspapers.

Brad took a closer look, impressed at the collection. His mother, who was several years younger than Marla, had always said that Marla never threw anything away, and the more he saw descend from Marla's attic, the more he believed this to be true.

A few weeks earlier, Marla had told him she had been born in 1922 and had begun saving keepsakes when she was nine years old. On the table in front of him lay what had to have been at least fifty years' worth of articles and magazines of African-American interest. She had told him that the bulk of her collection was in books and newspapers, but he hadn't thought much about it until now. What she had was priceless, and he couldn't wait to bring his students over to see it.

"I've been sorting through this all day," she said. "What do you think? You're the history expert. Do we have the beginnings of a museum here?"

"Definitely," Brad told her, nodding vigorously. "This stuff is extremely valuable. I almost hate that we have to display it. We'll have to find some way to display it under glass, especially the older ones."

She grinned. "I'm ahead of you there. I've been calling around to some of the stores here trying to find out how much glass display cases cost. I've already ordered several."

He looked at Marla, surprised. "I'm sure they're not cheap. I'd be willing to put in some money, if you need me to."

Marla shrugged. "You can if you want to, but I've got some money saved up. Remember, I've been planning this for a while."

Brad nodded, still looking through the goods on the table. "You've got a big chunk of our history here, Marla, and not just locally. Some of the bigger Black history museums would love to get their hands on this."

Marla shook her head. "This is for the people of Sterling," she replied firmly.

Brad nodded gravely. "The people of Sterling are blessed to have you here, making sure we know and remember our history," he said.

"I couldn't do all of this without your and Natalie's help," she said.

"Did I hear my name?" Natalie's voice echoed from the hallway. He turned to see her standing in the kitchen doorway, dressed up and ready to go. She was wearing a long, sky blue dress with ruffles at the hem and on the short sleeves, and a matching set of pearl earrings, necklace, and bracelet. Her hair was held up off her neck and shoulders somehow, even though stray curls had escaped here and there.

He held back a smile, thinking that she might be a tad overdressed, but opted not to say anything. He was relieved that he had actually worn a suit and tie, having had a feeling that Natalie still enjoyed getting dressed up, as she had throughout her school years.

"Well, aren't you all dressed up?" Natalie asked. Brad instantly realized that he hadn't yet complimented Natalie on how she looked, and he felt embarrassed that she had beaten him to it. "Thanks," he said, walking toward her. "You look very pretty, too." Feeling the need to say more, he touched the edge of her sleeve and added, "I like the ruffles here."

Natalie gave him a curious look and giggled. "Thanks, Brad." Silence settled between them, and after a moment,

Natalie added, "I like your jacket. The dark gray is a good color on you."

From the other side of the kitchen, Marla cleared her throat. "If you two keep standing there complimenting ruffles and jacket colors, you'll miss the dinner." Brad didn't have to look at her to know she had a big smile on her face.

He took Natalie's hand and said, "Marla's right. Let's get going." To Marla, he said, "We'll be gone a couple of hours at the most. It's just the same old, same old every year." Casting another glance back at the kitchen table, he added, "We might even be able to sort through some of that together later this evening."

Natalie groaned, but she didn't truly sound upset. "Oh, let's not think about the museum tonight. We'll come back to the house, but let's not work, okay?"

Marla nodded. "I've about done all I'm going to do with this anyway. Call before you head home, and I'll get some popcorn ready. We can sit in the upstairs family room and watch one of Natalie's old movies."

Brad really would have preferred doing museum work, but he was clearly outnumbered, so he just agreed with the two women. He knew Natalie could sit for hours watching old mysteries, and he found himself hoping that whatever they watched wouldn't be exceptionally long. Maybe tomorrow they could look through Marla's things.

The dinner turned out to be just as he'd predicted. A meal of Caesar salad, baked chicken, asparagus, wild rice, and strawberry cheesecake in the school cafeteria, mingled with smells of lunches that had been prepared and served in the cafeteria the previous school year. The principal got up and gave his carbon-copy speech about how he hoped this would be the best

school year ever at Sterling High, etc., etc. Brad was one of the
five unmarried faculty members, so his having brought Natalie
as his date caused somewhat of a stir. Everyone did a great deal
of looking, but no one actually asked any questions about
whether or not he and Natalie were a "couple," something he
found surprising since his coworkers were all life-long citizens
of Sterling.

They, like most everyone else in town, usually had the same
penchant for being "detail conscious," as his mother liked to term
gossipy behavior. Brad was relieved, though, for Natalie's sake;
since he knew that the fact that everyone seemed to know everything about everyone else really bothered her. She was a little
quiet and reserved in the beginning, but she grew more relaxed
when it became apparent that no one was going to pry into her life.

By the time the assistant principal got up to give the closing
remarks, Brad glanced at his watch, noting that this year, the
festivities had clocked in at an a hour and forty-five minutes.
He and Natalie hung around for a little of the after-dinner conversation, then said their good-byes.

"That wasn't too bad, was it?" he asked Natalie, once they
were in the car, heading back to her house.

She looked across at him. "Who said it would be bad? I
wasn't expecting anything less than a good time." She grinned.

Brad was surprised. Natalie didn't strike him as the type of
person who would actually have fun at one of those dinners.
He didn't dislike attending the yearly event, but he had never
considered them to be fun. The people who really had the
most fun were the teachers who brought their spouses along,
and they had a good time because they all spent time with one
another outside of faculty events. Brad usually sat at a table
with Mrs. Spelle and Mrs. Kapren, who were widows, along

with Ms. Cone and Mr. Macon, who had never been married. They were all nice to him, but those four teachers were in their sixties and all had been his teachers when he was in high school. He never quite felt as if he fit in with them, and they often treated him as if he were still a student, rather than a colleague.

He was one of the youngest members of the faculty, and sometimes he wondered if he had made the wrong career move. Some of his old school friends had decided to become teachers, but none of them had come back to teach in Sterling.

"So tell me," Natalie persisted, now laughing openly, "did you invite me only because you thought I would be bored?" She leaned back in the seat and crossed her arms. Shaking her head, she said, "And I thought you really wanted to go on a date with me."

"I did ask you because I wanted you to be my date," Brad answered honestly.

"I had a good time, you know." She looked across at him and paused.

Brad nodded, waiting for her to continue.

"I talked to Essie Lyn Briggs for a long time. She was my English teacher, always pestering me to turn in better work. And she knew my heart wasn't in it, because she was also the drama teacher, and she directed all of the plays."

"She still does, you know."

Out of the corner of his eye, he saw her nodding. "I do know. She told me all about it. She fussed over me so much about how talented I was, I almost felt like a real star." She stopped abruptly and looked away, out the window.

Brad had become aware that Natalie was uncomfortable talking about her life as an actress, and while *he* had been careful to steer clear of the subject, he couldn't prevent her or anyone else from bringing it up.

He reached over and took hold of her hand, "You'll get there someday, Natalie. I know you will." He didn't know all of the details of her life, but he knew she wasn't where she wanted to be.

She didn't question his comment, but whispered, "Thank you."

They turned the corner to Marla's house, and he wondered how much she had really enjoyed the evening. Would she be willing to spend more time with him? He cleared his throat and asked, "So you did have a good time?"

She nodded.

"Would you go out with me again?" he asked.

She nodded again. "When do you want to go out?"

After a moment of consideration, he suggested, "Sunday after church?"

"I'll look forward to it," Natalie said. He pulled the car to a stop, and they made their way up the stairs to the front door.

Inside, they were greeted with the smell of freshly popped popcorn. Natalie grinned. "I guess Aunt Marla's all ready for this movie."

"Come on upstairs! I've got the movie ready to go," Marla called from somewhere on the second floor.

Natalie and Brad went upstairs and found Marla in the old guest bedroom that Marla and Natalie had transformed into a very serviceable family room. Brad sat down on one of the sofas, but Natalie hesitated, standing in the doorway.

"Don't tell me you're backing out on this movie," he teased.

She shook her head. "No, I'm just going to change into jeans or something. Go ahead and start, though. I'll be right back."

Natalie left to change and Marla started the movie. Brad did his best to concentrate on the plot, which was moving rather slowly.

"So what did I miss?" Natalie whispered when she came back.

Brad shrugged. "I wasn't really following it that much. I figured you've seen this one before. You've seen one mystery, you've seen 'em all."

"I have seen this one," Natalie said, reaching for the popcorn. "But it's a romantic comedy, not a mystery, Mr. Smarty Pants," she teased.

Brad watched for a while, but after nearly an hour, his thoughts wandered elsewhere. After getting off to a rocky start, the couple on the screen was starting to realize how much they cared for each other, and they were well on their way to a happy ending. There would be no big surprises in the ending.

Brad's mother was an avid fan of a good love story, in either book or movie form, and he had once asked her why she even bothered, when she knew how the story would end.

"It's all the same," he'd told her. "They meet, and they might hate each other, or they might fall in love at first sight. Something happens in the middle, but in the end, they fall in love, and it's over."

She had answered that she enjoyed them because she liked to watch the *process*, which varied from story to story. He'd been skeptical, but she had assured him that he would understand one day when it happened to him.

As the years passed and he remained unmarried, he had doubts that he would ever understand the appeal of a good love story. He sometimes wondered if he would end up like Mr. Macon, a great teacher but still single at the age of sixty-two. Brad sometimes wondered if he should have done what many of his peers had done and moved to a bigger city.

After college, he had given thought to moving elsewhere but had ultimately decided to come home and build his adult life in the place he'd always lived; overall, he had no serious regrets about his decision.

Occasionally, he did struggle with concern for his future social life, or the lack of it. Currently, his main activities consisted of going to church, working, and grocery shopping. His older brothers had moved away to attend college in St. Louis and hadn't come back to live in Sterling; they married women whom they met at school and opted to stay where they were. He sometimes hung out with his good friends Eric Summers and Jake West, but they had wives and children and didn't always have time for men-only events. Lately, they, in addition to his parents, had been pointing out some of the single women at church, hinting that maybe it was time for him to start thinking about marriage.

Brad knew they were trying to help, but their constant "concern" sometimes rankled him. He did think about marriage, and the more he thought about the idea, the more he realized that he didn't have any interest in the women who were available. They were nice women, he couldn't deny that; but none of them had ever made a deep impression on his heart—the type of impression that made him think, She's the one.

Until now. Lately, he'd been shrugging off feelings that he may have found his future wife. And this wasn't the first time he'd had this feeling about someone. The problem was, both times the feelings had surfaced when he was around the same woman . . . Natalie Jacobs.

The idea that Natalie might be "the one" was an uncomfortable one, given that she would never be happy in Sterling.

Deciding not to think about it for the time being, Brad returned his attention to the movie. Right on cue, the couple re-alized how much they cared for each other, and the credits started to roll.

Natalie looked at Brad and nudged his arm. "Did you like it?"

Brad shrugged. He hadn't exactly watched the whole thing, so he couldn't very well give the film a glowing review. "The ending was nice," he said, smiling. "Such a happy ending."

Natalie burst out laughing. "Oh, sure, like you were paying attention. You were zoning out for most of the time. What in the world were you thinking about?"

Brad shook his head. "Doesn't make any difference—" An unexpected yawn interrupted his sentence.

"Was it that boring?" Natalie asked, a smile tugging at the corners of her mouth.

Brad stood up. "No, it wasn't that boring, but I probably should get home. I've had a long day."

Natalie nodded. "Me, too. I'll walk you down to the door."

When Brad opened the door, a gust of cool early-autumn air wafted inside the house. This year, summertime had seemed to make itself known earlier than usual, bringing higher tempera-tures and more thunderstorms and severe weather. For several weeks Brad had been looking forward to cooler temperatures, and if the seventy-degree highs of the past few days were an in-dicator of things to come, his favorite season was closer than its official start date on the calendar. Brad stepped out on the front porch and Natalie followed him.

"Thanks again for coming tonight," he told her.

She shrugged. "I really did have a good time. And I'm look-ing forward to Sunday."

He blinked, having almost forgotten that he had asked her out for Sunday. He had half expected her to turn him down, so he hadn't planned anything really special. Now he would spend tomorrow trying to think of something to do that Natalie might enjoy, and that might be difficult, considering the types of activities available in Sterling. He frowned slightly, wondering if he should have kept his mouth shut and left well enough alone. She had gone with him to the dinner, and that was good enough. He was pushing his luck to try taking things any further.

Natalie must have realized he was feeling hesitant. "You haven't changed your mind, have you?" She looked genuinely disappointed, and that made him feel a little more confident.

He shook his head. "No, I haven't forgotten, but . . . it probably won't be anything fancy or exciting. Maybe you and Marla can come over to my mom's for dinner. She gets kind of lonely sometimes. After that, I don't know. I need some time to think of something." He shrugged and looked at her. "You can back out now, if you want." He decided it would be best to lay all his cards out on the table so she wouldn't feel as if he had tricked her into anything.

"You could come over tomorrow and look at all of those magazines Marla dragged out," she suggested. "I have to start designing the display for the den, so I'll be here all day."

Brad rubbed his chin. "What are we doing with the den? I keep forgetting."

"I want to make it look like the interior of a sharecropper's cabin, and I think your students can really help with that room in particular. I have some ideas to make it look very realistic."

He nodded. "I'll look forward to hearing all about it in the morning, then." He waved good-bye and got into his car to head home. The evening had gone well, better than he had dared to hope it would. As to the matter of spending more time with Natalie, he would have to wait to see how things went. If she didn't mind hanging out with him, he wouldn't object to going out every now and then. He would just have to keep in mind that she would be leaving soon, and when she left, that would probably be the end to anything that might remotely resemble a relationship between them.

Eight

Natalie was busy working on a sketch for an old kitchen display when she realized the group of students under her direction was no longer working. She stared across the room where they were laughing and joking and making a mess in the process. "Hey, watch it over there," she said, rushing to where they sat in the entry hall. "Those walls haven't even been painted for ten days," she continued as she knelt down on the floor next to them. They were supposed to be brushing a mixture of tea and water on sheets of newspaper to make them look older. The task wasn't all that exciting, and they had spent the last few minutes flicking drops of tea on one another instead of on the paper. They looked at Natalie guiltily and sat still. "Look, I know this isn't necessarily *fun*, but the next time we divide up jobs, I'll see if Brad can assign you all to something more interesting."

They nodded their agreement, and Natalie stood up. "How-ever," she added, a hint of sternness in her voice, "if I find any flecks of tea on the walls in this hallway, I will not hesitate to drag you all out of your beds during fall break and have you come over to repaint. Show some respect for the kids who painted here last week, okay?" Looking thoroughly chastised, they returned to their job. Natalie held back a grin. Having got-ten to know these kids over the past three months, she was pretty sure they would return to the tea-flicking war within a matter of minutes.

Natalie longingly glanced outside where a group of kids was measuring pieces of lumber for the den. Although Thanksgiv-ing was a couple of days away, the weather was still rather warm, so working outdoors was enjoyable. The leaves were a breathtaking variety of fall colors, and the bright sunshine seemed to reflect down through the branches, casting a golden glow on the ground underneath. People were already burning wood in their fireplaces, if only for the atmosphere.

The steady sound of loud hammering echoed from the den down the hall. Natalie closed her eyes briefly, wondering how six kids who usually looked for any excuse not to do their as-signed job could wholeheartedly embrace this particular job, keeping up a constant stream of noise for what had been well over an hour.

"I need a break," Natalie murmured under her breath. She couldn't blame those kids she had just chastened for getting antsy. She wanted to go outside herself and take in a little fresh air.

She turned her attention back to the small group. "I have an idea," she announced. They looked up at her expectantly. "Let's take a fifteen-minute break and get some fresh air." No one moved, and they looked at her as if she had sprouted another head. Usually Brad was the lenient one, while Natalie pushed for more work to be completed.

"I mean it. Really," Natalie told them. "Now go outside and have some fun." They didn't move, so Natalie turned and left the room. If they didn't want a break, that was fine with her, but she needed one. Rubbing her temples, she made her way to the den, better known today as Noise Central. Looking around the room, she had to admit they were doing an excellent job.

In order to make the room look like a sharecropper's cabin, Natalie and Brad had decided to cover the smooth white walls of the den. In photos they had looked at, the walls of such cabins had been made of slats of wood, and sometimes the windows and parts of the walls were covered with old newspaper. Natalie had wanted to go with that theme, but Brad had adamantly resisted the idea of using Marla's authentic newspapers, which was why Natalie had commissioned several students to "age" some current newspapers.

Natalie and Brad had then been faced with the task of transforming the walls and flooring. They decided they could either paint the walls and floors to look like old wood, or they could somehow affix boards to the existing walls and floors. The students had actually pushed for a way to use real wood, because they thought it would appear more realistic.

Together with some of his students, Brad had designed a way to build a frame within the walls and floor, allowing the students to affix the old wood to the frame rather than the actual walls, leaving the walls unharmed in case Marla ever wanted to change the den display to something different.

Natalie ignored the loud hammering as she glanced around the room. The floors were in place and two of the walls were already finished. The lumber had been donated by different citizens of Sterling who had old or scrap wood lying around, so much of it didn't match, but in Natalie's opinion, it looked good. The room was starting to look like a real cabin, and when classes resumed after Thanksgiving, Marla would take a group of the kids and begin furnishing it to look like a one-room house, complete with an old wood-burning stove that had belonged to Marla's grandparents.

"Hey!" Natalie yelled, trying to get the kids' attention over the noise. When they finally took note of her, she told them they could take a fifteen-minute break as well. They headed outside excitedly.

Natalie checked the kitchen and the dining room to make sure she hadn't forgotten anyone, then went outside herself.

Most of the kids had taken full advantage of the break, but a few were still busily sawing pieces of wood, with Brad hovering nearby, stopping to check on their progress.

Natalie watched him for a few moments, realizing, not for the first time, how handsome he looked.

As Natalie walked toward him, Brad glanced up from the ever-expanding notebook of plans and ideas he carried around with him, a curious look on his face. "Everything okay?" he asked.

She held back a smile, realizing Brad was puzzled about her sudden command for everyone to go outside. "It is now."

Chuckling softly, Brad took her hand and led her to one of the picnic tables he had been using as a workbench. "What happened?" he asked. "The kids giving you trouble in there?" He sat down on the table and patted the space next to him.

Climbing up on the table, Natalie inhaled deeply and shook her head. "Not exactly. Several people in there were getting antsy, including myself, so I just gave everyone a break."

"Aha," Brad said, a look of recognition spreading over his face. "You're always the last person to suggest a break."

"I just have a strong work ethic, that's all," she explained, grinning. "And," she added, "you don't truly appreciate quiet until you've tried to ignore six teenagers doing nonstop construction work for over an hour."

"I knew there was some underlying reason," he said.

"So," she said, gesturing toward the stack of lumber that had been cut. "Do we have enough wood to finish off the cabin?"

He glanced toward the pile, a thoughtful look on his face. "I think so, if we cut everything correctly and don't waste very much."

Natalie lifted her eyebrows slightly. "That's your department, all of the measuring and cutting. My work is more in the finishing-touches arena."

"Don't worry. I'll take care of the man's work. You can decorate all you want." She knew he was teasing her, so she didn't respond with a retort.

They both laughed, and Brad reached over and covered her hand with his. Natalie allowed his hand to remain for a few moments, and then, reluctantly, she pulled her own hand away. Brad looked at her for a moment, not saying anything. Clearing his throat, he opened his notebook and began poring over some of the pages.

I did it again, Natalie thought, feeling guilty. Lately, her time spent with Brad had gone much like this. She and Brad spent a good deal of time together, whether it was attending church, working on the museum, or just hanging out alone together, or with Marla, or his mother, or sometimes even Janet and Eric and their little ones.

Natalie could not deny that she definitely had feelings for him, and those feelings grew deeper and stronger every day.

She also guessed that, although he hadn't said as much, Brad might have similar feelings for her. The problem was, even though her heart didn't mind when Brad held her hand, or hugged her before they parted company, the logical side of her mind did. She now found herself jumping away from Brad as if he were made of fire whenever he touched her. They hadn't discussed this yet, so she wasn't entirely sure what he was thinking. It was a carefully avoided subject, and she would rather they didn't put a damper on the coming holiday by trying to grind out a definition for their relationship. She had puzzled over this herself many times, and she still hadn't been able to determine that they were anything less than or more than friends. They were in the middle, a very comfortable place to be as far as she was concerned. In some respects, Brad was more faithful than some of the people in Kansas City whom she considered good friends. Maila had suggested that it could be due to the fact that Natalie and Brad weren't in a competitive friendship, trying to get the same job.

Natalie didn't know for sure what made him so different. Regardless of her opinion as to *why* he was a good friend, he was a good companion, and he seemed to understand her. She admired his devotion to his students and the way he encouraged her in her faith. He had a great sense of humor, and he dealt gently with everyone he knew, but no one ever thought of him as weak.

Sometimes she felt guilty because she didn't know what she could be to him in return. Natalie glanced at Brad, who was now writing in his notebook. It was a good thing that she would be leaving soon. As things stood, she could very easily allow herself to fall in love with Brad, and that realization had jolted her into devoting more time and energy into getting her finances back in order as fast as possible. The sooner she left, the better. She would miss him when she left Sterling again, but that would be all. She hoped.

The kids had apparently decided their break was over and were heading back to their work. Natalie was impressed, noting that maybe she should offer more unexpected breaks to keep the morale up.

"Natalie?" One of the girls who had been coating the newspaper with tea stood on the front porch, holding the cordless phone. "The telephone's for you," she said.

Natalie went to retrieve the phone, wondering who was calling. Marla was up in the attic, sorting through her treasures, and since she had moved back to Sterling, Natalie rarely got phone calls from her friends who lived outside of Sterling.

"Thanks, Regina," Natalie said, taking the phone. "Hello?" she asked.

"Natalie, it's Kimbra."

"Hey, Kimbra." Natalie took a seat on the porch swing. "This must be important. I haven't heard from you in ages. How's Chicago?"

"It's very important, long-distance calls are expensive, and Chicago is great," Kimbra said, answering all of Natalie's questions at once. "Anyway, I'm not made of money, so I have to be quick. I talked to Kelly last night, and she thought I should call and let you know about this." Kimbra paused and Natalie waited for her to continue. Brad got up from the table and walked toward her on the porch.

"You know the play I'm in, *The Case for Clark Chester*."

"Ummm-hmmm. Kelly told me it's getting a lot of attention. Do you like it?"

"I love it. It's not the biggest company, but this play is extremely well written, so the critics love it."

"I'm so happy for you," Natalie admitted. "I hope to get up to Chicago soon, and if it's still running, I'd like to see it."

"You might do better that." Kimbra laughed. "One of the girls in the play is pregnant, and her husband wants her to quit at the end of January. They're having auditions right before Christmas, and I wanted to give you a heads-up to come and try out."

Natalie was flattered. This could turn out to be the break she needed. "Seriously? Is Kelly going to audition?" Brad walked up the porch steps and sat down next to her.

"I asked her if she wanted to, but she thinks she's landed a new role at a dinner theater back in KC. But when I told her about the part, she and I agreed you'd be perfect for this one."

"Thanks," Natalie said.

"And I told the director that I knew someone who could handle the role. It's not a guarantee, but . . . there's a good chance it could pan out."

"Wow," Natalie said. "It sounds great."

"So will you come audition?"

"I don't know. I was planning on coming for good later in the spring, and I don't have the time or money to go early and look for an apartment or anything."

"I think I can help there. I need a roommate because my bills are getting a little stiff. We could go fifty-fifty, and that would make things easier for both of us."

Natalie thought for a moment. "I'd like to think about this and get back to you."

"Okay, but let me know so I can talk to the director again."

"Yeah, I will. Maybe I can call you back and get a little more information about the part."

"I'll put a script in the mail for you, and it should be there the Monday after Thanksgiving at the latest. I know you'll love it."

"Sounds good. I'll get back to you as soon as I read through it."

"Okay, I'll be waiting to hear from you," Kimbra told her.

Natalie hung up the phone and looked at Brad. He had a re-signed look on his face, and Natalie wondered once again how deeply he cared for her. "You got offered a job in Kansas City?" he asked.

"Not exactly," she admitted, shaking her head. "I have a chance to audition for a part in Chicago."

"When?"

"Middle of December, about three weeks from now."

"So when do you leave?"

"I haven't decided if I will yet. I don't really want to leave here until I'm ready to go for good. I might pass up this chance and start auditioning when I'm ready to move."

"But what if you do decide to go and you get the part? I thought you wanted to stay here until your finances were all in order."

She shrugged. "If I get the part, I'll have a paying job. If that's not enough, I'll get a part-time job. I've done it before, and lots of people other than me have, too. Plus, my friend has offered to share her apartment with me, and we'll split everything fifty-fifty, which will be a lot easier."

"Oh." He stood and opened the front door.

Natalie stood and laid her hand on his arm. "You don't think I should go?"

"It's not my job to tell you what to do, and if I tried, you'd be upset with me anyway. Why are you asking?"

"I don't know . . . I just want your opinion."

"Why?" He looked her directly in her eyes, and his gaze didn't waver.

Because I want to know if you care about me even a little, her heart wanted to say. She sighed. "I just . . . I really respect your opinion, that's all." There was no way she was going to say what she really wanted to say. Even if he did care, a little, what would be the point? He was rooted in Sterling, and she hated to bring more than one bag with her when she visited. They would never be happy together because no matter where they lived, one of them would always feel misplaced.

Brad glanced inside the door, then back at Natalie. "I'd have to get back to you on that one."

"When?" she asked, feeling bold.

"When it's time. Is that okay?"

"Of course." Brad didn't go inside but remained where he was. Confused, Natalie asked, "I thought you were going inside."

He looked down at his arm, where she had placed her hand. "As soon as you let go of my arm . . ." He grinned.

Embarrassed, Natalie snatched her hand away. What had she been thinking, demanding that Brad give her his opinion? He probably assumed she was flirting with him. No wonder he hadn't answered.

Natalie let Brad walk ahead of her, but once they were inside, she fled upstairs to her room. In addition to having a lot to think about, she had a sudden headache, and she couldn't take another minute of listening to the hammering that had already resumed.

"Hold the frame still, please," Brad told André, one of the students who had been working on the den/sharecropper's cabin. The room was nearly completed, and he was proud of his class for accomplishing so much so soon. The way things were going, Marla might get this place open a great deal earlier than her target date.

One last part of this room's makeover was attaching the old screen door to the doorframe of the den. One of the students had actually found the old screen door in his grandparents' cellar and had donated it to the museum.

This was another reason Brad was so happy to be involved with this job. So much of African-American history was sitting around in people's houses, not being used and being forgotten. When people heard that Marla was going ahead with her museum idea, people started hunting around their own homes and bringing in items they thought might be useful. In addition to Marla's extensive collection, they also had old dishes, furniture, books, quilts, farming and household tools, and many handmade items.

Some of the more significant pieces neighbors had contributed were an overseer's whip and over-the-shoulder bags that were used to hold the cotton slaves had picked.

The evening Marla had called him to tell him about them, he had rushed over, just to get a look. Touching them in awe, he felt nearly ready to cry.

Those items were foreign to his own life, but they had been a reality back when his great-great-grandparents lived. When he brought his students over, he sensed they felt the same sense of gravity and gratitude.

Although nearly everyone in town knew he was a Christian, Brad had never used his status as a teacher to preach in the classroom. His students knew his views and his standards, and if one had questions, he was happy to talk with them, but only if someone specifically asked. However, as he stood in Marla's living room, holding a whip in one hand and a cotton bag in the other, he hadn't bitten his tongue or held back how he really felt. "It is by the grace of God and only God that most of you have never even seen these things," he had said. "Sometimes it feels like we never seem to have *everything* we want in life, and I know it can be frustrating. But I'm not kidding when

I say that we should be thanking the Lord every day that our lives are not dictated by whips and cotton crops anymore."

As soon as the words left his mouth, he'd wondered if one of the students would complain to the principal or the school board, but he had spoken those words nearly a month ago, and so far he hadn't heard any negative feedback.

What he *had* seen was a new intensity from the kids in their level of participation, both in the classroom and here at Marla's house. Many of them even stopped by on weekends and on days when Brad hadn't required them to put in time. They did whatever odd jobs Brad had for them, and when he wasn't there, they helped Marla and Natalie.

For some of them, it was the first time they had even been able to touch their history and see it all laid out before them in a tangible and recognizable form. And because they had hands-on experience at the museum, what they read in their textbooks became more alive to them.

Brad's heart swelled with pride for his students when he saw how much they had grown over the past few months.

"Mr. Owens?" asked André.

"Yeah?" Brad said, trying to make sure the doorframe was screwed in securely.

"Some of us were wondering about something."

Brad got down on his knees to check the last hinge. "You can let go now, André. I think it's on there pretty well." André stepped back while Brad swung the door open and shut a couple of times. When he was satisfied the door was in working order, Brad stood up and stood back to admire the entire effect of the room. Looking over at André, he asked, "What do you think?"

"Looks good," André answered.

"So what was that question you all had?" Brad asked, stepping inside the room to check the progress of the kids who were attaching the slats to the walls. Brad grinned.

"Well, we wondered who's going to take the people through and give the tours when the museum opens."

Brad rubbed his chin while he thought. "I don't know, I guess Marla will."

"All of the time? What if she needs to go somewhere?"

Brad shrugged. "Don't know. She's in charge of the hours, so she'll do what she thinks is best?" He looked around the room. Several of the students had stopped working and were listening carefully. "Why?" he asked, realizing they probably had cooked up some plans. "Did you all have some suggestions?"

Kyra, another of the students, spoke up. "We thought since we know so much about all of the things that will be on display, we could sometimes do the tours ourselves, maybe on weekends or after school. Lots of us want to help, and we can make out a schedule."

Brad looked around, and took note of several students nodding their heads. He admired their enthusiasm but didn't know how long it would last. "Well, I'd have to talk it over with Marla and Natalie and see what they think. But I'd have to be sure you guys would be committed enough to stick with it. And then what about next year? Would you guys still want to do this, even though you might not be in my class?"

Several nodded, and André spoke up again. "And you could make your classes next year help out as part of their class requirements. That way, the museum could be open a lot without Marla having to run it herself all the time."

"You guys have some good points. I'll check it out; meanwhile, you all start coming up with a schedule you can really stick to. Remember that Sterling is a small town, and even though we might get visitors from nearby towns, the museum doesn't have to be open every day from nine to five, okay?"

"We understand, Mr. Owens," said Kyra. "You want us to help Marla, but only if we're going to stick with it, so our schedule should be pretty honest."

"Right," Brad agreed. "And it looks like we can close up shop for the day. Why don't we clean up what we can, and we'll get back to work after the holiday?"

The students quickly straightened up their messes and headed home for the holiday weekend. Just before Brad left, Marla came downstairs to check the progress of the room.

"This is excellent, Brad. This looks like the real thing," she told him, her hands clasped together. "I can't believe this used to be a plain old den."

"It's a pretty big transformation," Brad agreed. "I've gotta get home and get some rest before tomorrow. I promised my mom I would help her clean her greens for Thanksgiving dinner."

"Then I guess we'll see you Thursday at your mom's," Marla said. Because Brad's older brothers wouldn't be able to get back to Sterling until Christmas, his mother had invited Marla and Natalie, along with Eric and Janet and their kids, to have Thanksgiving dinner.

"I think we'll have a good time. I know I'm looking forward to your apple shortcake."

Marla shook her head. "Natalie's making the cobbler this year. I'm just going to do the rolls."

Brad looked around. "Where is Natalie?"

"Upstairs with a headache," Marla sighed. "And trying to decide if she wants to audition for this play."

"I heard," Brad said, surprised at how flat his voice sounded. "Will you miss her if she goes?"

Brad chuckled. "Miss Marla, why are you asking me? If Natalie wants to know if I'll miss her, she can ask me."

"She said you wouldn't give her your opinion about whether she should go now or later."

Brad couldn't be upset with Marla for trying to get information from him, but he didn't want her to take on the role of go-between for him and Natalie. "Let me ask you something, Marla. Will *you* miss Natalie if she leaves?"

"Of course."

"But does it really make any difference to get all up in arms about the situation. She's already planning to leave in the spring anyway. So she leaves earlier. What difference does it make?" Marla didn't answer, so he gathered up his things and headed toward the front door. "See you Thursday," he called over his shoulder.

"So is that your opinion? You'd rather she leave sooner instead of later?" Marla called after him.

Laughing softly, Brad turned to answer her. "I told Natalie I would give her my opinion when the right time comes. I don't think now is that time." He gave Marla a little wave and headed out to his car.

Natalie silently closed the door to her room and returned to lie on her bed. She hadn't meant to listen to Marla and Brad talking, but she had been on her way downstairs to get some tea and had heard her name. She had figured Brad had gone along with the kids when they left earlier, and she was surprised to find he was still downstairs.

Natalie cringed, realizing Brad probably thought she had sent Marla down to pepper him with questions. Of course, she hadn't, but sometimes Marla just had to try and help things. So far, Marla hadn't accomplished anything, except Natalie had heard with own ears Brad pretty much admit that she was going to leave no matter what, so there was no reason to "get up in arms about it."

She leaned back on her pillows, noting that her headache was getting worse. This was getting too confusing.

For all of her efforts to stay emotionally aloof from Brad, he seemed to mean more and more to her. Not only did she care about his opinion, she was upset when he refused to tell her his thoughts.

Natalie turned on her side, blinking rapidly to hold back a wave of threatening tears.

Her initial guess had been correct. Brad didn't care for her as much as she cared for him. After carefully guarding her emotions for years, she had allowed herself to fall in love with someone who didn't love her back. Natalie inhaled deeply in an effort not to cry. There was no reason to upset Marla. She would be upset enough when Natalie left to go to the audition in Chicago.

Nine

*T*he night before Thanksgiving, Brad spent the night at his mother's house, helping her get the house ready for the holiday. He hadn't lived at home for several years, and it felt strange to sleep in his old room once again. He partially felt as if he was a little kid again, but the fact that his brothers weren't there with him made him feel empty, and even a little lonely.

The next morning, Janet and Eric arrived a little after ten o'clock. Brad greeted them at the front door, and while Janet got little Eric Jr. and Olivia unbundled from their coats and blankets, he and Eric Sr. unloaded items from the car.

"What all's in here?" he asked Janet.

She nodded. "Your mom wanted to make some of the dishes this morning, so she asked us girls to come over and help this morning."

"Who are 'us' girls?" Brad asked.

"Me, Natalie, and Marla."

"So they're coming early, too?" Brad glanced out the window.

"They should be."

Brad's mother came out of the kitchen. "Janet, you're just in time."

"How are you this morning, Rhetta?" Janet asked, hugging Mrs. Owens.

"Just fine. I talked to Marla ten minutes ago, and she and Natalie will be here shortly. I guess we can go in the kitchen and get started." Brad's mother turned and disappeared back into the kitchen.

Janet glanced over at Brad and Eric. "All right, you two. That means you are in charge of Eric and Olivia. Can you handle it?"

Eric put his arms around Janet. "Honey, of course we can. You don't have to worry about us. The kids'll be fine, so you can just enjoy your day off."

Janet rolled her eyes playfully. "Are you kidding me? I'm going to be in the kitchen all day, either cooking or washing dishes. You call that a day off?" She kissed Eric and said, "Don't worry. One of these days I'm really going to take a day off, and then you *can* watch the kids *and* cook *and* run errands, *and* do everything else I normally do."

Janet went to the kitchen, leaving Eric and Brad with the kids. "I'll do my best, but I don't change diapers," Brad told Eric.

Eric grinned. "Don't worry, I'll teach you."

"So what do we do?"

Eric handed Eric Jr. a duffle bag. "Play with your toys, buddy," he told him. Then he glanced over at Olivia, who was asleep in her carrier. "We watch TV until one of them starts crying," Eric told Brad, grabbing the remote and turning on the television.

"And when they cry?" Brad asked, leaning back on the couch.

"We check their diapers, feed them, and play with them."

"Simple enough," Brad said.

Eric shrugged. "It can be more challenging, but, really, I love being a dad."

Moments later, Natalie and Marla arrived, and they hurried to the kitchen. Natalie quietly said hello but wouldn't meet his eyes. Brad returned his attention to the television, hoping Eric wouldn't notice the coolness between him and Natalie. Although Brad had called and left a message for Natalie yesterday, he hadn't seen or talked to her since their discussion about the audition in Chicago.

The more he thought about the conversation, the more frustrated he became. For the past few months, he had been watching Natalie reintegrate herself into the town and had deluded himself into thinking that she was learning to love the place. He had envisioned her telling him that she didn't want to leave again. He had hoped that she cared for him more than she cared for just a friend, but she had proven him wrong. The minute a hint of a job in another city presented itself, she was ready to go running off, chasing after fame and fortune, leaving the people who really loved her behind, like Marla . . . and himself.

Of course, she had tried to hide her own excitement about the job, but he had seen the joy that filled her eyes when she was on the phone. If she hadn't looked so happy, he would have asked then and there that she not go. It might not have been very good for his pride, but he had been willing. But he could tell she had already made her decision, which was why he'd been so aggravated when she'd actually asked his opinion. If he had thought there was a chance that she really hadn't made a decision, he would have asked her to stay, but it made no sense when he could tell that her mind was already made up.

Her only decision was whether she should go right away or later. Staying in Sterling was not even an option to her, and Brad wasn't going to lay his heart out on a platter for her to laugh and say, "But you've known this entire time that I was going to leave. I'm sorry, but it's not practical. We should just forget each other and get on with our lives."

The sound of Olivia crying made Brad forget his own troubles for a minutes. Eric quickly picked her up and determined that she needed her diaper changed.

Eric Jr. suddenly decided that his toys weren't fun anymore. He grabbed hold of his dad's arm while Eric was trying to change Olivia's diaper. Eric gently hugged his son, then said, "I'll play with you in just a minute, buddy. Why don't you ask Brad to read you a story?" He pointed the boy in Brad's direction, and in a matter of moments, Eric Jr. was climbing up on the couch next to Brad with a picture book in his hands.

"Stowy," Eric commanded, holding out the book.

Brad took the book and began reading aloud, but Eric, disgruntled that he didn't have an optimal view of the pictures, clambered onto Brad's lap. After listening to the story three times in a row, the boy fell asleep.

"What should I do now?" Brad whispered to Eric.

Eric searched the diaper bag and pulled out a blanket. "We'll put him down on the floor for right now. But we'll have to wake him up pretty soon, or else Janet will be upset that he'll stay up all night."

Olivia had also fallen asleep, so after the two kids were put down for their naps, Eric sat on the couch next to Brad. "I can turn back to the game," Brad offered.

"Good idea. And on the commercials, we can talk about you and Natalie."

Brad wanted to groan. What did Eric know about him and Natalie? "What are you talking about?"

Eric pointed to the television and shook his head. "I said, we'll talk on the commercials."

Brad turned his attention to the TV but couldn't concentrate on the game. As soon as the commercial break came, he turned back to Eric. "Okay, what's up? Why did you mention Natalie? Did Janet tell you something?"

"What is this, an inquisition?" Eric laughed.

"You're the one who brought it up," Brad countered. "What's with the subject of me and Natalie?"

"Nothing, really," Eric said, looking puzzled. "I just wondered why she wouldn't even look at you when she came in. You guys have a fight or something?"

Brad didn't answer right away. He didn't know if he wanted to give Eric the details of how he was feeling. They had been friends for a long time, but this was pretty personal. He took a deep breath and decided not to get unnecessarily lengthy with his answer. "I guess so. The bottom line is, she still wants to leave Sterling, and I didn't really want to believe it until a couple of days ago."

"So? What does that mean to you?"

"What does what mean?"

"Her wanting to leave. Natalie has always said she could never live here. She needs to be in a bigger city where she can get theater work."

"Yeah, I know."

"So why are you so worked up about it?"

"Because I don't want her to go."

"So tell her," Eric suggested.

"I can't. She wouldn't change her mind anyway. She'd think I was trying to run her life."

"So take a chance and see what she says. The worst she can say is no."

"I don't need to take a chance," Brad's voice rose slightly.

Eric glanced at Eric Jr. and Olivia. "Okay. Do whatever you want, just don't wake up my kids."

"Sorry," Brad said.

The football game came back on, and they watched in silence for the next several minutes. Janet came in to check on the kids and was pleasantly surprised to find them both napping. "Now I see why you guys aren't yelling and shouting at the TV. We were starting to wonder if something was wrong," she teased.

"We're letting them sleep for as long as we can," Eric told her.

"But not too long," she warned. "Otherwise, you can stay up when they won't go to sleep tonight."

"I'll wake them up in a half hour," promised Eric.

"Good," she said before departing to rejoin the group in the kitchen.

"Have you ever considered moving away from Sterling?" Eric asked on the next commercial break.

"No. I don't want to."

"Why not?"

"Because. I don't need a reason. This is my home," Brad said, feeling defensive.

"Then you can't get mad at Natalie. She has a right to live where she feels at home, just like you."

"Yeah. I never said she didn't. I just figured that if I meant anything to her, she might reconsider."

"Does she mean anything to you?"

"Well, yeah."

"So why don't you reconsider?"

"Me? I don't think so."

"Why not? You want her to do the same thing," Eric challenged.

"It's different. I'm already settled here. I have a job, and students, and a home, and my church. She doesn't have any of those things. It would be easier and more practical for her to stay here."

"Because you're the man, right? She should do everything you suggest," was Eric's casual reply.

Brad leaned back, silent. Eric had laid a trap, and he had fallen right in. Did he sound bossy and archaic? Was that how Natalie saw him? "Never mind, you're on her side," Brad grumbled.

"Who said I am?"

"You didn't have to say it." Brad felt angry. It seemed as if his own friend was betraying him.

"Look, Brad, we can drop this subject now. I'm just saying you should think about it. You have a good job, but schools are always looking for good teachers. You can get a job anywhere. You want to pretend it would be so simple for her to stay here, but when you think about doing the same thing yourself, it's out of the question. If you're going to suggest it, you need to be willing to do the same thing yourself. You'd have to love her that much, or your relationship would never be strong enough."

"Thanks for the advice, Eric. I assume your marriage must be perfect."

Eric gave him a surprised look. "What's wrong with you today? I don't think you've ever been so hard to get along with. I have a good marriage, and I don't appreciate your saying that I don't. All marriages have ups and downs, but don't even go there with me."

Brad closed his eyes and ran his hands over his head. He had totally lost his temper, and the bad part was, he knew Eric had a point.

"Listen, Eric, don't be mad at me. I'm sorry. You brought up some good points, and you were right. I want her to be willing to do something I can't imagine doing. I'll think about it, but let's change the subject before things get worse. We're supposed to be having a good time."

"Good idea. Now be quiet, the game's back on." Eric grinned.

Natalie stared at the pile of potatoes she was supposed to be peeling. Normally she loved to cook, but today her heart was definitely not into the activity.

"Ahem." Janet looked over her shoulder. "I speak for myself and probably everyone else when I say that most people like their mashed potatoes cooked. So, if that's going to happen, you need to finish peeling so we can get them on the stove."

"I know, I know, my mind is just in a million other places right now," Natalie answered, getting back to work.

"Like in the living room with Brad?" Janet grinned. "You still not speaking to him because of this audition thing?"

"Pretty much. I wouldn't know what to say anyway. If I'm misreading signals, then I'll feel like an absolute clown when he says he's only interested in me as a friend."

"You want me to talk to him? Or maybe Eric can," Janet suggested.

Natalie whirled around to face her friend. "No, don't do that." Lowering her voice, she added, "He already thinks I asked Marla to talk to him." Natalie made sure Marla and Rhetta were busy at the other end of the kitchen. "Janet, please promise me, you're not going to get into this. I think I'm old enough to solve my own problems."

Janet hesitated for a moment. "Are you sure? Maybe it's a misunderstanding."

Natalie shook her head. "I totally know where he's coming from. I don't need anyone to ask questions for me. I want to leave well enough alone, so don't make things more difficult."

Glancing again toward the other end of the kitchen, Natalie added, "And please don't talk about this with anyone, okay? It's my personal business and I don't want it spread all over Sterling by tomorrow afternoon."

Janet sighed deeply. "Okay, it's up to you, and I'll do like you asked me to do. I won't discuss you and Brad with anyone."

Brad and Eric were busy playing with the kids when Rhetta peeked into the family room to inform them dinner was ready. "Bring the kids to the dining room so Janet can get them in their highchairs," she instructed. "Then you two wash your hands so we can have dinner."

Just before they entered the dining room, Brad pulled Eric back for a moment. "Hey, I know we put this to rest earlier, but I don't want you getting any bright ideas to help me out."

"What?" Eric asked, switching Olivia from one arm to the other.

"Don't discuss me and Natalie with anyone else. It's my business, and I can handle it. She already sent her aunt to ask me a bunch of questions, and it didn't help matters."

"Are you upset with Marla?"

Brad shook his head. "Marla's a good friend, and she wants to help, but if this is going to get worked out, it'll have to be me and Natalie doing the working, okay?"

"Got it. I won't mention our conversation to anyone," Eric said.

The rest of the day passed in a blur for Natalie. Brad was exceedingly polite to her, but their closeness had evaporated. The following Monday, the script from Kimbra arrived in the mail. Natalie read through it after work and decided that it was a project she'd be interested in trying.

The part of Laurel, the new college graduate unhappy with her career, was a good fit for Natalie. The character was facing some of the same ups and downs in her life as was Natalie. The major difference between Natalie and Laurel was that Laurel was married, but that small difference wouldn't hinder Natalie from playing the role. She was an actress, and her job was to act.

Natalie picked up the phone and called Kimbra to let her know that she was planning to come and audition. Kimbra was thrilled and immediately began planning for Natalie's stay.

After she hung up the phone, Natalie sat in her room, listening to the students working downstairs. She had excused herself from the project today, but she was starting to feel guilty, remembering how Brad had once questioned if she would stick with the job until it was finished.

"It looks like he knew me better than I did," Natalie said to herself as she left her room to go downstairs.

Brad was in the living room, guiding the students through

building display cases. "Hey, how are you today?" he asked when he saw Natalie.

She nodded. "Good. And you?"

"Great."

"Have you seen Marla lately," she asked him.

"Actually, she just left to go to her sewing circle meeting."

"Oh." Natalie looked around the room, wondering if she should offer to help or just go back upstairs.

"We're about to finish up here, so do you want to go and get something to eat afterward?"

Natalie couldn't decide how to answer him. She wanted to spend time with him, but she also realized that every minute she did spend with him would make it harder to leave for good when the time came.

"Listen," he said, his voice quiet. "I'm sorry about the other day. I think we're both still upset, and we owe it to ourselves at least to talk about it."

His sincerity put her at ease. And he was right; they did need to talk. "Okay. About how long before you're ready? I need to get some things done," she explained.

He looked around him. "No more than a half hour. Is that okay?"

"Perfect," she said, checking her watch. "I'll see you in thirty minutes."

Natalie took the opportunity to call around and check prices for an inexpensive flight to Chicago. By the time she got off the phone, she had reserved a reasonably priced seat leaving from KCI on December 16.

That left her with twenty-something days to devote to the museum project, so Brad couldn't truthfully accuse her of dropping the ball. She didn't know if she would get the part, but if she did, she wanted to be ready to take it and move to Chicago as soon as she could to start rehearsals.

She slipped into a sweater because the T-shirt she was wearing wasn't warm enough, then went downstairs to see if Brad was ready to go.

Ten

When she reached the top of the stairs, she saw Brad sitting in a rocking chair in the front hallway.

"You're just in time," he said.

"Nice chair," she said, admiring the elaborate detail that had been carved into the wood.

"Thanks, my great-grandpa made it, and my mom decided to donate it to the museum."

"Wow," said Natalie. "Is she sure she wants to do that? It's beautiful."

"You know Rhetta. She made up her mind, and I'm not going to argue with her," Brad said, standing. "You ready?"

"Definitely. Where do you want to go?"

Brad opened the front door for her and led the way to his car. "I don't care. What do you prefer?"

"Peace and quiet," she admitted. "Nothing fancy."

"We could get burgers and do the takeout thing. Maybe go over to the park and eat."

"Sounds good," Natalie answered, stepping into the car.

They picked up sandwiches from a fast-food place and drove to the park, where they sat across from each other at a small picnic table.

They talked about the museum for a few minutes, and Brad informed her that several of the students wanted to work there after it was opened. Natalie couldn't muster up much enthusiasm for the museum right then, but she could honestly say that she was pleased that Marla would have some help. After the museum topic was exhausted, they ate in silence until Brad finally broached the subject they both wanted to discuss.

"You know, I might have overreacted a little the other day," he admitted.

Natalie's heart sank at those words. She'd spent the whole weekend thinking he hadn't reacted enough. She wouldn't exactly call his way of "not getting up in arms about things" overreacting. She cleared her throat, aware that he was waiting for a response from her. She chose her words carefully, not wanting to tell him that she didn't think his actions were too extreme. If she told him that much, he might guess how she had wished he'd reacted, and she wasn't sure she wanted him to know her deepest feelings. At least, right now she didn't.

"Well, I guess I maybe overreacted a little, too," she said, trying not to let her face betray how she really felt. "I guess . . ." she trailed off, trying to think of something more to say.

"You thought I was trying to tell you how to run your life," Brad answered for her.

Natalie nodded, unable to say more. She would have loved

for him to ask her to stay, and she wouldn't have felt he was intruding on her life or trying to be overbearing.

"Well, I'm sorry," he told her. "I'm trying to be more sensitive. I just thought maybe you would have changed your mind about leaving. You were starting to look like you enjoyed it here."

Natalie's ears perked up. "I am enjoying myself here," she admitted without even giving her words a second thought.

Brad's eyes widened. "You are?"

Natalie nodded, swallowing deeply. Had she and Brad had a misunderstanding, just like Janet had suggested?

"But I thought . . . I thought you couldn't wait to get away from here. And when the audition came up, well, you looked like you were mentally packing your bags and leaving us all behind."

"Who are us?" Natalie asked, her heart growing softer with each passing moment.

Brad exhaled and seemed to look at a spot somewhere over her head. She reached across the table and touched his hand. "You can look at me instead of behind me, you know."

Brad grinned, and their gazes met.

"You were going to tell me who all was going to miss me," she reminded him.

"Well, lots of us," he began. "Probably everyone you know will miss you in some way or another."

"Humor me and give me some specifics." She smiled.

"Marla, Janet, Eric, my mom, the kids who've been helping with the museum," he said.

Natalie lifted her eyebrows slightly. He must think this was pretty funny, making her pull answers out of him. "Anybody else?"

Brad laughed and stood up. He gathered up the wrappers from their meal and took them to a garbage bin several feet away. When he returned, he sat next to her.

"You know," he said quietly, "I think Eric Jr. and Olivia might miss you, too."

"Really?" Natalie inquired, amused. "What makes you think so?"

He shrugged his shoulders. "I can't say for sure. I just had a feeling."

"Oh, I see," Natalie said in mock seriousness. "They can be pretty tight-lipped, those two. I guess we won't know how they feel for sure unless I actually leave."

"Yeah, you're right." Brad laughed. He suddenly grew sober, and said, "But they may make it pretty hard for you. You know how they are once they make up their minds about something." He shook his head and looked off into the distance, apparently thinking about something.

"I'm not sure I understand," Natalie told him. "How do they get when they make up their minds about something?"

He looked at her almost condescendingly, but she could tell by the grin threatening the corners of his mouth that he was kidding with her. "Oh, you know, the usual. Crying, whimpering, etcetera." He sighed. "They might even go for the ear-limb attack."

"The what?" Natalie was incredulous.

"The ear-limb attack. I've seen it work on many adults. It's a great immobilizer."

"Explain how it works so I can be prepared," she said dryly.

"It's pretty simple, actually. Eric will probably wrap his arms around your leg, throwing twenty-five pounds of dead weight onto your frame, making it incredibly hard for you to walk, let alone catch a plane. Meanwhile, Olivia will be screaming at the top of her lungs, making you want to sit down and cover your ears."

Natalie burst out laughing. "Oh, stop it." She looked sideways at him. "I can't believe you even managed to keep a straight face through all of that. Shame on you, talking about babies like that."

They both started laughing again, and Natalie felt even more tension melt away. Leave it to Brad to come up with something so utterly silly and hilarious at a time when a comic interlude was so necessary.

Natalie swallowed the last of her giggles and said, "Even so, I don't think the ear-limb attack could keep me from leaving if I really wanted to."

"Do you really want to?" Brad turned to face her, completely serious now.

Natalie looked away, just over his shoulder, not sure how she should answer. Brad's fingers softly brushed her cheek, turning her face back to him. "Do you?"

Natalie looked in his eyes for some sign that he wanted her to stay. She saw something there, a glimmer of sadness, and she realized he might not be so nonchalant about her leaving after all. Throwing caution to the wind, she asked, "Do you want me to? Would you miss me, too?"

She watched Brad swallow several times, his Adam's apple bobbing up and down. "Yes," he whispered.

As a wave of relief blanketed Natalie, her eyes filled with tears. He did care about her, at least she knew that much. "I would miss you, too," she told him, her voice breaking.

Brad pulled her into his arms, and she felt the steady thump of his heart beating as she softly cried tears of relief. Brad ran his hands over her hair and patted her back, trying to comfort her.

When she finally stopped crying, another concern made its presence known in her mind. Now that they had both admitted deeper feelings for each other, had their relationship hit a turning point?

The ticket, her conscience reminded her. *Are you going to tell him about the plane ticket?* Natalie tried to ignore the thought. True, she had purchased a ticket. But she hadn't used it yet, and the ticket wasn't of any use for two and a half weeks.

She reluctantly pulled away from him and wiped her eyes. "Sorry about that," she apologized. "I just got . . ." she shrugged, unable to put her emotions into words.

"Don't worry about it," he told her, and she noticed his own eyes were damp. "So now what?" he asked her.

"I don't know," she admitted. "I never expected this to happen."

"I can't say I didn't expect it, but I didn't think my hopes would ever materialize," he said. "So I guess before we go any further, I need to know how you feel. I care about you so much, and I don't want you to leave. How do you feel about me?"

"The same way," she said nodding. "Except, in my case, I don't really want to leave and be away from you."

"So then it's settled. We both agree that you shouldn't leave."

Natalie looked away. Something inside of her didn't want to admit that she owned that ticket. And worse yet, she didn't like the fact that he had seemingly just settled things for her, deciding that she wouldn't go. Did he not see a need for the two of them to talk out all of the pros and cons, then decide what was best for her and for them?

If she didn't leave, *she* would be the one walking away from a future, not him.

Brad had a concerned look on his face. "Am I right?"

Natalie felt pinpricks of pain pulsing through her heart as she looked him in the eye. "I don't know, Brad. I'm sorry."

He back away from her, looking shocked and hurt. "Why? I thought you said you cared."

"I do, but I have to be positive about what I should do."

"But why would you leave now? You just said you didn't want us to be apart."

"I know." She nodded. "But I can't just throw my whole future away. People fall in love all of the time, and sometimes they look up later and realize they don't love each other anymore."

Brad shook his head. "Yeah, that happens, but what does that have to do with us?"

Natalie opened and closed her mouth, trying to find the right words. "What if I decided to stay here, and maybe six months from now, we decide that we don't care about each other like we thought we did? Then what happens?"

"It wouldn't happen," Brad said, sounding urgent. "It won't."

"But hypothetically, what if it did?"

He looked bewildered. "I don't know. We'd forgive each other and move on with our lives."

"That's my point. Except I would have the hardest time of it. You have a life here and a job here. I don't, not really. I'd be stuck here, trying to make a living doing something I hate, like being a secretary, and everyone would feel sorry for me. I would hate myself for not having taken this chance for the job in Chicago."

"But you've said yourself there are always lots of acting jobs," he protested.

"Yeah, but in case you haven't noticed, I haven't landed any. This is what I went to school for, what I've been waiting for. I don't want to throw it all away for something that might not ever pan out."

His laugh was humorless. "That's how you see this? Some kind of business deal, like playing the stock market?"

"Why not?" she retorted. "Aren't relationships based on taking chances, from the first time you meet someone and ask them their name, right down to when people march down the aisle?"

"Sure, you take chances, but the Lord has a say in things, too. At least, He should."

Natalie nodded in agreement. She had prayed about her feelings for Brad, but she hadn't really gotten an answer yet. "You're right. But consider this. If I stayed here, I would be building a whole new life. You, on the other hand, would just be continuing your everyday habits and patterns. And if we were wrong, then I would suffer the most."

Brad held up a hand. "Can we please stop discussing a situation I hope we never face?"

"Okay," Natalie said, looking down at her hands.

Several moments passed in silence, until Brad reached for her hand again. She looked up at him, and neither one of them said anything for a long time.

Brad cleared his throat. "So you're going to go." His remark was more of a statement than question.

"I think I should at least give myself that chance," she said softly. "You're still not the one being asked to walk away from your dreams."

He winced, and Natalie felt a twinge of remorse. Even so, between the two of them, someone needed to be honest. "Look, I'm sorry, I shouldn't have said that," she said gently.

He shook his head. "No, you're right. I know that. I just

thought if we loved each other, it wouldn't be a big deal. But maybe we don't love each other."

Natalie's heart jumped into her throat. This was the first time either of them had spoken the word *love*. Was he saying that he could possibly be in love with her?

She swallowed before she spoke, trying to hold back tears. "Or maybe we just haven't given ourselves enough time to find out how much we care . . . find out if we love each other. Maybe we do."

"Look, Natalie," he said, taking her other hand. "Let's not rush ourselves. It's almost Christmas, and I had hoped we wouldn't have something like this hanging over our heads. When is the audition?"

"The seventeenth."

"So, why don't we both calm down and try not to stress about this. It's ultimately your decision whether or not you should leave, and I won't try to make you do things my way, okay?"

She nodded, feeling better about the whole thing.

"In the meantime, let's not talk about this," he suggested. "Let's spend time together like we normally do and try to enjoy the holiday season."

Natalie hated to bring up another sore point, but she had to make sure Brad wasn't asking her to ignore the situation altogether. "But what if I do decide to go?"

He sighed, looking away for a moment. When he looked back at her, his eyes were filled with heaviness. "We'll take it a step at a time. I'll try to be levelheaded about whatever you decide. If you go to the audition, I'll try to be cool with that. If you get the part, I'll try to be cool with that. If you don't get the part, and you decide to move to Chicago like you originally planned, I'll try to be cool with that."

Natalie smiled, genuinely touched by his efforts. "You will? I'm so proud of you," she admitted.

He laughed softly. "Don't get all excited. I said I would *try* to be cool with it. But I do respect your decision making, and we can both pray about it and see what the Lord wants us to do, okay?"

"All right," she agreed.

The two of them sat on the bench for several more minutes until Natalie grew too cold to keep sitting still. "It's getting pretty chilly out here, don't you think?"

"Yeah, I guess I should get you back home. Marla's probably back from her meeting and wondering where you are."

They headed to the car, and during the ride home, they talked about creating a schedule for the students to work at the museum. When they reached the house, the lights inside were burning brightly. They figured Marla must be home. Brad walked her to the door and promised he would either come over or at least call the next day. His students would be doing less work at the house during the month of December because they had to study for finals, and Brad didn't want to compromise their time.

"I will pray about all of this," Natalie told him, just before she went inside.

"I will, too," he assured her. "I know that if we trust the Lord, He will work all of this out."

He hugged her, then turned and made his way back to his car.

Natalie felt a pang of sadness watching him walk away. For all of her promises to pray, she didn't feel comfortable letting go of her say in a situation so important to the rest of her life. Right now, she was incredibly torn between going away and staying here to be with Brad, and she didn't think she would ever be able to decide on one of the two and be at complete peace with herself.

She closed her eyes and prayed silently. *Lord, I want to do what You think is best for me, but I have a hard time understanding how I could be happy choosing either one of these things over the other. Please help me to understand Your will for me, and give me the courage to do what You want. Amen.*

A peace settled over Natalie, and she went upstairs to get ready for bed with a new sense of confidence that she was on the right track.

Long after he got home that evening, Brad couldn't relax. He tossed and turned, unable to sleep. On one hand, he was relieved that he and Natalie had actually had a discussion about their relationship, but part of him worried that she would still leave and go to Chicago. He had promised to respect the decision she eventually made, but in all honesty, it would be difficult for him to accept her leaving.

His conversation with Eric echoed in his mind. Asking Natalie not to pursue her career choice was asking a lot. Eric and Natalie had told him as much, and he knew they were right. He had struggled with this over the past few days, wondering if he would be willing to leave Sterling and follow Natalie where she went. If was only fair for him to ask himself to do so, but the more he thought about it, the more he knew he couldn't make that decision.

He belonged in Sterling, and he felt as if Natalie belonged there with him. His conscience was calling him a hypocrite, and he was starting to feel incredibly selfish.

The thought of leaving everything he knew to be home was

scary. So scary, in fact, that he wouldn't dare mention the idea to Natalie. If she knew how he felt, she would never make an honest effort to do the same by staying here.

Brad sighed deeply and closed his eyes. *Dear Lord,* he prayed. *Am I being unreasonable? I want Natalie to stay here, but I can't imagine ever doing what I'm asking her to do. I put this whole situation in Your hands and I ask that You would help us both to make the right choice. I would like to think that Natalie is the one You have for me, but if things are going to work out between us, one of us is going to have to give up something important to us. And no matter how much I try to ignore it, I'm not willing to move away from this town. So, if I'm wrong, show me, and if Natalie should stay, please show her as well. Amen.*

Brad lay very still, knowing that he still felt exactly the same, but knowing that if he needed to change, the Lord would show him.

Eleven

Natalie sat at Janet's kitchen table, holding Olivia and looking at Eric's immense collection of crayon and paper artwork, while Janet took a tray of cookies out of the oven. Christmas was a couple of weeks away, and Natalie was feeling the Christmas spirit more than she had in a good many years.

"Oh, that's wonderful," she told Eric as he held up another picture for her approval. "Did you do that all by yourself?"

"Uh-huh." He nodded solemnly.

"Wow," she said, watching him beam with pride.

"Who taught you how to make such nice pictures?"

"Mommy and Daddy!" he said, laughing.

Janet smiled at them from the other end of the kitchen. "Hey, look over there, buddy," Natalie told him. "Your mommy is getting ready to decorate those cookies. You should help her and get those cookies looking as good as your pictures."

While Eric trotted off to help Janet, Natalie bounced Olivia on her knee. Olivia gurgled a happy laugh, her dark eyes sparkling. "How are you today, pretty baby?" Natalie singsonged to the little girl. Olivia cooed even more. "Hey there, precious . . . yes, you are precious. Are you your mommy's sweetheart? Hmm?"

"You're spoiling her." Janet laughed.

"You do the same thing; don't try to deny it," Natalie said, grinning.

For the next hour, they took turns entertaining Eric and Olivia until Janet decided it was time for the kids to take their naps.

After Eric and Olivia were asleep, Janet and Natalie sat down to have tea.

Janet wasted no time getting right to the point. "So have you decided what you're going to do? You have six days until the audition; today's the eleventh."

Natalie nodded. "Yeah, I know, and that means I have five days until I have to decide about my ticket."

"You didn't return the ticket?" Janet asked.

Natalie shook her head. "Not exactly."

Janet took a sip of her tea, looking thoughtful. "And I'm guessing you haven't told Brad about the ticket."

Natalie sighed heavily. "No. But only because he said he didn't want to discuss it."

"Have you prayed about it?" Janet looked her in the eye.

Natalie squirmed uncomfortably. She had prayed about it, but she wasn't sure she was hearing a clear answer. What she *did* know was that with every passing day, she wanted more and more to go to the audition. She couldn't deal with the idea of passing up the chance. "I have prayed, Janet, but I still don't really understand why God should care about my career choice."

"God cares about every aspect of our lives," Janet replied.

"I know, and I don't mind asking Him what He thinks I should do. It's not like I'm trying to do something wrong."

Janet nodded, but didn't say anything.

"And He gave us a free will to make decisions, right?" Natalie pressed further.

"Yes, He did."

"So why does God care about what I do for a living? I mean, do we all have to pray and ask what jobs we should do? Do we have to pray about what we study in college?"

Janet shrugged. "We don't have to, but part of being a Christian is making sure we always stay in God's will. Think about some of the people we study in history, like the ones who made some great scientific discovery. What if they had decided they didn't want to be in science and had chosen a totally different field? Maybe we wouldn't be able to benefit from what they had learned."

"Still, someone else could have come along later and made the discovery."

"You're right, but how many people would have gone without until the next person came along?"

Natalie considered Janet's reasoning. "Okay, you have a point, but I'm not in any scientific field. I'm an actress, and God also gives us creativity and talent. Wouldn't I be wasting my talent if I decided to ignore it?"

Janet nodded. "God doesn't gift us for no reason at all, but it helps to make sure we're using our gifts in the way He wants. Take, for example, someone who was gifted in science and they chose one field, but the Lord had really gifted them to make a discovery in another field. They would still be using their gift, but if their mind was focused on a different part of their gift, they might not realize what the Lord had originally planned for them."

Natalie nodded. Janet was making sense. Maybe she had approached her prayers in the wrong way. She felt sure that God wanted her to use her acting ability, but she hadn't been able to find assurance that her place was in Chicago. She'd had some ideas about ways to incorporate acting into her life here, but since she'd always planned to leave soon, she hadn't discussed the ideas with anyone or even given them much serious consideration.

Janet poured herself another cup of tea and passed a plate of cookies to Natalie. "You know, we're supposed to be having fun. It's Christmas." Patting Natalie's hand, she added, "Don't worry about it, just keep praying, and the Lord will show you what to do."

"I will," Natalie agreed.

Three days before the audition, Natalie sat in Sunday-morning service, still unsure of her decision. True to his word, Brad hadn't asked her what she was going to do, and although she knew he was wondering what she would decide, Natalie didn't want to back herself into a corner. Once she made her decision, she would stick to it, and she didn't feel that she could make a decision. The theme of the sermon was Proverbs 16:9. When the pastor first read the verse, Natalie instantly felt a connection between her own life and this scripture.

" 'In his heart a man plans his course, but the Lord determines his steps.' "

Natalie sat quietly considering her own life. Was this the answer to her prayer? Were her plans in contrast with what God had in mind for her?

Natalie prayed during the entire sermon that she would be able to reach the correct decision, but when she and Brad filed out of the pews, she still felt no closer to having an answer.

That evening, she and Brad sat in the kitchen, sorting through old books and magazines to create a timeline of African-American history for the main display in the living room. Natalie hesitantly decided to speak to Brad about her difficulty in making a decision.

She shared with him all that she had been puzzling over, including her conversation with Janet and the relevance of the morning's service. "I've been praying, but I still haven't felt that one choice is better than the other," she concluded.

He flipped through another magazine, then put it aside. "You know, I wonder if we should display all of the old clothes and accessories in the parlor. With all of the donations, we have such a big assortment that I don't know how to integrate them into the other rooms. Maybe it could be a women's display, and we could do something on black hairstyles, too. What do you think?"

"I think that's a good idea. That way we have more room for the invention display in the living room. And, I also think you should help me out here. I can't decide. I can't tell where the Lord is leading me, but I know without a doubt that I shouldn't ignore my talent."

"I can't help you, Natalie," he said, flipping through another magazine. "This is up to you. Plus, you promised you wouldn't bring it up until you made your choice. A deal's a deal."

"Please," she asked him. "If I don't have some help, I'm going to have to go, just because time is running out and I don't want to lose the money I spent for the ticket."

Brad's head snapped up from the magazine. "You already have a ticket? Since when?"

Natalie bit her lip, feeling both relieved and worried she had admitted to already having the ticket. "Since the day we went to the park and decided we wouldn't talk about it until I made a choice."

"So you agreed to pray about it and then went home to buy a ticket?"

She shook her head vigorously. "No. I bought it before we even left the house."

"Oh. So what was the deal in the park? Was that some kind of an act, since you had apparently decided already?"

"No, no. I mean, yes, I had the ticket, but by the time we finished the discussion that night, I didn't want to cause any more problems by telling you I had the ticket. I didn't want you to think I was hanging it over your head."

He was quiet for a long time. Then he calmly stood and put his coat on. "You're right. I didn't need that hanging over my head. It feels so much better to realize now that you knew what you were going to do all along. Thanks, Natalie, for not bursting my bubble. I really appreciate it." His sarcasm hurt because she knew he was right.

"Brad, I know I was wrong," she said, rising from her seat. "I just didn't know how to fix it."

He shook his head. "No, no, that's not it. The point is, can we be totally honest with each other?" His gaze was intense, and his eyes seemed to look straight through her. "How about it? Let's tell each other exactly what we feel about this once and for all." He took his jacket off and tossed it over the back of a chair. He took his seat once again and gestured for her to do the same. "Natalie, I'm tired of this. I'll be honest with you if you can be honest with me. What do you really feel? How are you leaning in this decision and why?"

Natalie decided not to hold anything back. "I'm torn, that's all. I really enjoy my life here, but I can't ignore this chance. I would always question what might have happened if I had not gone. It's nothing against you personally, because I do care about you."

"Then I think you should go," was his simple answer.

Natalie blinked. "Are you sure? You don't mind?"

"I mind, but I agree with you. I don't want you to waste your talent, either. You should go and not feel guilty about it."

"And what if I get the part?"

He considered for a while. "We'll have to work something out. And don't worry about it. Just go, do your best, and we'll see what happens."

She smiled, relieved. Brad told her he needed to get home and grade some papers before his classes the next day, and Natalie spent the rest of the evening getting clothes together for the trip.

The next few days were spent in preparation for the audition, and Marla and Janet even helped her go over scenes.

The day before her flight, she drove to Kansas City and spent the night at Kelly's apartment, getting very little sleep because her old roommate wanted to catch up on what was new.

Kimbra met her at the airport, thrilled to see her, and they spent the rest of the day sight-seeing and shopping. The day of the audition, Natalie went to the theater early with Kimbra and sat in on a morning rehearsal.

That afternoon, she had her audition with the director, producer, and two of the actors in the show. Afterward, she and Kimbra went back to the apartment to take a breather before they had to return for the evening's performance.

Kimbra gave Natalie a ticket for the show, and Natalie was thoroughly impressed with the entire production. This was the kind of play she'd always hope to work in, and she already got along well with the other cast members she'd met.

When it was time for her flight home, Kimbra told Natalie that she hoped the audition panned out so they could see each other again soon. "Whatever happens, keep in touch, girl-friend," Kimbra told her. "If you don't get this part, I'll be on the lookout for other things, and I'll keep you updated."

"Thanks," Natalie told her, and she promised to call once she heard any news. On the plane to Kansas City, Natalie day-dreamed about getting the part and being up on stage in front of hundreds of people every night. She was born for the stage, and she had known it all her life.

She felt herself nodding off, and she didn't fight her fatigue. Just before she drifted to sleep, she wondered how Marla and her friends in Sterling would react to her excitement. Willing herself not to worry about it, Natalie pushed the thought away and slept soundly.

Brad sat on Marla's front porch, ignoring the cold, watching for Natalie to return. He felt silly just sitting there, but for the past three days since she had left for Chicago, he had done every kind of busy work he could imagine in order to keep his mind occupied. Now that he had run out of projects, sitting and wait-ing seemed the logical thing to do.

As the sky grew darker, he hoped she would arrive soon. The drive from Kansas City to Sterling was relatively quick and easy during daylight, but the roads were harder to navigate when it was dark.

However, when she called to say she had arrived in Kansas City safely and was heading home tonight, he hadn't tried to discourage her because he missed her.

Now, sitting in the old rocker, he forced himself to face the growing sensation of dread that she might actually get the job.

He couldn't deny the fact that she had talent; yet, part of him hoped she wasn't right for this part, or any other part. He wanted her here with him, and even though he knew he was being selfish, he couldn't force himself to change his mind.

And no matter how hard he worked to convince himself, he knew there was no way he could tell Natalie he would follow her if she did get the job. He wanted her to be his wife, but not at that cost. That thought worried him, because he knew she may eventually ask him if he would be willing to come with her. If she had to go, then they would probably have to part for good, and that would hurt them both.

Brad pushed his hands into his pockets, trying to keep them warm. Maybe he was going to end up a bachelor after all. Several months ago, before Natalie had come back, the idea hadn't been too disturbing, but now that their relationship had deepened, he knew that he really desired to be a husband and father. He doubted he would ever love anyone as much as he loved Natalie, and he suspected he was on the verge of losing her.

The glare of car headlights coming down the block pulled him from his mournful thoughts. Natalie pulled her car into the driveway, and Brad was at her side before she could get out of the car. They immediately hugged—a long, silent embrace, full of unspoken joy and fear. He carried her bags inside, where Marla served them coffee and refreshments from her never-ending supply of Christmas cookies.

Natalie filled them in on all the details of her trip and told them that she probably wouldn't know for several days whether or not her audition had gone well enough for her to get the part.

"Well, until then," Marla said, "I want us to enjoy the holiday. We won't worry about whether or not she's leaving. I know we've all prayed about this, and God will let His will be done." Marla affectionately squeezed Natalie's hand and added, "Honey, I'm proud of you no matter what. You know that, don't you?"

Natalie's eyes grew damp, and she nodded vigorously. Wiping her eyes with the back of her hand, she teasingly complained, "Marla, you said we were supposed to enjoy the holiday, and in the very next sentence you make me burst into tears."

At that, Marla started crying as well, and the two women hugged and wept. Not wanting to interrupt such a bittersweet moment, Brad quietly said his good-byes. "I'll let you two catch up tonight, but I'll be over tomorrow after school gets out so Natalie and I can spend some time together."

He let himself out the front door and wearily drove home. At least she was home. That alone made him feel somewhat better. As for the play, there were seven days until Christmas, and he hoped the director would wait until after the holiday to inform them of the decision, whatever it was.

Natalie and Marla stayed up into the early hours of the morning, talking. Natalie knew she hadn't always been as gracious and respectful to Marla as she should have been, and she wanted to make sure her aunt would not have any objections to her leaving to try to get her career started.

Marla accepted Natalie's apology and explained that even though she would miss her, she would never want to prevent someone from doing what the Lord wanted them to do. "As long as you're doing what you're supposed to be doing, honey, I'll never complain. I'll miss you because you're my family, but don't ever feel guilty that I never had a family of my own. As far

as I was concerned, when the time came to raise you, you became my own, because there was no way I was going to let
someone else take you."

When Natalie noticed the distant look in Marla's eyes, she
had the feeling that Marla had not told her the whole story.

"What do you mean?" Natalie asked, touching her aunt's
sleeve. "Did someone else want to adopt me?"

"Child, yes," Marla said emphatically. "When your parents
disappeared, the story was in several papers."

Natalie was surprised. "It was? You never told me that."

"It never seemed like the right time," Marla said. Chuckling,
she added, "Truth was, it was such an ordeal the first time, I
didn't want to think about it anymore. But now, I think you
should know."

Natalie listened intently as Marla explained what had occurred. "When the story came out in the papers, people started
calling, hounding me nonstop. I had announced that I was going to take care of you, and people assumed that raising you
alone would be too difficult for me."

"So, you were my only living relative. Didn't that make a difference?"

"I thought it should, but adoption agencies came saying they
had people who were willing to take you, and individual couples offered to raise you. Most of these people I didn't even
know, and most of them accepted my answer. But there were a
few who threatened to take me to court to prove I was unfit,
that I would be too old to take care of you. They said you
should have the opportunity to live with parents who would be
able to keep up with you better."

Natalie was speechless. She didn't remember much about
what happened after her parents were first considered missing,
but she did know that having Marla with her had been a great

comfort. She would have been terrified to have been taken away from her aunt at such a young age.

"Did I know any of this?" she asked.

Marla shook her head. "I wouldn't let the media near you. I kept you in the house, and I don't think you ever suspected."

"So what happened?"

Marla shook her head. "I prayed and prayed and prayed some more." She chuckled. "I had my friends and people at church praying, and finally those others just gave up. I just knew the Lord wanted me to keep you. I had a feeling He had something special planned for you, and I wanted to bring you up so you would know and obey Him from the very beginning."

"Wow," Natalie breathed. "I'm totally shocked. I can't imagine not growing up here with you. And I'm even more grateful that you fought so hard to keep me here."

"I am, too, honey," Marla said warmly.

The two women were silent for a long while, Natalie reflecting on all she had learned. "You know, it's really terrible, but all these years, I've taken for granted what you did for me, not even knowing what you just told me. When I was little, I used to wish my parents would come back so that we could move to a different city. I hated living in a small town."

"There's nothing wrong with feeling like that," Marla told her.

Natalie nodded. "I know. The strange thing is, knowing how much you went through to keep me here, I wonder if I need to be here. I always felt like there was some big magnet keeping me connected here in some way, and I hated it. When I came back a few months ago, I was so angry."

"I know."

"So why didn't you yell at me? Tell me to get my act together?" Natalie wanted to know.

"I knew that even with your frustration at having your career ambitions come to a standstill, in your heart you still loved the Lord. I *could* have yelled and fussed, but I thought the Lord would be more effective in bringing you closer to His heart."

"I think you're right about that. I knew I was being rude and sharp sometimes, but I always felt so terrible afterward. I kept promising myself I wouldn't do it again."

"See," Marla said. "I told you the Lord would do a much better job than I could."

Natalie laughed. "I don't think I'm a saint yet. I haven't been consistently nice to Brad and Janet, either, but they must have turned me over to the Lord like you did. And I've had to apologize every time. They probably think I'll never change."

"I don't know about that. They seem to have put up with you this long. And right now, you're doing way better than you did when you first got here."

"Aunt Marla?" Natalie said quietly.

"Yes?"

"I'm scared."

"About what?" Marla sounded surprised.

"About everything. I've changed so much, and I don't want to stop making progress. I pray more than I have in a long time, and I feel myself getting closer to the Lord. I worry that if I leave, I might lose that closeness with Him."

"Now, why is that?"

Natalie shrugged. "I guess because you and Brad and my friends from church wouldn't be there with me."

"That's not a good reason, Natalie."

Natalie looked at her aunt, feeling confused.

"All of us here," Marla continued, "are not the ones who determine your relationship with the Lord. It's like your relationship with Janet. Only you and Janet can decide how much you want to put into your friendship. The more you give, the closer you become, and it's the same way with the Lord. He's always ready to get closer to you, but you have to make the decision to spend more time with him, to give more of yourself."

"I just feel like I won't be so faithful about it if I leave. I wasn't very dedicated in going to church and reading my Bible when I didn't have you all around."

"So, if you leave now, you'll have to make better choices. It's good to have people to keep you accountable, but you shouldn't sit around waiting for someone to tell you what you already know you should be doing." Marla smiled and patted Natalie's shoulder.

"The strange thing is, I never really felt like I belonged here all of this time, until recently. And now, even though I want this job, I feel reluctant to leave. I have you here, and I've mended relationships with Janet and Brad and other people."

Marla nodded, but didn't comment.

"I wonder if I should just back out of this audition before I even find out how I did," Natalie mused.

"That's up to you," Marla said. "I won't tell you how to make your decision."

Natalie nodded. "I know you won't. I wonder if Brad will understand if I decide to go. He says he will, but I know that our relationship would be pretty much over if I did. He wants me to stay here."

"I take it from the way you're worrying over this that you care for him quite a bit," Marla said.

"I think I love him," Natalie admitted. "And I think he loves me, too, but we've never actually said we do."

"Well, if you two love each other, you should be able to

come up with something that makes you both happy, don't you think?" Marla yawned, covering her mouth. "I guess I'm up way past my bedtime." She grinned.

Natalie yawned and nodded her head. "Me, too," she agreed. "I guess we should get some sleep. Tomorrow I'll be able to think about this some more."

Marla stood and headed out of the room, still yawning. "Good idea. But don't get all worked up about it. Remember, we're about to celebrate Jesus' birthday, and the focus should be on him."

"I won't," Natalie promised as she followed Marla's example and went to her own room. She tucked herself into her bed and fell asleep immediately, a contrast from the two previous nights she'd spent in Kansas City and Chicago where, even after her girl-talk sessions with Kelly and Kimbra, she'd been unable to enjoy a peaceful rest.

Twelve

*T*he next few days passed rather quietly as Natalie prepared for the holidays. She and Marla attended special Christmas services at church every night, and they spent time with their neighbors at holiday parties.

They planned to spend Christmas Eve at home, and Brad and his mother were invited for dinner. The next day, they would spend the holiday with Janet's family.

Christmas Eve afternoon, Natalie was in the kitchen, concentrating on kneading a batch of rolls for Marla's dinner that night and Janet's dinner the next day, when the phone rang.

Natalie let it ring three times before she realized Marla was making the rounds to several of her friends' homes, taking them sweet potato pies.

Wiping her floured hands on a towel, Natalie answered the phone just before the sixth ring. "Hello?" she said, feeling impatient.

"Could I speak to Natalie Jacobs, please?" a woman's voice on the other end said.

"This is Natalie," she answered, realizing the voice seemed very familiar.

"This is Cam Phillips, the director of the play you auditioned for last week," she announced.

"Oh, yes," Natalie said. "How are you?"

"I'm fine, and I know it's Christmas Eve, but I thought I'd go ahead and tell you now. We decided that we'd like to have you join the cast. How's that for a Christmas present?"

Natalie was too shocked to say anything at first. She'd tried to ignore the possibility that she might get the part, halfway hoping that she wouldn't, and now that she had won the role, she was thrilled. "That's wonderful," she managed to tell Cam.

"Of course, you'll want to know when you start," Cam said.

"Yes," Natalie said. "What's the schedule look like?"

"Well, we'd like to get you in here as soon as possible. Julie, the gal who has the role right now, is quitting at the end of January, so we'd like to get you in rehearsals right after the New Year. You seemed to have a pretty good handle on the script at the audition, but we need to get your blocking set so you don't confuse the rest of the cast."

"That sounds fair enough," Natalie admitted.

"We think so, too. It's sometimes easier to assemble an entire cast than to pluck one actor out of the ensemble and put someone totally new in there. Of course, we're totally thrilled with your audition, and we know you'll do fine," Cam reassured her.

"Well, thanks. I'm flattered, really," Natalie said. "Now I've just got to tell my family," she said, thinking aloud.

"Oh?" Cam said. "Parents, brothers, sisters?" Cam sounded somewhat wary.

"Actually, my great aunt and a few friends, that's all."

"Oh, I see. I was thinking husband or fiancé, which had me worried for a sec. We lost Julie to the demands of her husband, you know. She was willing to keep working for another couple of months, but he insisted."

Natalie nodded, even though Cam couldn't see her. A knot formed in her stomach, and Natalie slowly realized that Cam was probing to see if she wanted to back out.

"You're not engaged, are you?"

"No, not engaged."

"I see. So does it look like you're clear to come and start maybe around the second or third of January?"

"I think so, but is it all right if I get back to you, maybe the day after Christmas? There is someone who would appreciate my discussing this with him before I just decide to leave." Natalie bit her lip, knowing she was treading on shaky ground. Cam could very well go out and hire a new actress and not even inform Natalie until after the fact. "Is that okay with you?" she added, hoping Cam would be gracious.

A deep sigh sounded from the other end. "I guess that would be okay. It is Christmas, after all."

"Thanks so much. I'll get back to you soon."

"All right. Happy holidays," said Cam.

"Merry Christmas to you, too," Natalie said cheerily before she hung up the phone. With a heavy heart she returned to kneading her bread dough. Why did she have to get the call right before Christmas? Now she was going to have to explain this to everyone tonight or tomorrow, which would not be very pleasant.

Natalie shaped her rolls and put them aside to rise, then wrote a note to Marla, letting her know that she was going to go for a short walk.

Before she reached the end of the block, Brad pulled alongside her in his car. "I was just coming to see you." He smiled. "Why don't you get in and we can go get a cup of coffee or something?"

Natalie had thought she wanted to be alone to think things out, but as soon as she saw Brad, she knew she would rather be with him.

They got coffee to go at the café and took them back to Marla's since Natalie wanted to put her rolls in the oven. Sitting on the front porch sipping coffee, Natalie listened while Brad did most of the talking. For whatever it was worth, he seemed much more conversational than he had been in recent weeks; in fact, he was almost chatty. He jumped from one topic to another, and even though he looked relaxed, Natalie could sense an undercurrent of expectancy.

Could he somehow know that I got this job? Natalie wondered. She sat still, drawing up all her courage reserves. She had nearly decided to tell him right then and there when he suddenly turned to her and took hold of her hands.

"You know, I don't know why I'm doing this."

"Doing what?" she asked, concerned. She hadn't been following his conversation too closely, and now she wondered just how much she had really missed.

"No." He was quiet for a long time. "No, I do know why I'm doing this. I had wanted to do this later on, maybe tonight or tomorrow, but I have a feeling that now is better."

Natalie's stomach flip-flopped as she started to suspect what he might say.

He reached into his coat pocket, pulled out a small jewelry box, and held it out to her.

"Okay, I know I'm not doing this the right way, but I couldn't decide exactly what to say." She hadn't reached for the box, so he opened it and took out a small silver band with a blue gemstone.

"Oh, it's so pretty," Natalie said, covering her mouth in surprise.

"I know we haven't talked about this, but I know I love you. And I hope you love me, too. Please say you'll marry me."

Natalie looked from the ring to Brad and then back to the ring. Her conversation with Cam played over in her head, and she felt so confused. "But, but what about—"

"The play?" Brad said. Natalie nodded. "We'll just have to work something out. I love you, and I won't lose you." He took a deep breath. "If you get the part, that's fine. I could move there after school gets out and find a job there. Lots of schools need history teachers, and I've already made a few calls."

"Are you sure?" Natalie asked in disbelief.

He nodded. "One hundred percent. Here, put this on," he said, holding the ring out to her again. "You're making me nervous since you haven't put it on yet."

Natalie burst into tears and buried her face in her hands.

"Hey," Brad said, gently placing his arms around her. "Aren't you happy? This is what you wanted, right? Now we can be together, *and* you can be an actress."

Natalie nodded. She was happy. "It just seems so . . . I don't know."

"Are you happy I asked?"

"Of course I'm happy. I love you, too," she told him.

"Good. Now that's out of the way, and we can go from there." He kissed her hands, then her forehead, her cheeks, and finally her lips. Natalie kissed him back and then leaned her head against his shoulder while he held her. Several moments later, she reluctantly pulled away, ready to face the truth.

"Here, put the ring on," he said.

"First, I need to tell you something. I got the job. The director called me just before you saw me walking earlier."

He looked surprised, but he still held the ring out to her. "That's okay. I'm happy for you."

He reached for her hand and Natalie allowed him to slide the ring onto her finger. "So," he said, after he had finished. "When do you have to leave?"

"Right after Christmas. She wants me there by the second or third of January."

"Wow. That's fast. It doesn't give us much time to say good-bye, does it?"

Natalie shook her head sadly.

"I'm glad I asked you when I did," he told her. "I got so nervous, I didn't know if I could do this in front of everyone."

Natalie laughed. "You did fine. It was very romantic."

"Oh, right." He grinned. "If you can really call me shoving a ring at you and saying, 'Hey, how about it?' romantic."

The two of them laughed at this for several minutes.

"Okay, it was a little . . . unusual, but I still loved it." Natalie looked at the ring on her finger, then back at Brad. "When I woke up this morning I didn't dream that I would be engaged by the end of the day."

"Well, I had my hopes, but I passed by your house three times before I got the nerve to stop. And by then, I saw you walking down the street."

"You didn't seem nervous when you stopped," she pointed out.

"I was. Believe me."

"Brad?" Natalie asked.

"Yes, darling?"

Natalie grinned. "What's the 'darling' for?"

He shrugged. "Isn't that what they always say in those old movies you like? I figured maybe I should try to pick up some phrases since I'm marrying an actress." He paused. "It did feel kind of strange to say it, though."

"That's because it's an outdated word. I don't think I've ever heard anyone in real life say it."

"Then we'll be responsible for reviving the word . . . darling. So what were you going to ask me?"

"I just want to make sure we're totally in agreement about my taking this job. I know we've been over this before, and you said it was my choice, but I told the director I needed a couple of days to talk this over with some people I care about, and since we're engaged, I think it's more important that this be a joint decision."

"You told her that? I'm flattered."

"So what do you think? At least right now, what are your feelings about it?"

"Same as they were ten minutes ago," was his confident reply. "I'm willing to go with you. I've been able to do the job I've always wanted to do, and you should have the opportunity to do the same thing. The only problem is, we both know you can't do that here in Sterling, so it's only fair that you should be able at least to try. I love teaching, and I can teach anywhere." He leaned back in the swing seat. "That's the way I see it. How about you?"

"I would like to give it my best shot. It is what I've been wanting for a long time, and I'm pretty excited. Although it's even more exciting since you've decided that you'd be willing to move there, too. But I don't want you to feel like you have to."

"I *want* to," he said firmly.

"So, it looks like we're in agreement," she said.

He shrugged. "Yeah. You can call the director back now, if you want to. I promise I won't change my mind."

Natalie shook her head. "I don't want to think business right now. I'll call her back after the holiday, like I planned."

Just then, Marla pulled into the driveway. "I thought you were baking the rolls," she said as she got out of the car.

"Don't worry about the rolls," Natalie said. She grinned at Brad, and whispered, "Should we tell her now?"

"No," he answered. "Let's tell everyone tomorrow."

"Don't think I don't see you two whispering," Marla said, walking inside. "I'll figure out whatever it is you're talking about sooner or later."

Natalie giggled softly after Marla was inside. "She'll see the ring, you know."

"Okay, you win. Let's tell her then. Then we'll go over and tell my mom. I think they'll think it's a pretty good Christmas present."

The rest of the week passed quickly. Natalie and Brad were the subject of the day during Christmas festivities at Janet and Eric's. Brad's brothers and their families arrived early Christmas morning and planned to spend the rest of the week in Sterling.

Natalie got along well with Brad's brothers, sisters-in-law, and nieces and nephews, and they were happy to hear that their brother and uncle was ready to get married.

They spent the following days arranging Natalie's travel plans. One day, they drove to Kansas City to collect the belongings that Natalie had stored at Kelly's apartment, and the next day they shipped those items to her new address in Chicago.

Every once in a while, one of them would get a little melancholy about the prospect of being apart for several months. But they didn't allow themselves to stay that way for long, because they didn't want their last few days together to be overshadowed with unhappiness.

"Well, this is the last bag," Natalie said, coming down the stairs. Marla and Brad were going to drive her to Kansas City to catch her flight, and even though she hadn't left, Natalie was feeling an emptiness settle over her.

"Are you sure you didn't miss anything?" Marla asked.

"I'm positive," Natalie said. "Are you ready to head out?"

"I think so," Marla said.

"Where's Brad?" Natalie asked, looking around.

"He's outside, warming up the car," Marla informed her. Marla hurried to the door and opened it, waiting for Natalie.

When they stepped out on the front porch, Natalie stopped in her tracks. "What is it?" Marla sounded anxious. "Did you forget something?"

"No . . ." Natalie bit her lip. "I wonder if I should stop by Janet's and tell her good-bye."

Marla took Natalie's hand. "Come on now, honey. You and Janet talked for hours last night. We've got to get moving if we're going to get you to Kansas City in time for that flight."

"I know," Natalie said, following Marla to the car. Brad saw them coming and took Natalie's last suitcase and put it in the trunk. "Is everything okay?" he asked, putting his arm around her. "You don't look too happy."

"I don't feel too happy," she admitted. "I was just thinking I needed to stop at Janet's and say good-bye one more time."

Brad's face softened. "I thought you and Janet said good-bye last night."

"We did, but I miss her already. And the kids, too." Natalie felt as if she was going to cry.

"Okay, don't worry about it," Brad said. "I think we can stop for maybe five minutes maximum. Would that be enough time?"

Natalie nodded. "Yes, that's perfect." She walked around to the passenger's side to get in the car, when Janet pulled up in her minivan. Happily surprised, Natalie ran over to meet Janet.

"I just had to tell you good-bye again," Janet said as she got out of her car.

"We were just about to stop by your house," Natalie said, hugging her friend. "You had perfect timing."

"I'll miss you, Natalie," Janet said, looking teary-eyed. "This is almost worse than when you first went off to college."

"I know. I don't know how I'm going to make it without all of you guys there with me."

"You will," Janet said. "And don't forget to call."

"I won't," Natalie promised. "And I'm already looking forward to you and Eric visiting next weekend." Janet and Eric were going to drive Natalie's car up the next weekend, then stay for day or two.

"I am, too," Janet said. "I'm already packed for the trip."

"Are the kids in the car?" Natalie asked.

"Yes. They're still in their pajamas, but I brought them anyway since it was going to be such a quick little trip."

"Can I take a peek at them?"

"Sure." Janet went around to the side of the car and opened the door.

Natalie grinned when she saw Eric Jr. and Olivia staring up at her with sleepy eyes. They were probably wondering what had brought them out of their warm beds so early in the morning. She hugged them and kissed both sets of plum-shaped cheeks, savoring their sweet baby smells. "I'm going to miss you two," she said. "You be good and don't grow up too much before I get to see you again, okay?" Natalie said softly.

Janet laughed. "I don't think they're going to grow up much before next weekend, Natalie."

"I know, I know." Natalie said, closing the van door. She stood quietly, enjoying the early-morning quiet, feeling even more reluctant to leave.

"Ladies, I hate to interrupt," Brad said, joining them, "but if I'm going get my darling to the airport on time, we have to leave now." He and Natalie grinned at each other because of his use of the word *darling*. He used it all of the time now, and both of them thought it was a little corny, but sweet.

"Oh, I'm sorry. Don't want to hold you up," Janet exclaimed. She hugged Natalie again and said, "You don't forget us this time, girl."

"I won't," Natalie said, heading back to the car.

When Natalie was settled, Marla asked, "So, are we sure we have everything?"

"I hope so," Natalie answered.

"If you don't, we'll ship it later on," Brad said. "For now, we've got to go."

The ride to the airport was much too short. And because they had gotten off to a late start, once they arrived, they spent their time scurrying around trying to get Natalie's luggage checked. When the time came for her to board the plane, Natalie didn't think she could go.

Marla hugged her. "I'll miss you, child," she said, starting to cry.

"Me, too," she said. "I don't want to go," she whispered.

"Is that how you really feel?"

Natalie considered for a moment. Even though she was sad,

she still wanted this job. "No," she admitted. "I just feel like that right now."

"Then you go," Marla said. "You'll be okay. And when you get homesick, just pick up the phone and call somebody."

Natalie nodded. An announcement over the intercom informed them that her flight was now boarding.

Brad hugged her. "You don't want to miss your flight," he reminded her.

"I know. I'll miss you," she said.

"Me too. Working on the museum won't be the same without you."

"I'll miss working with you, too."

He kissed her quickly and released her from the hug. "They just gave another boarding call."

"I know." Natalie kissed his cheek. "Then I guess it's time for me to go." She took a deep breath and gathered up her purse and her carry-on, then waved to Marla and Brad. "I'll probably call you guys all of the time," she informed them.

"We don't mind." Brad grinned.

Natalie laughed. "I guess I should get on the plane now. Are you leaving right away?"

Brad shook his head. "We'll stay here until it takes off."

Natalie nodded, but didn't move.

"You better go now, before they leave without you," Brad's voice was gentle.

"Okay." Natalie turned and walked the few steps to get in line with the other passengers. Just before she went down the long hallway, she turned and waved one last time to Brad and Marla. She hoped she was doing the right thing.

Thirteen

"Natalie and Peter, that was great," said Cam from her seat down in the darkened auditorium. "However, the blocking was pretty chaotic there, especially toward the end. You two nearly ran over each other during that bit about the Cornish hens. Let's take ten, and run the second half of that scene again, starting at . . ." Cam flipped on her flashlight and looked down at her script, just as her cell phone started ringing. Looking up at the stage, she said, "We'll pick up at Peter's line when he says, "I think I'm allergic to Rosemary." Cam closed her script and answered her cell phone. Peter sighed and stalked off to the other end of the stage.

Natalie nodded, feeling overwhelmed. The past two weeks had been filled with strenuous rehearsals, both for herself and the other cast members with whom she shared scenes. Cam called rehearsals at odd hours, whenever she could fit them in around the existing rehearsal schedules and performances.

Natalie knew the script like the back of her hand, and she knew the blocking fairly well, but every once in a while, she would forget where she was supposed to stand and end up on the other side of the stage, then have to cross in a hurry to reach some prop, or open the door of the apartment where her character lived.

She felt guilty whenever these things happened because it was her responsibility to get these things right, and when she didn't it meant extra time and practice for the rest of the cast.

Natalie sat in an old armchair in the wings, checking the blocking notes in her script. Part of the problem in that last scene had come when Peter tried to help her remember that she needed to stand downstage during part of the dialogue. Natalie had gotten confused; and when the time had come to cross the stage, she and Peter had nearly bumped into each other. Now that she saw the mistake, she made a mental note to correct the mistake.

"Hey there, you," Kimbra came around the corner and stopped at Natalie's chair. Covering her mouth, she stifled a yawn. "You certainly left early in the morning, didn't you? What time did Cam start your rehearsals today?"

"Six A.M.," Natalie said, resisting the urge to yawn herself.

"You've been here for four hours already?" Kimbra exclaimed.

"But we've made a lot of progress," Natalie told her.

"Good. Hopefully you won't have these crazy schedules right up until your first performance." She grinned. "Just two more weeks before your opening night. Are you excited?"

"Very," was Natalie's emphatic reply. "And Cam said that next week she won't run us so ragged with these rehearsals. That is, if we do really well this week."

"You'll do fine," Kimbra said, pulling up a small wooden

stool. After she sat down, she said, "Meanwhile, it didn't make any difference that I didn't have to rehearse so early. I've been up for hours anyway. Your aunt called at like seven-thirty, and we ended up talking for a half hour."

"Really? Marla called?" Natalie asked, pleased. "What did she say?"

"She told me that that museum you guys were working on is almost finished. The grand opening will be on the same weekend of our spring hiatus here with the show. She said she wanted to make sure that you could come."

"Oh, that's great," Natalie said. Mentally, she counted the weeks until the opening. "That's the end of April, and I can hardly wait."

Kimbra laughed. "Well, here's something even more interesting. She talked me into coming to the opening. Said she thought I might enjoy it."

Natalie laughed. "That's Marla for you. But I thought you and Cate were planning to go someplace warm that week."

Kimbra shook her head. "No, I decided that going to Sterling, Missouri, would be way cheaper than Mexico or somewhere else, and since I need to save the money, it was not a hard decision to make."

"Did you tell Cate yet?"

Kimbra shook her head. "Haven't seen her this morning, but it won't be a problem since we hadn't made any reservations yet; I know she won't be mad at that. Plus, I know girlfriend's credit cards are maxed out just like mine."

"Talking about me this early in the morning, Kimbra?" Cate said from the opposite side of the stage.

"Mmm-hmmm," Kimbra said. "Just told Natalie I was too broke to go anywhere expensive during the week off, so I'm going home with her."

"Oh really?" Cate said, crossing the stage. "It just so happens my parents sent me a little money, but maybe I'll come with you two and use the money to pay those people at the card company who keep hounding me. Is that okay?"

"Fine with me," Natalie said. Listening to everyone's money woes made her even happier she'd gone home to get her savings built up.

"Thanks, I appreciate it. So how has your morning been so far?" asked Cate.

"Long. But lots of progress."

"And Peter?"

"Moody," Natalie answered.

"He's still upset she keeps turning him down," Kimbra added. "But what's she supposed to do? She's engaged."

"He can't get mad at you for wanting to be faithful," Cate jumped in. "And we've all seen pictures of Brad, who happens to be just gorgeous."

"Has he got any brothers?" Kimbra wanted to know.

"Sorry, but they're married," Natalie said.

"Oh well, someday *my* prince will come." Kimbra laughed.

"I hope he's a lawyer, because you'll need one, with the bills you have." Cate laughed.

"Girl, please. Nobody goes to jail for not paying their bills."

"Maybe, maybe not. But it doesn't do anything for your credit," Cate argued. "I'm about ready to move back with my parents and do what Natalie did."

"Yeah, and it wouldn't hurt to get engaged, while you're at it," said Kimbra.

"Oh, here comes Mr. Moody," Cate said, glancing in the direction of Peter, who was crossing the stage.

Natalie, who had been studying her script again, hoped he was in a better mood. When she messed up a scene, he was usually the one who got the most extra work. He was playing her husband, and most of her scenes were with him. To make matters worse, he had asked her out several times over the past couple of weeks, and he was having a hard time accepting her answer.

He cleared his throat. "We have a couple of minutes before Cam starts again, so maybe we should run through the blocking really fast," he suggested.

"Good idea," Natalie said, standing. "I'll see you ladies later."

Natalie and Peter quickly marked through the blocking, and when Cam ran the scene again, it was flawless.

"Good job, guys," Cam praised from her seat in the audience. "Now let's run through the rest of the apartment scenes and see how we do. If they're anything like the one you just did, I'll cancel the night rehearsals for the rest of this week."

Amazingly, the next scenes, while not perfect, were exceptionally good, and Cam decided that she wanted to end Natalie's rehearsals for the day.

Instead of staying to watch the regular rehearsals, as she often did, Natalie decided to go home and get some much-needed rest. She stopped by the dressing room to say good-bye to Kimbra and Cate, then headed home to the apartment.

There was cold coffee in the kitchen, probably brewed by Kimbra that morning, but Natalie skipped over it in favor of milk and cereal, since she planned to sleep and didn't need a caffeine rush.

After eating breakfast, Natalie called Marla back, and they had a long, pleasant conversation. Marla filled Natalie in on all of the news in Sterling, and Natalie told Marla about her role and the actors she had met.

Afterward, she fell asleep and didn't wake until much later, when Kimbra came home from rehearsal.

"I'm making spaghetti," Kimbra called from the kitchen.

A few minutes later, Natalie forced herself to wake up and join Kimbra. Natalie chopped lettuce for a salad, while Kimbra tossed the pasta and the sauce together.

When everything was ready, they sat down to eat. Kimbra described to Natalie how the day's rehearsals had gone, and Natalie listened intently. Kimbra sighed as they finished their meal. "Are you coming to watch the performance tonight?"

Natalie yawned, covering her mouth with her hand. "I think I need to stay home tonight."

"That boring, huh?" Kimbra grinned.

"Stop it," Natalie laughed. "I'm just worn out. I'll look over my blocking and try to relax a little. I need the rest because I have another six o'clock tomorrow morning."

"Don't I know it," Kimbra said. "Cam's letting Peter come in at ten, so you'll be doing some scenes with the rest of us. I don't know how I'll make it." She grinned. "You'll probably have to roll me out of my bed and just let me fall on the floor. That way, I know I'll at least wake up in time."

Natalie laughed. She glanced at her watch, noting that the time was nearly four o'clock.

"You have an appointment or something?"

"Not really, I was just wondering if Brad was home from school yet."

"Is he?"

"I think so. I'll call him after we finish."

"How sweet. I think I'll take a short nap. Could you wake me up around five-thirty?"

"Sure."

Kimbra stood up and took her dishes to the sink to wash them.

"You go on and get some rest. I'll put the dishes in the dishwasher."

"Thanks a lot, Natalie." Kimbra ran off to her room while Natalie cleaned up. Just as she finished, the phone rang. Natalie picked the receiver and was pleased to find that Brad was on the other end.

"I was just about to call you." She smiled.

"We think alike," he said, teasing.

They chatted about many subjects for almost an hour, and when they were about to hang up, Natalie asked if Brad was still planning to come to her fist performance.

"Well," he cleared his throat. "I have some bad news, I think."

"What?" Natalie asked.

"I just found out the school is having parent-teacher conferences that night. Any other day, I would take off and get a substitute, but I feel like I personally should be there to talk with the parents, you know?"

"Oh. You're right, of course," Natalie said, trying to not to sound upsct.

"Are you okay with that?" Brad said. "I could try to get a sub, but he wouldn't know what to say to the parents."

"No, no, that's fine. You should be there." She remembered something else. "I guess if you're not coming, Marla probably won't either."

"I'll try to come up the next week, and I'm sure she'll want to come then," he said. "I promise."

"Okay. I'm disappointed, but I know you're doing the right thing."

"Thanks, Natalie. You're special, did you know that?"

She laughed. "You know, this guy named Brad tells me that all the time."

"He's right, you know. Don't let anyone tell you anything different."

"All right," she said. "I'll let you go then."

"I miss you," he said.

"I miss you, too," she told him.

"Love you," Brad said.

"Love you, too," she answered. "And I'll call you tomorrow, okay?"

"Okay, 'bye, darling."

"Good-bye, darling," she said.

Natalie hung up the phone.

"You guys are too cute," Kimbra called from her room.

"And you are such an eavesdropper," Natalie called back, laughing.

"I am not," Kimbra protested. "It's not my fault that I can hear through these old vents," she called.

"Just take your nap," Natalie returned.

That night, after Kimbra left for the theater, Natalie experienced her worst bout of homesickness since she'd arrived in Chicago. She hadn't even felt this lonely the day she'd first arrived. Kimbra had worked overtime trying to cheer her up, and it had been successful.

Now, she was home alone, feeling sorry for herself because Brad and Marla wouldn't be able to make it to her opening.

She dialed Marla's number, but the line just rang. Natalie remembered that Marla had already left to go to her sewing circle, and she wouldn't be home until later because Wednesday-evening service was held right after the sewing meeting.

"Stop feeling so selfish," Natalie told herself. "Brad didn't sit around moping because I came here. He was happy for me, and he's proud of me. If he can do it, then you can, too," she said, giving herself a pep talk.

Looking around for something to do, she decided she needed to get out of the apartment.

Natalie's gaze fell upon her Bible, sitting on the coffee table in the living room. Church. She had attended one Sunday-morning service in the past two weeks but hadn't had time to go to any of the other services. She wasn't sure if the church she'd visited was the one for her, but she pulled out of her Bible the bulletin she'd gotten to see what time their Wednesday service started. Even if she didn't join this church, it would be refreshing to go to fellowship with some other Christians.

Kimbra was a Christian, but her relationship with the Lord was a lot like Natalie's had been before she'd gone home. She didn't spend time with the Lord on a regular basis; so while she didn't object to conversation about Christianity, she rarely initiated the topic. Natalie hadn't had much time to discuss her faith with many of the others she worked with, but she hadn't seen much to suggest that the group was overwhelmingly Christian.

She went out to car and made the short drive to the church. She was surprised that several people remembered her from last Sunday's service, and she met quite a few new people.

The service was a satisfying meal for her soul, and Natalie was glad she had come. She promised herself that she would come back, and often. She was doing well keeping up with her personal Bible study, but she enjoyed being with her brothers and sisters in the Lord.

The day of her first performance, Natalie was surprisingly free from any jitters, partly because she was too tired to be nervous. Cam had wanted to give her and the rest of the cast more time to rest, but some of the scenes demanded their attention, and they worked long, hard hours smoothing out the rough spots.

She was in the dressing room, getting ready for her first scenes when Kimbra knocked on the door. "Hey, you. You look great. A little tired, but great." Her friend grinned.

"So do you," Natalie teased her back. "Maybe a little more tired than me, but still great."

"Hey, can you come with me for a sec?" Kimbra turned and began walking down the hallway that led to the stage door.

"Umm, wait a second. I'm not ready yet. I still have to do makeup."

"Doesn't matter," Kimbra called over her shoulder. "We have at least a half hour before the first act."

"I know, I know, I just like to be ready."

"You have plenty of time."

At the end of the hallway was a large empty room. Natalie looked around. "So. What is it? I thought you needed help with a costume or something."

"Sit down," Kimbra commanded.

"Why?" Natalie was starting to get annoyed. Kimbra was such a practical joker, and she could never be sure if her friend was being serious. Natalie sat hesitantly.

"Now close your eyes," Kimbra said.

Natalie narrowed her eyes, glancing around the room again. "If you dump something on me, I will *not* be happy."

"I promise, no buckets of water. I learned my lesson." A few days earlier, Kimbra had rigged a bucket of water to fall on Natalie when she opened the kitchen door. Natalie had come home at nearly midnight, exhausted. After the bucket had spilled its contents, she had stormed into Kimbra's room, fully ready to argue.

Kimbra had been very contrite and offered profuse apologies. She had also been the one to mop the kitchen floor in the middle of the night. Since then, the practical jokes had all but ceased.

"Now close your eyes, it's important."

Natalie obeyed, hoping she was not being too gullible. She heard a door open and footsteps across the room. She shifted in her chair, wondering what this was about. "Kimbra . . ." she said, her voice an indicator of her wariness.

"Okay, open them," Kimbra said.

Natalie opened her eyes to see Brad and Marla standing in the room. She jumped out of her chair and ran to them. "How did you guys do this? Brad, I thought you had conferences."

Brad hugged her tightly. "The date on the memo was a typo, and when I found out, I just decided that we would surprise you. Are you surprised?"

"Of course!" Natalie couldn't contain her excitement. She hugged Marla, who was grinning from ear to ear. "I had totally convinced myself that I was going to be okay with you guys not being here, but I'm so happy you made it."

"We are, too," Marla said. "I almost let the secret slip so many times, but Brad said if I told he'd be really disappointed. He just had to surprise you."

"I love it. This is the best surprise I've ever had." She laughed. She turned to Kimbra, who was standing a few feet away. "And I thought for sure you were going to dump another bucket of water on me." She hugged Kimbra, too.

"Oh, believe me. The look on your face the other night has put my pranks on hiatus for a long time."

The four of them chatted until a call came over the intercom. "Fifteen minutes to curtain. Cast in your positions, please."

"Well, we need to finish getting ready," Natalie said. "Do you know where your seats are?"

"Yes, you go on ahead and get to where you're supposed to be," Marla prompted her. "We'll see you after it's over."

"Okay." Natalie hugged them both one last time, then returned to her dressing room to finish getting ready.

Natalie's performance was a success. Cam and the rest of the cast thought she had done a great job. Brad and Marla said that she was "incredible" and they were very proud of her.

After the performance, they took her to a late dinner at an all-night diner, where they talked for hours. That night, Marla stayed at the apartment with Natalie and Kimbra, and Brad checked into a hotel for the evening.

They left the following morning, and Natalie spent the afternoon missing them. She was, however, cheered by a review of her performance, written by a local theater critic. The article stated that "the transplant of Natalie Jacobs into Julie Wold's role was seamless, and one could not guess that Ms. Jacobs has not held the role of Laurel since the play began its run last September. She has done a superb job in assimilating with the rest of the cast, and she was a delight to watch. One could safely assume that she will not have any trouble finding new roles, and she will likely become a household name in Chicago theater productions, should she not choose to leave for the theater community of New York."

Natalie fell asleep that night with the review still in her hands. She was thrilled to have finally gotten this type of review. As far as New York was concerned, she no longer had the same desire to go so far from home. Chicago would be just fine, especially once she and Brad were together again.

Fourteen

*T*he rest of February passed uneventfully. Brad was unable to make the trip to Chicago for Valentine's Day because his mother caught a bad cold, and Natalie thought he should stay with Rhetta. He sent three dozen roses and a long letter, telling her how much he missed her. Natalie put the letter in her scrapbook, pleased to have a tangible connection to Brad.

She continued to go to church on a regular basis, and she grew to love the members of the congregation more and more as the weeks passed.

By mid-March, she was counting down the six weeks until the museum's grand opening. She was having a particularly hard time trying to shake a bout of homesickness that even regular conversations with Janet, Brad, and Marla couldn't dampen.

The fact that Marla came down with a cold similar to the one Rhetta had didn't make matters any better.

Natalie called several times a day to check on her aunt, even though Brad and Janet assured her they were taking good care of Marla.

One afternoon, she called Brad to see how Marla was doing. "She's fine, but she was so tired that we canceled work on the museum for the rest of the week. I thought we were disturbing her too much."

"Is she feeling any better?"

He sighed. "She is, but I think her spirits are a little low. Maybe you should call. It might cheer her up."

"I was thinking about calling her, but the last few times I called in the afternoon, she was napping, and I woke her up. But if you think it's okay, I'll call now."

"I think it would be a good idea," he said. "I love you, and I can't wait until you come back for the opening."

"I love you, too, and I can't wait either." Natalie hung up the phone and hurriedly dialed Marla's number. Her aunt answered the phone sounding tired, but she seemed to cheer up when she heard Natalie's voice.

"Brad said he didn't think I would disturb you if I called," she explained.

"No, you're not disturbing me. I was trying to take a nap, but I couldn't seem to get comfortable."

"Are you taking it easy?" Natalie asked. "No working, no lifting, nothing like that."

"I'm not doing anything except working on this quilt for the sewing circle."

Natalie made a *tsk-tsk* sound. "You're not supposed to be running around, going to meetings. You're supposed to be in bed resting."

"Oh, I am. I'm just working on this quilt, and I'm doing it here, at home."

"Oh," Natalie said, feeling relieved. "So tell me how Eric Jr. and Olivia were the last time you saw them." Marla launched into a story, and Natalie listened to her aunt relate the latest news. When it became apparent that Marla was tired, Natalie hung up the phone after making Marla promise that she would get some sleep.

After hanging up, Natalie sat thinking. She didn't like the idea of Marla being in that big house alone, even if friends and neighbors were checking on her regularly. Her aunt insisted that she wasn't too old to be alone, and Natalie didn't argue with her. Marla was perfectly competent, but Natalie sensed that her aunt had been very tired for some time. Natalie had been examining her life and her level of happiness for several weeks now, and she wondered if this was the time to make some changes. She had been through all of the pros and cons several times over, but she knew she had to do something different.

Without hesitating, she picked up the phone to call Cam. It was time for them to talk.

"GOOD-BYE, NATALIE . . . WE'LL MISS YOU!" read the banner in the conference room.

Natalie looked around the room at the people she'd spent the last three months working with. They were enjoying this party, and while they mourned the fact that Natalie would be leaving the cast so soon, they were also celebrating that they had just finished the last performance before the weeklong spring vacation.

Since she'd told Cam that she needed to leave the show six weeks ago, they had been highly supportive of her reasons for doing so. Even Cam, in her own way, had managed to joke about it. "I guess the part of Laurel is doomed to become a revolving role," she'd laughed after announcing to the rest of the cast that Natalie had resigned.

The past month and a half had been filled with a desperate shuffle on Natalie's part to get things in order. Not wanting to leave the show in a lurch, she had offered to stay on as long as she could before leaving; thankfully, Cam had hired her replacement not even a week after she'd announced that she wanted to return home.

Natalie had spent the next five weeks rehearsing with April, the new actress, filling her in on the details of the role, and she was doing a fine job. She knew the role well enough that Natalie would not even have to return after the break.

The best part of the deal was the fact that no one at home knew she was returning for good. They still assumed she was coming for only a week, and Natalie couldn't wait to see the looks on their faces when she told them.

"Well, Natalie," said Cam, who had walked up beside her. "You were a joy to work with. After you get married, if you and your husband ever decide to move here, I want you to look me up. You have a lot of promise as an actress, and I know you'll be able to find work."

"I can't promise you that I'll come back, but if I do, I will find you," Natalie promised.

After Cam had hugged her good-bye, Natalie moved around the room, saying her good-byes to all of her new friends. Many people, including herself, got teary-eyed, but inside Natalie was excited. She was going home tomorrow, and she could hardly wait. She decided to leave the party before it ended; it had started well after eleven o'clock, and she was ready to get some rest. Just before she left, Kimbra decided to head home with her; they both had an early flight the next morning.

They also reminded Cate that she needed to get some rest.

"If you're not at the apartment by five-thirty, we're leaving," Kimbra warned.

"Don't worry, I'm going home now, too," Cate told them.

Natalie forced herself to sleep, knowing that she was going to need all of her energy during the coming week for the busy schedule her friends had planned for her.

When the three women stepped off of the plane the following afternoon, Brad was there, waiting for them.

"Remember, no one knows I'm going to stay," she instructed her two friends. "So don't tell. It's my surprise to them."

"Gotcha," Kimbra said. "Now go hug your fiancé."

Natalie didn't need to be told to hug him. She ran to meet him, and they kissed. "I can't believe I'm really here," she said.

"I can," Brad said.

Natalie reintroduced him to Kimbra and also introduced Cate. "Well, let's get your bags so we can get on the road," he said. "Marla wanted to come, but she didn't know if we'd have room in the car. I had to borrow Eric and Janet's minivan."

During the ride home, the four of them chatted about different things, and Natalie felt herself growing impatient to see Marla and everyone else.

When they were twenty miles away, Natalie turned to Brad. "Aren't you driving really slowly?"

He laughed. "No. Just calm down, we'll be there soon."

As they pulled into the driveway, Natalie couldn't wait to get out of the car. As soon as Brad stopped the minivan, she jumped out and ran to the front porch, where Marla was standing.

Her aunt looked thinner than usual, but she seemed to have her strength back. "I missed you," Natalie said, hugging Marla.

"I missed you, too. It's been a long few months. Having you here last fall made me forget how lonely I could get."

"I'm sorry you got lonely," Natalie said.

Marla laughed. "Don't feel too badly. I more than had my hands full with all of Brad's students. They pop up all the time now, wanting to do some work, and I tell you it's like having a bunch of extra kids."

Natalie motioned for her friends to join them, and they went inside to get a look at the museum.

"It's pretty much done now," Marla said proudly.

Natalie was thoroughly impressed with the progress they had made. Indeed, the museum was nearly complete. The living room was now overflowing with the different artifacts and items collected, and each item was identified with a small card, explaining what it was and who had donated it. The dining room was a chronicle of famous persons in Black history and a display of Black inventors and their inventions.

The den was now a fully furnished one-room cabin, and the library held display cases full of Marla's old magazines and books, brimming with African-American history, both happy and sad.

"This is so awesome," Cate said. "I can't believe you guys just had the stuff to put this together."

"It is amazing," Natalie agreed. "For a long time, I could never understand why Aunt Marla had to save everything, but I'm so glad she didn't let me talk her into getting rid of any of these things."

"And there's more to come," Brad added. "We've got ideas for the rooms on the second floor. Before we know it the museum will have taken over the house."

"Oh, great," Natalie said, smiling. "Guess that means Aunt Marla and I will have to move into the attic."

"You mean just Aunt Marla," he corrected. "We're not planning to expand the museum this week."

Natalie exchanged glances with Kimbra and Cate. She suppressed a smile at the fact that she still hadn't revealed her secret.

"I told Brad you guys are going to have to get down here this summer and help me get started on the rest of the museum, since he won't be teaching here next fall."

"And all of my students have volunteered to help with second floor," Brad said.

"But where will you live if that happens?" Natalie asked Marla.

Marla sighed. "Well, I was going to tell you later, but I've decided that this house really is too big for just me. And Rhetta is in her house all alone, so she asked me if I would move in with her. So that means the museum will expand, and you and Brad won't have to worry about Rhetta and me being alone."

Natalie gently hugged Marla. "Okay, I won't worry about you living alone, but how are you going to run a museum by yourself?"

Marla shrugged. "The whole town wants to help now. They are excited to see how far it's come, and they want to see it continue. Eric and Janet help quite a bit, as well, when they can get keep those little ones from getting into things."

"I didn't know that," Natalie said.

"Janet wanted to surprise you," Brad said, "and Marla just ruined it."

"Oops. Sorry," Marla said, wincing.

"Well, enough of this small talk," Brad said. "I'm sure Natalie and her friends need to get unpacked."

"And I'm sure Natalie and Brad need to spend some time together," Kimbra said, mimicking him. "Don't worry about us, we'll stay out of your hair." She laughed.

"Yes, thank you for letting us come," Cate told Marla.

"You two are perfectly welcome. It'll probably be the only time I have three famous actresses under my roof at one time," said Marla. "Let me show you where your rooms are."

After the trio made their way upstairs, Natalie turned to Brad. "This museum is amazing. You did an excellent job."

"Thanks," he said, looking around. "My only regret is that I won't be here to oversee the second phase. I have some great ideas."

Natalie didn't say anything, but she took his hand so they could go out on the front porch. They sat talking for a long time, until Natalie started yawning. "I'm sorry," she told him. "I had a late night and an early morning."

He laughed. "You always have late nights and early mornings. Kind of makes you wonder when we'll ever see each other once we get married."

"Are you trying to back out of the engagement?" Natalie teased.

"Never." He kissed her forehead. "But I am going to let you get some sleep. The grand-opening party is tonight, and I want you rested up so you can be with me the whole time." He stood up. "I'll be back around six or so."

Natalie yawned, standing up. "I forget. What time are the festivities supposed to start?"

"Seven," he said. "Anyone who wants to can walk through the museum, and the students will be giving tours."

"I bet they're excited about that," Natalie said, remembering their enthusiasm for the project.

"Excited?" Brad said. "Nah, not really." He laughed. "They've been giving me 'practice tours' that put my longest lectures to shame. They want to explain each and every detail, you know?"

Natalie shrugged. "Like teacher, like student, I guess."

"I guess so. See you soon," Brad said, walking away from the porch. "Get ready for another late night. They've been planning a block party that could last for hours."

"Okay, I'll be ready for it, but I don't know if Kimbra and Cate can last that long," Natalie said.

After Brad's car was out of sight, Natalie went inside and took a nap, just as her friends were doing. She would tell everyone her surprise later on.

The museum opening was a great success. Although many of the people had already seen parts of the collection, they were impressed with the finished product, and everyone was excited about the next phase. Natalie spent the better part of the evening with Brad, making the rounds to talk to old friends, including Janet and Eric. Little Olivia had grown so much, but she seemed to remember Natalie, and so did Eric. She spent a long time with two little ones, who seemed delighted to see her again.

Around ten-thirty, someone spotted smoke coming from the back of the house.

Brad ran around to the back to see what was going on, and when he came back, he yelled, "Call the fire department! The kitchen's on fire!"

Natalie's heart beat double time. "Lord, please don't let the house burn down," she prayed. "Marla would be heartbroken if it's ruined."

The firefighters arrived quickly, and while they fought the blaze, everyone ran around in a frenzy for the next half hour.

Natalie stood next to Marla with her arm around her shoulders, praying that much would not be harmed.

Finally, the firefighters came back outside. "It was just a small fire," one of them said. "Probably started in the oven, but we contained it, and it didn't leave the kitchen. The kitchen doors were closed, which helped contain the smoke, but you might want to go inside and remove anything you think might get damaged from smoke. You'll need a new kitchen, but the rest of the house will be fine once you air it out."

The crowd breathed a collective sigh of relief. Then Brad began barking orders. He put his students in charge of removing delicate items from different rooms, and the townspeople helped.

Natalie also pitched in carrying items outside. In the middle of working, she looked up, happy to see Kimbra and Cate helping as well. The job was done in less than an hour, and when they were done, people headed home to bring portable fans to help air the rooms out. Afterward, Brad organized groups to take the museum items to Rhetta's, where they would remain until they could be placed in the house again.

When everything was done, the gathering broke up for the evening. The opening had still gone well, and thanks to everyone's help, none of the items had been ruined. By the time Brad left, Natalie had forgotten about her surprise, and she, Marla, Cate, and Kimbra wearily went to bed.

The next morning, everyone at Marla's slept late, but they got up around noon when a steady stream of people started arriving at the house, checking to see if there was anything more they could do to help. Natalie got dressed and went downstairs just in time to see Charles Warden, a local contractor, pull up in his truck.

"What's going on?" she asked Kimbra.

Kimbra shrugged. "I have no idea."

Brad came out of the library. "Good morning."

"I didn't even know you were here," Natalie said. She self-consciously put a hand to her hair.

"Your hair looks fine," Brad assured her. "Charles is going to replace Marla's kitchen."

"You're kidding."

"Free of charge," Brad said.

"Wow," was all Natalie could think to say.

Marla came from the kitchen, her hands sooty. "A pot of black-eyed peas," she told them. "I can't believe I forgot they were on the stove."

"Don't worry," Natalie said. "There was so much going on, none of us remembered. And Charles is going to fix the kitchen free of charge."

"Oh, my," Marla said. "Is that his truck out there?"

"Yes," Brad said. "He's here to get some plans together and take measurements."

"Let me go out and thank him."

"Wait," Natalie said. Everyone turned to look at her. "Since it looks like today it going to be a busy day, I wanted to go ahead and say this now."

"Is something wrong?" asked Brad.

She shook her head. "I just wanted to tell you both that I'm not going back to Chicago. I'm staying here."

"What?" Marla and Brad said simultaneously.

"I'm staying," she repeated.

"Are you sure about this?" Brad asked. "I hope you're not doing this for me. I'm prepared to move."

"No, it's for all of you guys, but mostly for me. I can't stand being away from here, and even if Brad came to Chicago, he couldn't bring Marla or the museum, or any of the wonderful people here."

Brad grinned. "I'm not going to argue with that. What are you going to tell your director?"

"She already told her," said Cate.

"Thanks a lot, Miss Chatty," said Kimbra. "Let Natalie tell her news."

"Cate's right," Natalie informed them. "I told my boss back in March, and she's already hired a replacement who's ready to start next week."

"So you don't even have to go back for a little while?"

"Well, eventually, I'll need to get my stuff out of Kimbra's apartment since Cate's moving in with her, but I'm pretty much home for good."

At that, Marla and Brad cheered and rushed to hug her. Kimbra and Cate went outside, leaving the three alone.

When they had quieted down, Brad asked, "Are you one hundred percent sure about this, darling? This doesn't fit in with what you originally wanted for your life, and I know you're a good actress."

She shrugged. "Every good actress knows you have to be versatile, and I'm beginning to think that the script I wrote for myself wasn't perfectly matched with the one God had for me." She laughed. "The last few months have been wonderful, but really empty, because I was longing to be home, and now I don't want to leave again. I'm still interested in theater, but maybe I can do something here, like start up some community plays or direct something in conjunction with the museum."

"That would be wonderful." Marla smiled.

"It sounds perfect already," Brad agreed.

"Do you think you can keep your teaching position?" Natalie asked.

"I know I can."

"I hate to interrupt, but I need to get this soot off my hands," Marla said, heading upstairs.

"So," Natalie said, "when do we start work on this next phase of the museum. I want to do a room about the contributions that African Americans have made to the performing arts."

"Wait just a minute," he said. "I've been waiting for you for a long time, and I think phase two can wait until after we've planned our wedding and walked down the aisle."

"Good idea," Natalie said.

Brad leaned down and kissed her. "It's good to have you home," he said.

"It's good to be home," she answered.

About the Author

LILLIAN MEREDITH is a writer who lives in the Midwest. She enjoys telling a good story, and hopes that the Lord will use her stories to touch the lives of the people who read them.

Someone for Toni

CECELIA DOWDY

Prologue

"*I*ris, I don't want to hear any more about your Christ or your God!"

Toni Brown peeked out into the living room from behind her bedroom door just in time to see her father turn and smash his fist into the wall, leaving a jagged hole in the fake paneling. She sighed. How many times before had she seen this kind of behavior? She'd lost count years ago.

Toni swallowed her pain as she turned back to her bed and threw another pair of jeans into a suitcase. Tomorrow couldn't come soon enough as far as she was concerned. Finally she'd be able to leave this dump and start a new life at college. If it hadn't been for that track-and-field scholarship, she didn't know what she would have done to get away. But she was certain of one thing: she would have managed to escape somehow.

A sudden quiet caught her ear. For the past two hours, her

father had been drunk, yelling and screaming, while her mother sat at the kitchen table, looking calm and serene. Mom had been praying, although why she bothered, Toni certainly couldn't say.

The silence was broken by sounds of her father stumbling down the short hallway to his bedroom. The door slammed shut. Soon his deep snores filled the house. He always liked to sleep off the effects of his liquor.

John Brown had been an alcoholic for most of Toni's life, but from hints her mother had let drop over the years, Toni gathered that he had been well thought of when her mother met and married him. As a young man he had been handsome, charming, and successful. Toni could barely remember the small house where they had lived when she was very young. In those days her father had sold structural steel products up and down the East Coast for a large firm based in Baltimore. He earned good money but began to rely on drinking to cope with the pressures of business. He lost one job after another until no one would offer him another sales position. Eventually he was forced to settle for production line work in factories. Even there he had not been able to advance beyond low-paying work because of his inability to stay sober for more than a few months at a time. More than once Toni had heard her parents arguing because her mother had discovered that her father had shown up at work drunk after his lunch hour.

Toni stared out her bedroom window at the street that stretched alongside their trailer park. How she hated her home. Everything always looked worn, frayed, and tired. They'd had the same furniture for fifteen years, and it showed. She'd always been too embarrassed to invite friends over and had tried to keep them from knowing she lived in a trailer.

"Why don't you have some friends over?" her mother would insist. "I could cook some hot dogs on the grill."

Toni would groan and say she would think about it. Her classmates were far from rich, but she had seen their homes during parties and sleep-overs and knew they were much nicer than hers.

Getting along with the kids at school had never been very hard for Toni, but she did not consider them to be friends. She had learned early on how to steer conversations away from herself. She could talk for hours about homework, fashion, and the latest movies. But if anyone asked direct questions about her, she always found a way to make some general, uninformative comment and then change the subject. She wished things could be different—that she could have a real friend, someone she could trust to keep her secrets, someone who would still accept her after discovering where and how she lived. It was lonely not to have anyone with whom she could share her hopes, fears, and dreams.

It had taken her a long time to find her first friend. Toni had carefully observed Sheila Robertson from a distance for a whole year. There was something different about her. She didn't talk about other people behind their backs. Her language wasn't full of street slang and profanity. She treated everyone respectfully, even kids who were troublemakers or outcasts. As she watched, Toni realized that Sheila made her feel safe. And for the first time, Toni Brown found herself wanting to talk to someone about the drabness of her life in the small and tattered home. Soon they developed a comfortable camaraderie that gave Toni someone she could lean on and trust. But even then Toni didn't want to show Sheila where she lived.

"How come we can't go to your house, Toni?" Sheila asked one day when the two girls were about ten years old. They were enjoying an afternoon at Sheila's house, watching television and drinking sodas.

Toni rolled her eyes. "Sheila, you know my dad drinks. He's not always the most pleasant person to be around."

"So, he doesn't come home until late. You said so yourself."

"We couldn't watch TV over there. My family doesn't have cable, and the picture on our old set is pretty bad," Toni insisted. Sheila's family was so . . . so normal. Her father came home on time and sober every night, and they always seemed to have enough food on the table.

A few weekends later, Toni heard a knock at her door. She looked up in surprise. Her father had gone fishing at the creek, and they weren't expecting company. "I'll get it, Mom," she'd called to her mother.

She opened the door. There stood Sheila and her mother. "Toni, I had no idea you lived—"

"Come in," said Toni's mother warmly, rescuing the two friends from what was obviously an awkward situation. Toni watched numbly as her mother made the two visitors comfortable at the worn kitchen table, quickly prepared tea, set out the best pieces from their small collection of china, and served everyone homemade cookies she had baked that morning. It suddenly occurred to Toni that her mother was very good at putting people at ease.

The two mothers spent a few minutes getting to know each other. After that the reason for the visit became clear. The church congregation Sheila's family belonged to had grown so large that they had built a new building. Individual members had volunteered to visit families in different parts of the city to invite them personally to attend a special series of services in the new facility. Mrs. Robertson handed Toni's mother a flyer, explaining the location of the new church and the times for services. Toni's mother had taken that flyer eagerly and carefully hidden it away where her husband wouldn't find it. She began to attend regularly and ended up joining the church two years later.

After that unexpected visit, Toni had been terrified that her friendship with Sheila would end, but it hadn't. Sheila had never said a word to anyone about where Toni and her mother lived. She didn't even bring the subject up unless Toni mentioned it first. Sheila did begin to talk more about her faith in God, but Toni never could understand why Sheila considered her religious commitments so important. Eventually Toni found the courage to invite Sheila to her house regularly, and the two girls became even closer.

Sighing, Toni pulled her thoughts to the present. She turned from the window and opened an envelope on her desk. It contained the tips she had earned from her job at the country club, where she had worked since she turned sixteen. She recalled the conversations she'd overheard while busing tables and taking orders. Wealthy people made her sick. They had no idea what it was like to stand in line at a grocery store, holding food stamps and feeling people's angry stares. They couldn't imagine the embarrassment of hearing the checkout clerk proclaim loudly, "I'll have to ring those cough drops separately. You can't use food stamps to buy medicine."

But in spite of her resentment, Toni felt attracted to wealthy people. She heard the country club members speak of vacations on the French Rivera, cruises to the South Pacific, private schools, and college funds. Eventually she began to take every opportunity to eavesdrop, hungry for bits and pieces of news about the lives of the rich patrons. Their money seemed to give them power. It was a power that enabled them to do just about anything. And Toni felt increasingly powerless. She couldn't lift her family out of poverty or control her father's drinking.

By her senior year in high school it was more difficult for Toni to endure the situation at home. True, her father had managed to hold the same job for several years, and his conflicts with her mother were less frequent and less violent than they had once been, but grinding poverty still haunted their daily life. The gold paint decorating the exterior of their trailer faded to light yellow and began to peel off. Several windows cracked as the cinder-block foundation settled unevenly. There was no money for new paint or glass and not much for anything else. Her parents refused to let Toni spend any of her savings on repairs to the trailer.

Sometimes she put on her track clothes and ran to escape the misery at home. By running, she could get away from the torment of her father's alcoholism. She could forget about the garbage, the rats, and the squalor of being poor.

Toni wanted a life in which her father loved her mother and never touched a drop of alcohol. He'd have a great education and make lots of money. They would live in a big house—perhaps in a neighborhood like the one she remembered from her earliest childhood—and eat fancy food every day. She would be respected and admired by others. Everybody would know Toni Brown.

The sound of her mother's soft steps interrupted Toni's thoughts. She turned to busy herself with a suitcase, but from the pleasant scent of her mother's inexpensive perfume, she knew the older woman was standing in the doorway.

"I don't know why you let him treat you that way," remarked Toni angrily as she zipped the suitcase shut. It was heavy, and she struggled to move it to the floor. Her mother rushed forward to help, and the aging trailer creaked as they set the luggage next to the wall.

Iris laid her cool brown hand on Toni's shoulder.

"Antoinette, I've tried to explain it to you," the woman began.

Toni huffed and turned away. "I don't want to hear that garbage anymore." Toni flopped onto her bed. Hot tears began to spot the worn quilt her mother had made so many years ago.

"Toni, I think you need to hear it one more time. You're leaving home tomorrow. You're about to become an adult. There are some things I may not have another chance to explain to you. Your father knows there are limits. He didn't always, but he does now. It's been years since he laid a hand on me, and I don't tolerate any profanity from him. He may not like it when I talk about the Lord or spend time at church, but he knows that God and God's people are looking out for me—and for you, Toni. He knows that if he crosses that line, the people from the church will take us out of here and put us in a safe house. He'd be alone. And your father is afraid of being alone.

"But I don't think it will ever come to that," Toni's mother continued, "because I believe that God is already answering my prayers to preserve this family. I still love your father, Toni, and I believe that God is slowly changing him. But it's a long, hard process, and I need the help of my church family to hang on while God works. I don't go to church because I love your father or you any less than I did before I became a Christian. I go because I love both of you more."

Toni wiped at her tears as she glanced up at her mother. She was still the short, dark-skinned woman Toni had known all her life, but there was something different. Toni had grown used to thinking of her mother as a victim, but the women standing in her room radiated a feeling of subdued power.

Toni looked down at her worn quilt again. Tonight she was the one feeling weak: weak and scared. Tomorrow she was going away to college and leaving behind everything she had ever known. Her father wasn't the only one who was afraid of being alone. She had leaned on her parents her entire life, and now they would be far away.

Her mother's quiet voice broke the silence that had fallen between them. "I'm proud of you, Toni. You're going off to college tomorrow. Haven't been many people in my family who've made that trip. And it's not like you've never been away from home before. You got on well enough with your aunt and uncle a few years ago."

Two years ago, she'd lived all summer with Aunt Grace and Uncle Bob in the small town of Blue Spring, Maryland. Robert Fitzsimmons was her mother's brother. He and his wife, Grace, owned Blue Spring Baked Goods, a small but very prosperous bakery. Toni had worked with them and found it unexpectedly relaxing. She had enjoyed the process of baking and was surprised by how close she felt, after only a few weeks, to many of the bakery's regular customers.

All that summer she'd enjoyed the warm, cozy atmosphere of the bakery and felt surrounded by love and affection. All that summer, the three of them lived together as friends and partners, sharing the common goal of making the bakery thrive.

Toni would have been glad to spend every summer in Blue Spring, but she soon found she could make more money for college by working at the country club year-round. When the scholarship offers had started to pile up during her senior year in high school, she regretted not spending more time with her aunt and uncle.

Toni's mother bent over and kissed her daughter's cheek.

Then she held out a small package wrapped in lavender paper and tied with a white bow. "This is your going-away present."

Toni fingered the pretty paper. She'd always been drawn to lavender. Her mother loved wrapping presents and giving gifts. No matter how little they had, the woman always found something to offer others. When money ran low, she gave time. Iris Brown spent hours each week helping out at the battered women's shelter downtown.

"Go ahead, open it," her mother urged, gesturing toward the package.

Toni untied the ribbon and opened the paper carefully. She wasn't surprised to see that the gift was an expensive-looking black leather Bible. Silently, she reopened a suitcase, placed the Bible on top of the packed clothes, and zipped the luggage shut. "Thank you, Mom." Toni honestly didn't think she would ever read the book, but she appreciated how her mother must have sacrificed to afford it.

Toni had never managed to get beyond just tolerating her mother's faith or that of her best friend. And Toni herself was certainly not a believer. She had attended church a few times, but she refused to take their religious beliefs seriously. Toni just couldn't see how faith in God had solved any of her mother's problems.

If anything, Christianity had caused more conflict between her parents. Her father had been outspoken in his disapproval of church. To him, time in church meant less time for important household chores, like fixing his breakfast. To avoid trouble, her mother made his breakfast on Sunday mornings before she left so that all he had to do was heat it up in their battered microwave when he got up.

Sure, her father's attitude had softened over the past six

years. He used to fuss about her mother's Christianity all the time. Now he got angry about it only when he was drunk. But they were all still stuck in a twenty-year-old trailer, in an ugly "manufactured home development." The fancy name didn't make the sewer system work any better. Any time there was a heavy rain, pools of smelly, gray water still appeared in the same old places.

"So, are you all packed?" asked her mother as she glanced into the empty closet.

Toni nodded, then asked, "What time did Mrs. Fielding want to leave tomorrow?" Mrs. Fielding was a member of her mother's church who was giving the two women a ride to college. Toni's mother had never gotten a license, and even if she had, the family car had been repossessed the previous year.

"She said to be ready early tomorrow morning since it will take about three hours to get there. Once we get you settled in the dormitory, she suggested that we might have lunch on campus."

Toni nodded, barely listening. She had waited all her life for this moment. She would not be afraid. Beginning tomorrow, the world would see what Toni Brown could do.

One

Ten years later . . .

Toni rang up the order. "That'll be six dollars and thirty cents," she said.

"How come you don't have any of those sugar cookies, you know, the ones with the red icing?"

Toni sighed as Mrs. Turner, an elderly customer, gave her a ten-dollar bill. The woman was getting senile. She had asked that same question a few minutes ago. Toni reminded herself to smile and repeated her previous answer. "I'm all sold out of those. Since I'm getting ready to close, it doesn't make sense to make more. If you come back tomorrow, I'll make sure to save some for you." She wrapped the chocolate chip cookies in waxed paper for her customer.

A few moments after Mrs. Turner left, the bell rang again above her door, signaling the arrival of another customer. Toni was so tired she was tempted to say she was closing, but when she gazed into the stranger's dark brown eyes, her ability to speak seemed to vanish. The man had a strong face and a firm chin. He was bald, and he calmly stroked his mustache.

"Can I help you?" she managed to say after a few moments of silence. Her voice sounded dry, as if she needed a drink of water. These long hours really were getting to her.

The man rewarded her with a slow smile. He had even white teeth and a dimple in his left cheek. "Do you serve coffee?" His deep, mellow voice filled the empty bakery.

She nodded. "Regular or decaf?"

He chuckled as he continued to look at her. "Regular is fine. I need the caffeine to stay awake." Dark circles were noticeable under his eyes. He sat down at a table near the display cases containing her cakes and looked around the shop as she went to get the coffee. No matter how intently he examined the cookies, pies, bread, pastries, and many other things, his eyes seemed always to return to a sign at the top of the nearest glass-fronted cabinet, advertising made-to-order cakes for Mother's Day. REMEMBER MOM ON HER DAY, it read. As she served the coffee, a look of tired sadness passed over his handsome features.

She had learned long ago that food could sometimes change a person's mood. For some reason, she wanted to make him feel better. She arranged cream and sugar on a plate and then cut an extra-large slice of apple pie to serve him. Her customers always said her apple pie tasted great with coffee. She placed the pie on the table along with the cream and sugar.

"But I didn't order pie," he lightly protested.

"Are you on a diet?" she asked. He looked nice and trim, and she doubted he needed to worry about calories, unlike some of her customers, who had created a demand for her low-fat/low-calorie desserts.

"No," he responded.

"Well, go ahead and eat the pie, then. It's on the house."

She was surprised when he lowered his head in prayer. She wondered if he was a Christian like her mother. He lifted his head and took a bite of the pie. Surprise and pleasure erased much of the fatigue on his face. "I'll pay to eat pie that's this good," he exclaimed. "It's almost as good as my momma's."

Toni's own fatigue melted away like warm butter as she cleared the other tables and placed the dirty plates and utensils on a cart hidden behind the counter. She wanted to ask him where he was from but thought better of it. She didn't want to seem nosy.

Walking to the front of the bakery, she placed the CLOSED sign in the window. "Is there a hotel around here?" he asked.

She nodded as she emptied garbage into the trash can. "But it all depends on what you're looking for. If you're after a five-star fancy place, then you'll need to travel a bit farther. But Mrs. Dukes owns a bed-and-breakfast that's a few minutes from here. She orders pastries from me every day," she said.

He asked for directions, and Toni drew a map on the back of a napkin. "By the way, I'm Jason Matthews," he said as he folded the napkin.

"I'm Antoinette Brown, but everybody calls me Toni." She shook his hand and felt a firm grip. He seemed strong and confident, even if he was tired. She liked that.

"Are you planning to stay in town for a while?" she asked.

"I'm not sure," he said, turning his attention back to the pie. She thought it was odd not to know how long one was staying in town.

"I just asked because Mrs. Dukes gives reduced rates to people who plan on staying awhile. She can tell you more about that once you get there," she explained.

"Do you own this place?" he asked, changing the subject.

She nodded and flashed him a proud smile. "I have for the past three years. My aunt Grace died and left it to me in her will."

Toni removed the cart with the dirty dishes from behind the counter and rolled it into the kitchen. Her mind flashed back to memories of the summer she had spent working at the bakery with her aunt and uncle. A few years after Toni had gone to college, her uncle Bob had died. Aunt Grace had continued to run the business until her own death.

They had one daughter, Eva, who was five years older than Toni. But Eva had no interest in the family business. She didn't like the early mornings and long hours. She had run away from home when she was seventeen, so Toni never got to know her cousin very well. Every once in a while, Eva stopped in the bakery with her husband, but the two cousins still weren't close. Toni remembered her aunt and uncle saying that they never heard from Eva unless she needed money. Toni couldn't understand it. She had always enjoyed working here.

One good thing had come out of the situation with Eva, however. Uncle Bob and Aunt Grace had hired Catherine Wellstone. A friend of the family, she was more than ten years younger than Toni's aunt and uncle. Cathy had helped out at the bakery for years. She usually worked part-time and occasionally took a few months off to visit friends or family. Cathy had been gone the whole summer Toni had worked at the bakery as a teenager. But when her aunt and uncle wanted to take a vacation, Cathy often ran the shop herself for a week or two at a time. After Uncle Bob died, Cathy had helped Aunt Grace recover from her loss. And when the business had been passed on to Toni, Catherine Wellstone had made the difference between failure and success for the new owner. Toni sometimes wondered what she would do when the woman finally decided to retire.

She returned from the kitchen, bent down behind the counter, and began removing empty racks from one of her display cases. "You seem kind of young to be owning and running your own bakery," Jason said, interrupting her thoughts.

Toni straightened up quickly, intent on defending her honor. "I'm not that young. I'm twenty-eight. My aunt trained me well, and one of her friends has helped with the things Aunt Grace never showed me. Besides, I'm pretty good at learning things on my own by reading or just by trial and error. I'm even famous around here for my mistakes."

She tried to moderate the irritation she heard in her voice and worked to summon up a smile. Her face felt frozen somewhere between a scowl and a grimace. "I usually experiment on the weekends, and on Monday, I give away any failures that are edible. They're always gone by ten o'clock, and the extra people they bring in improves business at the beginning of the week. Trust me, I'm completely capable of running my own place."

"I didn't mean to imply that you weren't." He looked puzzled, but his face also held the hint of a smile. Jason finished his apple pie and drank the last drop of his coffee.

"So, you're twenty-eight. Well, I don't think you look a day over twenty-two—a very pretty twenty-two."

Toni felt her cheeks warm with embarrassment. "Thank you," she whispered before she took his empty plate and cup away.

"Thanks for giving me the directions, Toni. I'll be seeing you soon." Giving her a warm smile, Jason left the bakery. The bell tinkled as the door closed behind him, and Toni watched him walk to his car across the street.

As she finished closing her bakery, Toni wondered once again why Jason Matthews had stopped in the small town of Blue Spring, Maryland.

*T*wo

*A*s Jason pulled into the parking lot of Mrs. Dukes's bed-and-breakfast, he remembered the pie and coffee. He hadn't paid for them. His first instinct was to rush back to the bakery, but then he remembered that Toni had been about to close. As thoughts of Toni Brown swirled through his mind, he almost forgot the money again. Just being around her made his composure melt like ice during a spring thaw. Her creamy brown skin, pretty eyes, and tall, shapely figure were enough to distract anyone. He could have sat and chatted with her for hours.

The last thing he had wanted was to imply that she was too young to run a business! Why had that comment made her so angry, anyway? He considered how to apologize as he knocked on the front door of the bed-and-breakfast. He imagined himself returning to her bakery the following day, smiling humbly. While leaving his money for the bill, plus a huge tip, he would issue such a sweet apology that she'd never be able to resist his charm.

"Well, if this don't beat all!" boomed a loud, friendly voice. It belonged to a woman standing in the doorway. She was short and plump. Her light brown hair was streaked with gray. Fine wrinkles lined her mouth and eyes, but her face still reflected the youth and vitality in her voice.

"H-h-hi," Jason managed to stammer.

"Ain't you the handsomest man who's graced my doorstep in ages! But don't let my husband know I said that," she whispered, giving Jason a teasing wink. Jason smiled, and she invited him inside.

"I'm Mrs. Dukes, by the way, and I suppose you're looking for a place to stay," she began after they were seated. Gospel music played in the background, and he heard people in the adjoining room talking as they watched television.

"Uh, yes, I am," he answered and then introduced himself.

"How long you planning to be in town? Are you visiting relatives or something?"

"No, I guess you could say I'm just passing through," he said.

"Passing through? Really? Where are you from?"

"Chicago," he replied, barely suppressing a yawn.

"How did you find out about my bed-and-breakfast?"

He sighed as he rubbed his hands across his eyes. Waves of fatigue washed over him. How long had he been on the road? For a moment he couldn't remember. Three weeks, no, longer. Yes, of course, it would be four weeks this coming Sunday since he had left the bleakness of a Chicago winter behind. After staying in a half dozen hotels along the way and eating in a different restaurant for almost every meal, he was more than ready to stop traveling.

"Toni Brown told me about your place," he answered. How

much longer would he have to wait before she offered him one of her rooms? This woman was nice enough, but she seemed to have an endless supply of questions!

"Ah, Toni told you. If that don't beat all! She's such a nice young lady and pretty to boot. I've always wondered why she's still single. Are you married, Mr. Matthews?"

Jason smiled again, trying desperately to hide his fatigue. "No, I'm not." Thankfully she didn't know just how close he had come to getting married. "Please don't call me Mr. Matthews. You're welcome to call me Jason," he said as he stood. He yawned as weariness continued to envelop his body.

"Oh, well, I guess I should show you to your room, shouldn't I?" Mrs. Dukes led him to the front desk, processed his credit card, and then gave him a key and led him upstairs. Pausing in front of a door, she said, "This is one of my more masculine rooms."

When she opened the door, Jason smiled with pleasure. The room was decorated in dark shades of blue and gray. The blinds were open, and afternoon sunlight poured in. There was a twin bed, a dresser, and a desk with a chair. A Bible sat on top of the dresser. "You're fortunate to get this room because it has its own bathroom. I only have two rooms that have their own bathroom. The rest of my boarders have to share."

Jason entered the room and sighed with contentment. This place reminded him of home. The adjoining bathroom was white and clean as a whistle. The shower curtain and matching rug were light blue.

"So, do you like the room, Jason?" Mrs. Dukes asked, smiling. He nodded. Tonight, he would have no problems falling asleep. "Well, if you're agreeing to take the room, there's a few things I need to go over with you. First off, since this is a bed-and-breakfast, I do serve one meal a day, and that's breakfast.

It's available from six to ten each morning, and it's the best deal in town, if I do say so myself. Also, I'm a Christian woman, so I don't allow my boarders to have overnight guests," she said.

"Don't worry, Mrs. Dukes. I'm a Christian man myself. As a matter of fact, can you let me know where you attend church services?"

She beamed at his request and mentioned the most popular churches in the area, offering to give him further details once he had gotten some rest. She also described the church she and her husband attended. "You're welcome to come with us if you'd like," she offered.

He smiled. "I'd like that, Mrs. Dukes. Say, do you know what church Toni Brown attends?"

She sadly shook her head. "Toni doesn't go to church. She told me that a long time ago when she first came into town to take over her aunt's bakery."

A wave of disappointment washed through him. "Don't look so glum, Jason," Mrs. Dukes said. "We all have to find the Lord in our own time."

He gave her a small smile before she left the room. Jason gazed at his luggage, thinking he should unpack and arrange his things. He walked over to the bed and sat down to test its firmness. Suddenly unpacking didn't seem so important. Jason collapsed sideways onto the bed, kicked his shoes off, and was deeply asleep less than a minute after his head hit the pillow.

When he awakened a few hours later, his fatigue had vanished completely. After he had showered and changed, he opened both of his suitcases. Laundry was next on the agenda, and Mrs. Dukes had already told him where the town's Laundromat was located. He put his clean clothes on hangers and in drawers while tossing his dirty clothes into a garbage bag. Grabbing the bundle, he walked to his car.

Jason rolled his window down and enjoyed the fresh breeze. The April evening still held some of the day's warmth. The sun had just set, and the sky was beautiful. Blue was fading into pink over the horizon. Jason never ceased to be amazed at the wonders of this earth that God created.

He drove slowly through town, observing his surroundings. A sign at the edge of the road stated, WELCOME TO BLUE SPRING, MARYLAND, POPULATION 2,000. This really was a small town! He now understood why the speed limit was so low. Children darted into the street. He stopped his car as they ran in front of him and into the video arcade across the street. A woman pushed her baby in a stroller. A man sat on a bench smoking a cigar. There was only one supermarket, and it was already closing its doors for the evening. He passed a thrift store, a beauty parlor, and a clothing boutique. The local high school was a brick one-story building equipped with an athletic field. The town's only coffee shop was still open, and people lingered inside. A small bookstore adjoined the coffee shop, but its doors were closed.

Jason's stomach rumbled with hunger. Spying a Chinese restaurant, he parked the car and ordered shrimp fried rice with egg rolls. After he finished his dinner, he continued the drive through town, turning on his headlights as the afterglow from the sunset faded.

Toni's bakery was located at the corner of Maple and Pine Streets. It was a small white building, and it stood alone, separated from the other stores on the street. He stopped his car and stared. A long, narrow wooden sign was mounted across the front of the building. The words BLUE SPRING BAKED GOODS were clearly visible in the light of the three antique fixtures that illuminated it from above. A street lamp beamed down into her yard. The small plot of earth was neatly mowed, and yellow flowers bordered the sides of the building. He gazed up into the second-story window. The lights were on, and a shadow passed the closed curtain. When a woman walked by on the sidewalk with a screaming child, the curtain parted. Jason quickly drove away, not wanting to be caught staring at Toni's window.

It was easy to find the Laundromat in such a small town. Two men sat outside on a bench, reading newspapers and talking. They greeted Jason as he entered. The place was practically deserted so late on a weekday evening. Only a few of the washers and dryers were being used, and he was the only person in the building. He took a roll of one-dollar bills from his pocket and got change from the machine. As he threw all his clothes into the washer, he realized he hadn't brought detergent. The vending machine for laundry supplies was empty, so he strode back out to the two men.

"Hey, can I bum some soap powder from either of you?"

"Yeah, man." Both men were elderly and resembled each other. They looked like brothers. One of them followed Jason back in and gave him his box of laundry soap. "Use as much as you need."

"Thanks. I don't need much. I'm only doing the one load," Jason said.

The man kept looking at him, his dark eyes full of curiosity. "Hey, I don't recall ever seeing you around here before. Are you new here?"

"Yeah. I'm not staying for very long, though." He returned the soap powder and found a newspaper on the counter. He began reading, and the man finally left. With the exception of Toni Brown, the people he'd met so far in this town were certainly nosy.

By the time his clothes had been washed and dried, Jason had read the entire paper. Nothing exciting seemed to happen in Blue Spring. The lead story on the front page was about a boy who had found his dog that had been missing for more than two months.

Jason threw his clothes back into the garbage bag and left the Laundromat. He drove through the streets of the town until he found the small church Mrs. Dukes had mentioned. The dark sky was littered with tiny white stars. Lights shone through the stained-glass windows of the church. A few cars were parked in the lot. He stopped and stared at the cross on top of the steeple. The sound of singing voices drifted through the open door, and he figured they were having choir practice. It was beautiful.

He closed his eyes and enjoyed the sweet music. A sigh escaped as he thought about all that had happened in his life over the last few months. At times, he felt as if he'd reached the end of his rope.

Someone rapped against his partly open car window, and Jason jumped. A middle-aged man in a white shirt and blue jeans gave him a small, curious smile. His skin was the color of dark coffee.

Jason lowered his window the rest of the way.

"Are you all right?" the man asked.

Jason blinked, wondering if he should answer the question truthfully. "I think so," he managed to say.

"I'm John Wilkins. I'm the pastor of Blue Spring Community Church."

Jason hesitated before he shook the man's hand and introduced himself. The music had stopped, and the night was filled with silence. Only a few lights remained on in the church.

"Choir practice is over," said Pastor Wilkins as he looked toward the church. "Since the deacon isn't here today, I'll need to lock up. I heard a car drive up a while ago, and I just wanted to make sure everything was okay."

People began coming out of the church and walking toward their cars. The stream of choir members broke up into smaller clusters, and some of them drifted toward Jason's part of the parking lot. He heard friendly banter as well as quieter, more serious conversations. The members of the nearest group laughed together and exchanged a few hugs as they said their good-byes.

Jason felt a familiar burning sensation in his eyes. He swallowed hard to hold back the tears. Sometimes the sadness from his recent loss hit him unexpectedly. Reverend Wilkins continued to gaze at him, concern mirrored in his dark brown eyes. What should he say? He certainly didn't feel like burdening the pastor with his problems. After all, he barely knew the man.

"Reverend, what time does your church have worship services?" Jason finally managed to ask.

Blue Spring Baked Goods was full to overflowing with customers, and Toni Brown was a mess. She hadn't been this flustered since her first few days in the bakery as a teenager. She wanted to pull her hair out, but there was no time. How was it possible for an entire day to become a total loss before nine-thirty in the morning? She was worried, she was frustrated, and it all just got worse from there.

What was she going to do?

A long line stood at her counter, and a snide woman was returning a cherry pie she had purchased the previous day. She claimed the concoction was too sweet. Toni didn't feel like arguing. Customers were always right, she reminded herself, no matter how unreasonable they seemed. But how could this woman claim a pie didn't taste good and demand a refund when only one piece was left in the pie tin? Toni took a slow, deep breath, the kind her track coach in college had taught her to take just before a race. She forced herself to smile, then gave the woman her money and began filling the next order.

What was she going to do?

Cathy had been early for work. Nothing out of the ordinary about that—she often showed up about four-thirty. But today she brought disturbing news. Her daughter and son-in-law had been involved in a serious car accident the night before. They were in the hospital. And Cathy was already packed and on her way out of town. She hoped to arrive at their home in Virginia before noon.

"I'm sorry to do this to you, Toni," she'd said. "And I can't even tell how long I'll be gone. I think you'd better plan on a couple of weeks at least. I'll call you tomorrow night. I should know more by then."

"Don't worry about me. I'll be fine," Toni was quick to respond. But now she wasn't so sure.

What was she going to do?

As she rang up an order for a dozen éclairs, the bell on the door jingled again. Glancing up, she noticed Jason walk in. She didn't have the energy to return his smile. Her eyes swept quickly around the shop, noting that most of the customers sitting at the tables needed coffee refills. There was no way she could get to them until the line at the counter was a lot shorter.

"Toni, did you need some help?" a deep voice asked from behind her. Startled, she turned. Jason was standing behind the counter with her.

Her first instinct was to say no, but she was so backed up that she couldn't refuse his offer. "Yes, can you refill the coffee for the people at the tables? The regular is in the brown pot and the decaf is in the orange," she explained as she gave him an apron. "And make sure you wash your hands before you start." She managed to soften her words with a smile, adding, "We need to keep the health department happy."

She continued to ring up orders as Jason refilled coffee cups. When he finished, he asked what he could do next. "You can get the people what they want while I work the register," she instructed.

Requests poured in for tarts, pies, pastries, and donuts. Jason found most of the items quickly. When he couldn't, Toni pointed him in the right direction. After an hour and a half of hustle and bustle, the bakery was suddenly empty. The peace and quiet was soothing, but also a bit of a shock. Toni knew she needed to force them both to slow down and take a break. She poured a cup of coffee for herself and one for Jason, and then she pulled out her famous chocolate éclairs.

As they sat at a table to enjoy their snack, she said, "Okay, Jason, can you please tell me why you're here this morning?" She took a large bite of her éclair and a sip of coffee. She had worked up a real appetite and was eager to hear what Jason had to say.

Jason sipped his coffee and took a bite of his éclair. "Hey, this is good!"

"Of course it's good," she protested. "People wouldn't be lined up at the door every morning if what I make didn't taste a lot better than what they can buy at the grocery store."

Jason smiled apologetically. "I didn't mean to offend you," he said. "And the reason I showed up is because yesterday I forgot to pay for my pie and coffee. How much do I owe you?" He stood and removed his apron, then reached into his back pocket and pulled out an expensive leather wallet. She recognized the Ghurka logo from her years at the country club.

"Jason, after all the help you gave me this morning, I owe you money! Why did you do it? And where did you learn so much about pastries? Most men can't tell an éclair from a cream puff."

Jason looked away from her. His easy smile dissolved into a pained grimace, which was quickly followed by a thoughtful expression. He replaced his wallet and slowly sat down. Staring out the front window of the bakery, his eyes seemed to lose their focus. "I learned the difference between an éclair and a cream puff from my mother," he said in a soft voice. "She was quite a cook. And I suppose I learned about helping people from her, too—and from Dad."

He sighed deeply, and a weak smile returned to his face. He turned back to face her. "Look, Toni, when I see somebody in a tough spot, I stop and help if I can."

She frowned. "You would help anybody?"

"Usually, sure. The Lord wants us to help one another." He polished off the éclair and helped himself to a second cup of coffee.

When he returned to the table, she asked, "Do your parents live near here? I don't think I've ever heard of a Matthews family in this part of the state."

"No, they live in Chicago. I mean, well . . . my father still lives in Chicago." A look of complete despair passed over his face. The next words came out in a choking whisper. "My mother is . . . she . . . she died." Tears filled his eyes, and she could see his jaw muscles working as he fought to control the spasm of grief.

Toni was stunned. She searched for something to say. "I'm sorry, Jason. That must be so hard. I can't imagine what it would be like."

"It's all right. I don't expect you to understand." A single tear escaped from his left eye and ran down his face. His voice seemed to gain strength. "I probably shouldn't have said anything. I try to keep reminding myself that she's with the Lord, but that doesn't seem to help much. I guess I just need to learn how to trust God to bring something good from all this pain."

"You sound like my mother," she said softly.

"Your mother is a Christian?"

Toni nodded. A tendril of her dark brown hair had escaped her bun, so she pushed the stray lock behind her ear. "Mom has faced a lot of disappointment and pain in her life, and she always says that God is going to turn it into something good."

"What sort of disappointment and pain, Toni?" Jason's voice was suddenly strong and filled with concern.

She thought about the conflicts she'd witnessed between her parents. She remembered her father's alcoholism, their small trailer home, her mother's deep faith in God, and how that faith never seemed to make their hard lives any easier. "My parents fought a lot when I was younger, mostly because Dad drank a lot," she began.

What was she doing? She didn't know this man. Could she trust him? She had learned in college that most men were after only one thing. After a few dates, they made you feel as if you owed them something. So far, she had followed her mother's advice to stay away from such entanglements, and she was glad she had. But there was something different about Jason. He felt safe. It was nice just sitting here alone with him in her bakery.

Jason gave her a peculiar look, waiting for her to continue.

The next words came tumbling out before she could stop them. "Dad had trouble keeping a job, and Mom didn't work. We were poor. It was . . . very hard. And I hated it." More words threatened to escape. She didn't want the conversation to end.

And she didn't want anything to disturb the warm glow she felt from being near Jason Matthews. He felt comfortable, familiar. Suddenly Toni was afraid. She had let down her guard once before.

A gentle ache in her heart reminded her of the only serious relationship she'd ever had. She and Brian had been star members of the college track team. She admired his competitive streak. They dated for a full year, and she had been in love. Shortly after graduation, they both found jobs for the same international company. They were engaged a short time later, and she had eagerly planned her wedding. But when she discovered that he had been unfaithful to her, she broke the engagement. She shook her head as if to drive further thoughts of Brian from her mind. Instead she gazed at Jason.

"Are you all right?" he asked.

"I'm not sure. I was just thinking about a lot of things from my past. Things I'd rather forget. I'm not sure how much I want to tell you about them."

"Believe me, Toni, I don't want you telling me anything that makes you uncomfortable. We just met yesterday, after all. And I've seen what poverty can do to people. It's terrible, and you had every right to hate it."

There was something different about him. What kind of man would come into a bakery for a cup of coffee and end up serving the customers? If someone had predicted this would happen, she would have thought he was crazy.

She stole a look at Jason's car, parked across the street. He drove a black BMW four-door. It seemed to be crouching in the shadows under the huge maple tree, ready to spring away from the curb. Something about it was familiar. Of course — the president of the bank in a nearby town owned one like it. He sometimes picked up boxes of baked goods on his way in to bank meetings. He'd once told her that his car was a special edition, that there were only a few hundred like it in the whole country. She remembered the car clearly now. It had been black, too, and it was always spotless. But Jason's car was so dirty it looked more gray than black.

"Who are you, Jason Matthews?" she whispered. It was only when the look of surprise crossed his face that she realized she had spoken her thought out loud. "I-I'm sorry, I didn't m-m-mean to be rude," Toni stuttered. She was making a fool of herself. Standing, she cleared their dirty dishes away, hoping the familiar task would restore her composure. She felt Jason's eyes following her, but he remained silent.

Who was this guy? His jeans and shirt were simple, yet expensive. The only jewelry he wore was a Rolex watch. There was no hint of the arrogance she usually associated with rich people, but everything else about him said that Jason Matthews had more money than he or any three other people needed. Yet he said he understood the pain of poverty.

Since she'd moved away from home, Toni's fascination with money had grown. She paid close attention to the wealthy people she met just as she had done when she'd worked in the country club. She usually found that there were two groups of wealthy people. Some grew up with money and usually took their possessions for granted. But those who became wealthy as adults often flaunted their new status. Their expensive cars always sparkled like new, and when they went on exotic vacations, everyone around them got a full report. Jason looked, sounded, and acted like old money, but she was sure that was only part of his story.

As Toni walked back to the table, she gazed at his left hand and saw no wedding band. At least he wasn't married. She wondered if he was divorced or if he had any children. The problems of the world seemed to rest on his broad shoulders. She understood something of that burden now, but even the loss of his mother didn't seem enough to explain the brooding melancholy that so often erased his wonderful smile. What was a young, handsome, wealthy black man from Chicago doing this far from home? How could she find out more about this mysterious stranger without seeming to pry?

"Jason," Toni said quietly, "why are you here in Blue Spring? Are you on a business trip?"

Before he could answer, a group of customers entered the bakery. Toni stood and filled their orders for sodas and cookies. After they paid, she returned to the table.

"It's kind of complicated, Toni," he responded. "My mom died last fall from brain cancer. I watched it slowly killing her for over three years. My family owns a business in Chicago, and we've all worked together for years, so there's a unique bond between us. We're used to solving problems and offering support. It's not just what we do for a living; it's who we are as people. So, when Mom got sick, the cancer was just another problem for us to solve. But we couldn't solve it. And no matter how much help we gave Mom, she just kept getting worse."

He paused, and Toni said, "It sounds like you were all feeling kind of helpless and maybe useless, too."

"Yeah, that's it exactly. And I'm not used to feeling helpless, much less useless. I'm a Christian, Toni, and I believe God is working to change me from the inside so I can be a better person. And I also believe He gives me opportunities to change the world around me. Following Christ means serving other people. Christians aren't supposed to be helpless when they face suffering. We're supposed to make a difference.

"My whole family wanted to transform Mom's suffering into something less painful," he went on. "Most of all, we didn't want her to face the cancer alone. All of us were determined to go through the whole terrible process with her: the tests, the treatments, the moments of hope, and all the disappointments. And I suppose we were able to do that, but it didn't feel like we were making things better.

"When it was clear nothing more could be done for her, she wanted to die at home, and we were able to arrange that for her. The night she died, we were all there. She was never alone. But in the end, there was nothing we could do to help her, because we couldn't stop the cancer. And when she died, we all died with her. Ever since that night, I've felt like my own life is some sort of illusion. It's like I'm suddenly powerless to have any sort of positive impact on the world around me. I'm afraid that the things I think I'm accomplishing will all turn out to be meaningless."

"So, you feel like you failed your mother because you couldn't cure her?" Toni asked.

"Yes, and I've got to admit, I think God failed her, too. And I don't know what to do with all the feelings of pain and anger and fear and— I don't even know what all the feelings are. Anyway, the holidays were awful for all of us. After the first of the year things got a little better for everyone but me. Winter in Chicago is gray, damp, and raw. It's hard enough to endure when things are going well, but this year every new storm seemed to suck more life out of me. After Valentine's Day, I could hardly make myself get out of bed in the morning."

Jason paused and shook his head, remembering how lost he had felt. "By that time even my dog was worried." A small smile returned. He was looking directly at her now. "My dad, my brother and sister—they all told me that I needed to get out of town. They suggested I hop a plane for somewhere warm. Dad even offered the corporate jet, and he's never done that for a nonbusiness trip before. But I felt like driving. I guess it's a form of therapy for me."

Jason stared down silently at his empty plate.

She waited, expecting him to continue. Finally she asked, "How long have you been on the road?"

"It will be a month on Sunday."

"Jason, I don't think you failed your mother. And I'll bet she didn't think so either. You loved her—all of you did, together. Do you have any idea how rare that kind of experience is? I think most people would be willing to face anything, suffering and death included, if they could be sure they would be loved like that. I would."

Jason's head came up slowly. A strange intensity filled his eyes, and they were glassy with unshed tears. "How could you know that?" The words came out in an amazed whisper. "The last few weeks before she died, Mom kept saying to us, 'When I've gone to be with the Lord, I don't want you to think that you've failed me. Even in the midst of sorrow and suffering, God is teaching us that His love is stronger than the grave.' "

Jason reached for another napkin and blotted at his eyes. Toni was stunned by all that she had learned about him in such a short time and by how much she had revealed about herself. She struggled to think of another question to ask. A strange gurgling sound broke the silence. Toni glanced toward the kitchen, wondering if it was a plumbing problem. "What was that?" she asked.

"I'm afraid it's me," Jason said sheepishly.

Toni turned back to him just in time to hear the sound

again. It was his stomach, and it was very loud. In spite of her best efforts, she started to chuckle. "Did you want another éclair?" she asked.

Suddenly, they were both howling with laughter. After a minute or so, relative calm returned.

"I haven't laughed that hard in a long time," he confessed. "And no, I don't want another éclair. But it is about time for lunch." He stood and stretched.

Toni glanced at the black-and-white clock on her wall. They had been chatting for over an hour! It was eleven-thirty, and she wanted to eat lunch, too.

"Did you want to go out and get something to eat?" he asked.

She shook her head. "I can't leave the bakery. I live on the top floor of this building. It has a small apartment with a kitchen. I usually just make a sandwich and eat it down here. If somebody comes into the bakery, I hear the bell from upstairs," she explained.

Jason agreed to watch the bakery while she went upstairs to make their sandwiches. Customers began to come in to pick up various things for lunch, so their own lunch was delayed for more than an hour. It was nearing one o'clock before they started eating their tuna fish on rye with potato chips, and then Toni explained about Cathy's departure for Virginia.

"I'm glad she decided to go and help her family, but I don't know how I'm going to keep this bakery running without her help," she finished.

"Look, Toni, I'm tired of traveling. I have nothing but time on my hands for at least the next few months. I can help you out."

She was so startled by his suggestion that she was momentarily speechless. "Yesterday, it sounded like you weren't planning to be in town for long. I guess I can understand now why you want some peace and quiet, but why on earth do you want to work here? You've seen how crazy this place gets sometimes."

Jason wiped his mouth with a napkin, rolled it into a tight ball, and threw it across the room. It unerringly hit the bottom of the trash can.

"A lot's been happening in my life over the past couple of years and especially over the past few months," he said. "And you're right, I have been looking for a quiet place to rest. I think I found it when I drove into Blue Spring yesterday. I like the bed-and-breakfast, and I like your bakery. Let me work here for a week, and then we'll see how things go. If either of us is uncomfortable, I'll help you find another replacement for Cathy. You can pay me minimum wage. I bet that's less than you were paying her. I may not know as much as she does, but I learn fast, and I already know quite a bit about running a business." He smiled. "I even know a little about baking."

Another group of customers came into the bakery, and the next few minutes were taken up with helping them. Afterward Toni asked, "What kind of business does your family own in Chicago?"

"It's called Matthews and Company. My father founded it about fifteen years ago, but we didn't become an important player in the telecommunications industry until about ten years ago. We make some of the hardware and software products that allow the Internet to function. Have you ever heard of devices called servers or routers?"

"Yes," Toni replied. An eager light appeared in her eyes. They were familiar terms from her years of work in the financial industry.

"That's the kind of hardware we build—machines to move

information back and forth across the Internet. But we're best known for our custom-designed software, which makes the routers and servers easier to run and easier to fix when things go wrong. And believe me, that's important, because things always go wrong. My father, Kevin Matthews, is an electrical engineer. He graduated from MIT in the early sixties and has been involved in developing several important computer-programming languages. Dad is the CEO, and I'm the CFO, that's—"

"Chief financial officer," she said, finishing the sentence for him. "You probably have an MBA and a degree in computer science."

"Actually, I have two degrees in computer science, but you're right about the MBA."

She reminded herself not to have too much fun at his expense, but she couldn't resist asking, "Don't you think you're a little overqualified to work in a bakery?"

"My mom never thought so," he replied. "Robin Matthews was famous all over the Chicago area for her pies, cakes, pastries, and other baked goods. She donated hundreds of them to charity auctions and programs to feed needy families. She also liked to give large parties for all sorts of people several times a year. She was constantly coming up with creative things to do for Valentine's Day and Easter, but her favorite holidays were Thanksgiving and Christmas. And I was always her chief assistant."

Toni suddenly looked confused. "Let me see if I understand what you're saying. Your mom owned a bakery in Chicago and you worked in it part-time?"

"No. I'm sorry, I'm not explaining this very well," he replied. "Mom did all her cooking and baking at home. My parents bought and remodeled a huge old house that had originally been built in the 1920s. They put in a big commercial kitchen, with large refrigerators, special stoves and ovens, cooling racks, floor-mounted mixing equipment—everything you would find in a well-designed restaurant or small bakery. But entertaining was a hobby for her. She worked as the manager of charitable giving for Matthews and Company. Mom created the Matthews Foundation and acted as its chief administrator. The foundation provides college scholarships for low-income students from poor neighborhoods in and around Chicago."

Toni sat quietly and tried to make sense of all that had happened since yesterday. She had lost an employee who had been with Blue Spring Baked Goods almost as long as she had been alive. A wealthy, successful, and handsome man with chocolate brown skin had walked into her small bakery and offered to help run her business. And while he had not filled out a job application and she hadn't checked any references, she felt more comfortable hiring him than she'd ever felt hiring anybody else. Jason made her feel safe.

"Mr. Jason Matthews," she announced, "you've got yourself a deal." They were both smiling as they shook hands.

Three

*T*oni watched Jason walk across the street. A few women stopped and stared as he unlocked his car. She knew they were wondering who he was. One thing she didn't like about living in a small town was the lack of privacy. Everybody was so nosy.

Several customers had watched Jason with open curiosity as he poured coffee earlier that day. She hadn't figured out yet how she was going to explain his presence to the members of this tight-knit community. In the past, vague answers and silence had been her two best weapons when people asked questions she didn't want to answer. Everyone already knew that, except for Cathy, she usually hired teenagers because she couldn't pay more than minimum wage. Perhaps that would be a good place to start. She imagined herself carefully describing the tragedy in Cathy's family (once she had more information to give) and adding a brief comment about the son of a bakery owner who was vacationing in the area. She suspected that nothing she said would keep them from thinking she simply wanted to spend more time with the good-looking stranger.

A few minutes later, Toni placed the CLOSED sign on her door and covered the leftover food with plastic wrap, ready to be sold the next day at half price. It was just after three in the afternoon, and she was tired. She had often considered keeping her bakery open in the evenings, but simple fatigue discouraged her from making the attempt. Even with Cathy's help, part of the morning and all of the lunch hour were extremely busy, so by the time the middle of the afternoon arrived, she was ready for a change of pace. Not that she could simply lock the door and disappear. She sighed as she got out cleaning supplies and began attacking the dirty tables.

About an hour later, she tossed a garbage bag in the Dumpster, locked the back door, and took one last look around the bakery to make sure everything was in place. She yawned and stretched before turning off the lights and walking up the stairs to her small apartment. Unlocking the door, she smiled in contentment as she crossed the living room to open the blinds. She was always glad to return to her cheerful home after a hard day of work.

The cream-colored walls were decorated with pictures of the ocean in various moods. Fluffy carpet matched her walls and set off the light lavender couch and overstuffed chair, positioned to take best advantage of the television, stereo, and VCR. Beside the television stood a bookcase that held her collection of books on cooking and related topics. She also had a wooden CD case full of classical and jazz disks. She placed a recording of Beethoven's "Moonlight Sonata" into her player and turned it on. Soft notes filled the air and soothed her tired body.

Kicking off her shoes, she walked into the small kitchen, surprised to discover she was hungry again. The day must have been even busier than she remembered. Throwing together a Caesar salad and grabbing a glass of lemonade, she collapsed into the living-room chair and enjoyed a quiet meal.

Just as she finished, the phone rang. She quickly walked into her bedroom and answered it. Would it be Jason? Her heart raced. She had given him her phone number earlier that day in case he needed to contact her after working hours.

"Hello?" Her voice was breathless and full of hope.

"Antoinette, you sound mighty happy this evening," said her mother.

Her heart slowed immediately as she sat on her bed. "Oh, hi, Mom." She smoothed imaginary wrinkles from her blue bedspread. "How've you been?"

"About the same. I just called to find out when you were coming home again."

Toni sighed. Home was more than two hours away. Her bakery was open six days a week, closing only on Sundays. Sometimes, when Cathy's schedule allowed, she would take over and Toni would go down for an entire weekend, provided there were enough pastries to last through Saturday. "I'm not sure," she said. As impressed as she was with Jason, she didn't yet know how much knowledge he actually possessed. It would take time to determine where his strengths were and whether she could trust him to run the bakery on his own.

"Well, your father hasn't been feeling well lately."

"What's wrong?" she asked, her voice full of alarm.

"Nothing serious. We're getting old, Antoinette. Your father just needs to take it easy and watch his diet."

Toni was glad to hear that it wasn't serious. She worried about her parents. They were still married, and their relationship had improved over the years since she had left home, but she could still sense that something was wrong. They didn't fight any more, and her father even went with Mom to church sometimes.

Apparently, the foreman at his current job had gotten to know Dad and liked him. After a few months, Toni's father discovered, almost by accident, that the man belonged to the same church her mom attended. With gentle encouragement on the part of his new friend, her father had begun to deal more effectively with his alcoholism. He was gradually beginning to see church attendance as part of that process.

But over the last year, Toni's father had often seemed distant when she visited. He acted much more tired than usual. Toni worried that his body was finally wearing down after years of abuse. Whatever the reason, he had certainly become a lot more dependent on her mother recently.

But that wasn't the most surprising change Toni had observed. Mom no longer pressured the rest of the family to come to church. Occasionally she would talk about something that had happened during a service or at the women's shelter, but such conversations were friendly, rather than sermons in disguise. Toni was grateful that her mother had never asked what had become of her going-away present from all those years ago. The Bible was carefully stored, along with other important documents, in a fireproof box on a bottom shelf in the bakery kitchen.

"Your father misses you, Toni, and so do I," said her mother, interrupting Toni's thoughts. "I know you can't always leave the bakery when you want to. I could come and visit you if you'd like, or maybe the both of us could come up," she suggested.

Toni tried not to laugh at the idea of her parents traveling together. Neither of them could drive. Her mother couldn't see well enough, and her father had gotten his driver's license revoked a few years after Toni had gone away to college. He had been caught driving drunk one too many times. Now he was sixty years old and still working at the factory. He caught rides to work with the same friend who had helped him face his drinking problem. Her parents would probably have to take a bus if they ever wanted to get to Blue Spring.

"That's okay, Mom. I'm sure I'll be able to visit soon." Toni hesitated. She had always been fairly close to her mother, but how much should she tell her about Jason Matthews? What did she really know? "I've hired a new employee. Cathy had to go to Virginia to take care of a family emergency." Toni described what she knew of the situation.

"Oh?" her mother said in surprise. "Well, who did you get on such short notice?"

Without intending to, Toni began to discuss Jason's sudden appearance in the bakery and the mark he had already left on her life.

"He sounds like a nice man, Toni. Maybe something will happen between the two of you. After all, I still want to see you get married and have children someday," she added hopefully.

Toni rolled her eyes as she flopped back on her bed, cradling the phone. Mothers! Did they ever give up? She stared at the stucco pattern on her ceiling. From what she could gather, Jason was intelligent, sensitive, and very honest. But she had learned that first impressions were sometimes wrong. It was way too early to be thinking about marriage. She quickly bid her mother good-bye, assuring her that she would try to visit as soon as she could.

The phone rang again, and she recognized Cathy's voice. "Toni, how are you doing? Did you get through the day all right?"

"I'm doing fine. Nobody in my family was in a traffic accident last night. Shouldn't we be talking about how you're doing?"

"Oh Toni, I'm so thankful to God. They're all right, though there are some broken bones and a lot of bruises. They'll be in the hospital for a week or so, but then it's going to be a month or more before either of them is going to be able to work again. I really need to stay here and help out with the kids and the housekeeping chores until everyone is back on their feet. Is there any way you can find someone to replace me for a couple of months?"

"You're not going to believe this, Cathy, but I already have. I'm glad to hear that things aren't too serious. Take as much time as you need." Toni explained about the situation with Jason.

"My, my, my," chortled Cathy, "sounds like I should go away more often. But I am glad to know things are covered on your end. Well, I've got to run. Lots to do and not enough time. You take care of yourself, and I'll be in touch in a couple of weeks."

Toni smiled as she put down the receiver. She wondered what interesting new developments she would have to share with Cathy when they spoke next.

The next morning Jason showed up at the bakery at seven-thirty, as planned. He helped Toni with the busiest part of the morning and the noon hour. During lulls between customers, Toni gave him a detailed tour of the front of the bakery, explaining each item she sold and describing which customers usually bought it. She also showed him where price information was kept next to the cash register. When business tapered off shortly after one o'clock, Toni went upstairs and fixed Greek salads that they ate with a fresh loaf of *ciabatta* bread she had made that morning. For dessert, Toni introduced Jason to her famous baklava.

As they worked their way through that layered delight, accompanied by strong coffee, Jason said, "You really enjoy working here, even with the odd hours and long days. Why is that?"

Toni paused to consider the question. "I'm creating something unique, something people enjoy. And I'm in control of my own future, as much as any of us can be at least. And I'm continuing something my aunt Grace and uncle Bob gave most of their lives to." She described what it was like to work with her aunt and uncle.

"Sounds like they were remarkable people," Jason responded. "I guess I agree with you on the importance of creativity. When I'm working on new systems or trying to solve a problem in an old one, I often feel like I'm helping to create the future."

She smiled. "So, you're telling me that you want to put God out of a job?"

Jason laughed. "That's going a little too far. But there was a Christian philosopher who said that when we discover new things or create new things, we are thinking God's thoughts after Him."

"My turn to ask a question," she continued. "What do you dislike about working at Matthews and Company?"

"The computer business can be really nasty," Jason answered immediately. "Everybody wants a piece of the future, and they'll go to almost any lengths to get it. Every time I go into work, I have to pass through several layers of security. There are retinal scans at the main entrance. To get out of the elevator on the floor where my office is, I have to pass a fingerprint scan. After that I get to spend all day wearing this nifty little ID tag that tracks my movements all over the building. It even shows when I'm in the bathroom. To get my computer running in the morning, I have to go through a security firewall that uses voice-identification software."

He shook his head and chuckled. "One day I came to work with a cold, and the computer refused to recognize me. I had to get our chief of security to enter an override code. It was crazy."

He paused and then asked, "What do you dislike about Blue Spring Baked Goods?"

Toni sat silently for a long time. Jason waited patiently. Finally she took a deep breath and said, "I'm afraid that I'm going to fail. That I'm programmed to fail and can't rise above the limitations of my parents. I'm afraid I'm going to end up trapped in poverty again. That everyone will abandon me because I'm poor and I'll be alone."

She described her life before leaving for college. "I know it's been more than ten years since I left home, but my parents are still suffering, and I can't help them yet. Mom keeps saying that God will take care of them, but I don't see anything changing."

She paused and looked at Jason. "Please don't take this wrong, but it seems to me that God is pretty good at making rich people richer, but He hasn't quite figured out how to help poor people escape poverty. Growing up poor makes me doubt God the same way watching your mother die makes you doubt God. In fact, poverty is a lot like cancer. It just takes longer to kill people."

"Toni, it's okay to be angry at God. And I agree, poverty is a slow cancer. But I'm not sure that God is the problem here. I wish I had a great explanation for suffering, but I don't. And I've got to admit that I'm angry at God some of the time, too. All I can offer you is my friendship. Maybe if we talk more about some of the things we've been through, both of us can find some answers. There's a passage in the Old Testament, in Proverbs, I think, that says wisdom is found in a multitude of counselors. We aren't exactly a multitude, but two is sure better than one."

Toni said, "That's the best offer I've had in a long time."

The jingling bell announced the arrival of more customers, and Jason and Toni were soon caught up in the rush of afternoon business. During a quiet moment, Toni introduced Jason to the joys of running a commercial dishwasher, and before they knew it, closing time had arrived.

"I'll show up early tomorrow morning so you can give me more training before we open," Jason promised as he left.

After locking the front door, Toni finished cleaning the front of the store and then moved to the kitchen. Having put everything in order for the next day's baking, she took a careful inventory of her sugar, flour, spices, fresh fruit, and other baking supplies. By six o'clock she had an order ready for her wholesaler. She was entering it on the computer in her small office next to the kitchen when the phone rang. It was Sheila, who had remained her best friend all through college and during the years that had followed.

"Girl, what've you been up to? I just got off work. I stopped by Chan's to pick up some takeout, and I heard people talking about some tall dark stranger at your bakery. You've been holding out on me, girl. I want to know all about this Jasper."

Toni chuckled. People in this town could really spread a rumor. Too bad they couldn't keep the facts straight. "His name is Jason, not Jasper," she said. "If you want to know the whole story, why don't you come by? We can have dinner together. A lot has happened in the last couple of days, so I didn't get a chance to call you."

In college, both Toni and Sheila had prepared for careers in

the financial world. Toni had gone into international investment, largely as a result of the things she had learned from her
uncle. Sheila had been vigorously recruited by three different
banking firms and had accepted a position with one of them
before she even graduated. A year after Toni had come to Blue
Spring to take over the bakery, her friend had been offered a
position as branch manager of the only bank in town.

Fifteen minutes after making their plans, Sheila arrived.
Toni unlocked the door and led her upstairs to the apartment.
Sheila was petite and dark-skinned. She always wore her long
dark hair in a bun, and she dressed conservatively. That
evening, she was wearing a simple white T-shirt, a pair of blue
jeans, and some light, airy sandals. In her hands were two large
sacks of food.

"Looks like you brought enough to feed a small army," said
Toni.

"It's been a long week, and you know how hungry I get
sometimes."

Toni envied Sheila's ability to eat like a horse and not gain
an ounce of weight. She had to watch every bite and work out
at the local gym regularly to avoid extra pounds.

"So, tell me about Jason," Sheila said, as she opened the
containers of food. Toni grabbed some plates, cups, and utensils. Then she joined Sheila at the kitchen table and filled her
in on the bakery's new employee.

"I agree with your mother—he does sound nice," Sheila
commented as she sipped on a large mocha from the coffee
shop. "And it sure sounds like he's taken a pounding lately. But
it seems so strange that he'd offer to go to work for you like that.
I admire his vision for Christian service, but his actions just
don't fit his background. This guy comes from a family that
lives by strategic planning—the kind of long-term goal setting

we learned about in college. They consider and debate and gather information. They don't make snap decisions. Why do you think he went to work for you?"

Toni considered the question for a moment. "I think the bakery reminds him of home—home before his mother died. I think he feels, well, comfortable here. And I have this sense that I can trust him. He certainly works hard, and he treats my customers like he's known them for years."

"I think, maybe, you should be a little careful, Toni. I doubt that Jason is looking at you as a mother figure." Sheila stood up, disposed of her trash, and gathered her purse. "Why don't you keep the leftovers? I've gotta go. There's a meeting at church tonight."

Toni looked up at her. She spoke softly. "Sheila, why did God let Jason's mother die?"

"You think I'm a theologian?" Sheila rolled her eyes. "All I know is we've all got to—"

"Give Jesus a chance," said Toni, finishing Sheila's sentence for her. A sudden anger erupted within her, and she glared up at her friend. "You've told me that about a million times since we were kids. Do you have the faintest idea what those words mean? Jason's whole family gave Jesus a chance, and nothing happened." She looked at her friend sadly, "And you wonder why I get so negative when you start talking about how great the church is."

"I'm sorry, Toni, I don't have time to discuss this with you right now. I'm late. Take care of yourself, okay?" Sheila hurried out the door, down the stairs, and disappeared into the fading light of evening.

Toni sat for a long time without moving. The darkness grew, and she watched it creep up the stairs toward her. Finally she got up slowly and locked the doors to her apartment. She had just returned to her kitchen when the phone rang. She ran to answer it, thinking it might be Jason.

"Hello," she said excitedly. Silence. "Hello?" she repeated.

"Be careful, or you'll be sorry," a gruff male voice grunted into the phone.

"Who is this?" Her voice quivered. A cold feeling crept down her spine. The question was swallowed up by unyielding silence. Suddenly there was a harsh click and the irritating buzz of the dial tone. The black cordless phone rattled back into its cradle, dropping from fingers that seemed no longer her own. Toni collapsed into a nearby chair. Her body shook uncontrollably. After a few moments, the worst of the shock had passed. With her heart still pounding, she picked up the phone and rapidly punched in the code that would identify the number of the last caller. It didn't work. The number was untraceable.

Four

The threatening voice greeted Toni on the phone three more times in the next few days. Two calls came in the evening, once on Saturday while she was fixing dinner, and a second time just before she went to bed on Monday. The third one caught her early Wednesday morning as she was getting ready for work.

By Thursday, she was having trouble hiding the growing panic within her. All day, Jason's presence in the bakery made the difference between her going on or collapsing. He also helped her keep ahead of the steady flow of customers, and Toni did not know how she would have managed without him.

"So," she said to Jason after the last customer had left for the day, "we've been through our trial week. How are you feeling about things?"

Jason smiled. "It's been great. I still have a lot of things to learn, but I hope my work's beginning to make up for all the time you're spending training me."

"Actually, you've picked up on things more quickly than anyone else I've trained. And if you're willing, I'd like you to stay around until at least the Fourth of July. By then I'd have a better idea of how Cathy's family is doing and when she'll be able to be back."

Jason beamed. "It's a deal."

"Then I think we should celebrate," Toni said.

"Sounds like a good idea," Jason replied. "Let's go out to dinner for a change."

"I have a better idea," she replied. "I'll fix us dinner, and afterward we can wash that insanely expensive car of yours."

"Why do you—"

"It hasn't been washed or cleaned out since you left Chicago, has it?"

He shook his head sheepishly.

"Well, don't you think it's about time? After all, you've cleaned my tables, my display cases, and even my windows all week. And I must say," she added in a teasing voice, "I just love a man who does windows." Switching to her normal voice she concluded, "Turn about's fair play, don't you think?"

Jason smiled slowly and replied, "Toni Brown, that's the best offer I've had in a long time."

Toni thoroughly enjoyed her evening with Jason, but her peace was short-lived. At one thirty-six A.M., the sound of a ringing telephone woke her from a sound sleep. Her tormentor had returned. She spent the rest of the night shaking, crying, and sleeping very little.

Jason hurried to the bakery early the following morning. Toni had promised to begin showing him how she created her masterpieces. Part of him was genuinely excited to compare his mother's techniques with the traditions of Blue Spring Baked Goods. Another part of him, one he tried to hide even from himself, knew that every hour spent learning was another hour alone with Toni.

He smiled as he approached the bakery. It was five o'clock, the sky was still full of stars, and the bakery doors wouldn't open until six-thirty, just at sunrise. The front of the bakery was dark, but lights were on in the kitchen. The smell of baking bread wafted through a partially open window. It was wonderful. Jason was surprised that being here felt so natural. He rapped on the front door.

Toni emerged from the kitchen, peered toward the door, and then hurried out to unlock the deadbolt. Jason's smile faded as he noticed her haggard appearance.

"Toni, what's wrong?" he asked softly. Her beautiful brown eyes were red with fatigue, and her pretty features were set in a frown.

"What makes you think something's wrong?" she mumbled as she walked into the kitchen. The room felt warm and comfortable.

"You look like you didn't sleep very much last night," he observed. She was trying to lift a huge bag of flour and move it from a storage shelf to the floor by a work table. He grabbed the awkward load, lowered it to the floor, and opened it for her.

"Thank you," she said softly as she began measuring the main ingredients for her donuts into a huge bowl.

"Well, are you going to tell me what's wrong?" he probed.

She sighed and pulled a stool up to the table. Jason joined her. "It's really nothing," she began.

"Why don't you tell me about it, and we'll see."

She placed her hand to her temple and rubbed her forehead. "I think I have a headache."

"Would you like an aspirin?"

She shook her head. "Maybe later. I get headaches when I worry about things." She paused before continuing. "I got a phone call last night." In a few brief sentences, she described the disturbing call of the night before. "It was probably just a joke," she insisted. "But it's the fourth time in the last week this has happened." Her eyes reflected fear and doubt.

"One call might be a prank, but four—that's a serious matter," Jason insisted. "Why didn't you tell me about this before?"

"I didn't want to bother you," she quickly replied. "And besides, I'm used to fighting my own battles."

Jason fought down the urge to ask her if she had lost her mind. He waited a few moments longer until he was sure he could remain calm and then asked, "Have you noticed any strange people coming into the bakery lately?"

She shook her head. "No. Most of my customers are regulars, and I know almost everyone in town—I've been living here for three years now."

Jason was worried. He hoped the phone calls were just pranks, but years of experience with security issues in the computer industry had taught him not to take anything for granted. "Do you have a girlfriend who could stay with you for a few days? I'd feel better if you weren't left alone."

She shook her head, and a new look of anguish passed over her face. "Normally I could ask Sheila. We've been friends most of our lives. But the last time we spoke, we had a disagreement, and I really don't want to see her right now." She turned away from him and concentrated on combining the dry ingredients.

Jason studied Toni, wishing he could erase the fatigue and worry from her beautiful features. "May I ask what happened?"

It was too much. She was exhausted. The feelings of fear and anger wouldn't stay inside any longer. The memory of her last meeting with Sheila surged to the surface. She turned on Jason, her eyes wild with pain. "We had a fight—the ultimate fight. The same one we've been having for twenty years. We had a fight about Jesus—and both Sheila and Jesus lost. Okay? And by the way, where do Christians get off thinking they can sell people this sort of bumper-sticker religion?"

"Whoa, hold on a minute, Toni," Jason said, holding up one hand. "Maybe you'd better back up so I have half a chance of understanding what's going on here." He took a deep breath. "What exactly happened between you two?"

"Oh, it wasn't much," Toni said in a voice dripping with sarcasm, "I asked why Jesus let your mother die, and Sheila walked out on me. Said she was late for church. Tried the same old 'give Jesus a chance' stuff she's been spouting for years." Toni looked directly at Jason. "You know what I told her? I told her that your whole family gave Jesus lots of chances, and He didn't do anything." She regretted her words the moment they left her mouth.

Jason just sat there, looking stricken, all the color drained from his face.

"Oh, Jason, I'm so sorry. I'm an idiot. I had no right to . . . to . . . to add to your pain." She reached over and squeezed his shoulder. "I'm just so angry at her. She's been my best friend forever, but ever since we were teenagers, I've felt like I came in a far second to her church life. Then the other day I wanted an answer—a real answer—and she wouldn't give me one. She wouldn't even stay around long enough to admit that she didn't have one. She was so busy rushing off to church that she didn't have time to talk about Jesus."

Jason recovered slowly from his shock. He rubbed at the back of his neck and looked out into the darkened front of the bakery. Then he turned back to her, shaking his head. "You have a right to be angry. Sheila made a mess of that situation, though I don't know if I could have done any better. And I've had a lot longer to think about it."

"Wait, Jason. You don't have to answer that question. I don't want to tear open an old wound."

"Toni, the wound has never healed over," Jason said quietly. "There's nothing to tear open. And maybe it would be good for me to talk about it with someone." He paused, collecting his thoughts. "I'm a Christian, but that doesn't mean that I have all the answers to life's mysteries and tragedies. I'm a long way from being perfect—I don't even manage to make it to good most of the time. But following Jesus isn't about knowing everything or acting correctly in every situation. It's about being forgiven for all we don't know. And even more than that, it's about being forgiven for all the things we do wrong. Like running out on a friend who's in pain, because we're scared."

Jason took a deep breath and then continued. "I don't know why God allowed my mother to die, but I'm sure of this: Jesus Christ has never run out on anybody. The night Mom died, all of us had a sense that Jesus was with us in that room. It was still terrible, but we weren't alone. For all of us, and for me especially, the real sense of despair came later. The next day, the next week, the next month. I no longer felt Christ's presence the way I did before Mom died—still don't, for that matter. But even though I don't feel His presence, I believe that Jesus has remained close to me during these dark times.

"Notice, I only said I *believe*. I'm still trying to work my way back to the place where I *know* that Jesus is near. And I can't say when I'll reach that place. Maybe I'll never find certainty again in this life. But I'm determined to go right on believing until I can know for a certainty again. And I'm gradually reaching the point where I'm willing to let God deal with the issue of certainty. I don't know if that makes my commitment to Christ and faith in God weak, strong, or something in between, but that's the best I can do right now. And, you know, I think God accepts that."

After a few moments of silence, Toni said, "My aunt Grace used to say that faith in God is a lot like baking. You begin with a recipe that you got from someone else. The process it describes sounds nothing like what you're trying to create, but you go ahead and mix all the ingredients together anyway. Many times, even after everything is mixed, what you're left with looks nothing like the finished product. Then you put it in an oven at a specific temperature for just the right amount of time, and in the end, something wonderful happens. The process is never the same twice, even when you're making exactly the same thing, and it takes lots of practice to get good results."

Jason smiled. "That's an interesting analogy—though I'm not sure how I feel about being a half-baked Christian." They both laughed. "And speaking of baking, I think we'd better get to work."

"Okay, let's see what I can teach you that you haven't already learned from your mother." Jason was glad to see her mood brighten as she took up a familiar task.

Toni pulled a huge black binder from a shelf near her office door. As she flipped through the pages, he saw that most of the recipes were handwritten. "My aunt and uncle never had a computer or typewriter. I guess they were kind of old-fashioned. I've typed all these recipes, and I keep them on my computer. I also have them stored on a disk that I keep in a safe-deposit box at Blue Spring National."

He touched one of the pages. It felt dry and wrinkled. "You

have to go through all that trouble to keep these recipes? Aren't they printed in any cookbook?"

She slammed the book shut. "Jason, these recipes aren't printed anywhere. I just want you to understand that by allowing you into my kitchen, I'm placing a great deal of trust in you."

He pulled his hand away from the book. "Toni, please don't be upset. I was just wondering. Most of the recipes my mom used came out of books."

"I'm sorry, Jason. I hardly slept at all last night, and I'm really on edge today." She took a deep breath. "How 'bout if I start by explaining how I organize and run my kitchen. Every baker has their own way of doing things."

He nodded his agreement.

"Well," she said, pointing to a counter, "I have three large mixers. I found that I needed extra ones to be able to make enough dough." She showed him the beaters and the special spiral attachments used to mix heavy dough. After adding liquid ingredients and turning on the mixer for the donut dough, she next gestured toward the floor-to-ceiling shelves that ran along one long wall. Fifty-pound bags of flour, various types of cane and confectioners' sugar, and brown sugar were stored on the lower shelves. She also had large containers of baking powder and baking soda. Huge bottles of vanilla extract stood on the upper shelves, as well as supplies of countless other flavorings. Jason recognized many of the same brands that his mother had used.

Two huge refrigerators took up most of the space along the short wall, and she opened them to show him where she kept the fresh fruit. "I use fresh fruit for most of my pies. I only use canned fruit for the cherry pies and tarts."

Next she turned to the massive commercial oven. The

dough for the donuts had finished mixing by that time. She showed him her technique for rolling out the dough and cutting out donuts with a round cutter. Then she placed the round circles of dough into the preheated oven to bake.

They returned to the large table located in the middle of the room. She began mixing another batch of dough for her pastries. Butter and eggs were already on the table. "It's best to use the butter and eggs at room temperature. It mixes into the dough better that way," she explained.

By the time the pastries were ready for the oven, the donuts had turned golden brown. She pulled several trays of the raised donuts from the oven and placed them on cooling racks. Then she mixed together a glaze. Jason noticed how she smiled as she explained everything to him. She answered his questions clearly and carefully. A lot of what she was explaining was familiar to him, and before long he was helping her with the preparations. Soon fresh glazed donuts were in the glass display case, and it was almost time to open for business.

Toni bustled around, making sure she had everything in place before the first customers arrived. She removed cherry tarts from the oven and smiled at the perfect triangles.

"Toni, can I ask you something?" he said quickly.

"Sure, Jason. You can ask me anything you'd like."

"Well, when I asked you about the recipes earlier, you seemed upset. And not just because you're tired. I wondered if there was something more you wanted to say about them."

She sighed and sat on a stool. They both knew that this would be their last quiet moment until after the morning crowd left. "Yes," Toni admitted. "Donut and pastry recipes are pretty much alike. Mine are a little different than most, but not much. Please don't repeat this to anyone, but you can find donuts and pastries just as good in almost any bakery."

Jason was surprised. He thought that Toni would claim all her sweets were the best in the world.

"This is awkward for me, Jason, but I have to tell you that the cookie recipes are off limits. Nobody knows those recipes except me. They were my aunt and uncle's secret recipes, handed down for generations."

Jason glanced around the kitchen. He noticed that cookies were the one item they had not made. "I bake the cookies by myself in the mornings. Usually I'll have someone to wait on the tables while I make them. That way, nobody can see what I'm doing."

"You're a shrewd businesswoman," he said with a smile.

"Well, I have to make a living, Jason. That's the way Aunt Grace and Uncle Bob did business, so I'm following their example."

"But what do you do when you're gone for the weekend? I know you must take a Saturday off once in a while."

She explained that for some of her pastries, the dough was made a day or so before it was baked. She prepared dough in advance during slow periods when business tapered off. "I didn't take the time to do this yesterday, though." She also explained that if she had someone working for her whom she could trust, that person would run the bakery for her on the rare Saturday she took off.

Promptly at six-thirty, Toni left the kitchen and went to the front of her bakery. Jason watched her as she flipped her sign to OPEN and returned to the kitchen to get more fresh pastries and donuts. She placed them behind the glass showcases where her customers could clearly view the items. Five minutes later, the bell above the door rang, and the first customer entered the bakery.

"Hi, Karen. Do you want the usual?" asked Toni as she opened a cardboard box. Jason had already observed that

Karen was one of Toni's regular customers. She came to the bakery at least twice a week to get donuts for her office staff meeting.

Soon the bakery business settled into a busy but pleasant rhythm. About an hour later, Jason noticed a strange woman entering the bakery. Her clothes were clean, but worn and frazzled, and she was mumbling. Her brown hair was streaked with gray, and she had tiny wrinkles on her white skin. Jason watched her like a hawk as she shuffled to the counter.

"I want my donut. Toni always lets me have my donut." She sounded like a child. She rubbed her wrinkled hands together as if she were cold. Her deep blue eyes glanced around the bakery as if she expected someone to attack her. Jason had no idea what to do. He was rescued from serving the customer when Toni came from the kitchen.

"Martha! I was wondering when you were going to show up. I haven't seen you in a few days!"

"I told this man that you always give me my donut. Can I have a chocolate one?" she asked eagerly.

Jason watched Toni speak with Martha as if she were any of her other customers. She placed two chocolate glazed donuts into a bag and poured a large cup of coffee for the woman. He noticed that she didn't ring up the order. Martha left without paying a cent. "Who was that?" he whispered when everyone else was out of earshot.

"That's Martha," Toni explained. "The people in town call her Crazy Martha, but I refuse to call her that. She lives in town with a relative. From what I understand, she's got mental problems, but she's harmless. She once told me that she likes coming here since I make her feel like a normal person."

The morning was almost over when a tall, dark-skinned, thin woman entered the bakery. Her companion was large and broad-shouldered. He reminded Jason of a football player. His black jeans had holes, and his T-shirt was ripped. A gold tooth gleamed from his mouth as he smiled. She was dressed in a thin, diaphanous, tangerine-colored dress. It flowed over her legs and clung to her small waist. Her dark short hair was slicked with gel. She pursed her lips as she glared at the customers. Finally she looked behind the counter.

"May I help you?" asked Jason. Her eyes were just like Toni's, with one important difference: malice and hatred filled the stranger's eyes. Jason thought she might be an attractive woman if she'd drop her tough attitude.

She licked her lips and grabbed his hand, hooking it firmly in place around the crook of her arm. "I've never seen you around here before, handsome," she cooed.

Jason quickly pulled his hand away.

"Eva, what I tell you about flirting with other men?" said her companion gruffly.

"What can I get for you?" Jason asked again. Toni was in the kitchen making cookies, and he didn't want to disturb her.

"You can get me your phone number," Eva said with a laugh. Her friend squeezed her thin arm. "Ouch, you big oaf! You're hurting me!" She pulled away and rubbed her arm. Toni came out of the kitchen, hearing the commotion.

"Eva, what do you want? You haven't been here in weeks," Toni said. She glared at Eva and her companion.

"I came to get some donuts! What's the matter? You don't want to serve me and my husband, Hank, no more! We're here to stay, cousin dearest, and you can't ignore us!"

"Did you want me to take care of this?" Jason asked Toni.

"Who are you, her knight in shining armor?" Eva's shrill voice dripped with sarcasm as she glared at Toni. Jason just wanted to get these crazy people out of the bakery.

"Eva, what do you want?" Toni spoke slowly, as if she were talking to a naughty child.

"Give me six donuts and three of them tarts."

Toni opened a box and placed the items into the container. She closed it and rang up the order.

"I'm not paying you!" Eva declared. "After all that's happened to our family, you owe me this!" She clutched the box in one hand and grabbed Hank's arm with her other hand. Customers turned and stared as the couple exited, Eva's high heels drilling the floor. As they walked out the door, Eva began yelling at Hank. The customers shrugged and turned back to their interrupted conversations.

"So, that's your cousin," Jason commented in a carefully neutral tone of voice. "I see why you didn't have much to say about her the other day. And I can certainly understand why your aunt and uncle wanted you to have this place."

"As far as I'm concerned, the less said about Eva and Hank, the better," Toni said bitterly. "And I've still got more cookies to make."

Jason watched the rigid plane of her back as she strode back to the kitchen.

Five

ason got up early Sunday morning for Palm Sunday services. As he had anticipated, a crowd was already gathering when he arrived. He parked his BMW and followed other worshipers into the foyer of the church. To his surprise, a lovely young woman greeted him before he had walked more than twenty feet toward the sanctuary.

"Hi Jason, my name's Sheila," she said, holding out her hand and smiling broadly.

He shook it with a bemused expression on his face. "You must be Toni's friend." The smile faded a bit.

"Yes, that's right. She told me what you looked like, and I thought you might be coming today. Since you're new here, I thought we might sit together. Why don't we get you a name tag?"

"I think I'd rather remain anonymous, if that's okay. But I'd be happy to sit with you."

Sheila found them a place three rows from the front and made quiet introductions to the people sitting near them just as the musicians began playing a prelude. Jason found himself enjoying the service. He and Sheila sang harmony parts during some of the praise choruses, and he felt completely at home until the pastor began preaching.

The sermon was about suffering: the suffering of God, the suffering of the fallen world, the suffering of Jesus, and the suffering of those who follow Jesus. Jason could feel his composure slipping as the pastor moved toward his conclusion.

"Jesus asks us to go to the cross with Him this week. To share in His suffering. We in America want to be successful and powerful and secure. We think it's our right. We even think God has ordained it.

"But this is what God has ordained—that the cross comes before the resurrection. The pain comes before the power. The trials come before the triumph. When Jesus calls us, He calls us to come and die."

Jason felt the tears begin to slide down his face. Sheila leaned over and put a hand on his shoulder.

"And this is not simply a theological proposition," the pastor continued. "It is a living reality that we have to be ready to face in our own lives. As the disciples walked into Jerusalem on that first Palm Sunday so long ago, they thought they were going to see the crowning of a king. But Jesus knew they were going to see the redemption of the world. And He knew that there was only one way for that to be accomplished."

Jason glanced over at Sheila and saw that her face was wet with tears as well.

"Yet, by the end of that first Holy Week, even Jesus was looking for another way. Even the Son of God feared the cross. And that is why, when we face our own crosses—and, my friends, we will all face them — that is why we can be sure that He understands our suffering.

"That is why we can say with the prophet Isaiah, 'Surely he hath borne our griefs, and carried our sorrows. . . .' That is why we can be sure that He is with us even unto the end of the world.

"The power to be changed ourselves and to change the world only comes to us through the suffering of the cross. Our instinct is to run from it, but God asks us to consider another option. To go through it with His Son as our guide. To hang there with Jesus. Trusting, like the thief on the cross next to Him, that, 'Today shalt thou be with me in paradise.' Waiting there, with Jesus, for the end of all things. And for the beginning. Let us pray together."

Neither Jason nor Sheila were quite sure how they made it to the front of the church when the pastor gave the invitation to come forward for prayer. They simply found themselves there, along with many others. The pastor himself prayed with them. Jason heard Sheila's anguished story of how she had failed her best friend and her Lord. Sheila heard Jason pour out his pain and doubt over his mother's death. And by the time they left the church together, each of them realized they had made a new beginning with God and discovered a new friend in each other.

After church, Jason and Sheila agreed to eat lunch together at Chan's and took Jason's car, leaving Sheila's in the church parking lot. After they had been seated and checked over the lunch specials, Jason said, "I was glad to hear your side of what happened with Toni the other night. It helps me to understand some of things she said about it."

"I'm glad she told you, though it is a little surprising. She has some good reasons not to trust guys."

"Can you tell me what those might be?"

"I'd rather not. Toni is a very private person. She needs to feel safe with people before she really starts opening up. That's why I'm surprised that she has already told you so much. But then I guess you've told her quite a bit, too. Maybe you can help me with something."

"I'm willing to try."

"From what Pastor Wilkins said, it's clear I've got to go to Toni and ask her forgiveness for leaving so abruptly last week. For running out on her. But I don't know how to go about it."

Jason chuckled. "Asking for forgiveness is never easy, but which one of the typical dozen or so problems it may create are you wrestling with?"

"I don't want to make Jesus look bad."

Inwardly, Jason winced and fought the temptation to tell Sheila what a mess she had already made of things. Instead he asked, "Why don't you tell me how you think asking Toni to forgive you would make Jesus look bad."

"Aren't Christians supposed to have answers for the questions nonbelievers ask? I don't have any answers for her. I can't explain why your mom died. I can't explain why her life has been so tough. If I can't answer her questions, I'll make Jesus look bad because I won't be able to give her the kind of information and comfort He wants to offer to her through me. The Bible even says we're supposed to be ready to answer any questions people ask us about our faith: 'Always be ready in season and out to give an answer to those who question you about your faith.' Isn't that the advice that Peter gave to Christians who were facing persecution?"

For a moment, Jason studied the place setting in front of him. Then he looked up at Sheila and gave her a sympathetic smile. "I understand your struggle," he said. "I've wrestled with it myself. But I think you're feeling responsible for something God hasn't asked us to do. And I think the misunderstanding begins with the verse you just quoted. You got it almost right, but you made a mistake at the end. Let me get my Bible from the car, and I'll show you."

He returned quickly. "The verse is at the end of First Peter. And it is addressed to Christians who are suffering persecution. In fact, the whole book is about the relationship between faith and suffering. This is what Peter tells them to do in verse fifteen of the third chapter, 'But in your hearts set apart Christ as Lord.' But look at how he advises them to make that lordship real in their daily lives. Read the rest of verse fifteen and then verse sixteen." He slid the Bible across the table to her.

Sheila began reading: " 'Always be prepared to give an answer to everyone who asks you to give the reason for the hope that you have. But do this with gentleness and respect, keeping a clear conscience, so that those who speak maliciously against your good behavior in Christ may be ashamed of their slander.' "

She looked up, and Jason continued. "Look at what it says and what it does not say. It does not say that we have to be ready to answer any kind of question we are asked. It says only that we are to be ready to answer questions about the hope we personally have in Christ. And the answers we give are supposed to be gentle and respectful. That's all. We need to be ready to talk about how Jesus gives us hope. We don't have to explain suffering, in general or in a specific situation. All we are responsible to talk about is our personal experience with Jesus. And if there are things that Jesus has not yet made clear to us, then we need to have the courage to admit that they aren't clear."

Sheila held up one hand. "Okay, let me see if I understand. It isn't what we know that defines our faith, but who we know."

"That's it exactly."

"But don't we have to study the Bible to learn about Jesus and to learn how to live our lives according to biblical principles?"

"Of course, but we aren't responsible to explain all the complexities of Christian theology and daily obedience to Christ to anyone who asks, any time they ask."

Sheila looked confused, but just then their food arrived. They paused long enough to pray and serve themselves from several steaming platters. Then Jason tried another approach. "Can I ask you a few questions about your conversation with Toni the other night?"

"Sure, anything you like."

"Tell me two things: what went wrong, and when did it start going wrong? And if you want to think about it for a few minutes before you answer, that's fine."

Sheila ate quietly, obviously thinking about the disastrous evening. Finally she said, "It had been a long, hard week, and I was tired. I was hungry." She smiled and looked directly at Jason, "I wanted to hear all about you." He returned her smile, and she continued. "I didn't realize how late it was, and when I did, I started worrying about being late for church. Then Toni asked why God let your mom die. I just freaked out inside. I was terrified. I felt stupid and useless. I couldn't get out of there fast enough."

Sheila took a few more bites, while Jason waited silently. "I think, maybe, things started going wrong before I ever got to Toni's."

Jason nodded. "That's a very perceptive observation. But what went wrong after you arrived?"

"Well, I stopped paying attention to Toni, because I was worried about being late to church. Then, when she asked the question, I just blurted out the first thing that came to mind. I guess I was so worried about making Jesus look bad, that I ended up making him look awful."

"We've all been there, Sheila," Jason said quietly. "So, what you're saying is that you were hungry, tired, and scared, which made you angry. I'd say you had a lot pushing you in the wrong direction. But even with all of that weighing on you, the situation didn't explode until you stopped treating Toni with gentleness and respect."

"Yes, I can see that now. But how does that help me with asking her to forgive me?"

"When any of us ask someone, even God, for forgiveness, we have to begin by facing the specific things we've done wrong. Our repentance has to be specific or the other person can't offer us any meaningful kind of forgiveness, and our relationship with them can't move on from the point where the damage was done. You need to begin by telling Toni that you let your fatigue and hunger keep you from treating her with gentleness and respect."

"And I need to tell her that I got scared when she asked me a question that I couldn't answer, which made me angry." Sheila paused. "I also need to tell her that I still don't have any answers, don't I?"

Jason nodded.

"But what is she going to think of me? And, more important, what is she going to think of Jesus?"

"That depends on what you tell her about you and Jesus. On how you explain the hope you possess because you've surrendered your life to Christ. And on how gentle and respectful you are when you explain that to her."

"So, Jesus comes out looking good because He offers me hope?"

"Yes, but more important, Jesus has an opportunity, through you, to offer hope to Toni. I don't really understand how this all works, but here's some of what I've come to understand in the last few months. The only thing that Christians have to fall back on when we face suffering and doubt is the knowledge that Jesus is with us. That we are not alone. The answer to the fear of the unknown is not more information; it's being able to face the unknown with Jesus. The presence of God in our lives is the one comprehensive answer to all the impossible questions we ask and all the painful situations we face. It's often the only answer we're given in this life, but it also offers us more real, practical help than anything else could.

"If you ask Toni to forgive you and then work to restore your friendship with her, you'll be showing her what it means not to be alone. You'll be showing her something of what it's like to have a personal relationship with Jesus Christ."

Sheila smiled. "So Jesus comes out looking good, even though I'm admitting that I'm a fool, because He gets a chance to offer Himself to Toni through me?"

Jason nodded. "Yes, at least that's the best explanation I've managed to come up with."

They finished their meal in companionable silence, and then Jason took Sheila back to the church to pick up her car. As she got out, Sheila turned and smiled at him. "Well, Jason Matthews, since you're such an expert on the presence of God, and forgiveness, and all the rest of this stuff, you'd better be praying for me—and for Toni."

"You can count on it," he replied.

Sheila got into her car and immediately headed for Toni's home. Two hours later, Toni and Sheila were standing in Toni's living room, hugging and crying. Toni said, "I was so afraid I'd lost you after all these years. I'm so glad I haven't."

"Toni, I promise, I'll never run out on you again. If I'm late for church, they'll just have to survive without me. And, girl, if you ever see me acting like a pious phony again, you've got my permission to whup me up side of the head."

On Monday morning, Toni explained to Jason all that had happened with Sheila. "After I told her about the strange phone calls, she was more than happy to stay with me for a while," she concluded.

During the rest of the morning they fell into the routine they had established during the previous week. Jason found himself so comfortable with Toni that he talked a little about the new perspective he had gained on suffering. Toni was genuinely interested. When they stopped for a coffee break at ten-thirty, it seemed the most natural thing in the world for Jason to say, "I'm really looking forward to Easter Sunday services, in a way I haven't for a long time. How would you feel about coming with me?" He stirred cream and sugar into his coffee and waited for her response.

Toni hesitated as she sipped at her own hot brew. "I don't think I'm quite ready for that yet, but I appreciate your asking. It does sound like some interesting things go on there."

Their quiet time was cut short by the sound of the bell, announcing another customer. A tall, slim man with copper-colored skin entered. He wore a dark business suit and carried a briefcase, and Jason noticed that the man smelled as if he had used a whole bottle of aftershave. The stranger pushed his spectacles over his aristocratic nose as he announced, "Well, well, well, it's true after all. Toni, I can't believe you gave up your career to sell donuts! Girl, where's your pride and dignity?"

Toni clutched her coffee cup. "Brian, what do you want?" she asked harshly.

"Don't get so riled up. Can't I visit an old friend? I've moved back to take a job outside of Baltimore." He bent to try to kiss her cheek. Toni pushed his head away, twisting his neck painfully in the process. He stumbled away from the table.

"You stay away from her." Jason's voice was like steel. He stood and gave Brian a long, cool look.

Brian regained his balance quickly, rubbing his neck. "Calm down, man. I just heard that Toni owned this bakery now, and I had to come and see for myself. You've got quite a place here," he said sarcastically. He barely glanced around the bakery before his eyes rested on Toni again.

"Well, you've seen my place, and now you can leave," replied Toni coldly.

"Leave?" Brian glanced uneasily at Jason. "Hey, Toni, is there somewhere we can go to talk alone?"

"No, Brian. And unless you're here to buy something, get out. Now!" She stood, marched to the front door, and held it open.

"I'll be back," Brian said as he left. "We still have some unfinished business to discuss."

Silently, Toni picked up her banana-nut muffin and began tearing it into bite-sized pieces. She finally looked up at Jason. "I suppose I owe you an explanation for that outburst."

"Toni, I don't want you telling me anything you're not comfortable with," Jason replied quietly.

Toni ate her muffin and sipped her coffee mechanically for a couple minutes. "I haven't seen Brian in more than three years, and we didn't part on the best of terms." She chuckled wryly. "That's what happens when you discover that your fiancé is cheating on you."

"That explains a great deal," Jason said with a pained expression on his handsome face.

"Last I heard of him, he had moved to California. I wish he'd stayed there. I can't imagine why he would go to the trouble of trying to find me. He's definitely not a small-town person." Toni's throat suddenly felt dry. She tried to take a sip of coffee, but the hot liquid was slopping out of the cup and onto the table.

Jason quickly moved to her side. He touched her shoulder. "You're shaking," he said.

Using both hands, she carefully set the cup down on the table. "Brian gives me the creeps. I can't stand him." She was surprised at the anger in her voice.

"Why?" Jason asked as he worked to clean up the spilled coffee.

"Because I trusted him, and he betrayed me. Because I revealed too much about myself to him without considering what he might do with that knowledge. Because I let him see my weaknesses, and he used them all against me. He's the kind of man who gives friendship a bad name and turns the beauty of romance into something ugly. Everything Brian touches comes out twisted."

Jason got her a fresh cup of coffee and asked, "What did he mean about unfinished business?"

"I really don't know, and I don't want to find out." She looked out the large front windows of the bakery at the sunny glory of the spring day. She cast a quick glance at Jason, who was busily eating his donut. He had a serene manner, even though his face was still touched with sadness. She recalled how her mother had often found a similar peace, even in the midst of her struggle to make ends meet. How was it that faith and suffering could coexist? Both Jason and her mother had found their own, very personal answers to that question. Their lives were clearly more complete because God was at work in their suffering.

"I'm glad you're here with me, Jason."

He smiled in surprise. "That makes two of us." He lightly touched her arm, and she giggled. Jason made her feel safe and comfortable. She hoped those warm emotions would last for a very long time.

Later that day, Jason helped Toni empty the garbage, as he had done each afternoon. But this time he noticed a stray cat near the Dumpster. Toni called to it, and the large orange tabby came over and rubbed against her legs. She petted him and then disappeared for a moment back into the kitchen. When she returned, she was carrying a double-sided cat dish with water and food. She set it down, and the tabby greedily crunched his way through every bite and lapped up every drop.

Jason was amused. "Do you make it a habit to feed strays?" he asked.

"Yes," she replied, a smile in her voice. "I know I shouldn't feed them because that just keeps them coming back, but I can't help it." She paused, glancing at him and lifting one eyebrow. "Maybe that's why my bakery is a success."

Jason laughed as he followed her back inside. They washed their hands, and she showed him where she kept the deposit slips and the canvas money bag. "I don't feel comfortable keeping large amounts of cash overnight, so I make a deposit each day. The drive-through window of Blue Spring National is open into the evening, so I usually just go through there to deposit my money."

Jason noticed how hard she concentrated as she counted up

the day's gross receipts. She seemed to take joy in handling the bills. He'd seen that look before. Did she believe that money equaled power? He'd certainly known enough people who believed money was the key to all the finer things in life, and he couldn't completely disagree with them.

Promptly at three o'clock, Toni placed the CLOSED sign in the window and shut the blinds. She sat at a table to relax, and Jason joined her after first gathering all the stray newspapers on the tables and offering them to her. She subscribed to four different papers since her patrons liked reading while eating their donuts and drinking their daily cup of coffee. He watched her look through the various selections until she found the *Wall Street Journal,* and he was mildly shocked when she immediately turned to the exchange rates.

"Why are you looking at the exchange rates?" He regarded her with curiosity. Toni seemed so domestic, a real homebody. Foreign exchange rates should be the last thing to interest her.

She gave him a mysterious smile. "Well, I guess you could say that old habits die hard."

"Old habits?"

She nodded. "Checking the exchange rates was part of my job before I inherited this bakery."

Jason ran his hand over his clean-shaven head. Toni seemed happy and content running this business. It was easy to forget that she'd had another life and another job before her aunt died. "What kind of a job did you have?" he asked.

"I was an international accountant."

He was momentarily stunned into silence. Finally, he managed to ask, "Did you like it?"

She gazed at the closed shades as if she were reminiscing. "Sometimes, sometimes not. It was a job, but it wasn't like the work was my whole life. I majored in international business while I was in college, and got a job with a multinational after I graduated. They liked my GPA, and I'd held several internships with them between terms."

He nodded. "You must miss it if you're still reading the exchange rates every day," he observed.

"Honestly, I don't. I just like seeing what's going on outside Blue Spring. I like looking at the rise and fall of the mark, franc, and pound sterling." She smiled as she folded the paper. "I don't really miss my job, but I never want to forget that there is a world full of fascinating people and possibilities outside the walls of my little world here in the bakery." She frowned.

"What's wrong?"

"I was just thinking about Brian's visit. We were working for the same company when we broke up."

"So Brian was your coworker and your boyfriend?"

"Yes, but no more talk about Brian." She paused. "You know, Jason, I really like money," she admitted. "Isn't it amazing the way so much of our lives is tied to the value of the dollar and other currencies?"

"Money is fascinating," he responded. "My father has always said it's a tangible reward God gives us for hard work. But it can be a terrible thing, too. I've seen it make the best-intentioned people lose sight of other things that were much more valuable—like faith in God and relationships with other people." He gazed at Toni as she looked through the financial and business sections of the other three newspapers. "Toni, I want to ask you something."

She looked up from her paper. "Yes?"

"Well, I figure you made a really good living as an international accountant. Didn't you mind giving that up to take over your aunt's bakery?"

She sighed as she set her paper aside. "Well, to tell you the truth, Jason, when I first heard that my aunt had left me her bakery, I immediately wanted to hire somebody to run it. I figured I could use the profits as another source of income."

"Why did you change your mind?"

She removed a napkin from the dispenser to wipe the newsprint off her hands and slowly began to rip it to shreds. "My aunt had a stipulation in her will. She said that in order to inherit the bakery, I would have to run it myself, hands on. If I didn't, then the bakery would no longer be mine. It would go to someone else."

Jason nodded. "So you decided to give it a try?"

She gave him a thoughtful smile. "Yes. I gave notice at my job and moved here to Blue Spring a few weeks later." She sighed. "I'd just broken up with Brian, and I was eager for a change. Aunt Grace and Uncle Bob had always been good to me. The summer I'd spent working with them in their bakery was one of the best times of my life. I also liked being with them because it was such a relief to be around two people who were obviously in love. They hardly ever argued, and they got along so well," she said wistfully.

"Your parents never got along?"

"No, they didn't." She moved quickly back to the original subject. "Even though the bakery is very profitable, I made more as an international accountant, but I still end up further ahead by working here. I don't have to pay rent or mortgage because the bakery is already paid for. So even though my revenue is lower, my net income is higher."

Jason smiled at the authoritative tone that crept into Toni's voice as she described the financial condition of the bakery. It still seemed strange to imagine her sitting behind a desk in an office while she analyzed exchange rates day after day.

"Also, I loved that summer so much because I discovered my

love for baking," she continued. "I found that making pies, cakes, and cookies, and seeing people enjoy them, made me feel good. I understood that there were people behind the numbers I was studying at my old job, but here I'm face-to-face with the results of my work every day.

Jason gazed at Toni. She was full of surprises. It would take time to get to know her well, but he was willing to be patient. As he sat there quietly, he made a promise to God: Whatever happened, he would treat this remarkable woman with gentleness and respect.

Six

"Toni, I promised I wouldn't pressure you about church anymore, and I won't, but is it okay if the people at church tonight pray about those strange phone calls you've been getting?" Sheila gathered her purse and Bible while she waited for Toni's response. She was dressed in a striking pale-pink dress, and she was wearing heels. There was a quiet strength to her youthful face.

Toni muted the television and thought for a moment. "That's all right with me. I'll take help from anyplace I can get it." She smiled. "Have a good evening."

Sheila had been staying with her for nine days. During that time there had been two more harassing phone calls, and both had come in on the business line. One arrived early in the morning, before Jason got to work, and the second occurred in the late afternoon, after he'd left to drop off the daily receipts at the bank.

Jason was concerned that someone was watching the store, and Toni was worried that he might be right. It was clear that he wanted to take more aggressive action to protect her and the bakery, but she wasn't ready for that yet. He had agreed to wait but had asked her to let him know if the threats became more specific. Toni kept telling herself that it was silly to be so concerned over a few threatening phone calls, but she found herself suspicious of just about every customer who entered her bakery.

She stared at the television, daydreaming. Jason Matthews was turning out to be the most interesting person she had met in a long time. She admired the way he clung to his beliefs, even after all he had been through, even though he freely admitted that he didn't have all the answers. She found his openness, sensitivity, and strength of character very attractive. As she reviewed their most recent conversations, her eyes began getting heavy. Soon she was dozing on her living-room couch.

Jason entered the sanctuary of Blue Spring Community Church. Several other people waved as he took his seat. Since the day he had gone forward for prayer, he had decided that this would be his temporary church home. The congregation was small and friendly, and he felt as if he belonged.

Jason noticed Mrs. Dukes and her husband enter the sanctuary. He had discovered that they were one of the older couples who took a special interest in the single people in the area. She spoke to Jason before they took a seat in the front. He gazed around the now-familiar building. The church was small and white. The stained-glass windows held a dull shine in the fading evening sunlight. The deep-cranberry carpet contrasted nicely with the light wooden pews. Each bench held two Bibles as well as a hymnal.

Jason smiled when Sheila entered the church. She looked lovely in her pale pink dress. Giving him a warm smile, she sat beside him. "Hi," she whispered. "I'm so glad I made it on time. I decided to walk from Toni's for the first time, and I wasn't sure how long it would take."

"How is Toni this evening?" He knew that she had been increasingly worried as the number of anonymous calls mounted. She had been tired and irritable. Even a strong person could take only so much of this harassment.

"I don't talk about it much, but I think it's eating away at her. The people who come into her bakery are like family to her, and the idea that one of them might be doing this really upsets her," Sheila whispered back. "I'm not sure if my staying with her is helping very much. The calls have stopped coming to her home number since I moved in."

Just then Pastor Wilkins walked up behind the pulpit to start the Wednesday evening worship service. Most of the people in the congregation were between twenty and forty. They sang praise choruses, and then people stood to give testimonies. One young woman thanked God for helping her find a job after being unemployed for several months. A retired businessman, who acted as a mentor to many of the singles, thanked the Lord for returning him to good health. There were also a few prayer requests, and Sheila took the opportunity to mention Toni's problem. After prayers had been offered, Reverend Wilkins started his sermon.

The minister preached about the importance of having a fear of the Lord. "It is a good kind of fear," he said. "We respect and honor our heavenly Father, and we fear His vengeance when we don't respect his wishes. Turn in your Bibles to Psalm 111:10. Please stand and read aloud."

Jason and Sheila turned their Bibles to the appropriate passage and stood with the rest of the congregation. "The fear of the Lord is the beginning of wisdom; A good understanding have all those who do His commandments; His praise endures forever."

For the next half hour, Reverend Wilkins talked informally about the healthy fear of God. When he was finished, the group sang another hymn, and the service closed with prayer. As he left the church, Jason decided that he didn't want to return to the bed-and-breakfast only to sit alone in his room. He noticed that Sheila still seemed pensive as they approached the parking lot. "Would you like to join me for a cup of coffee?" he asked. "There's that place down the street that's still open. We could easily walk there."

Sheila nodded in agreement. Once they arrived at the small coffee shop, they noticed a few groups of single people from the church and waved as they took their seats. Pictures of wild horses decorated the rough pine walls. Deep jade curtains covered the windows and lent a homey feel to the place. The coffee machines sputtered as workers prepared lattes and cappuccinos. Toni had mentioned that she served custom-roasted coffee from this shop and that the coffee shop had a standing order for her pastries. Since each business was open at different times of the day, they both benefitted from the arrangement. The shop served elaborate coffee drinks, tea, sodas, and a fine selection of baked goods. After ordering their drinks, Jason again asked Sheila about Toni.

"If the scary phone calls don't stop, I'm not sure what's going to happen to her," remarked Sheila. The waitress returned with their coffee, and Sheila added cream and sugar before she stirred her steaming drink.

He nodded. "You know, Sheila, Toni told me before Easter that she might be interested in coming to church sometime."

"Well, that's a milestone for you. I've known her a long time, and she hasn't been very interested in either God or church. I think that God has finally convinced me to let the Holy Spirit change her mind, rather than trying to do it myself."

Jason nodded. "I think I've discovered some of the reasons why she's sensitive about the whole subject of Christianity and religion, but I'll bet you know a lot more than I do."

Sheila sighed as she sipped her coffee. She frowned and toyed with the silver spoon. "Look, I'm not sure how much I can tell you. Most of it isn't my story to tell. Toni and I have been best friends since we were kids, so I know all about her life. But I don't want to violate a confidence."

Jason nodded in understanding. He waited while Sheila weighed her next words carefully.

"We grew up together. A few years ago, I grew tired of life in the big city. Toni suggested I move to Blue Spring. She'd just inherited her bakery and . . . well, she'd been going through a difficult time herself. So I found a job in this area and moved here."

"If you're talking about Brian, she has explained some of that situation to me," he replied. "But it was also clear there were things she didn't want me to know yet. It's frustrating. I want to know more about a lot of things in her life, but I'm trying to be careful not to press her too hard. It's so hard to wait sometimes."

Sheila's dark brown eyes were full of concern as she rested her small hand over his. "You really care for her, don't you?"

He was shocked to realize that Sheila might be right. He quickly looked away, not wanting to confirm her observation. Once before he'd fallen for someone too quickly, and the whole experience still haunted him. He could not let that happen again. He'd barely known Toni Brown three weeks, and already he was looking forward to every day he spent with her.

"Jason?" Sheila asked, bringing him back to the present.

Realizing he hadn't answered her question, he took a sip of coffee and then said, "I suppose I do, but I don't want this situation to get out of hand. As far as I know, she's not a believer yet. I don't want to interfere with what God is trying to do in her life. But I want to help her with her search for an authentic faith, with those crazy phone calls, with the bakery. I just don't know what to do."

"I understand, Jason." She removed her hand from his and looked pensively out the window. "I've prayed for Toni for years, and I want to help her, too."

She turned to look at him, "I've been a part of a Christian family since I was a little girl, but Toni's family had very few contacts with the church until she was ten." Briefly, Sheila related the story of how Iris Brown had been converted. "Her decision split the family, and I think that's where some of Toni's problems with the church started." She paused, looking uncomfortable and uncertain. "And I'm afraid that's all I feel free to tell you about Toni's spiritual life."

Jason was grateful to hear that much. "That fits in pretty well with some of the things she has mentioned, but it does give me some added information. Can you tell me anything about her cousin Eva? Both she and Brian have been to the bakery recently, and Toni wasn't happy to see either of them."

"Brian came to the bakery?" Sheila was clearly alarmed. "Toni didn't tell me that. What did he say?"

"Very little, but it was all nasty. He said something about unfinished business, and that has me worried. Toni had to throw him out of her place. She gave me the bare outline of a story, but it seemed like a lot of details were missing."

"When it comes to Brian, even I don't know the whole story, and beyond that, my lips are sealed. But Eva and Hank are definitely bad news. They're never up to any good."

"I was afraid of that," said Jason. They finished their coffee, and Jason offered to walk Sheila back to Toni's bakery.

Toni awoke when the door to her apartment opened. She blinked when she saw Jason and Sheila framed in the doorway. Jason was wearing a suit that drew attention to his wide, muscular frame quite nicely. She noticed the easy camaraderie he shared with Sheila, who was laughing at something Jason had just said. She gave him a charming smile. The two seemed like a happy couple.

Toni sat up, suddenly wide awake. Sheila liked Jason! It was quite obvious they shared something special. She rubbed her eyes as they entered her living room. Sheila smiled as she sat next to her on the couch. "Did you have a good nap, Toni?" she asked.

"Uh, yes." She sounded nervous and flustered.

"Are you okay? Did you get another threatening phone call while we were gone?" Jason sounded worried.

She swallowed hard, trying to manage a weak answer. "No, I'm fine." She didn't feel fine, though. She sensed that a bond existed between Jason and Sheila. It was a bond that did not include her, and it hurt.

"You look awful, Toni. What's the matter?" asked Jason firmly.

I'm jealous. I'm upset because you and Sheila seem to be so happy together, Toni thought. What was happening to her? Sheila was her best friend. They had just resolved some difficult issues from the past, so they were closer than they had been in some time. She enjoyed Jason's company and appreciated his help at the bakery. She respected him. He was a friend, but was he becoming something more to her? And was it possible that Jason had feelings for Sheila? Maybe he preferred Sheila's company because they shared the same deep Christian faith.

"I'm fine, Jason. I'm just tired. I think I'll go to bed," Toni mumbled.

When she slept, she dreamed about Jason. He was packing his suitcase and leaving Blue Spring forever. He kissed her cheek and said it was time to return home. She screamed at him, "Why can't you stay with me forever?" But he still turned away and disappeared into the darkness. Suddenly Sheila ran into the black void after him. "Wait for me!" yelled Toni. But they didn't listen. They left her behind, and she awoke in a cold sweat.

Toni glanced over at the clock by her bed. It was three in the morning, almost time for her to start making her pastries for the early-morning crowd. She rubbed her eyes and got out of bed. Then she reached for the phone and punched in her mother's number.

"Hello?" Her mother's voice was thick and groggy with sleep.

"Hi, Mom," greeted Toni.

"Antoinette, is everything okay?" Mrs. Brown's voice was filled with concern.

Toni sighed as she toyed with a piece of paper. "Yes, I mean no. Mom, I wanted to ask you something," she began.

She was silent for a few moments as she tried to put her thoughts into words. She still couldn't believe that seeing Jason and Sheila share a happy moment together could make her so paranoid. How could she have such strong feelings for Jason after knowing him for only three weeks?

"What's the matter, Antoinette? I can tell something is bothering you." She waited patiently for her daughter to speak.

Toni sighed. "Mom, I wanted to ask you something. If a man is a Christian, wouldn't he want to be with a woman who is a Christian, too?"

Her mother was quiet for so long that Toni wondered if she was going to answer her. "Antoinette, that's a strange question to ask. I take it you've fallen for a man, and he's a Christian, right?"

Toni swallowed and clutched the receiver. "I don't know," she responded in a hoarse whisper.

"Is it the man you've hired to work in your bakery?"

"Yes."

"Antoinette, I think you know what my answer will be. Think of the way you grew up. There were conflicts in our family before I became a Christian, but a lot of new ones developed after I was saved. Now, I will admit that some of those problems were my fault. I was real clumsy in trying to share my faith with you two. But some of the difficulties we faced came from the fact that your father and I were approaching life from very different spiritual viewpoints. That's why the Lord doesn't like couples to be unevenly yoked. Hold on for a minute, dear." Toni knew her mother was going to get her Bible.

"Let me see," the woman mumbled when she returned to the phone. "The Scripture I'm looking for is Second Corinthians six:fourteen. It says, 'Do not be unequally yoked together with unbelievers. For what fellowship has righteousness with

lawlessness? And what communion has light with darkness?'
I'm glad you called me about this, Antoinette. The minister
gave a sermon about this subject last Sunday. God doesn't like
for the ones in his flock to be unevenly yoked. Of course, my
circumstances were a bit different since I was saved after I married your father, but . . ."

Her mother continued to share her views, but Toni was no
longer listening. She felt sick inside. Of course Jason preferred
Sheila's company. They were both Christians. She could never
share in the deepest parts of his life until she took more time to
examine the spiritual values that were so important to him.

After she finished talking to her mother, Toni brushed her
teeth and took a quick shower. She was careful to be quiet so
she wouldn't disturb Sheila. Her friend was still sound asleep
on the couch, and with any luck she would sleep for another
two hours. Quietly, Toni slipped out of her apartment and tiptoed downstairs.

Placing her white apron over her clothes, she opened her
kitchen for the day and began making dough for the pastries
and donuts. Her mind was spinning as she tried to sort out what
she needed to do next about Jason, the spiritual dimensions of
her own life, her friendship with Sheila, the threatening phone
calls. It was all too much.

She shifted her focus and concentrated on the routine tasks
of her day. Within the confines of her kitchen, life still made
sense. Here she could find a place of refuge, where she could
calmly consider the shape and direction of her life. Her aunt
had said that baking was like faith, but what did that really
mean? She considered the question while she measured and
mixed.

After her first batch of donuts was in the oven, she started
preparing the fillings for her cherry and peach tarts by opening

a can of unsweetened dark cherries and pouring them into the bowl. Then she crossed to one of the refrigerators and removed the peaches that she had sliced and seasoned the previous day and began spooning them onto the raw dough. Just as she placed the first tray of pastries into the oven, she realized what she needed to do.

Shortly thereafter, she heard Jason's soft knock at the front door. Jason washed his hands and followed her into the kitchen, beginning his usual routine of assisting her with the food preparation.

Suddenly he stopped. "I know something was bothering you last night, Toni," she heard him say. "I wish you'd tell me what it was." His voice was deep and strong, and Toni longed to tell him of her apprehensions. But if she told him that she was jealous of his budding relationship with Sheila, she'd only cause bigger problems, and besides, she had something much more important to tell him.

She looked over to Jason, who was waiting for her response. "I can't tell you about it now, but I will have something to tell you later today," she said confidently.

He seemed hurt and confused as he abruptly turned and continued mixing the pie dough. She heard him sigh.

"Toni, I really care about you." He stopped mixing the dough, and Toni turned and gazed into his deep brown eyes. He certainly did seem to be concerned about her, but she didn't know if he cared because he felt it was his Christian duty to feel this way, or if he had true feelings for her.

But that didn't really matter, did it? Somewhere during the morning hours as Toni had thought about her aunt's words, she had understood something very important. Jason and Sheila and her mother, and even her aunt and uncle, had been trying to hand her a new recipe for life. Some of them had been offering it to her for years. The only way for her to understand it was to mix it up, put it in the oven, and see what happened. That was more important than her feelings about Jason, or Jason's feelings about her, or Jason's feelings about Sheila. It was even more important than crank calls.

She smiled at Jason. "I'm sure you do care about me. And I'm glad you do, but we have some work to get done. We've got to keep all those strays happy, don't we?"

Never, in the entire time she had known him, had Jason Matthews looked so confused. When they opened at six-thirty, Toni was sure it was going to be a good day.

The morning was busy. Martha arrived to get her donuts and coffee. A few people greeted her as she entered the bakery, but Jason heard others call her Crazy Martha. Toni heard the comment, too. She spent more than twice as much time with Martha as she usually did.

Afterward, she had a quiet word with the people who had made the comments. "If you want to keep coming in here," she said in a carefully neutral voice, "you will never again use the name 'Crazy Martha' in this establishment. Is that quite clear?"

Jason was glad when they finally stopped to eat lunch. While Toni fixed tuna-fish sandwiches, Jason wondered what had happened between last night and this morning to change her from a frightened and exhausted young woman into an energetic, confident moral crusader. When she came back downstairs, he looked at her carefully. She still looked tired. There were circles of fatigue under her cocoa brown eyes. He wondered what was on her mind.

Toni served the sandwiches and got them both something to drink. "Jason, I've made a decision," she began.

"Yes, Toni?" He held his breath, wondering what she would say next.

"I want to go to your church on Sunday. Not with you. Just by myself. I need to start trying to figure out what this recipe called faith is all about."

"That's great," said Jason enthusiastically. He reached across the table and squeezed her hand. "But are you sure you want to go alone?"

She smiled and nodded. "Just don't be surprised if I sit in the back. And I'd better ask you some questions about what goes on during a typical service." Just then a group of customers poured into the store, and Toni's questions had to wait.

Later that evening, when Jason returned to the bed-and-breakfast, Mrs. Dukes met him at the door. "My goodness, Jason, I've hardly had a moment to chat with you since you've moved in. Seems like you've been living at Toni's bakery. How is she doing anyway?"

Jason smiled at Mrs. Dukes as she followed him into the living room. "Toni's fine. But she's had a lot on her mind lately."

"I heard Sheila mention those crank calls last night. And I wish I had some idea who was behind them. I'd give them a piece of my mind; you can just bet I would." She frowned and looked thoughtful. "It's hard for me to imagine that anyone from Blue Spring would treat her that way. She's too well liked around here. But her uncle Bob and aunt Grace had a daughter. What was her name? Oh yes, Eva. She left home when she was a teenager, but I think she's still living somewhere in the area. Folks say she married a man who was even wilder and nastier than she was. Together, who knows what they might do."

Jason nodded, "I've met Eva and Hank. Toni says they're bad

news, and I'm inclined to agree. But crank calls seem a little too sophisticated for them. I'd expect them to drive by at night and toss a rock through the front window. Except that they'd probably miss the whole building and then crash their car into a telephone pole on the way out of town." They both laughed, but then Jason turned serious again.

"I'd like to just laugh the whole thing off, but I'm afraid the situation may be more serious than anyone imagines. The calls have been going on for too long to be simple pranks, and it appears someone is keeping track of Toni's movements. Sheila has been staying there in the evening for more than a week. After she arrived, the calls shifted from Toni's personal line to her business phone. Toni told me this afternoon that she doesn't think Sheila's presence is doing any good. I convinced her to try a rotating schedule where Sheila stays in the apartment with her a couple of different nights each week for the next few weeks. But I've got to tell you, it was a hard sell. Toni doesn't like inconveniencing her friends, and it's not easy for her to accept help."

"She's always been a strong woman," Mrs. Dukes added. "And that can be both a blessing and a curse. If you don't believe me, just ask my husband."

"But there is some good news," Jason continued.

"I'm always ready for that," Mrs. Dukes replied, smiling.

"Toni wants to come to church. We talked about it this afternoon."

"Now that is good news. I wasn't sure I'd live long enough to see the day when Toni Brown would darken the door of a church."

After a few more minutes of conversation, Mrs. Dukes excused herself and went into the kitchen to get ready for breakfast the next morning. Jason climbed the stairs to his room.

After he showered, he pulled out his Bible and read a few verses. Then he sat on his bed and absently stroked the book's black-leather cover. It was worn from years of use. He'd been using the same Bible since he was eight years old, when his parents had given it to him for his birthday. He was glad they had raised him in the Christian faith. He wondered how different his childhood had been from Toni's and if that had something to do with her feelings toward God.

Before he fell asleep that night, he prayed for his family and for Toni. Much as he wanted to help her, he knew the answers she was seeking could come only from God. Just as he was drifting off to sleep, it struck him that Toni had come to the same conclusion.

Seven

*T*oni sat curled up on the couch in her quiet living room. She was staring fixedly at the mystery novel in her hand. Every so often she changed position slightly, but that was the only hint she gave of any connection to her immediate surroundings. She was, in fact, far away, both in time and place, on a journey of discovery, in the company of a twelfth-century monk from Shrewsbury Abbey in southwestern England.

Uncle Bob and Aunt Grace had both recommended the Brother Cadfael novels by Ellis Peters to her during the summer she had lived with them. They had suggested that the books addressed issues of faith from an unusual perspective. When she had begun to examine the idea of a personal faith in God for herself four weeks earlier, she had remembered her aunt and uncles's recommendation. Much of the couple's large collection of books had gone to the local library after her aunt's death, so it seemed only reasonable to ask the librarian where to find them. Toni had been deeply engrossed in *A Morbid Taste for Bones* for the last two weeks. She was discovering, to her surprise (and secret delight) that extremely religious people were often the greatest enemies of real faith.

And the same message had come to her from the last place she expected to hear it—Blue Spring Community Church. When she started attending Sunday services just after Easter, Toni had been shocked to learn that Jesus had been killed by some of the most powerful religious leaders of his day. The pastor had preached about the resurrection on Easter and had been talking about the responses of the early Christians to that event ever since. As Toni quietly sat in the back of the church and took notes, she began to absorb stories from the last few chapters of all four Gospels. One thing quickly became clear, those disciples had been every bit as confused and fearful as she was. Peter had abandoned the Messiah business and gone back to fishing, until Jesus came after him. Thomas thought the resurrection was some crazy religious fantasy caused by intense grief, until Jesus appeared to him. Faith really was like baking; sometimes it was a total mess.

The sound of a car rolling to a stop on the graveled parking area behind the bakery reached her through the open window and broke her concentration. Toni had grown much more sensitive to noises of all kinds over the past few weeks. The harassment directed at her and at Blue Spring Baked Goods had slowly escalated. The phone calls had continued, though they did not come more than once a week now, and some weeks passed with no calls at all.

But that had only been the beginning. Spray-painted graffiti had appeared first on the Dumpster, then on the back of the building. Ten days ago she had discovered the word *garbage* marching across one of her front windows when she turned on the lights in the front of the shop at six o'clock. Last week, an anonymous report of unsafe practices at the bakery had been phoned into the health department. Yesterday, she had tried to process a credit card order at seven-thirty in the morning, only to discover that the bakery phone line was dead. It had been cut where the wire entered the building. Sheila had been staying with her a couple days each week for the last month, but that had made no difference.

Toni put down her book, walked carefully to the window, and peered around the edge of the partially open curtain. She was surprised at how relieved she felt when she recognized Jason's car, but the relief soon turned to irritation. Sheila and Jason were standing by the car. They were having a serious discussion, though Toni couldn't hear what they were saying. Sheila seemed upset, and Jason hugged her. Toni felt a twinge of jealousy. The two of them had left for the Tuesday night single's meeting at the church almost three hours ago. She couldn't imagine what the group could have been discussing for so long, assuming, of course, it was the meeting that had kept Sheila and Jason out so late.

Tears welled up in Toni's eyes. Jason and Sheila obviously had feelings for each other, and enough time had passed so they were probably more than just friends. Sheila was petite and beautiful. Men had always been attracted by her dark, cocoa brown skin and thick, lustrous hair. They got lost in her huge dark eyes and responded unconsciously to the sense of helplessness projected by her small size. But more than anything else, Jason would be attracted to Sheila because they each had the same deep faith in God.

Toni stepped away from the window and firmly reminded herself that their relationship was none of her business. She needed Jason as an employee and wanted him as a friend, but she wasn't sure yet whether she could ever share his faith. She did not want her examination of Christianity clouded or compromised by some premature romantic involvement. And she had already picked up some hints that he wanted to be more than her employee and friend. Yes, it might be just as well if Jason Matthews was distracted by Sheila for the time being.

"I still have some things to settle with God," she whispered. Toni was momentarily shocked by the sound of her own words. Had she come so far in only a few weeks that she was now accepting the idea that God existed and was personally interested in her?

The sound of Jason and Sheila on the stairs to her apartment interrupted her thoughts. She was surprised to see them laughing as they entered. It was almost as if they shared a secret joke, a joke that did not include her. "Hi, Toni," both of them said as they headed toward the kitchen.

She forced herself to smile, "Hi. How was your meeting?"

Sheila turned and answered. "It was great, Toni. You should come with us next time. We always have a lot to talk about since almost everybody in the group is single." She opened the refrigerator and poured two glasses of iced tea, offering one to Jason.

Toni joined them in the kitchen. "Sheila, I've been meaning to tell you something. You don't have to stay with me any longer. I know you probably want to get back to your own place full-time."

Sheila set her tea on the table and placed her hand on Toni's shoulder. "Toni, do you really think that's a good idea with all that's been happening?"

She sighed. "Things keep happening whether you're here or not. You were here Sunday night, neither of us heard a sound, and on Monday morning the phone in the bakery was dead.

You were going back home tonight anyway, and I just don't think there's any reason for you to keep disrupting your life. I really don't want to put you out anymore, and I'd feel better if you were sleeping in your own bed instead of on my couch, okay?"

Sheila gave her an irritated look and then reluctantly agreed. "You are a stubborn woman, Toni Brown." Then she turned to Jason. "Do you mind giving me a lift home? My car is in the shop again, and it'll only take a minute for me to throw my things together."

Toni glanced at Jason and noticed that he was staring at her even as he told Sheila he would be happy to take her home. His dark, warm eyes were full of concern, and she wondered if he thought she was making a mistake by asking Sheila to return to her own home.

As if in answer to her unspoken questions, he said, "I'm always worrying about you, Toni. You've seemed so tired and distracted lately."

"I haven't been sleeping very well," Toni replied. "But I'm fine. Really I am. I've just had a lot on my mind lately." Jason kissed her cheek, and she couldn't decide whether to laugh, cry, or get angry with him.

Just then, Sheila appeared with a garment bag and a carry-on case. Jason and Sheila said their good-byes and headed out to his car.

During the rest of the week, Jason and Toni worked companionably. He continued to show up at the bakery first thing in the morning, both to help with the baking and so that she wouldn't be working alone. She enjoyed the time they spent together at the crack of dawn, but she reminded herself each day that there was no way to predict where this relationship was going. And as hard as she tried, Toni could not entirely ignore the apprehensions she felt about Jason's relationship with Sheila.

"Jason, I feel that I can trust you with a secret," she said as she unlocked the door that Friday. It was four o'clock in the morning, and the dark sky was just beginning to lighten. Awakening birds twittered in the trees.

"Trust me? With what?" He smiled as he washed his hands and placed a crisp white apron over his lean body.

She grinned, touched his cheek, and beckoned him into her kitchen. "I haven't shown you how to make the cookies yet. The chocolate chip and the lemon sugar were my aunt's secret recipes."

"Toni, are you sure that's a good idea?" He spoke levelly, but there was a look of frank amazement on his face.

"Jason, I trust you. I need somebody else to know the recipes besides me. Cathy isn't going to be back until at least the middle of July. You've been here for a month and a half, and I'm a pretty good judge of people. If you were dishonest, I think I'd have figured it out by now." She chuckled over his apparent speechlessness and began measuring flour and sugar. "Now, I always make a batch with milk chocolate chips and a batch with semisweet chips. Remember, the butter has to be at room temperature because it's easier to mix that way. I also make sure the eggs are at room temperature."

"Toni, you really don't have to do this," Jason began.

She touched his hand. "But I want to, Jason. I don't mind sharing my secrets with you. I know you won't tell. Now," she continued, "I use fresh lemons in the sugar cookies. That gives them a sharp, tart flavor. I also use lots of yellow food coloring to make them bright."

During the next hour, she explained everything she knew about making her trademark cookies and found herself enjoying life more than she had in ages. When the cookies were cooling on racks, she smiled at her stunned assistant.

"Jason, I don't care if you use the recipes to make cookies for yourself. I just don't want you to give them to anybody else. This bakery is my livelihood, and these cookies are the most popular things that I make. They're also the most profitable."

He looked at her with genuine surprise. "I had no idea. But your secrets are safe with me."

Suddenly Jason looked uncomfortable. His eyes were filled with the same deep sadness she remembered from his first day in the bakery.

"What's the matter, Jason?"

"I'm just thinking about secrets and the terrible price we pay for them. Sometimes they don't seem worth it . . . no matter how profitable they are. And you're right, keeping secrets can be a matter of life and death, both for businesses and for individuals."

"What secrets have caused you so much pain?" she asked quietly.

He sighed, "It's a long story, and we have cookies to make."

"We've gotten an early start—there's plenty of time. And I think it may be good for you to talk about this. I can take care of this batch while you tell me your story." She watched him consider her offer.

Finally, he asked, "What do you know about the beginnings of the Internet?"

She smiled. "Not very much."

"The ideas and basic technology for what we call the Internet were developed by the Defense Department, some of it more than thirty years ago. They were looking for a secure communications system that could continue functioning after a nuclear attack."

Toni looked stunned, and Jason continued. "My father graduated from MIT in the sixties, and he got involved with some of the earliest work on the system through his contacts there. A lot of the work Matthews and Company does today is for projects funded by the military. Most of it is top secret, and there are a lot of people who would do anything to get their hands on the research and products associated with that work. So, you see, I understand the importance of keeping secrets."

Jason paused. "I've told you before that I don't like the security systems I have to deal with at Matthews. What I didn't explain was that some of them are managed by the military and are designed to keep members of my family from being kidnapped or killed. For example, I don't usually drive myself to work. I'm driven to work in an armored sedan, using several different routes. There are two National Security Administration agents with me in the car, and two more sometimes follow us in another vehicle. My home and those of other family members are under twenty-four-hour-a-day surveillance. When I go on business trips, I usually have two body guards. One of the biggest concessions made to me when I decided to take my leave of absence from work was that I be allowed to go alone. At least I think I'm alone." He offered Toni a smile and pointed at the work table. "Who knows, maybe those chocolate chips have listening devices in them."

"That's an amazing story, Jason, but I have one question." Toni suppressed a giggle. "Do you have a high enough security clearance to do the next batch of cookies on your own?"

Out of habit, Toni awoke early that Sunday morning. She had plenty of time to get ready for church because services at Blue Spring Community didn't start until eleven o'clock. She got out of bed, fixed her morning coffee, and nibbled on a donut as she surfed channels, finally settling on a Sunday morning news program.

A few hours later Toni opened her closet to select her outfit. Since she no longer had to dress up for work, she didn't have a lot of fancy clothing anymore; she'd given most of her skirts and dresses to a homeless shelter. Studying the clothes that remained, she eventually settled on a pale-peach dress that always drew compliments when she wore it. She also selected the string of pearls that had been a gift from her parents when she graduated from college. After she applied her makeup, she picked up the Bible her mother had given her so many years ago, which Toni had retrieved from the fireproof box in the bakery kitchen. Grabbing the padded portfolio where she kept her sermon notes, Toni headed downstairs to the front door. As she walked to her car, she realized it was hot as an oven outside. She gazed into the distance and saw the waves of heat. The television meteorologist had predicted record-breaking temperatures. For once he might be right.

Toni arrived at the church doors just as Mrs. Dukes and her husband began walking up the steps. "Toni, it looks like you're in danger of becoming a regular around here!" Mrs. Dukes gave her a hug and her husband did the same. Toni smiled. Even after a few weeks, she was still trying to adjust to the older couple's effusive greetings.

"Did you come alone again?" Mrs. Dukes asked as they entered the church. Toni nodded. The woman invited her to sit with them, and Toni politely refused, as she had every week since she had started coming. She took her accustomed place toward the back of the church and looked at the bulletin to prepare herself for the service. She marked the Bible passages that were listed as references for the sermon and looked through a hymnal to try to familiarize herself with the words and music.

She sighed as she glanced uneasily around the small church. The sun poured through the stained-glass windows, spilling a rainbow of blue, green, red, black, and yellow on the dark-cranberry carpeting. The pews were made from light oak. It was a nice building, and the people were certainly friendly enough. But she still had doubts about the trustworthiness of God. She looked up at the pulpit and saw the cross. The pastor had said a few weeks ago that all the most important questions in life ultimately found their answers at the foot of the cross. Was it possible that was actually true?

Just then Sheila entered the sanctuary from a side door. She gave a little wave to Toni and joined her near the back of the church. The pews in front had already been filled. The organist began to play a tune that sounded vaguely familiar.

Suddenly, the side doors near the pulpit opened, and a long line of men streamed in. They were dressed in black and white suits, and they were humming. Toni immediately spotted Jason amid the crowd. His broad muscular body looked nice in the dark suit. His clean-shaven head shone under the church lights. "He's so handsome," she breathed.

"What did you say?" whispered Sheila.

"Nothing," Toni responded softly, biting her bottom lip in consternation. The last thing she needed was for Sheila to discover her carefully concealed feelings toward Jason.

The organist continued to play, and suddenly the men's voices burst forth. "Amazing grace, how sweet the sound, that sav'd a wretch like me!" The men's voices joined in unison, creating a deep, powerful sound that seemed to come from the soul of every man in the choir. Toni closed her eyes and enjoyed the music. Several members of the congregation joined in.

When Pastor Wilkins came onto the platform, the music stopped. Toni opened her eyes and discovered her cheeks were wet. She wiped her tears and gazed at the men's choir. She looked at Jason, and their eyes locked. He gave her a faint smile just before the pastor led the congregation in prayer.

When the prayer was finished, Toni felt different. She felt something, but she wasn't sure what it was. She felt as if something or someone was silently beckoning to her.

"Now, everyone, I want to give a sermon about a subject that is near and dear to all of us." Pastor Wilkins's deep strong voice carried over the pulpit. "I'm going to preach to you today about the subject of money."

Toni's eyes widened with surprise. Here was a subject she already knew a lot about. As a child, she'd learned how financial hardship could cripple a family. As an adult, she had tracked the influence of money on economic development, politics, and the shaping of whole societies. Since inheriting the bakery, she had kept a close watch over her income and expenses. At almost any point in the year, she had a good idea of what kind of profit or loss her business was generating. What could a preacher have to say to her on this subject?

"Let's begin with the Old Testament. If you'll read with me Ecclesiastes 7:12 and then turn to Ecclesiastes 10:19." He read the verses and emphasized how money protected against poverty and created a way to procure things such as food and clothing that were necessary for survival.

"But sometimes we begin to place our total trust in money for security. We all need to be reminded that money does not provide total security. Only the Lord can provide that." He paused, allowing his words to have an effect on the congregation.

Reverend Wilkins spoke of people in debt, living beyond

their means, struggling to make the next credit card payment. He spoke of people who were millionaires and had so much money that they didn't know what to do with it. He spoke of how money dominated people's lives, and he stressed the error of falling victim to the power of silver and gold.

He ended his sermon by reading 1 Timothy 6:10–11: "For the love of money is a root of all kinds of evil, for which some have strayed from the faith in their greediness, and pierced themselves through with many sorrows. But you, O man of God, flee these things and pursue righteousness, godliness, faith, love, patience, gentleness."

When he quoted verses, Toni followed carefully in her own Bible. Twice the pastor referred to passages in the Gospels that were not printed in the bulletin. Toni was surprised when she was able to find them without difficulty. His words echoed in her mind as he reached the end of his sermon.

The sound of the men's choir interrupted her thoughts. "Go tell it on the mountain," sang their deep voices, blending together so smoothly, it was almost as if they were being led by angels. The musical notes drifted through the air, and Toni felt as if she were conquering an internal battle. The words of Scripture ran through her mind.

When she left, she shook the preacher's hand. "I'm glad to see you again this morning, Toni," he commented. Toni had been pleased to find that the man was just as friendly at church as he was when he made his regular trips to Blue Spring Baked Goods. She smiled warmly as she shook his hand and then turned to find Sheila among the crowd.

"Toni," her friend said, "I was wondering if we could go someplace for lunch. It's been a long time since we've done anything fun." Sheila looked flustered, as if she had something on her mind.

"Let's go to Lottie's Diner," Toni suggested. "We'll take my car and come back to the church later to get yours."

A few minutes later they were seated in a corner booth of the small diner. After they ordered, Sheila took a sip from her water glass. "Sheila, I can tell that you've got something to say to me," said Toni. She was still thinking about the morning's sermon, but she forced the preacher's words from her mind as she gave Sheila her full attention.

Sheila offered a weak smile. "Toni, we're best friends. But recently I've sensed that there's been a rift in our relationship. Is something wrong? Is everything okay?"

Toni sighed as she sipped her soda. Apparently she had not been as successful as she had hoped in hiding her feelings about Jason. She didn't know how to tell Sheila that she was jealous of the close relationship she seemed to share with him. She didn't even want to admit to herself that she had feelings for him. Most of all, Toni didn't want to damage the new rapport that she and Sheila had achieved. She thought back to that tearful Sunday afternoon. It suddenly occurred to her that their friendship would never have grown that day unless both of them had been willing to take risks.

"Sheila, it's about Jason," Toni began. The waitress returned with their food. Sheila paused to pray silently, then cut her spaghetti and meatballs. Toni gazed at her lamb chops and mashed potatoes. She took a small bite of her food.

Sheila looked up at her and asked, "What about Jason? He's still working out at the bakery, isn't he? I thought you told me that he was the best employee you'd ever hired."

"He's great, Sheila. I'm just worried and confused about a lot of things these days."

"What sort of things, Toni?" Sheila put her fork aside and looked deeply into Toni's eyes. "I've known you for most of my life, and there aren't many things we don't know about each other. But you have been acting kind of strange lately. Did something else happen at the bakery?" she asked in alarm.

Toni pulled a paper napkin from the dispenser and began ripping it into tiny pieces. She was suddenly upset, and her appetite had vanished. Sheila placed her hand over Toni's.

"Toni, your hands are cold. I can tell you're nervous. Now please tell me what's the matter," she said quietly. She released Toni's icy hand.

"I've noticed that you and Jason have gotten close lately." Toni swallowed and willed her erratically beating heart to slow down. Sheila continued to gaze at her steadily with her large brown eyes.

"Yes, we have gotten closer since he started going to the church. Pastor Wilkins even made him an honorary member. He said that he could become a full member once he decided to move here." She laughed lightly, but Toni did not return her smile.

"Sheila, this is just so hard for me to discuss," she admitted.

"Did you and Jason have an argument? Is that why you're upset, Toni?" Sheila's voice was full of concern.

"No, that's not the problem. The truth is that I've felt something has been going on between you and Jason. It makes me uncomfortable because I have feelings for him. If he doesn't share my sentiments, then I need to know now."

Sheila's large eyes widened with surprise. "So you think that Jason is interested in me?" She dropped her napkin and smiled. A few seconds later she started laughing, and soon tears were rolling down her dark cheeks.

Toni was stunned. "What's so funny?

"Toni, forgive me, but why would Jason be interested in me, of all people?"

"But you two have been spending so much time together lately. You go to worship services and singles meetings together. You're always having these long, intense conversations about the Bible and your faith and your lives."

"So? Listen, Toni. When you're a child of God, you share lots of things with fellow believers. I love my church family. I love every single person in the congregation, including Jason."

"But you two seem to enjoy each other's company so much," Toni began.

"We do, Toni, but we're just friends! There are other men in the congregation I speak with as well. I'm even interested in someone in the singles ministry, and I can guarantee you that it's not Jason." Sheila grabbed Toni's hand again. "Listen, Jason only has eyes for you. No one else."

"Are you sure?"

"Yes. He's told me so. He even wants to know more about why you have an aversion to church and organized religion. I told him that I couldn't break your confidence since you were my best friend."

Sheila took a deep breath and squeezed Toni's hand. "Jason cares about you, Toni. Jason and I share a commitment to Christ, and we both want to help you. But there's no way we're interested in each other romantically. That man is interested in only one person, and that person is you. Jason is kind, warm, and loving, just the kind of person you deserve." Sheila nodded emphatically as she released Toni's hand.

"I feel so stupid, Sheila. I can't believe you're not angry with me. After all, I've just accused you of something that you're not even guilty of."

"Toni. I'm just glad to hear that you have feelings for Jason. I'm sure he'd be as surprised as I was to hear what you had to say. We've been wondering what's been eating at you lately, and now I know."

"Jason's been asking you about me?" Toni's heart pounded with anticipation.

Sheila buttered a roll. "He sure has. We could tell that something was bothering you, but we weren't sure what it was. At first we thought it was all the stuff that's been happening at the bakery or the issues of faith you're wrestling with, but we both thought something else was going on, too."

"Too much is going on. And that's the real problem. I'm having trouble separating one thing from another. So you have to make me a promise, Sheila. Don't let Jason know how I feel about him."

"But Toni, that's crazy. And it's also a lie," Sheila insisted.

"No, it isn't. I really don't know what I feel toward him. And I refuse to find out. Right now isn't a good time for me to be slipping into a romantic relationship with anyone."

"Why?" Sheila asked emphatically. "Do you actually think you can turn your emotions on and off at will? No one can dictate —"

"I have to try. I've got to decide whether believing in God and having faith in Jesus makes sense before I let anything happen with Jason. In fact, I'm a little shocked that Jason would let himself become so interested in me when he knows I'm not a Christian. Who knows, I may never get there. I won't become a Christian in order to snare Jason. And he shouldn't be praying for my conversion in order to fulfill his romantic fantasies."

Sheila sat in stunned silence while Toni continued. "I grew up in a family that was divided by religion. And I am not going to set myself up for that kind of conflict and loneliness. Even if Jason was my worst enemy, I wouldn't want to see him suffer like that. And I'm sure not going to let it happen when I think I might be falling in love with the man."

Sheila shook her head. "Much as I hate to admit it, you do have a point. And I will keep your secret."

For the next few minutes they ate in silence, then Toni said, "Can I ask you a question about what it's like for you to be a Christian? And before you answer, I've got to warn you, this is a weird question."

"I'll give it my best shot."

"Who do you feel closest to: God, Jesus, or the Holy Spirit? Pastor Wilkins says they're all, what's the phrase he used . . . manifestations of . . . that's right, he said they're all manifestations of the same divine being. But who do you personally feel closest to?"

"I suppose I feel closest to Jesus because I've always thought of Jesus as a friend. I guess that's because, when I became a Christian, I surrendered my life to Jesus. And I suppose it's also because, when God wanted to show human beings what He was like, God sent Jesus. Jesus brought the message, but He also is the message. That's why Jesus is referred to in the Gospels as 'Immanuel,' which means 'God with us.' "

Toni looked sad and tired. The next words came out in a whisper. "I like the idea of Jesus being a friend. But it's so hard for me to trust God to be my friend."

Sheila leaned forward. "Why?"

"I need to be able to trust my friends to protect me, and I don't know if I can trust God to protect me. I'm not even sure I understand any more what protection means. I mean, God didn't exactly protect Jesus, did He? Jesus went to the cross, and those who follow him end up going to the cross, one way or another. I know that the resurrection comes after the cross, but sometimes it takes so long for Christians to get to the resurrection. I don't know how they do put up with the waiting. I don't think I could."

She paused and shook her head. "I've talked to my mom about this a lot, and she says that the Holy Spirit gives her strength when times are hard. But that's hard for me to understand. She's describing something that she already has, something that has been a part of her life for a long time. But that doesn't tell me where or how to find faith in the first place.

"You know, Sheila, I've even talked to my dad about this. He has always been a big fan of mystery novels, and we've both been reading the same Brother Cadfael book. He says it helps him understand the things he hears in church. Dad says he likes Cadfael because it shows how Christians are able to hold on to some small part of God, even in the midst of horrible situations. That's what faith means to him: finding some small part of God and holding on to it for all we're worth. He's been holding on to the Sermon on the Mount lately. The parts that all begin with the word 'blessed.' Last week he said, 'When I can't hold on any longer, I discover that it's Jesus who has been holding on to me all along. That's how faith works. You don't realize you have it until you can't hold on any longer.' "

Toni felt tears sliding down her cheeks. "I don't even know if my father's a Christian, and he's the only person I've ever talked to who has come close to describing faith in terms I can understand."

Sheila wiped at her own eyes with her napkin. "What does your mom say about your father's ideas?"

"Mom wasn't at home when we talked about it. But she hasn't said anything about him going forward at church or anything like that."

"Toni, it sounds to me like something is going on between your father and Jesus. I'm not sure what it is, but his description of faith is amazing. Sometimes, when people surrender their lives to Christ, the whole process is very quiet and very personal. They don't always go forward immediately or make any sort of public profession of faith. I think you'd better ask your mother about this the next time you talk to her."

"You're right. Mom would certainly want to know, and Dad didn't say I couldn't tell her." Toni blew her nose and then smiled. "And this conversation is getting way too serious." She leaned toward her friend, propped her chin on both hands, and raised one eyebrow. "So tell me, Sheila, which hunk in the singles group have you got your eye on?"

The two friends spent the rest of their lunch catching up on each other's lives. Sheila updated Toni on life in the singles group and at the bank. Toni told Sheila about life at the bakery and that she'd revealed her secret cookie recipes to Jason.

"You did? I'm surprised! You won't even tell me what those recipes are!"

"But you aren't Jason," Toni said. The two women laughed as they went up to pay their bill and make their way out to the car.

Eight

When she finally arrived back at the bakery, Toni was more than ready for a nap, even though it was only midafternoon. All the interrupted nights of sleep over the past weeks were catching up with her. She drove into the graveled parking area in back and walked toward one of the back entrances to the building. The door opened onto a first-floor hallway that led to the kitchen, her office, and several storage rooms. It also connected to a stairway that led up to her apartment above the shop.

As she walked across the gravel, she noticed strange reddish-white marks at regular intervals. She stopped, bent down, and looked at them closely. They were footprints. They led back toward the rear entrance of the bakery's kitchen. She followed them to the steps leading up to the kitchen door. The marks were clearer there, and she could see them glistening in the sunlight.

She started up the stairs, intending to unlock the door, but when her hand touched the knob the door swung inward. It wasn't locked. It wasn't even tightly closed. For a moment Toni wondered how she could possibly have forgotten to close and lock the door, then she looked into the kitchen and her mind went numb with shock. Before her lay a chaotic wasteland of flour, sugar, milk, cream, and spoiling fruit.

The counters and work table were covered with thick, sticky layers of the mixture. The mess on the floor was six inches deep in some places. Her expensive commercial mixers were dripping with a congealing red glaze. Out of the open door flowed the smell of apples and strawberries and disaster. She leaned helplessly against the doorjamb, trying to deny the evidence of her own eyes and nose. She looked across the kitchen and out into the front of the shop, but most of her view was blocked by a wall. There was no way to tell how far the devastation extended.

Toni stepped carefully down the back steps, avoiding the sticky tracks. She ran around to the front of the bakery and unlocked the front door with her key. A quick glance showed no visible damage, so she hurried behind the sales counter and approached the wide doorway leading to the kitchen. A few feet from the entrance, she stopped. An oozing beige tide was flowing out of the kitchen. A huge container of buttermilk had been dumped near the doorway and had apparently combined with spilled flour and baking powder to create a grotesque, bubbling mass that was slowly rising.

As Toni surveyed the damage in silent despair, more details registered in her mind. Large flour and sugar sacks, some still partly full, were draped over counters, tables, and machines. Several drawers of utensils had been pulled out and emptied onto the floor. One of the drawers had been thrown across the kitchen and had shattered into a half dozen pieces against the stainless steel front of her largest commercial refrigerator. Its point of impact was clearly marked with scratches and a small dent. Broken pieces of the Pyrex bowls she used to store fresh fruit were scattered across the floor. Her fire extinguisher had been sprayed around the room and then used to smash in the door of a large storage cabinet.

Toni backed away from the jumbled disorder and picked up the phone. The line was dead—again. Automatically she started for the stairs to her apartment, then stopped because the path was blocked by the mess in the kitchen. She quickly re-traced her steps to the back of the bakery and used the outside entrance to the stairway hall.

She ran up the stairs in a blind rage, taking them two at a time, grabbed her phone, called Jason. While she listened to his phone ring, she wondered who would do this to her. Who could hate her that much. It just didn't make any sense. By the time he answered, fear and sadness were beginning to replace the anger, and her hands were shaking.

"Jason! You've got to come over and help me," she screamed. Suddenly there were tears running down her face, and she was sobbing into the phone. "Somebody's . . . trashed . . . my . . . kitchen, and I . . . I . . . don't know what to do."

She tried to describe the incredible scene downstairs, but could get no more than one or two words out at a time between the sobs that were convulsing her. Jason had to shout from his end of the line to get her attention.

"Toni, Toni! Try to calm down. Take slow, deep breaths. That's better. Are you standing up?"

"Yes."

"It will help if you sit down. Can you do that for me?"

"Yes, I'm sitting down now."

"Good. Are you upstairs?"

"Yes, the phone downstairs doesn't work."

"Are you injured in any way?"

"No, except that I'm scared out of my wits."

"Good. Is the door to your apartment locked?"

"No, should I lock it?"

"No, Toni. Please go downstairs, leave the building, and walk to the front of the bakery. Take the cordless phone with you, and tell me what you're doing, as you're doing it."

She followed his instructions. "I'm standing in front of the bakery."

"I want you to wait there for me. Don't go back into the bakery. Don't touch anything on the outside of the building. Just sit down at one of the tables out front and wait for me. Can you do that?"

"Yes," Toni said weakly as she collapsed into one of the padded patio chairs. "I'm sitting down now."

"That's very good, Toni. I won't be long, I promise. I'm calling the police from here, and then I'll be right over."

Toni sat silently, clutching the phone and staring blankly through the front window of her bakery. She was shaking so badly that she couldn't make her finger push the button that would break the connection. A voice said, "If you want to make a call, please hang up . . ." The phone dropped from her cold hands, clattered onto the table, and went silent. Her heart was pounding, and she felt faint. "Lord, what's going to happen to me?" she pleaded.

Jason appeared in less than five minutes, and Toni ran to hug him. They stood together for some time while she cried into his shoulder. By the time she had stopped shaking and was able to talk, the police, one male and one female, had arrived. While Jason and Toni returned to the table where she had been sitting, the two officers drew their weapons and asked her permission to search the apartment.

"Why did you want me to come outside," asked Toni with a puzzled expression.

"I was afraid that whoever had vandalized the kitchen might still be in the building. That they might be hiding in your apartment. Apparently the officers are concerned, too."

Toni's face was a mask of shocked amazement. Jason waited for a moment and then quietly continued. "I'm sorry. I know this is a terrible shock to you, but have you recovered enough to tell me what happened?"

Toni described the condition of the kitchen. The expression on Jason's face grew more thoughtful with each additional detail. Just as she finished, the police returned from upstairs and reported everything to be safe. They asked for a brief description of the damage and then went in to see for themselves.

Jason squeezed Toni's hand and then looked directly at her. "This whole situation has just gotten a lot more serious. Someone who could do that much damage to your kitchen is capable of anything. We need to take some drastic steps to protect you personally and the investment you have in this business."

"If you're sure it's that serious, then, okay," Toni said doubtfully.

"I'm sure it's that serious," he said with grim intensity. "And I don't want to take any chances. I've had more than my fill of standing around, doing nothing, while people I care for suffer."

Just then, the woman officer returned and asked to interview Toni. After an hour of asking questions, taking pictures, and collecting other evidence, both officers left and told Toni it would be all right for her to start cleaning up the mess. She and Jason went upstairs to make some coffee and to plan how they would attack the job before them.

Toni dropped into her favorite overstuffed chair. She looked across to the couch where Jason sat. "I don't know if I've ever heard you sound quite so . . . well . . . desperate," she said. "I guess I'm not the only one who's feeling overwhelmed by that mess downstairs."

"I'm sorry, Toni. I was out of line. I should be helping you, not taking out my frustrations at your expense. But I am worried. It's always hard for any of us to imagine that someone we know would want to hurt us, but we all have enemies. And business owners often underestimate what their competitors will do to steal important information or simply destroy them. I made that mistake myself not so long ago." The look of thoughtful sadness that Toni had seen so many times over the last couple months settled on Jason's handsome face. She waited for him to continue.

"If some good people hadn't been watching out for me, I would have seriously damaged Matthews and Company and probably compromised national security."

Toni looked stunned and held up her hand. "Just because I showed you my cookie recipes doesn't mean you have to give away any of your corporate secrets. I'm already scared enough and angry enough to do whatever you want me to do as far as security around here is concerned."

"They're not just corporate secrets," Jason said. "They're personal secrets. They'll help you understand why I've been wrestling with God for so long. I need to tell you what happened, because it's part of the reason I left Chicago and turned up in your bakery." He looked surprised, and the next words came out almost as a whisper. "I hadn't thought of that before. I only made this trip because of all that had happened to me. I wonder . . ." Jason shook his head. "It's so strange the way things work out sometimes."

He looked across the coffee table at Toni, and a small smile began to form. His voice became stronger. "But I'm getting way off track. I want to tell you a story about corporate espionage, but I have to ask you not to repeat it to anyone without asking me first, okay?"

She nodded.

"I told you before that Matthews and Company works on classified projects for the military, but I did not tell you that several of those projects are very complex and extremely profitable. And one project in particular is very important for national security.

"It's known as BatCom, which is short for Unified Battlefield Tactical Communications System. It began as a simple, rugged, and secure communications system for use by a small number of military units fighting close together. It allowed them to track each other's movements electronically and discuss strategy without being located or overheard by the enemy.

"But that was just the beginning. Over the years the system was modified to give more information about individual soldiers and also to give those in command an accurate picture of a battle as it developed.

"The latest version provides detailed information on the exact position and physical condition of each soldier. The information is gathered by a full body sensor suit. It's a little like a set of long underwear, with extra pieces to cover the hands, feet, head, and neck. The data is so complete that medical personnel can use it to diagnose wounds or other injuries. They can even tell when someone is too hot, too cold, dehydrated, or has gone too long without eating.

"At the same time," Jason continued explaining, "commanders can see what groups of soldiers are doing. The information shows where individual combat units are located, what sorts of weapons they are carrying, how many transport and combat vehicles they have, how long they've been in the field, how many casualties they have suffered, and a lot of other information. This unit information can be scaled up to show how the individual units fit into larger structures, such as brigades or divisions. Even the positions of enemy forces can be displayed. And here's the most remarkable thing: Though the system was originally designed for the army, it's now possible for all branches of the American military to use it for combined operations."

Jason paused and looked at Toni, as if to make sure she was still with him. She nodded her understanding.

"Obviously this is a big deal," he continued. "But it's all useless unless the massive amounts of information flowing back and forth through the system can be kept out of enemy hands. Fortunately, everything is encrypted, using a special scrambling system that is constantly changing. The encryption codes are the heart of the system. And last spring, because I wasn't being careful enough, they were almost stolen.

"I was making a lot of trips to Europe on nonmilitary business, and I got to know a flight attendant who worked for Air France. I thought I was falling in love. What I didn't know was that she was a French intelligence agent. It turns out that Air France had been hiding surveillance devices all over the first-class cabins of their commercial aircraft for years. Whenever they picked up something interesting, they would investigate it. If it looked important enough, they would assign one or more agents to get more information. Often this was accomplished by getting close to individual business travelers. The woman assigned to me was good. She became a close friend over several months and then acted like she was interested in a much more serious relationship. After I had known her for six months, she came to Chicago to visit my family. She spent a lot of time with me at Matthews."

Jason paused again, this time because his mind seemed to be

a thousand miles away. Toni waited patiently for him to continue. Finally, Jason cleared his throat and looked across at her.

"Then she stole the encryption code generator program for BatCom and disappeared. At least that was what I thought had happened. Fortunately, my father and some of his friends at the National Security Administration had been suspicious about her. They actually used me as bait and offered her a great opportunity to steal a carefully disguised fake. After she stole it, they arrested her. All that she got was a very sophisticated computer virus that is doing damage to their military and academic computer systems to this day. Remember the big computer virus scare last spring? That happened because one small part of this program got passed on to an unsuspecting American university from contacts in Paris."

"Jason, that's awful. How could your father do that to you?"

"He didn't have a choice. Remember, I was the one who let myself fall in love."

"But you must have felt like a complete fool. And your mom was dying of cancer at the same time. No wonder you wanted to get away for a while."

"So, now you know the whole story. What's going on here in Blue Spring doesn't threaten national security, but it's still serious. We don't know who is doing these things, and we don't really know why. All we know is that the level of violence has been increasing for weeks, and it just went up again—way up. There's no telling what may happen next."

"So you've convinced me," Toni said with a forced smile. "What do you want me to do?"

"First, you need to call Sheila and arrange to stay with her for a few days. And then we need to get our hands on some timers to control the lights here, so it will look like you're still around at night."

"I'm afraid you're right." She sighed.

"All your locks look like they're about fifty years old. I don't think there's even one outside door with a deadbolt lock on it. I'll bet the person who messed up your kitchen used a credit card to jimmy the lock on the back entrance. You need new, heavy-duty lock sets with separate deadbolts on all the exterior doors. And I'd recommend the same thing for the most important interior doors: the one to your office, the entrances to the storage areas, and the interior door leading into this apartment. Locking devices should also be installed on all your windows, including the ones on the second floor."

"New outside locks have been on my to-do list since I inherited this place," she admitted sheepishly.

"You aren't the first small business owner to say that," he said, smiling his sympathy. "Now only one side of your building is illuminated by the streetlight at night," he observed. "You need to install several outside lights to cover the dark areas. They should all have motion detectors, so they come on automatically when anything or anyone gets too close to the building."

"That would also making coming home after dark much nicer," she added.

"You should also have a complete security system installed. Get one with an independent power supply, as well as both wired and wireless links to a twenty-four-hour monitoring service. That will protect you against break-ins, fire, and several other problems."

His suggestion surprised her. "A security system?" she protested. "Those things are expensive, and this is Blue Spring, not Baltimore."

"I know, Toni. But a security system would have stopped today's visitor in his tracks. The technology is a lot better and a lot less expensive than it was even two or three years ago. It will save quite a bit of money on insurance, too. I've seen how much you make here. You can afford to invest in your safety. And I also want you to get a cell phone and keep it with you at all times."

"A cell phone! I work here all day and live upstairs. I'm never more than thirty feet away from a phone."

Jason nodded. "I know, but what if someone comes after you when you're buying groceries or taking a trip to see your mom? What if you hear a noise in the night, wake up, and find that both your phone lines are dead?"

"I see your point," Toni agreed grudgingly.

"Now, all this is going to take time to set up, and we still have a mess to clean up downstairs. As much as I hate to say it, I'm afraid the bakery will have to remain closed tomorrow and maybe on Tuesday, too."

Toni was beginning to look a little glassy-eyed. "I guess that all makes sense, Jason. Though some of it sounds a little too much like something out of a James Bond movie for my taste. Or maybe it's more like the *X-Files*. Please tell me I'm not about to be abducted by space aliens on top of everything else." She managed a tired smile.

"No, actually this is the sequel to *Men in Black*, and I *am* a space alien."

"Well, that certainly explains a lot. I always thought you were too good to be true."

"Yes, and I have a dark and sinister plan—to abduct you and take you out to dinner. Have you noticed what time it is?" They both laughed.

"We could get pizza and bring it back here to eat," Toni suggested.

"That's a good idea," he replied, "but why don't you call Sheila first? I don't know if she's going to church tonight, but it's just past six-thirty, so she should still be home. I'm sure she'll be happy to let you stay with her for a few days, but you might as well give her as much warning as possible."

Sheila not only was happy to have Toni stay with her for as long as necessary, but she also insisted on picking up the pizza herself and then joining them in the cleanup effort. The three friends swept and shoveled the worst of the goo into a dozen large trash bags and deposited them in the Dumpster out back. Utensils of all kinds had to be extricated from the congealed mass on the floor, and most of them were placed in a sink full of soapy water and left to soak overnight. All of the ovens, cook-tops, and refrigerators were checked and found to be undam-aged. Each large stand mixer was cleaned enough to make sure it was still functioning. At nine-thirty that evening, Toni called a halt to the operation.

"We aren't going to get this done tonight. And even if we did, I need to reorder flour, sugar, and a bunch of other things be-fore this place is going to be back in business."

"All right," said Sheila. "I'll go home and get the sofa bed ready. How long do you think it will take you to pack?"

"I'm too hyper to sleep yet," Toni admitted. "Why don't you just give me a key and leave a light on? Thanks for your help, Sheila." The two friends hugged.

"I'll see you in the morning." Sheila made her way carefully to the back door and closed it behind her.

"Would it help you to take a walk?" asked Jason.

Toni surveyed the work remaining one more time and turned to him with a rueful grin. "That sounds like an excel-lent idea. Maybe some fresh air will help me relax and clear my mind." They locked the bakery and strolled out into the warm evening. The velvet black sky was littered with tiny stars. They walked toward the center of town in companionable silence for a few minutes.

"I'd be more than happy to give you a historic walking tour of Blue Spring, Maryland," Toni suggested. They stopped in front of the video store. "This store is owned by the Joneses. They had this great idea to open it when VCRs became popular nearly fifteen years ago, and they added DVDs when those first became available a couple years ago. They make a lot of money since they're the only video store in town." She pointed out the clothing boutique and the beauty parlor. "I go here twice a month to get my hair done, and they give me a discount since I come so often," she said with a grin.

They passed the tiny mall where teens congregated after school. The only business still open was the movie theater, and a crowd of kids was waiting in line to see the latest hit. As they walked by houses, Jason saw families sitting in their living rooms, reading, talking, and watching TV. He suddenly realized that he felt very much at home, and it surprised him that a city boy could become so fond of a small place like Blue Spring.

Toni's descriptions continued as they turned back toward the bakery. When they passed the police station, she fell silent, and Jason could see her worried expression. He reached over and took her hand. It was cold despite the lingering warmth of the night.

Toni glanced over at him. "That's a pretty bold move for a sinister space alien. If you're not careful, you might admit that you actually like working with me." She was shocked at the bitterness in her own voice. "I'm sorry. I had no right to say that. You've given me more help than I have any right to expect. I guess I'm finally getting tired enough so that my natural rudeness is starting to show."

Jason stopped, and she was forced to turn back toward him. "You are correct. You had no right to say either of those things.

You know that I enjoy working with you. And you do not have any right to put yourself down like that—it isn't healthy, and it isn't true. You're a remarkable person, and I . . . I . . . I'm very fond of you."

"Fond!" Toni wrenched her hand out of his, crossed her arms, and glared at him. "Fond! I'm *fond* of that scruffy-looking cat that keeps showing up at my back door. At least he knows what he wants. But you . . . you . . . you are the most infuriating man I . . . What is it with you? Are all Christian men so emotionally repressed? What was that word that you just couldn't bring yourself to say?"

Jason's eyes sparkled with anger and hurt. She could see his eyes filling with tears. He spoke in a tightly controlled voice. "I was taught by my parents that you never, never say certain things to a woman until you are ready to ask her to marry you. To do anything else is the worst kind of hypocrisy and emotional abuse. I am very fond of you. So fond that it keeps me awake at nights."

Tears began running down his cheeks. "So fond that I don't want to wait to see what will happen between us. But I'm going to wait because we're both wrestling with important issues of faith, and I know we'll both be in a better position in a few weeks or a few months to know what we really feel for each other. I'm so fond of you that I don't want to rush into anything. So fond that the thought of anything happening to you frightens me to death. So fond that the thought of losing you is intolerable. But the thought of winning you in the wrong way is more intolerable."

Toni reached up and slowly ran the tips of her fingers across one of his cheeks, trying to undo the hurt she had caused him. It wasn't enough. She had to do something more to make amends. She gently kissed his cheek and hugged him tightly. He returned the embrace.

Jason whispered in her ear, "I'm sorry, Toni. I'm just so scared. I'm afraid of making a mistake that will hurt us both."

"I know, Jason. I'm afraid, too. And you're right, we do have a lot of things to sort out. Both of us do. But we can help each other. We already have. Let's just keep doing that and see what develops. Maybe we just need to have more . . . well . . . more faith in the process. More faith that we aren't alone."

Jason let go and gently pushed her away, holding her at arm's length, with his hands on her shoulders. He looked deeply into her eyes, and his slow smile reappeared. "Faith that we aren't alone? That sounds like a fine place to start, especially when dealing with fear." He chuckled quietly, took her hand, and they continued walking back toward the bakery.

On Monday morning, Toni and Jason met at Blue Spring Baked Goods just before opening time and made two large signs to place in the front windows announcing that the shop would be closed until Wednesday due to vandalism. They then retired to the kitchen to continue their cleanup efforts.

By seven o'clock, several regular customers had come around back to express concern, and a couple had offered to help. Word of the damage spread through town, and soon a half dozen people showed up with their own cleaning supplies. They included the owner of a professional cleaning service, who quickly took charge of the whole operation.

Meanwhile, Jason had gotten the coffee machines going and was serving the growing group of visitors and helpers. Toni began giving away two-day-old donuts, éclairs, and other items from the display cases. She had just enough time to phone her insurance agent and then talk with her wholesaler to order replacements for the damaged sacks of flour, sugar, and other products before things really got busy.

Just before eleven o'clock, the locksmith arrived. Toni and Jason showed him around the bakery and the upstairs apartment. By noon, all the decisions about lock styles and positions had been made, and the locksmith was working on the front door. Just then, two large urns of coffee arrived, donated by the local coffee roasters where Toni bought her beans. They had not been sure whether her appliances were still working at the bakery, and they figured more coffee would always be welcome. About the same time a large delivery of sandwiches arrived from Lottie's Diner. It was more than enough to feed all the workers twice, but new visitors were happy to finish the leftovers. Work was suspended for lunch, and Toni gave away slices of pie and cake for dessert.

Shortly after the noon break, the chief of police arrived to clarify a few items from his officers' report. He assured Toni that he would step up patrols at night in that part of town for at least the next few weeks and asked if she had considered installing shatter-resistant windows. After discussing a whole range of security issues with Jason and Toni, the chief recommended a security-system specialist who lived in a nearby town, then left with a full thermos of coffee and two large sacks of pastries. Jason used his cell phone to contact the security consultant and made an appointment for the next day.

By midafternoon the phone company had sent a technician out to repair damage to the bakery's line. He offered to install a device for recording and tracing crank calls on both lines, and Toni gladly accepted.

Before the day was over, the kitchen was spotless and all the exterior doors had new locks. The locksmith promised to return the next day to finish the inside work. As everyone was packing up, a local remodeling contractor stopped by and offered to replace the damaged cabinet door and drawer for free. He took some measurements, collected the shattered remains of both items, and promised to return at noon the next day with replacements.

After the last volunteer left, Jason and Toni locked up the shop and joined Sheila at her house for dinner. Exhausted, the three friends made an early night of it.

Early on Tuesday morning, Jason and Toni met her wholesaler and helped him unload a large shipment of baking supplies. After he left, they moved the sacks and boxes into several storage areas near the kitchen. In the process, Toni discovered a number of items she had missed during her rapid inventory the previous day.

By midmorning, they were meeting with the security specialist. The three of them carefully examined the entire interior and exterior of the building and reviewed different options available for protecting it. He agreed with the police chief that shatter-resistant windows were important but suggested that they only be installed on the rear doors and the windows facing away from the street. At the end of two and a half hours, they had agreed on a security system with all the features Jason had recommended on Sunday, plus one or two more. Toni particularly liked the module that allowed the system to act as an electronic answering service for her business.

While Jason and Toni ate a quiet lunch, the contractor returned with the replacement door and drawer. Toni and Jason discussed installing exterior lights and shatter-resistant glass with him. He assured them that the lights could be done by the end of the week but explained that the glass would probably take several weeks, since it had to be custom ordered.

Later in the afternoon, Jason drove Toni to a large electronics store in a nearby town. They picked out a cellular phone, and he made sure she was thoroughly familiar with it by the time they reached the bakery again. "Make sure you keep that phone with you all the time," he reminded her as they walked upstairs to her apartment.

"Yes, sir," she answered with a mock salute. "Now," she added decisively as they entered the living room, "we've been working hard the last couple of days, and we deserve to spend some time celebrating what we've accomplished. I'm making dinner for us." She got out an embroidered linen tablecloth that her aunt had made to dress up the table and added some vanilla-scented candles to top it off. When Jason wanted to help, she put him to work polishing the silverware and getting out her best china. Meanwhile, she busied herself with dinner preparations.

Toni checked her refrigerator and cupboards and was pleased to see that she had all the fixings for a spaghetti dinner. She boiled the water for the pasta and put together the spicy ingredients for a homemade tomato sauce. She pulled down some stemmed glasses and filled them with sparkling water and lemon slices. When everything was ready, they sat down at the table.

"Jason, why don't you thank God for the food? And while you're at it, you could ask His protection of the bakery and help with our various questions, doubts, fears, and assorted frustrations." She smiled at the startled expression on his face.

"I'll be happy to," he said, puzzlement crossing his face, "but if I may ask, what brings on this request?"

"I guess I'm ready to agree with you that we aren't alone in facing all these things," Toni admitted, "so I'm ready to pray about them as well."

"I'm glad to hear that." They bowed their heads, and Jason prayed.

During dinner, the two concentrated more on eating than on talking. Jason complimented Toni on the tangy red meat sauce and ate several slices of garlic bread. After dinner, Toni pulled a rich chocolate cake from a box. "I saved one of these from the feeding frenzy on Monday," she announced. They enjoyed the dessert with vanilla ice cream.

"I'm stuffed. I can't eat another bite," Jason announced a few minutes later.

"Wanna walk off those extra calories?" she asked. They walked around town, holding hands, and eventually made their way to the park, where a half dozen different kinds of ducks were leaving crisscross patterns in the crystal blue water. They returned to the bakery in time for Jason to leave for the singles meeting at the church.

As he was leaving, Jason asked, "Is it okay if I tell the people at church what's been going on, so they can pray about it, too?"

"That's fine with me, but don't go into any details about our new security arrangements," Toni responded.

"Absolutely not," Jason agreed.

After Jason left, Toni went grocery shopping. As she pushed her cart down the aisle, searching through her purse for coupons, her cart stopped in a jarring collision with another customer's cart. "Well, Miss Toni, I'm glad to see that some habits don't change."

"Brian! What are you doing here?" Just seeing his smug face made her sick. All the love she'd ever felt for the man had completely vanished, and his repeated appearances in Blue

Spring over the last couple of months were like a recurring nightmare.

"I'm looking for you. I remembered that you used to go grocery shopping on Monday or Tuesday nights."

A cold shudder crept up her spine. "Have you been following me?" she asked in a hoarse whisper.

"Look, you've made it clear on more than one occasion that you don't want me showing up at your bakery, so I figure this is the only way to get a chance to speak with you."

She gripped the handle of her shopping cart and glared at her ex-fiancé.

"I have some important information I want to give you," Brian continued, seeming to ignore her obvious annoyance. "Something that might explain what's been going on at the bakery. Just give me five minutes, and I'm out of here," he said reasonably.

She nodded, and they pushed their carts to a deserted corner of the store. "Make this quick. I've got lots of things to do," she said tersely.

He licked his full lips as he assessed her from head to toe. She felt like a prize animal being appraised. "Look, I know we didn't part on the best of terms," he began.

Her mouth dropped open. "Best of terms? You stole money from me, you never paid me back, and on top of that you were unfaithful!" She was so mad she was shaking, and the thing that angered her the most was how he could still get her so riled. She slowly counted to ten and forced herself to remain calm.

"I know, Toni. I was not the best person in the world. But remember, we had some good times, and whose shoulder did you cry on when things got rough at college? I was always there for you," he said proudly.

She sighed and rubbed her temple. She felt a headache coming. "What do you want?"

"I want to be a part of your life again, Toni. Things are tough for you right now, and I want to help. Give me another chance," he pleaded.

"Brian, we're over, through. I can't take you back." Toni knew that Brian was used to getting what he wanted, but in this case he was going to be disappointed. She thought about the various acts of vandalism at the store and wondered what he knew. "What do you know about the things that have been happening at the bakery?"

"How much do you know about your new boyfriend?" he countered.

"He's not my boyfriend, and I know quite a bit about him. What are you trying to tell me?"

"You've always been naive and too trusting, Toni. And I think Jason is taking advantage of you," he said smugly. He touched her cheek, and she flinched. "And I may be able to help you."

Brian pulled a large manila envelope out of his cart. "I've been doing a little research on a Chicago firm that you might be familiar with. It's called Matthews and Company. Ever hear of it?" He noted the shock on her face. "I see you have. And I suppose you got your information from Jason. Well, I have fifteen articles here that you need to read. They're taken from several different sources." He ticked off the names of several leading newspapers and business journals.

"They paint a rather disturbing picture of the Matthews family," he continued. "I've even included a three-page summary for you, but here's the short version. They are high-tech robber barons, with powerful friends in the military. They like to steal promising technology from small firms that can't defend themselves. And sometimes they go after really big game. A few years ago, the French government accused Jason of acting as a spy for the U. S. Army. They claimed he had stolen classified information on a miniaturized nuclear weapon—the sort of thing that might fit comfortably in one of those large steel briefcases. There's some real nightmare stuff in here." Brian waved the packet.

"But it gets better, or worse, depending on your point of view. These folks have been investigated by Congress. Or should I say there was an attempt to investigate them. The military shut the whole investigation down—claimed it risked exposing national security secrets. Everyone thought that was just a little too convenient." He gave Toni a nasty smile.

"And one more thing. There's an article in here about Jason's mother. She's well known in the Chicago area for her charitable work. She likes to give lavish parties, and she's famous for her pies, cakes, cookies, and pastries. A few years ago she was exploring the possibility of opening a series of specialty bakeries in various parts of the country as a way to diversify the family's business holdings. And she's always looking for new recipes.

"So, Toni, I think you really need to ask yourself why a zillionaire like Jason would be interested in you and your little bakery. Maybe his family is looking for something else to absorb—or steal." He dropped the envelope into her shopping cart. "Yes, I think you could learn a lot by reading what's in there."

"You listen to me, Brian," Toni hissed. "Stay away from me. Don't come into the bakery, and don't ambush me in the grocery store—or anywhere else." Before he could comment, she fled with her cart into another part of the store.

But when Toni went home that night, the manila envelope

was tucked carefully into a shopping bag. Brian's words haunted her. Her mind was spinning with questions as she put her groceries away, sorted items to take with her to Sheila's, and checked her new locks twice. Was it possible that he was right about the Matthews family?

Brian could be dishonest and manipulative, but he was also one of the best corporate analysts she had ever known. And he was right about one thing. She had always been too trusting when it came to men. But she felt safe with Jason. And he had told her a lot about himself.

Toni shook her head. What if he were telling her half truths or even lies? Was Jason Matthews too good to be true? Was he or someone working for him the source of the harassment and vandalism directed at the bakery? Only one thing seemed certain: she needed to find out more about Jason Matthews and his family and the business ventures that had made them so wealthy. That was the only way she was going to put her mind at ease.

Jason saw Sheila from a distance and called out to her before they entered the church. They shared a brief, friendly hug.

"So, what's been up?" Sheila asked. "I've called Toni, but she hasn't called me back. I figure the two of you have had your hands more than full today."

Jason chuckled. "I guess there's nothing like a crisis to draw friends closer together. It's even been, well . . . romantic." He grinned sheepishly. "But we're both trying to ignore that." Suddenly he frowned as he thought back over the recent attacks on the bakery.

"What's wrong?" Sheila's dark eyes were full of concern as she touched his shoulder.

"It bothers me that I can't see any pattern to the vandalism at Toni's bakery. And I don't like the irrational violence that was displayed by whoever damaged her kitchen. I'm sure that Toni is in danger—personally in danger. This is about more than just the success of Blue Spring Baked Goods. But I don't know how to protect her." He described the most recent precautions Toni had taken.

"I've been praying for her safety."

Jason nodded. "So have I, and she gave me permission to have the whole singles group pray about the situation."

"That's great, Jason."

"Yeah, but I can't shake this feeling that I'm missing something obvious. I guess I'm just going to have to trust God to protect her. But boy, is that tough for me to do."

"It's tough for all of us, Jason." Sheila took his arm and playfully dragged him toward the meeting room where most of the singles had already gathered.

"Are there any prayer requests before we begin?" asked Thomas, the group's leader, as Sheila and Jason entered the room.

"Both of us have a request," said Jason.

"Yes, we do," said Sheila.

"We want to pray for the safety of our good friend Toni Brown," Jason said. "I'm sure a lot of you know her. She owns Blue Springs Baked Good, and some really strange things have been happening there lately." He briefly described the recent events at the bakery.

Thomas nodded. A few others had requests for sick loved ones and difficult work situations. Everyone joined hands. As Jason bowed his head, he added a silent prayer of his own: *Lord, please protect Toni Brown and help her to find a refuge in You from the storms of life.*

Nine

Weeks passed, and as news about the attacks against the bakery spread, many people in Blue Spring and the surrounding communities made it a point to express their support for Toni through cards, letters, e-mail messages, and purchases— lots of purchases. The rapid increase in business was almost more than Toni and Jason could handle.

The remodeling of the bakery went forward rapidly and without placing any added pressure on them, thanks to expert management of their contractor. Toni even had an idea for a new product—fruit pies made with uncooked fruit. The fresh strawberry pies were a success from the moment they were introduced, and she never seemed to be able to keep enough on hand.

One evening, near the end of June, Sheila called Toni and insisted they needed a girls' night out. They saw a movie at the local theater and then went out to dinner.

"Girl, you have been working too hard," Sheila said as they looked over their menus. "I've hardly seen you since you moved back to the apartment."

Toni smiled. "It has been a wild few weeks."

"You and Jason seem to be getting along," Sheila said quietly as she closed her menu.

Toni frowned.

"What's wrong?"

"I can't figure out how I feel about him. He's a great help around the bakery, and the customers love him. He's developed a real bond with Martha. I feel safer since we installed the new windows and the security system, but . . . well . . . You know, Sheila, I still wonder why he's here in Blue Spring." They ordered their meals, and then Toni explained what she had found in the packet Brian had given her.

"I can't believe it," Sheila said in shocked amazement. "Do you believe it? How can you trust Brian, after all he has done to you? Still, it sounds like there are some things Jason hasn't told you."

"Brian didn't make up those news articles. And the attacks haven't stopped, even with all the new precautions. The crank calls have continued. The phone company has been tracing them all, but it's not doing any good. They're coming in from isolated phone booths all over, some are forty or fifty miles from Blue Spring. There's no pattern to the calls, except that Jason is never with me when they occur.

More graffiti has shown up on the building. And a few days ago, a person tried to get into the kitchen by trying to smash the reinforced window in the back door. That set off the alarm system, and the police arrived in less than a minute, but they still didn't catch anyone. Whoever is doing these things is smart and careful."

The food arrived just as Toni finished her update, and she asked Sheila to pray before they ate. "But there is good news," Toni continued after a few bites. "I'm making more money than I ever dreamed of in this business. It's going so well I'm considering more improvements. I've been looking through trade magazines for larger commercial ovens and new, refrigerated display cases. And I think I'm finally reaching the point where I can buy my parents a new house. I've been waiting a long time to do that for them."

"That's not just good news, that's great news," Sheila commented enthusiastically.

"I think going to church regularly has changed the way I look at the obstacles in life," Toni admitted.

"Sounds to me like you're learning to trust God and take things one day at a time."

"You may be right, though I've still got a lot of questions. And I'm not really sure who it is I'm trusting. I've been feeling a lot more comfortable with the whole idea that God exists, but it's all kind of nebulous and impersonal. I guess I'll just have to wait and—"

"See what develops?" Sheila finished her friend's sentence with a smile. "You know, that would look pretty good on a bumper sticker."

Toni returned home a few hours later. She was humming her favorite song when she heard the phone ring. She jumped and a cold prickly feeling went up her spine. She lifted the receiver. "Hello," she said softly.

"Toni! It's Mom." Her mother's voice was agitated and almost unrecognizable. Toni had never heard her mother sound so upset.

"What's wrong?"

"It's your father. Toni, he's had a massive heart attack. And the doctor . . . doesn't expect him . . . to live," she sobbed.

"Are you by yourself, Mom?"

"No, dear. Some of the sisters from the church are at the hospital with me."

"Mom, I'm on my way!" Toni's hands were shaking as she replaced the receiver. She fought to regain control of herself, but she couldn't stop the tears from spilling down her cheeks. Oh, how she wanted her father to live!

The telephone rang again and she quickly answered it, assuming it was her mother.

"Hello!" she choked.

"Toni, what's wrong?" Jason's deep voice carried clearly over the line.

"Jason, my dad's in the hospital. I have to go home."

"Don't leave yet, Toni. I'm on my way." Jason arrived ten minutes later. Toni ran down the stairs and opened the door. She fell into Jason's arms, sobbing.

"Jason, I have to leave now," she said.

He wiped her tears away and kissed her cheek. "Toni, I don't think it's a good idea for you to drive right now. Let's wait a few hours for you to calm down." He took her hand and they went upstairs to her apartment. He fixed a pot of coffee and placed some lemon cookies on a plate. Toni drank two cups of black coffee, but she couldn't eat any of the cookies.

"I'll have to close the bakery for at least the next few days," she said as she removed her suitcase from the closet. He stood in the bedroom doorway and watched her haphazardly remove clothes from her closet.

"I could come with you if you'd like," he offered quietly.

"Thanks, Jason. But I'd rather go by myself. I'll call you if I need you to come later."

"Well, since you don't want me to go with you," he suggested, "how about I run the bakery for you while you're gone?"

"You'd do that for me?"

He nodded. "I still don't know how to make everything. But I would be more than willing to do what I could."

"Oh, Jason. Are you sure?"

"I'll do it under one condition. I want you to call me as soon as you need me to come to your parents' home. I hope your father is okay."

"I'll let you know," she promised, crossing over to him. "But right now I really need to get my stuff packed. Please let Sheila know what's happened and tell the other people at the church."

He reached out and gave her a comforting hug. She was surprised at the strength she drew from his embrace. He smelled like fresh cologne. It was a scent she had grown accustomed to. Reluctantly, she left his arms and continued packing. Being able to talk with someone had calmed her down considerably. She wiped away the few tears that kept escaping.

A few minutes later, she carried her packed suitcase out into the living room, where Jason was just finishing a phone call to the pastor.

"Toni, I don't feel right having you on the road in this condition. You're so upset." Jason took her hand. "Your hands are shaking. Please, don't drive now. At least wait until the morning."

She sniffed as she gazed into his nut brown eyes. "Jason, I have to leave now. If I wait until the morning, it might be too late."

"How long will it take you to get home?"

"A couple of hours."

"All right Toni, but call me as soon as you get there." He took a pad of paper and a pencil. "Just in case you forget, give me your mother's home number and your cell phone number. If I don't hear from you within three hours, I'm going to come looking for you," he warned.

Toni gave him the requested information and then threw herself into his arms one last time. "Oh, Jason, I hope Daddy's okay."

"Me, too. Toni, I'll be praying for your whole family, and I'll ask the church to do the same."

"Thank you, Jason. It's good to know I won't be alone."

After watching Toni's car disappear down the street, Jason drove back to the bed-and-breakfast and called Sheila, whom he'd been unable to reach earlier. This time she was home.

"This is awful," she said in a stunned voice. "I feel so badly for them. Toni was just beginning to reconnect with her dad. She was talking about building them a house earlier this evening."

Jason spoke with Sheila for a few more minutes before he got off the phone. He got ready for bed, crawled under the covers, and stared up at the white ceiling.

"Lord, how can I help her?" he whispered. He heard a sharp knock at his door. "Come in," he said.

Mrs. Dukes walked into the room. "You came tearing up here so fast, I just wanted to check and see if everything is okay." He explained the situation with Toni's father and asked her to contact the women's prayer chain.

"My goodness!" The smile on Mrs. Dukes's face disappeared and she dropped into a nearby chair. "I hope she'll be okay. I'll contact the prayer chain, and we'll include her family in our prayers."

"Thanks. You can never have too many prayers."

"I imagine Toni would agree with you these days. You've had quite an influence on that girl."

"Well, someone certainly has, but I'm not sure my name should be the first one on the list. By the way, I'm running the bakery while she's gone, so don't expect things to be running so smoothly when you get your pastries."

Mrs. Dukes sighed as she stood. "Well, I'd better let you get some sleep. The next few days are going to be tough. If you need some help down at the bakery, you just let me know." With those words, she walked out and shut the door.

Jason sighed with relief, but a moment later he wasn't so sure he liked being alone. There was still more than an hour before he could expect to hear from Toni. Most likely it would take even longer because she'd want to talk with her mother and see her father as soon as she arrived. He was too wound up to be able to sleep while he waited.

In desperation he crawled out of bed and fell to his knees. "Lord, I pray for Toni's safety as she drives to be with her parents," he said. "I pray for the recovery of Toni's father. Please let him live, Lord, if it is Your will. Also be with her mother. Please help her to deal with all that's happened. In Your name I pray, Amen."

He crawled back into bed and waited for the phone to ring. One hour passed. Then another. When the call came it woke him from a sound sleep. "Toni?"

"Yes, Jason, it's me. Jason, he's gotten worse," she sobbed. Her words ran together, and Jason could barely understand what she was saying.

"Toni, slow down. Just calm down, catch your breath, and tell me what's happening," he said.

"Jason, they don't expect him to live through the night. I just got here a few minutes ago," she said quickly. He heard her sniffles in the background, as well as what could only be the sound of a hospital P.A. system.

"Oh, Toni, I'm so sorry." He felt as if her pain were his own. A voice in the background called her name.

"Jason, I have to go. My mother needs me. I'll be in touch."

Jason had a hard time sleeping that night. He dreamed of warm cinnamon rolls, fresh from the oven at the bakery. He dreamed of Toni's light-brown face glowing in the moonlight. Several times he woke up, and every time he wondered if she would be okay. At three-thirty he gave up on sleep and got ready for a busy day at the bakery. By four o'clock he was pulling out the spare keys she had given him and opening the front door to the establishment. He gazed around the dark room before flipping on the lights. It felt odd being in Toni's bakery and not having her by his side. He straightened his shoulders and headed back into the kitchen.

"There's a job to do," he said quietly to himself. "And it really is like Toni says, we just have to hold on, have faith, and wait to see what develops."

Quickly he settled into the routine of fixing the donuts and setting them aside to rise, filling the pastries with fruit filling and putting them in the oven, and then preparing the cinnamon rolls. The last thing he finished before opening was the donuts. They had already risen, so he cut them into circles and baked them. While they were still hot, he drizzled the glaze over the yeasty circles. When it was six-thirty, he unlocked the door and let the first customers into the bakery.

"Where's Toni?" asked Karen as Jason filled her standing order of donuts for her office meeting.

"She had a family emergency. Hopefully she'll be back soon.

I'm trying to hold down the fort while she's gone." He rang up her order and counted back the change.

The morning was as hectic as usual, and he filled orders as quickly as he could. A few people wanted cherry tarts, but he had to patiently explain that this was one of the items he had not been able to get to before opening time. His stomach rumbled, and he soon noticed it was eleven-thirty. He sprinted upstairs and searched her small kitchen for something to eat. He found a loaf of bread and three cans of tuna. Quickly, he threw together a tuna-fish sandwich, grabbed a diet soda from the refrigerator, and ran back downstairs with his meal, thankful that the bell over the door hadn't rung during his absence.

Jason glanced out the front window and was pleased to see Sheila walking up the drive with her sack lunch. She came in and sat with him. He told her about his phone conversation with Toni late the previous evening. "If I don't hear from her by the end of the day, I'm going to call her. You know how much I worry about her, Sheila. It feels weird being in here without her."

"I can understand that," commented Sheila as she finished her sandwich. She went behind the counter and gathered two glazed donuts. She left the change on the counter to pay for her purchase.

"So, Jason, are you going to the service at the church tonight?"

He sighed. "I don't feel like doing much of anything, to tell you the truth. I'm so worried about Toni that I feel like I'm going crazy."

"That's usually the best time to go to church," observed Sheila as she bit into her donut.

"Amen to that," said Jason.

When they finished their lunches, Sheila got up to return to work. "Tell Toni she can also call me if she wants."

Jason smiled. "I'll be sure to do that."

The rest of the day dragged. After Jason locked up, he put the money into the canvas bag and went down the street to the bank to make the daily deposit. When he returned to the bakery, the phone was ringing. He hoped it wasn't another customer wanting to order a birthday cake. He'd gotten three calls that day, and he hated to turn the customers down. "Hello?"

"Jason, it's Toni." His heart quickened as soon as he heard the sadness in her voice.

"Toni, what's wrong?"

"Jason, Daddy died a few hours ago."

Ten

*F*riday morning, Toni sat in the living room of her childhood home, exhausted. The old trailer seemed so small, even smaller than she remembered. Although she had been home several times in the last few years, it was as if she was seeing everything with new eyes.

She was glad that she had managed to get her parents to let her make some repairs. The cracked windows had been replaced five years ago. The old electric furnace had been removed and a new heat pump provided both heating and cooling. The carpet and vinyl had been replaced two years ago. But she had never reached her ultimate goal: to purchase a new home for her parents in a better neighborhood, where they could enjoy their old age. Now it was too late for her father.

Her mother's soft sobs came from the bedroom, and several of the church sisters were seated in the living room. The doctor had given both of the Brown women a prescription for sleeping pills, but Toni wasn't interested in falling asleep.

Over the past two days, she had looked through every single photo album and studied every photo that included her daddy. She recalled the cake he had purchased for her birthday when she turned five. She remembered the first bicycle she'd received when she was six. She even chuckled when she thought about how he loved to watch horror movies on television. In spite of the pain and in spite of the arguments, he was still her daddy, and she would miss him. And she wondered what small piece of God he had found to hold on to during the final hours of his life.

"Toni, maybe you should try and get some rest," Mrs. Fielding suggested, her soft voice interrupting Toni's thoughts. "You need rest if you're going to make it to the funeral on Saturday." Mrs. Fielding had gotten older and grayer since Toni's high school years, but she was the best friend her mother had.

And Toni suddenly realized that Mrs. Fielding had been a good friend to her as well. "Thank you, Mrs. Fielding," she managed to say.

There was a knock at the front door, and when Toni answered it she burst into tears. Sheila and Jason were standing there.

"Jason," she sobbed, falling into his arms. A rush of strength and solace flowed from his embrace. She wanted to stay in those arms forever. She didn't care what he had done or what his family had done or what anyone thought of them. Sheila rubbed her shoulder, offering words of comfort.

"We came as soon as you called," Jason explained. "Sheila took a few days off from work, and I knew you wouldn't mind if I closed the bakery." Jason rubbed her back, and then he kissed each of her tearstained cheeks. His lips felt warm and soothing. "I want to be with you during this difficult time."

She gazed into his deep-brown eyes and saw that they were filled with sorrow. Jason knew very little about John Brown, but Toni sensed that he was sad because she was sad. She loved Jason—yes, she may as well face it. Even if he wasn't ready to return that love yet, she loved him because of his compassion and his strength. God would just have to understand, and in that moment Toni Brown knew that God did. She clung to that knowledge with all her might.

"Come on in," she said, taking a deep breath. "Let me introduce you."

All day Friday, the preparations for the funeral continued. Shortly after dinner, the church folk left, and by nine o'clock, Toni's mother had taken a sleeping pill and was headed to her bedroom. Toni followed to make sure her mother was comfortable.

"You know, Toni," the woman confided as she slipped under the covers of the double bed, "I don't know how I'm going to get used to not having your daddy here next to me."

Toni lowered the lights and bent over to kiss her mother's cheek. "I know how much you loved him," she whispered, "and I know that even with all his troubles, he loved us as much as he was able." She pulled a small chair next to the bed and sat, holding her mother's hand, until deep, regular breathing signaled that the exhausted widow was finally asleep.

Silently, Toni got up and slipped out of the room. She tiptoed down the hallway and entered the kitchen, where Jason was sitting at the table. Sheila had already said her good-byes earlier that evening and returned to her parents' house. She would return the next day for the funeral.

Jason got up and gave Toni a hug. "You must be exhausted," he said. "Are you ready to call it a night?"

Toni shook her head. "My mind keeps on racing," she said. "I can't seem to shut it off."

"Here," he said, "why don't you sit at the table with me. We can drink some herbal tea, talk, enjoy the quiet, and give you a chance to unwind. I've watched you today, and you're so busy taking care of everyone else that you haven't had a chance to think of yourself. You even made sure there were fresh sheets on your bed for that aunt of yours who just arrived."

She shook her head sheepishly and took the proffered chair. It was nice just to sit. Jason sat next to her, slowly stroking her hand. Then he stood behind her and massaged her shoulders. She could feel the knots loosen—knots that she hadn't even realized were there. Gradually, she relaxed and let her head rest in her arms on the table.

"Why don't you go to bed?" Jason's deep voice suggested. "Come on," he said, taking her hand. He led her to the living-room couch, which Sheila had made up into a comfortable bed. Toni crawled between the sheets and then grabbed Jason's hand as he started to leave.

"Please don't go, Jason."

"I won't leave you, Toni. I'll sit right here on the floor next to you until you fall asleep." She nodded and closed her eyes. For the first time in more than forty-eight hours, she finally managed to drift off to sleep.

Jason watched Toni while she slept in the faint light from the kitchen. He'd learned a lot about Toni Brown over the past few months, but here he'd finally discovered the core of her being. He gazed at the tarnished brown walls of the trailer. She had told him what it was like to grow up in poverty, but hearing words was different from seeing things firsthand. He felt claustrophobic in this old trailer, and earlier when he had helped get Toni's elderly aunt settled, he'd been stunned by the small size of her bedroom. There was barely enough space for a twin bed, small dresser, and a single chair.

Toni's deep, even breathing filled the room. Just seeing her suffer made him suffer. He wanted to wipe away her pain and anguish forever. How he wished that she shared his commitment to Jesus. He had talked with Mrs. Brown earlier that evening and witnessed the closeness she shared with her Christian sisters. The women had gathered around her, praying for the ease of her sorrow. Toni had joined the group, but she had been silent.

He blinked several times, trying to stay awake. Glancing at the lighted dial of his watch, he was stunned to discover that it was past two o'clock. If he didn't get some sleep, he'd never make it through the next day.

Jason yawned quietly and stood up. He tiptoed across the living room, grimacing as the floor creaked beneath his weight.

He checked the front door and noticed he would need to lock it with a key. Not wanting to wake Toni up, he glanced around the living room and kitchen. On the counter sat her purse. Her key ring was beside it. He scribbled a note, explaining what had happened to her keys and promising to return them the next day before the funeral. Then he moved her purse and the note to the center of the kitchen table where they couldn't be missed.

Once he'd stepped outside and had locked the door, Jason quietly walked down the steps and looked back at Toni's home. He compared it to the house where he had been raised. They always had an abundance of material possessions, and his father had purchased a new car for him the day after he had gotten his driver's license. He'd never fully appreciated the differences between his and Toni's childhoods. His faith had never really been tested until his mother had developed cancer. Until then he'd never needed anything that he couldn't buy. Now he understood what true neediness must feel like. And in spite of this background, Toni had survived and grown and was now clearly beginning to believe in God.

He walked to his car and started the engine. As he drove to his hotel, he thought about the questions he had thrown at God over the past months and years. Watching Toni face her father's death had brought back memories of the death that had so recently touched his own family. Fresh tears came to his eyes. He parked his car at the hotel and wept quietly for a long time. He still missed his mother. He missed her terribly. Spending time with Toni over the last three months had softened his grief somehow, but he still thought about Robin Matthews every day.

He remembered the songs she used to sing, the Bible stories she used to read. He thought about her love of flowers and cinnamon rolls. Small details about her life surfaced in his mind at the most unlikely times.

Jason walked into his hotel room and threw his keys on the dresser. He showered and fell into bed. He was so tired that he didn't read his Bible that evening, but before he fell asleep, he said a special prayer for Toni and for her mother and for himself—that they would find some small part of God to hang on to, and that when they couldn't hold on any longer, they would find God was still holding on to them.

Toni awoke early the next morning. She smelled freshly brewed coffee and headed toward the kitchen. Her mother sat at the table, reading her Bible.

"Hi, Mom." She kissed her cheek.

"Antoinette, you're up so early. Why don't you go back into my room and catch some more sleep? You won't be disturbed there, and the funeral isn't until two o'clock."

Toni wiped the sleep from her eyes and gazed at the sun shining through the window. She had to admit she felt bone-tired. "Mom, are you sure you don't want any company?"

"I'm fine, dear. The people from church will be here by noon to take us to the funeral," she said while pushing her reading glasses farther up her nose. Toni noticed that her mother's eyes were red and tired, but she sensed that reading the Bible gave her mother strength.

"Oh, and Antoinette," her mother added, "that nice young man, Jason, left this note for you." She pointed to the slip of paper by Toni's purse.

Toni read the note, smiled, and hid it away in her wallet. She kissed her mother's cheek again before heading back to bed.

Hours later, Jason's deep voice awakened her. She heard both him and Sheila talking to her mother and a few of the sisters from church. Toni jumped out of bed and quickly got dressed for the funeral.

She had chosen a black-and-white dress and a black hat. Jason was the first person she saw as she walked into the living room. He looked huge in the small space, and his voice carried over all the others.

Jason crossed the room in just a couple steps and pulled her into his arms. Then Sheila hurried over to give her a hug as well. Toni felt a huge lump in her throat, and she tried to suppress her tears.

"Have you eaten?" asked Jason quietly. She shook her head. Food was the last thing on her mind. He led her into the kitchen, and she managed to swallow some dry toast and tea.

Sheila reached over periodically to rub Toni's shoulder.

"Hang in there, Toni," her best friend murmured. Sheila mentioned that her family was going to be at the viewing and the funeral.

To Toni's surprise, the services were being held at the church Iris Brown had belonged to for so many years. Toni had not realized, until she heard the women from the church talking to her mother, just how regular John Brown's church attendance had become in the last year.

But her mother was still worried. Toni recalled the conversations she'd had with her while her father had been lying ill in the hospital. "I always wanted your father to go forward in church, so I would know he was saved," she'd said. "But he always said he wasn't ready to have everyone asking about what was goin' on between him and God. And now I don't know if I'll ever see him again."

Sooner than Toni expected, she found herself being driven to the funeral with her mother on one side and Jason on the other. She just wanted the day to be over. "*Lord, help me through this*," Toni whispered to herself.

As soon as he heard her words, Jason tensed. He gazed at Toni, but she stared straight ahead, her eyes full of tears. She was so beautiful that just looking at her made his heart melt. "Are you okay?" he murmured. She nodded slightly, not bothering to look at him. He wondered if she even realized that she had just called upon the Lord. Did she know?

They were riding in a large black limousine. One of the brothers in Mrs. Brown's church owned a limo service, and he was taking them to the funeral in style. He said that he ran a tight, fair business, but he never charged for funerals.

Jason held Toni's hand as they approached the church. He was surprised to see how many cars were in the parking lot. Once they got inside and people began introducing themselves, he got another shock. Many of the people here were friends of John Brown, and many of them had worked with him at one time or another. He signed the guest book and stayed by Toni's side the entire day. They gazed at the body in the casket. Jason was struck again by how much Toni looked like her father. Their facial features were almost identical.

When the coffin was closed, Iris Brown had broken down. As she sobbed out her grief, she kept repeating, "John, John, will I ever see you again?"

And Jason had been amazed to hear Toni respond, "Hang on, Mom. You've just got to hang on to the love of God. You've got to believe that God is big enough to take care of that. I believe He is, and if I can believe it, then anybody can."

Once the funeral was over, Mrs. Fielding invited everyone to her home for refreshments, Jason and Sheila stayed close to Toni the whole time. "I'm not leaving you, Toni," he had said as he squeezed her cold hands. Her light-brown skin looked pale. Her large dark eyes were tired and scared.

"And I'm right here, too," Sheila had added.

On Sunday, Jason and Sheila returned to Blue Spring. Toni promised to meet Jason in the bakery on the afternoon of the Fourth of July, even though he insisted he could handle things and Sheila had volunteered to help him. "What if you need to find something in my office?" she had asked. "Nobody knows where anything is in all those piles but me."

As Jason and Sheila drove home, he smiled. Sheila gave him a sharp look. "Jason Matthews, what are you smiling about?" she asked abruptly.

"Sheila, I didn't want to say anything."

"You didn't want to say anything about what?"

Jason told her what he'd heard Toni say while they were on their way to the funeral and later in church after the coffin was closed.

Sheila gasped. "Jason, does this mean that Toni's finding her way to Jesus? Do you really think she is?"

He nodded. "Something is certainly going on. I don't think she realizes how far she's come."

"She doesn't?"

"No. This is a very hard time for her and her mom. I know what it's like to lose someone you love, and it takes a while before the pain passes. It's hard to think clearly in the midst of all the pain."

"I hear you, Jason," she said soothingly as she patted his shoulder.

"I think it helped Toni for us to be with her over the last few days."

Sheila nodded. "I just hope her mom will be okay."

"She should be. She has her faith, and she has the support of the rest of her church. It helps when you have someone to help you through hard times."

"You know, I just remembered something."

"What's that?"

"Well, I know Toni doesn't have a lot of relatives, but I thought her cousin Eva would be there. She wasn't. I wonder why she didn't come to the funeral?"

"That's a good question, Sheila. Something tells me that

compassion isn't a strong point for Hank and Eva, but it's possible no one thought to contact them."

Sheila nodded. "I guess you're right."

They continued the rest of their journey in silence. It was evening by the time they arrived in Blue Spring. Signs had been posted throughout town about the annual Fourth of July celebration. The advertisements boasted a carnival, fireworks, and a parade. "It's the largest event of the year here in Blue Spring," explained Sheila.

Jason left Sheila at her door and then returned to the bed-and-breakfast. Once he reached his room and sat down, he was suddenly overwhelmed with fatigue. It had been a busy few days, and work at the bakery would start early the next morning. Offering another prayer for Toni and her mother, the exhausted man called it a day.

All day Monday, Jason and Sheila worked to prepare the bakery for the crowds expected on the Fourth of July. They got a great deal done and were feeling happy and tired by closing time. Sheila went home to fix dinner for both of them, and Jason worked to clean up the shop and then put together the bank deposit.

He had to go into Toni's small office to find where she kept the extra deposit slips, and he used her key to unlock the wide center drawer of the desk. There he found a large manila envelope marked BANK INFO. He looked inside, hoping to see more deposit slips. Slowly he examined what he found with growing shock, alarm, and disbelief. He carefully reviewed the unsigned, undated, three-page summary, the thick pile of articles, the detailed record of one small and painful slice of his family's past.

It was as compelling as it was incomplete. The summary did not mention the political enemies from Chicago who had spent years plotting this attack on his family. Nor did it contain one word about the extensive, written apologies that had appeared on the front pages of the papers that had carried the original accusations. After months spent revealing the supposed misdeeds of Matthews and Company and individual members of the family, they had been forced to admit that they had been taken in by a carefully designed misinformation campaign. They had acknowledged that it was one of the greatest journalistic blunders in modern American history.

As Jason sat and examined what he thought was Toni's investigation of his family, he could not summon the energy to be angry or even sad. He sat in numb disbelief. How could she believe these things? He had told this woman the truth, and she had used it to investigate him. She hadn't even bothered to follow the story to its conclusion. In time he began to feel anger, but before it had a chance to gain any momentum, it was replaced by a sense of hopelessness. What was the use of wasting energy on anger? There was nothing he could do. Once again he was about to lose someone he loved.

But he still had a duty to perform. He had promised to help through the crisis that had engulfed her family. God would hold him to that promise, and Jason refused to break his promises. He replaced the documents he had taken from the envelope and put it back where he had found it. He found the bank deposit slips, filled them out, and dropped the canvas bag at the bank. He would keep his word and do his duty before God, no matter what it cost him.

Jason was unusually quiet at dinner that night. When Sheila asked him what was wrong, he explained that he wasn't feeling well and had decided to go to bed early. Sheila wasn't surprised. The stress of the last few days had caught up with her as well. As Jason left Sheila's apartment, he was thankful that he'd had a good excuse for his silence. He wasn't ready to expose Toni's betrayal—especially not to her best friend.

Eleven

*T*oni returned to Blue Spring quietly and lost herself amid the crowds of people. It was the afternoon of the Fourth of July, and Blue Spring's big celebration was in full swing. She'd been gone for close to a week, but it felt as if years had passed.

That morning she had gotten up late and shared an even later lunch with her mother. Toni had urged the new widow to return to Blue Spring with her, but her mother had refused. "I just want to stay here, Antoinette," she'd said sadly. "You don't have to worry about me." Toni was relieved that one of the members of her mother's church planned on staying with her for a few days.

"I'll call you," Toni murmured to her mother as they hugged before she left.

The streets of Blue Spring were blocked for the parade, preventing her from parking near the bakery. She barely glanced at the red, white, and blue streamers decorating the sidewalks. The local marching band was playing patriotic songs while a young beauty queen, dressed in a tri-colored costume, sang the lyrics to an enthusiastic audience.

Toni was hot and sweaty by the time she reached home. It was close to one hundred degrees, and she was surprised that so many people were outside enjoying the holiday festivities. She opened the front door and glanced around the familiar bakery. It was packed. People were ordering pastries, donuts, and drinks. She was glad that Jason had ordered extra sodas. Her first year in business, she had run out of drinks on the Fourth.

Jason was behind the counter ringing up another order. She was surprised and pleased to see Sheila helping him. They both waved and when the last of the current customers had been served, Sheila came over and gave Toni a big hug. Jason disappeared into the kitchen and then busied himself restocking the display cases. She walked up behind him behind the main counter.

"Hi, Jason. Looks like a real madhouse around here."

"Yeah, I'm glad to see it, but the crowds are going to clean us out before the end of the day." He turned around far enough to glance at her while he spoke, but then immediately went back to moving pastries from a cart of racks to the display cases. Toni had been looking forward to a hug, but she turned away and pulled a clean apron down from a peg on the wall.

"Jason, I can't tell you how much the support you've given me over the last week has meant to me."

"You're welcome," he said to the display case in front of him.

Toni frowned but figured his odd behavior was due to fatigue. "Jason and Sheila," she said, "as long as you're both here, I'm going in the back to make some more donuts. Looks like we could sell out a few more batcnes before the fireworks are over tonight."

Jason stood up and turned toward her. "Are you sure that's a good idea? Maybe you should just enjoy yourself today. We can handle things here, even if we don't close until ten tonight."

She sighed. "Jason, I'm not that fragile. I'm upset about my father's death, but being in the kitchen will help me deal with everything. It'll give me something to do," she said.

He nodded as if he understood.

She went back and she began measuring flour and sugar into her mixing bowls, and Jason returned to the counter to wait on customers.

The day remained incredibly busy. They sold pastries, cakes, pies, and donuts until the display cases were all but empty. Countless sodas and other cold drinks flowed out the door. Toni was relieved to find herself so busy that she rarely thought of her loss or of Jason's coolness toward her.

"Let's close as soon as the fireworks are over," she told Jason and Sheila later in the evening. "Lots of people came into town for that, and I know we'll be getting business all evening, but enough is enough."

"You don't want to see the fireworks?" Sheila asked.

Toni shook her head. "Not really. I've never been much into fireworks. You or Jason can go if you'd like. I don't want to make you stay here if you don't want to. After all, fireworks only come once a year."

Just then Eva and Hank entered the bakery. Toni groaned. She did not need to have to deal with her cousin right now!

"Hey, Toni," said Eva. She was wearing tight shorts and a halter top, and she smelled as if she'd just stepped out of a perfume factory. Hank clutched her arm and grinned, his gold tooth flashing in the light.

"What do you want, Eva? I don't have time for your non-sense today."

Jason abandoned his post and came to her side.

"I heard your dad died. I'm sorry about that, Toni." Eva's voice sounded flat and emotionless.

"Thank you, Eva. What do you want?"

"Six glazed donuts and three tarts. You know, the ones you gave me last time were okay, but they didn't taste as good as my mother's," she added harshly.

Jason prepared the order and rang it up. Toni was relieved when Eva paid without putting up a fuss. They were too busy to deal with her childish behavior.

Sheila and Toni continued to ring up sales until the fire-works ended that night. Jason left earlier in the evening, saying he would return to help them close up when the display was over. He still wasn't back when Toni placed the CLOSED sign over the door and shut the blinds. Toni and Sheila opened the register and counted the money made that day. Sheila whistled softly at the total. "That's the most you've made ever," she said with admiration.

Toni gave her a small smile. "Yes, but we made so much only because it's a holiday." She locked the money in the safe, ready for the next day's deposit. They began clearing the tables. Several people had left empty bottles and cups behind. Toni froze when she spotted a white, business-size envelope. Her name was scrawled on it with bold, black letters. She suddenly felt cold. Slowly, she sank into a nearby chair.

"Toni, what's wrong?" Sheila dropped her cleaning cloth and came over to where Toni was sitting.

"Sheila, what's that?" Toni's voice was barely above a whis-per, and her brown eyes remained locked on the envelope. "It says Antoinette, not Toni. That's odd, don't you think?"

Gingerly, Sheila picked up the envelope and looked inside. She pulled out a single slip of paper. It read: *Get out of town or you'll be sorry.* She passed the paper to Toni.

"Oh!" Toni cried. Her hand was shaking as she covered her mouth.

Sheila reached for the paper and stuffed it back into the envelope. "I think it would be best if you stayed with me again for a while," she suggested calmly.

"Probably you're right," Toni agreed in a detached voice.

"I know you're scared, Toni," Sheila said soothingly.

"I'm not just scared, I'm tired. I can barely stay awake."

"Don't go to sleep just yet." Sheila smiled encouragingly. "I'll finish cleaning up down here. Why don't you go and get your things?" A short time later, they locked the bakery and set the alarm. Toni and Sheila got into Toni's car to drive to Sheila's house.

"I wonder where Jason disappeared to," Toni said as they pulled away from the bakery.

"I don't know," responded Sheila with a frown. "But he's been acting strange all day. I'll bet we're not the only ones who're beat." They both chuckled.

Shortly after the two women arrived at Sheila's, Jason called and apologized for not showing up in time to help them close the shop. When Sheila reported what they had found while cleaning up, he came right over.

"Tell me exactly what happened," he said once they were all seated in Sheila's living room.

"Well," Toni began, "I found this envelope on one of the tables and—"

"Which table?" Jason asked.

"I . . . I don't remember." She put her head in her hands and started to sob. Jason and Sheila looked at each other. Sheila pointed toward the bedroom, and Jason nodded his agreement.

"Toni, I think you need to get some sleep," Sheila said gently.

Toni struggled to get to her feet. She could barely stand, and the light from a nearby lamp revealed dark circles beneath her eyes. "I guess you're right. No more Superwoman act for this girl." Sheila escorted her guest to the spare bedroom. She returned a few minutes later and found Jason staring at the message.

Sheila dropped into an overstuffed chair across from Jason. "What do we do now?" she asked tiredly.

"I'm not sure," he replied, shaking his head. "Nothing I've suggested so far has done any good."

"Don't be so hard on yourself, Jason. It's not fair to you, and it doesn't solve anything."

He sighed. "You're right. I suppose the first thing to do is to have Toni stay with you for a few days. But beyond that, I just don't know." He paused, turned the sheet of paper over in his hands, and then examined the envelope once more. "We need to carefully review what happened in the bakery today. Was there anything unusual or suspicious? Do we have any idea when this message was left on the table?"

They discussed the events of the day, and Sheila described exactly where they had found the envelope. After a few minutes, Sheila said, "It was so busy that it's hard to remember what was happening at any particular time. I really have no idea when the envelope was left. It could have been any time during the whole afternoon or evening."

"You're right. I saw lots of new faces, and we don't know who we're looking for."

"That's true. But Jason, didn't you see anybody who looked at all suspicious today?"

Jason shrugged. "Eva and Hank came by, but they're not smart enough or disciplined enough to be the source of Toni's problems." He paused. "Though they certainly are vicious enough. What do you think?"

"Jason, at this point, I think just about anything is possible."

He continued. "A bunch of families came in and bought sodas. A few people wanted to purchase cakes decorated for the holiday, but I had to turn them away because Toni had been gone and I couldn't take cake orders. Martha came in for her donuts like usual. I was on my feet all day serving coffee and pastries. It's all such a blur."

"Well, do you remember who was sitting at that table?"

He sighed. "No. For a lot of the tables, I wouldn't pay attention to who was sitting there unless I had to refill their coffee cup. I wish I hadn't gone to watch the fireworks. I suspect that the message was dropped off late in the evening. If it had arrived earlier, someone would probably have brought it to our attention." He stopped suddenly and stared at the wall, deep in thought.

"What?" asked Sheila impatiently.

"I wonder if the person even lives in Blue Spring. It could be someone from out of town. But if it was someone far away, how did they know that the Fourth of July was the most crowded day of the year in Blue Spring?"

"I don't follow you," said Sheila.

"Well, the person doesn't have to live here, but he's very familiar with Blue Spring. Maybe he used to live here."

Sheila sighed. "It could be. Toni's aunt and uncle ran that bakery for years. Maybe it's an old customer who has a gripe with one of them. Since both her aunt and uncle are deceased, the disgruntled person is taking out his anger on Toni." Sheila suppressed a yawn. "I think we're both too tired to solve this problem tonight."

"I agree." Jason stood and walked to the door. He took Sheila's hand and squeezed it. "Thanks for being Toni's friend."

Toni opened her eyes and blinked. At first she was confused. She wondered why was she sleeping in Sheila's guest bedroom. Then she remembered the events of the previous day. She groaned. Bright sunlight spilled through the open blinds and she gasped. She glanced at the clock. It was already nine o'clock! She had overslept, and Sheila hadn't even bothered to wake her.

She jumped out of bed and an hour later was entering the bakery. She glared at Jason as he busily helped a customer. When he was finished, she confronted him. "Why didn't you call me at Sheila's when I didn't show up on time?"

"You needed the rest. You barely made it to Sheila's house last night without falling asleep, and you're still coping with a lot," he said as he squeezed her shoulder. "Anyway," he continued, "I'm glad you made it here. There should be enough donuts and pastries to last the rest of the day. A few people called with cake orders. I took their names and numbers down and left them by the phone. You can call them back." He glanced around the bakery. "I have an errand to run. Are you going to be okay here?"

"I'll be fine, Jason. Take your time."

"Do you have your cell phone?"

She lifted the phone from her apron pocket and flashed it in front of his face. "Are you happy now?"

The bell tinkled as Martha entered. Her nervous eyes darted

around the room. She was wearing a wrinkled pink dress, and her gray-streaked hair was mussed.

"Hi, Martha," said Toni. "What can I get for you today?"

"Can I have a glazed donut? Those are good," she said. Toni placed two glazed donuts in a bag and gave them to the woman. She also gave her a large cup of coffee.

"Where's Jason?" asked Martha. She didn't leave the coffee shop like she usually did. She sat at an empty table and opened her bag to remove a donut.

"He had to run an errand."

Martha began eating her breakfast. "He likes you, Toni. I can tell."

"What makes you say that, Martha?" she asked with a smile in her voice.

"Sometimes in the evening, I take long walks around town. He parks his car in front of your bakery and stares up at your window. Just like in that movie *Romeo and Juliet*. He would stare at her window." She giggled as she finished her donut.

Toni swallowed. Sweat beaded her forehead, and she wiped it away. Jason was peeping at her apartment window! "When did you see him doing this, Martha?" She tried to keep her voice calm.

"I don't know what days. I saw him doing it several times. Jason is in love. Just like in the movies; he's in love with you, Toni Brown."

Martha licked the sugary glaze from her fingers and took a sip of coffee. Fortunately they were the only people left in the bakery. Toni suddenly did not have the energy to wait on customers.

Martha giggled again as she started eating her second donut. When she finished, she stood up, took another sip of coffee, and left the bakery.

Brian entered just as she was leaving. He was wearing a custom-made suit and carrying his leather briefcase. "What are you doing here?" Toni grumbled.

"I came to see you, Toni," he replied. He placed his briefcase on the table and opened it. He removed a white envelope and held it out to her, but she refused to touch it.

"What's that?" Her voice was full of suspicion.

"It's the money I owe you. I want you to know that I'm serious about this. I think we still have a chance. I want to make things right between us."

Toni took the envelope and counted the money. "There's two hundred dollars too much in here." She remembered how much money Brian had swindled from her, down to the last penny.

"Consider that as interest on a loan. Toni, it's been three long and lonely years. I've thought about you so much." He touched her cheek, and she flinched.

"Don't touch me," she spat.

He stepped back. "Look, I came by to give you the money and to give you my condolences. I heard about your dad dying. That's awful. He was a good man."

"Thank you," Toni said icily. She swallowed hard and took a deep breath. "Brian, I told you we're through. I don't want you in my life anymore. Can't you understand that?" she asked.

"No, I can't. We're perfect for each other, Toni. You just haven't realized that yet." Brian paused, looking around as if to reassure himself that they were alone. "By the way," he said in a hushed voice, "I understand that someone has been threatening you and vandalizing the bakery."

Her heart skipped a beat. "Were you in here yesterday?"

"Why do you ask?"

She looked at him, trying to determine if he was hiding

something. His expression gave nothing away. Memories of their whirlwind romance flashed through her mind. She had been in love with Brian once, and now she wanted to be free of him.

"I still think you need to be careful about any entanglements with the Matthews clan," Brian added. "A woman living by herself can't be too careful nowadays."

Just then Jason walked through the door. He glared at Brian. "What are you doing here?"

Brian picked up his briefcase. "I was just leaving."

Toni stared after Brian as he walked down the street.

"Was he bothering you again?"

"He came to return something to me." They sat at a table, and she gave Jason the envelope. He looked inside. "There's over a thousand dollars in here! Why is Brian giving you this money?" His voice was full of suspicion.

She sighed. "Jason, there are some things I haven't explained about my relationship with Brian. You already know we were engaged. Well, after that, Brian wanted me to . . ." She paused and took a deep breath. "He wanted me to become intimate with him. My mother always taught me to wait until marriage, and I told him that it was against my beliefs to do something like that until we'd said our vows."

She paused again. "Well, he decided to take matters into his own hands and he went out and found somebody else who would satisfy his desires. And there's more. He used my credit card and charged a lot of stuff on it. Most of it was for his new girlfriend. Once I found out about all this, I had to break the engagement. Dishonesty and betrayal aren't much of a foundation for a relationship."

Jason sat silently, staring out the front window. Toni was surprised that he didn't have anything to say, but she had work to do. She took the money into her office and began clearing tables, but she couldn't stop wondering why Jason was so distant. Her thoughts went back to the things Brian had written in his summary. Was it possible he was right? Could Jason be trying to get the bakery from her?

Jason's voice interrupted her thoughts. "Do you think you can manage without me for the rest of the day? I'm really not feeling well. I wouldn't want you or any of your customers to catch something from me."

She tried to smile but couldn't manage it. "Sure, I'll be all right. Go get some rest."

He nodded sadly and walked out the front door.

Twelve

*T*he sound of Sheila's ringing phone shattered the silent night. Sheila came out of her bedroom, stunned. "Toni! That was the police. Your bakery is on fire—the alarm went off!" Toni jumped out of bed and threw on some clothes.

"I tried calling Jason's cell phone, but there was no answer," explained Sheila. "I called Mrs. Dukes and left a message on her answering machine."

Minutes later they arrived at the bakery. The police and fire departments had already arrived. Toni cried. She couldn't believe that her dreams were going up in smoke. The police were still running around, filling out reports and trying to discover if there were any witnesses. Sheila and Toni sat on the back of one of the fire trucks in stunned silence, watching the disaster unfold.

Finally, Toni said, "Sheila, I think Jason may have set this fire. In fact, I think he's been behind most of what's been happening at the bakery over the last few months. I think he wants to get his hands on my recipes and my business. He wants to make them part of the Matthews business empire."

"Oh, Toni. You're in shock, and you don't know what you're saying. Jason would *never* do something like this. How could you even say that?"

"Sheila, all these things started happening right after Jason arrived in town." Toni clung to her friend and sobbed into her shoulder.

"I'm not responsible for this." Jason's deep voice startled her. Standing just out of sight around the corner of the fire truck, he had heard everything she said. "I can't believe you'd think I'd do this to you, Toni."

"But, Jason, I—"

The orange flames flickered away, casting a strange glow on his broad shoulders and face. The shoulders slumped in defeat and tears fell from the dark eyes.

He walked toward her, ever so slowly. "Toni, I've done everything that I could for you. I wanted to protect you and the bakery. I've told you about my past. I've answered every question you asked. How could you believe the things you wrote about my family and its business? How could you believe them about me?"

Toni was speechless from shock.

"Oh yes," he continued, "I found your trenchant little analysis of our business ethics and personal morality in the drawer of the desk in your office. I was looking for extra deposit slips." His eyes blazed with anger. "While you were so busy doing all your extensive research, you could have at least bothered to get your facts straight!"

He turned and walked away. Toni wanted to call out to him, to explain, but her voice refused to work. Finally she managed to croak out a few words. "Jason, I didn't write those things. I don't believe them. It was Brian. It was Brian." She began to sob. "Don't . . . leave me . . . alone. . . . Jason, I love you." The roaring fire drowned out her words, and Jason slowly disappeared into the flickering darkness. Sheila held her shaking friend in speechless horror.

Jason drove back to the bed-and-breakfast. He ran up to his room, found his suitcase, and began throwing his clothes inside. His heart was pounding, and he felt as if someone had just carved his chest open with a knife. He sat on the bed as the tears continued to run down his cheeks. He loved Toni Brown. He loved that woman, and she thought he had burned down her bakery. Would she tell the police her theory? Would they soon be knocking on his door for questioning?

He gazed at the pile of clothes in his suitcase. He couldn't leave now. In spite of her slanderous accusations, he still loved her. He needed to know that she was going to be okay. Jason stretched across his bed. *Lord, help me . . . help me . . . please, help me with this terrible pain,* he prayed. He kept repeating those same words over and over again until he fell into a deep sleep.

It was four in the morning. Toni and Sheila had been at the scene of the fire for more than two hours. They were beyond tired. Just then, a policeman came up to them with surprising news. "There was a witness who got the license plate number of the car used by the arsonists. We've already apprehended them. They started the fire with a can of gasoline and some matches."

"Can we see them?" asked Toni.

"Yes, miss," the officer answered. "In fact, it would help us out if you could identify them and let us know of any possible motive they might have for destroying your business."

Toni's eyes were red and puffy from shedding so many tears. She wanted to inspect her home and assess the damage that had been done, but the fire chief had already told her that she wouldn't be able to do that until they had completed their investigation and were satisfied that the building was safe to enter. Anxious to see who was responsible for the disaster, she agreed to go to the police station. When Toni and Sheila were shown the suspects, Toni gasped.

"It's Eva and Hank," she said softly.

Her heart pounded as she approached the woman. Eva looked sad and tired. "Eva, why?" she whispered. "Why did you burn down the bakery? Your parents loved that place."

Eva stared at Toni coldly. "That place should've been mine, and you know it," she said. "If I can't have Blue Spring Baked Goods, then no one can have it. It would've been mine if you hadn't come along. One summer you spent with my parents— one. Three lousy months. That's all it took for you to steal everything that should've been mine. They cut me out of their will completely. They didn't leave me one thin dime."

"What else did you do to her, Eva?" Sheila asked in a low, hard voice. "What else did you and Hank do to Toni and the bakery? Did you cut the phone lines? Did you make all those crank calls? Did you wreck the kitchen? Did you leave a threatening note for us to find on the Fourth of July?"

"What note?" Eva asked in confusion. "We didn't leave no lousy note. What good would that've done?"

"Eva, shut up," Hank said harshly. "We ain't answerin' nobody's questions till we talk to a lawyer."

Suddenly, a great many things became clear to Toni. She turned to the police officer who was with them in the interview room. "I think I can tell you who did the other things. At least I think you'd better bring him in for questioning. His name is Brian Stevenson."

The following day, Toni got permission to enter her business and assess the damage. The kitchen was the most damaged part of the building. The whole room was black. She found her fire-proof box on the bottom shelf. It had done its job. Everything in it was in perfect condition. The same could not be said for the equipment. The refrigerators, commercial oven, counters, mixers—everything would need to be replaced.

Filled with dread, Toni next made her way up to the apartment. Her clothing reeked of smoke, and she wasn't sure even dry cleaning would remove the smell. Many of her few wools and silks were ruined from water. She sat on her soiled couch and sobbed. After a few minutes, she got up and went back outside. A police car pulled into the parking area behind the bakery as she was preparing to leave. Two officers got out and removed a handcuffed prisoner from the back seat. It was Brian.

One of the officers spoke first. "When we picked him up and asked him if he had anything to do with the fire, he denied it. Then he fell apart and started telling us about all sorts of other things. He asked us to find you so he could tell you about some of them."

"I'm sorry, Toni," Brian said. "I made the crank calls. I also cut your phone line, but I only did it once. And I bashed in the new window in your back kitchen door. I knew it wouldn't break. I didn't mess up your kitchen, but I did leave a threatening note on the Fourth. How was I supposed to know some-body would torch the place the next day?"

"What about the information you gave me on Jason?" she asked in a cold voice.

"It's true, but it's only part of the story. The congressional hearings ended because the charges of corruption were false. The whole thing was put together by some political and busi-ness enemies of the Matthews family. They even got the press to do some of their dirty work for them. When the papers dis-covered they were being used, they apologized to the family and printed front-page corrections to their previous stories."

"Why, Brian? Why did you put me through all that, and why did you accuse a perfectly innocent man of something you knew he wasn't responsible for?"

"Toni, when I got back in town, I knew I wanted you back. I wanted to be the shoulder you cried on. But you made it quite clear that there wasn't room for me in your life. I was desper-ate. Then I had an idea. Remember back in college that se-mester when there were some rapes on campus?"

She closed her eyes and nodded. "I remember I was scared."

"Yeah, you were scared, and you leaned on me. I liked being your protector, and I wanted to have that role in your life again. I figured if you got scared again, you would start leaning on me. I never figured you'd have somebody else in your life."

Toni turned to one of the officers. "I've heard enough." They put him back in the patrol car and drove away.

Suddenly it was all too much. Toni walked over to the back steps leading up to the bakery's kitchen and sat down heavily. She had just lost her father, and now she had lost her business. Her ex-fiancé had tried to scare her into dating him again, and her own cousin had plotted to destroy her life.

Then there was Jason. Had she lost him, too? She had accused him of arson. She couldn't blame him if he left town and never spoke to her again. She took a deep breath and tried to pull herself together. There was work to do, and the sooner she got a list of destroyed property to the insurance company, the sooner she could begin the job of rebuilding her life.

That evening, while she was eating dinner with Sheila, someone knocked at the door. "Come in!" Sheila yelled.

Toni gasped when Jason walked through the door. She had never seen him look so handsome. He was wearing the same clothing he had worn the first time she'd seen him: dark jeans and a T-shirt. Her eyes flickered over his lean torso and broad shoulders and finally rested on his face. He looked old and tired, like a man who had fought a desperate battle and lost.

"Jason," she breathed. She barely noticed Sheila leaving the kitchen. He walked slowly into the room. She had never been more ashamed of herself in her life. He didn't sit. He merely stood in the kitchen, watching her.

"I'm sorry, Jason. I am so sorry," she whispered.

He gave a curt nod, and she assumed he was accepting her apology. "Sheila came to the bed-and-breakfast today. She told me that Eva and Hank started the fire and that Brian was responsible for many of the other things that have been happening over the past few months." He paused. "Toni, I'm going home. I just stopped to see if you were okay before I left."

He pulled Sheila's grocery list from the refrigerator, flipped it over, and wrote something down. "Here's my address and phone number. Because of everything that's happened, I don't think we should talk to each other for a while. I think we need a lot of time to sort through everything." He gave her the slip of paper, and their fingers touched. A warm glow covered her hand.

"I didn't mean to hurt you, Jason. Really I didn't." Her throat felt dry and tight. He touched her cheek and quickly walked out the door. She parted the curtains and watched his black BMW disappear in the distance. "Good-bye, Jason," she whispered.

Jason's absence left a deep hole in Toni's heart, but she tried to cover the emptiness by keeping busy rebuilding the rest of her life. Fortunately, the fire had created plenty of work for her to do. She spent days at the building, sorting through her belongings and continuing to draw up a list of damaged and destroyed property for the insurance company. She threw away the ruined clothing and tried to be thankful that the TV and other electrical appliances in her apartment were still in working order.

Her insurance coverage included the cost of an apartment while her own living quarters were being rebuilt. Toni was grateful for that provision. While Sheila was more than willing to have her use the guest room, Toni knew that her friend valued her privacy. After a brief search, Toni found an apartment close to the bakery and settled in. But soon she had caught up with her paperwork and had nothing to do but wait for the rebuilding to be completed.

She spent a lot of free time in the kitchen. Sheila stopped by each morning for breakfast, and she usually visited during her lunch hour as well. Toni made bread and cakes and gave the food to the homeless shelter in town. Even with all those projects, she still had so much free time that she didn't know what to do with herself. She continued to attend church once a week, sitting in the back with her notepad and Bible. And she worked to find something more of God to hang on to.

Sometimes in the evening she would read the Bible her mother had given her, reviewing things that had been said in the pastor's sermon or just looking around to satisfy her growing curiosity. She often thought of her mother's kindness and her faith. The woman had always been there for her. When Toni called to let her know about the fire and who caused it, her mother had replied, "Oh, Toni. I'll pray for them. I'm just glad you're okay." Every day since then, Toni had gotten a reassuring phone call from her mom.

Throughout the years, Toni realized, her mother had always placed her faith and trust in the Lord. Over the last few months she had finally begun to understand how that process actually worked. God was personally involved in her mother's life in much the same way her mother had been involved in Toni's life for so many years. God had been there for her mother. God had been her friend.

When bad things happened to her mother, she felt their impact as much as did people who had no personal faith. But she was not alone, and those difficulties were only one part of a larger picture. The dominant element in that picture was a certainty that God was near her—actually personally present—no matter what threats or disappointments she faced. And Iris Brown believed that God would finally bring her to a place of fulfillment and rest that would make even the worst suffering unimportant by comparison.

Toni's mother actually lived in two worlds at the same time, something Toni still found difficult to understand. Her belief that Jesus was with her allowed her to live through the pain of the present by looking toward the promise of the future.

Toni often thought of her father, too. He had begun to understand the meaning of faith in the last years of his life. He had learned enough to show her how to begin holding on to God.

Then her thoughts wandered back to Jason Matthews. He was a good man with a kind heart. He was a Christian person, just like her mother.

She thought about Sheila, who had been her best friend since they were children. Sheila was always saying how much more fulfilling her life had been since she'd made the Lord the center of her existence.

All four of these people were important to Toni, and they all had similar things to say about God. They were all pointing her toward a personal relationship with God, a friendship. It had taken her a long time to understand where this journey of faith was going, but at least she now knew what the central issue was—and what she wanted more than anything else. Toni Brown wanted to have God for a friend.

One evening, as she was studying the pastor's latest sermon and flipping through her Bible, Toni prayed, *"Lord, how can we be friends?"* She was surprised to find tears rolling down her cheeks.

A few minutes later, an abrupt knock at the door interrupted her thoughts. It was nine o'clock, and she wasn't expecting company. She opened the door. Sheila smiled at her, then her expression changed to one of concern. "Toni, are you okay?"

Toni wiped at her tears as she invited Sheila inside. "Yes, I'm just a little bit teary tonight."

"Well, you've been through a lot lately, so you deserve to be teary." Sheila sat beside her on the couch and spotted the Bible. "So, what's your latest discovery about faith?"

"I've discovered that I want to be friends with God."

Her friend stared at her in amazement.

"Sheila, I want what you, Jason, and my mother share. I want to have the satisfaction of having God on my side. I want to know I'm not alone."

Sheila closed her eyes for a minute and then opened them. "Look, Toni, all of us are sinners."

Toni nodded. "Yes, I definitely agree with that." She picked up her Bible and turned the pages. "The pastor talked about that last week. But what does sin have to do with being God's friend?"

Sheila took a deep breath. "Can I borrow your Bible? Look Toni, sin is the one thing that keeps us from being friends with God. God sent Jesus to solve that problem. God sacrificed His Son just so we could be forgiven for our sins. Can you imagine that? Sacrificing your own son?"

Toni knew about Jesus dying on the cross. It was a subject her mother had spoken of often throughout the years. She knew they had nailed His hands and His feet on the cross and that He had suffered a lot.

Sheila continued. "He did that for us, Toni. You and me and all sinners in this world." She flipped through the Bible until she came to John 3:16. She pointed to the verse, asking Toni to read it.

Toni's hands shook as she took the Bible from Sheila. "For God so loved the world that He gave His only begotten Son, that whoever believes in Him should not perish but have everlasting life." Toni touched the page. Just reading the words made her feel good.

"Toni, God wants you to believe in Him. This sacrifice is a gift from the Lord. All He asks is that you accept it." Toni closed her eyes, and Sheila took her hand.

"I accept God's gift," Toni prayed. "I accept Christ in my life." Then she opened her heart and prayed that Eva and Hank would find a better life. She prayed for her mother, who would continue to grieve over the death of her husband for months to come. She prayed that Jason had made it safely to Chicago and that they could work out the problems in their relationship. She also thanked the Lord for Sheila's friendship over the years.

As she reached the end of her prayer, Toni cried for the second time that evening, thanking the Lord for allowing her to see the light, for opening her mind and her heart so that she could accept Him into her life.

It had been a full month since Jason had left town. Toni thought about him constantly. Her bakery was still being rebuilt, and it would be another month before she could move back in and reopen her business. She had spent most of the month becoming better friends with God. The whole idea still struck her as odd, but she was getting used to it. God no longer seemed far away, or at least the distance that remained didn't seem to matter as much. She felt no further from God than she did from Sheila, who worked a few blocks from the bakery during the day. She was as close to God as she was to her mother, whom Toni could speak to by just picking up the phone.

When she wrestled with the pain of her separation from Jason, God was by her side, helping her to endure. For the first time in her life, Toni was no longer alone with her pain. She had help for the present and hope for the future. She read her Bible regularly and was attending a study group at Blue Spring Community Church. She also went home to visit her mother a few times. She still smiled when she thought of her mother's exuberant reaction to the news that Toni had found God in her life.

Lord, what do I do about Jason? Toni prayed one evening. He was in her thoughts and dreams. She realized that she loved him with her whole heart, but the knowledge had come too late for her to tell him. She recalled her mother's advice about men. "You should never tell a man you love him first, Toni. When a man loves a woman, he'll let her know."

Jason had never said that he loved her, but he had said it wasn't something any man should say to a woman until he was ready to ask her to marry him. Was it still possible to believe that he might say those words to her someday? Was God willing to share her with Jason?

Sometimes when she thought of Jason she felt torn in two, like some essential part of her life had been ripped away. But the pain was only one part of a larger picture. She was not paralyzed by it. She was free to act with God's help. Suddenly, Toni knew what she needed to do. She dug out some stationery. She had nothing to lose by telling Jason the truth, and he deserved an explanation for her actions. Breathing a short prayer to her new best friend, she began to write:

Dear Jason,

First, I want you to know that I'm still holding on to God. And I'm waiting to see what develops. But the journey is not quite as lonely as it once was, because I have a new Friend to accompany me. I think you already have met Him. His name is Jesus. Yes, Jason, I've surrendered my life to Christ. Bet you thought it would never happen!

I'm studying the Bible, praying regularly, and spending time with a few other Christians. I'm going to church a couple times a week now, but I still insist on sitting in the back. I think it's easier to listen to God back there. So, one journey of faith has ended and another is just beginning. I want to thank you for the part you played in helping me find Christ. I know you took an awful risk by telling me so much about yourself and letting me see that you didn't have all the answers.

I'm sorry I hurt you. I was half out of my mind after the bakery burned. I never really believed what Brian had written, but that night it seemed like anything was possible. I miss you terribly. I miss seeing you at the bakery every day and working with you. I miss our long conversations and your humor and your cute shiny head.

I'll understand if you don't feel you can trust me again, but I want to make sure you understand I do love you and I do care about you. I'm sorry for the pain that I've caused you. I hope you're happy and doing well. Even if we don't have a future together, I'll always remember the time we did have. Whatever happens, I hope you can find it in your heart to at least be my friend in Christ.

Toni

Toni wrote her temporary apartment address and phone number at the bottom of the page. Then she read through the letter three times, folded it, and placed it into an envelope. She had memorized Jason's address and phone number long ago. After scribbling the address on the envelope and placing a stamp in the corner, she ran to the mailbox and threw the letter inside before she had a chance to lose her courage. There was no changing her mind now. Soon she would have some answers. It was just a matter of time—and eternity.

Jason stared out the window of his fourteenth-floor office. Several buildings loomed in the distance, and he could even see the Sears Tower. Chicago was a beautiful city, and it had always been his home. Sometimes when he just wanted to escape the stress of life, he found help by whispering a prayer to his heavenly Father and losing himself in the beauty of the view.

Bzzz! His thoughts were interrupted by the intercom.

"Yes, Connie?" His deep voice carried over the wire. He didn't like being interrupted, but he did have a business to run, after all.

"Marilyn is here. She wants to go over some numbers with you on the trial balance."

"Go ahead and send her in."

Marilyn sat on the leather chair across from Jason and gave him a coy smile. "You know we start closing the books tomorrow," she said.

He took the manila folder from her outstretched hand. "I know, Marilyn. And you've been doing a great job as usual." She was one of the best accounting managers they'd ever had, and he was painfully aware that his recent absence had made her job much harder. He checked the numbers for all of the accounts. After asking her a few questions, he returned the folder.

Once Marilyn left, Jason quickly concluded that he was too preoccupied to be of any use to Matthews and Company. He tied up some loose ends and told Connie that he was leaving work early. When he arrived home, he was greeted by Spike, his Saint Bernard. "You're hungry, aren't you, boy?" He filled the dog's dishes with food and water, then changed from his suit into sweatpants and a T-shirt.

He heard Spike chomping on his food and then lapping up his dish of water. Soon the big animal joined him on the couch. Spike placed his large head in Jason's lap and nuzzled his hand. Jason glanced around his small town house. It was located in an elegant neighborhood on the outskirts of Chicago. His lawn was mowed and trimmed weekly. The interior of the house didn't contain much of value since he had Spike to consider. It was hard to keep a nice place with a large dog running around. As if he knew what his master was thinking, Spike abandoned the couch and curled up in a corner for a nap.

Jason placed his head in his hands. He'd been irritable ever since leaving Blue Spring. He had not seen Toni for a month, and he missed her terribly. He still felt the sting of her accusations, but the pain seemed to lessen each day. Still, he missed getting up early each morning and helping in the bakery. Being with Toni seemed so natural and right.

Jason walked outside and retrieved his mail from the box. He returned to the couch and sorted through the bills. The last piece in the stack was a personal letter. There was no return address, but he recognized Toni's neat, feminine script. He touched the envelope, trying to find the courage to open it. His heart pounded.

Thoughts of Toni filled his mind. He recalled the light floral scent of her perfume, her thick dark hair pulled into a neat bun. He pictured the way she smiled as she baked pies and tarts. He remembered how her kind heart prompted her to feed milk to stray cats and give free donuts and coffee to Martha every day. He missed her so much that it hurt. He wanted to hold her in his arms and never let go. He closed his eyes and said a silent prayer as he opened the letter.

Slowly he read her words. Toni had found Christ. This was wonderful. She missed him? She loved him? How could he have been so blind! She hoped they could at least be friends in Christ? "Toni, my dear," Jason whispered to himself, "we can do much better than that."

He jumped up and grabbed the nearest phone, intending to dial her number. After punching three digits, he put it down again. He didn't want to discuss this over the phone. He lifted the receiver again and dialed his travel agent. "I'd like a round-trip ticket to Baltimore," he said.

Just as Toni was about to sit down for dinner, a knock sounded at her door. Curious as to who it could be, she crossed over to the door and opened it. "Oh, my," she squeaked. Toni blinked once, twice, but her eyes weren't playing tricks on her. It was Jason Matthews in the flesh. He was wearing a tuxedo, and he held out a dozen, long-stemmed red roses. She took the flowers and stared, resisting the impulse to pinch herself. She had been hungering for this man's presence for weeks.

"May I come in?" he asked quietly.

She felt silly, gawking at him like a schoolgirl. "Yes, come in," she said in a rush. Her heart was pounding. She found an empty vase in a kitchen cupboard and arranged the flowers in some water, all the while trying desperately to compose herself.

Returning to the living room with the fragrant bouquet, she noticed that Jason was still standing near the door. "Please sit down, Jason," she murmured while groaning with frustration. This was ridiculous. They were acting like polite strangers instead of like two people in love.

She tried hard not to stare at him, but it was impossible. He looked so handsome. The tuxedo fell from his broad shoulders appealingly. A sense of déjà vu swept over her as she sniffed his familiar citrus cologne. The room was silent except for the ticking of her wall clock. She took a deep breath as she tried to decide what to say.

"Toni?"

She swallowed. "Yes?" It came out as a whisper.

"You said in your letter that you would always remember our

time together." He had a smug expression on his face. "May I assume that you will remember it fondly?"

"Jason Matthews, you are insufferable."

"Good, we should get along just fine together." He grinned broadly and pulled her into his strong arms. All of the pain and anguish of the past month came to the surface, and she found herself weeping. Jason released her, took her chin in his hand, and gently kissed her tears away. "Why are you crying?" he asked.

"I don't know. I guess I'm happy to see you. But I'm upset about everything that's happened between us. Jason, I'm so sorry—"

He interrupted her words with a kiss on her lips. He tasted good and sweet, and she wanted him to kiss her again. But first she needed some answers. "Why did you come back to Blue Spring?"

He touched her cheek, and she quivered slightly. "Do you need to ask why, Toni? I came back for the same reason I stayed in the first place—because of you. I worked in the bakery because I wanted to be near you every day. I believe that God led me to you. I was still grieving over my mom, and I was still upset about the way I was deceived by that flight attendant. But after I met you, I felt so much better. You're an awesome woman, Toni, and I love you."

"Oh, Jason, I love you, too," she said. They fell into each other's arms, savoring each other's presence after so many weeks of separation.

A few minutes later, Jason pulled back. "So, what are we going to do about it?" he asked, the hint of a smile tipping his full lips.

"Do about it?"

Promises to Keep

"Yes, Toni. Let's talk about your bakery."

"My bakery? It won't be ready for a month yet."

"That's what I wanted to talk to you about, Toni. I have a proposition for you. I know you were thinking of expanding your bakery."

"Yes."

"Well, I figure we could go into business together. I could provide the money for expansion, and we could be partners."

"Partners?" she asked softly.

"Yes, partners. We'd be partners in business, but, more important, I want you to be my partner for life." He took a small box from his pocket and gave it to her. "Toni, will you marry me?"

"Oh, Jason!" she cried as he placed the ring on her finger. "I've been thanking the Lord for bringing you into my life," she said in a hoarse whisper.

"I've been thanking the Lord every day since I met you, sweetheart. You know, I think God wanted me to take that long trip a few months ago. He wanted me to stop in Blue Spring when I was tired. He wanted me to work with you in your bakery. God wants us to be together, Toni Brown."

Toni smiled and stared deeply into his dark eyes. "God wants us together, and so do I," she whispered. Joy flooded his face as he gathered her into his arms again.

Epilogue

One year later . . .

"*A*re you ready?" Jason hugged his new bride. They had been married for six months, and he never grew tired of being near her.

"Yes, I'm ready," Toni answered. "Look at that crowd! And we've still got fifteen more minutes before the doors open."

It was Saturday morning, and Toni's bakery was ready for its grand reopening. As Jason had envisioned, they had been able to expand. At first Jason's father had been disappointed that his son was leaving Chicago, but after he met Toni, his doubts disappeared. He kept Jason on the board of directors and enthusiastically supported the new couple's business.

Toni glanced at her display cases. They featured a new array of sweet, tempting treats as well as the old favorites. The grand reopening had been well advertised, and they expected good crowds throughout the day.

Promptly at six-thirty, Jason opened the doors, and people began streaming in. Toni was surprised by the size of the crowds. It was as busy as the Fourth of July. People even came from surrounding towns. At six o'clock that evening, the weary couple closed the doors. Most of the pastries were sold out, and they also had a stack of orders for special events. After they counted their earnings, secured the money in the safe, and cleaned the bakery, Jason drove them to their new home, a two-story white colonial house on the outskirts of Blue Spring. Toni sighed with pleasure as the house came into view. It had four bedrooms and plenty of space for entertaining friends.

After the couple showered and changed, Toni served Jason his favorite meal: salad, baked lasagna with garlic bread, and chocolate cake with vanilla ice cream. "I'm stuffed," he said as he ate his last bite of cake. "Why did you make such an elaborate meal tonight, Toni? You've been on your feet all day, so I know you must be tired."

She took his hand and led him into the living room. He wondered why she was acting so mysterious. He sat on a chair and pulled his beautiful wife on his lap. They shared a long, leisurely kiss. His heart was pounding. Toni seemed to have that effect on him.

"Jason, I made a special dinner tonight because I have some important news for you," she whispered in his ear.

His curiosity was piqued. He continued to stare at Toni as she took his hand and placed it over her stomach. "We're having a baby. I'm two months pregnant."

Jason's heart started beating even harder. He didn't think he'd heard Toni correctly. "We're having a baby?" he squeaked.

She nodded, and he was rewarded with her charming smile.

He smiled and kissed his wife again. "This calls for a celebration," he said.

"I couldn't agree with you more," she replied, snuggling closer to him.

Lifting her into his strong arms, he carried her to their bedroom.

About the Author

CECELIA DOWDY enjoys reading and writing. When she discovered the world of inspirational romance novels, she found the perfect niche for her writing. She is proud to pen stories that advocate a deep faith in the Lord. Six and a half years ago, she began writing novels. *Someone for Toni* is her first published romance. She currently resides in Maryland and is active in the singles ministry of her church.